THE PIER GLASS

THE
PIER GLASS

Nia Williams

HONNO MODERN FICTION

Published by Honno
'Ailsa Craig', Heol y Cawl, Dinas Powys
Bro Morgannwg CF6 4AH

First impression 2001
© Nia Williams

ISBN 1 870206 44 4

All rights reserved. No part of this book may be reproduced,
stored in a retrieval system, or transmitted, in any form or
by any means, electronic, mechanical, photocopying,
recording or otherwise, without clearance from
the publishers.

British Library Cataloguing in Publication Data
A catalogue record for this book is available from the British Library

Published with the financial support
of the Arts Council of Wales

Cover design by Debbie Maidment

Printed in Wales by Dinefwr Press, Llandybïe

'Your pier-glass or extensive surface of polished steel made to be rubbed by a housemaid, will be minutely and multitudinously scratched in all directions; but place now against it a lighted candle as a centre of illumination, and lo! the scratches will seem to arrange themselves in a fine series of concentric circles round that little sun. It is demonstrable that the scratches are going everywhere impartially, and it is only your candle which produces the flattering illusion of a concentric arrangement, its light falling with an exclusive optical selection.'

Middlemarch, George Eliot

Prologue

On the third of March, 1898, Alice Day received a proposal of marriage. Between hearing the question and giving her answer, Alice was seized with a notion. Not a thought – too fleeting and vague to qualify as a thought. It was a notion, of herself. Of Alice Day, here, in the market square in Castlebury; Alice Day, 18 years old, watching a phrase form on Ernest Butterworth's ugly lips. At the same time, it was a notion of another Alice: the Alice she would become. The real Alice, who would, at some point, be complete and self-contained – like a book, with a back cover and a front cover, with a first and a last word. This would be the Alice others remembered; the Alice pinned down in the memories of her friends, described by her children in their old age. The notion had passed in a moment, in the pause between Ernest's request and her reply. But during that breath-beat, Alice Day lived through the thrill of an unknown future, and knew the terror of an unalterable past.

PART ONE

They'll tell you that poetry and vision are the same. It isn't true. I was set to poetry before I could walk. It was my trade and my burden. It seeped into my blood and bones, through the long, red reflections of my instructor's lash. I built verses in the grate. I plucked rhymes from the chickens. I twisted and arched my tongue around the Themes and Adjectives, until they came trotting together at my command. I learned to howl odes and dirges across hushed halls and drunken brawls, as I learned to stop crying for my mother.

My gift of prophecy came much later.

I can't mark the day it came, exactly. My memory of events is a little confused. I know it was summer. I know it was cold – it was the damp, early cold, and the ache between my eyes, that coaxed me out of my dream. I lay there, cramped and weary, hoping to sink back into sleep. I shifted, creaking on the loose-strung bed. Or hissing on the straw-covered floor, maybe. Or feeling for the sacking that had rucked itself into a wedge in the small of my back. I don't know. I've slept in so many corners and sung under so many roofs. Fire-lit parlours, latticed with shadow and harpstring. Bare, dripping outbuildings, in among the spit and the dogshit. I've eaten roast venison and mutton *cawl*. I've tasted good claret and spluttered over bad ale. I've rested among linen and lavender, and settled among the retainers' grunts and farts. I can't recall, precisely, the time or the place.

But I can remember the dream.

It was the usual dream: the scene that had thrilled and plagued me night after night, for months.

A modest hearth. Logs crackling in the heat. I'm performing – telling tales; brave heroes, impossible tasks, magical creatures, all cascade from my mouth and whirl around my head, bright as stars, mingling with stray smoke from the fire. An angel with flame-gold hair flies after them, catching at them, turning and diving, chirruping and laughing.

I knew where this was – in a farmhouse, on a hill overlooking my birthplace. I had been welcomed there one infernal evening, the previous winter. The young farmer and his family took me in from the rain, and I repaid them with my best and longest stories. While his wife tucked their younger children into a crib and a truckle bed, one daughter – shy, wary – hid behind the settle. I began to spin my web. A terrible curse; a woman who became a bird; a potion that revived the dead.

And it caught her up.

Gradually she crept closer. Her eyes grew wider. She was no more than eight or nine summers old, with hair the colour of an autumn sun. She had invaded my sleep ever since.

So yes, I remember my dream. But when it slithered away, and I opened my eyes on that momentous day in August, where was I? I can only guess. The chances are that I breathed in the stink of sweat and stale vomit as I sat, swaying, among the ranked and mumbling heaps. I probably stood up, careful not to knock against these bellied thugs who sleep with their swords, and picked my way out into the open.

And now it doesn't matter where I was, or which verses had earned my supper there. Because the morning mist cleared, and the sharp, green, dank air slapped me awake, and the smell of grass and elderflower and sheep-shit and fresh running water was as vivid as the angel in my dream. I looked out across sodden black hills and shifting oakwoods. Words were already jostling, unbidden, into my head. Sent by the devil to gabble across the peace. In another part of my mind I searched for a suitable tunnel into the woods, where I could go and relieve my groaning guts. And beyond all that, beyond everything, a low melody: the first, whispered traces of a promise. The beginning of my first vision.

As I stood there, fighting the words and the nausea, the ground dropped away under my feet, and I rose like a kite. My insides seemed to lag behind as I soared – over the courtyard, the retainers' hall, the manor house. The oakwoods shrank away beneath me. I flew on, with no body, no breath to anchor me. I saw the accelerating retreat of mountains, heather, grass and rock, roads and walls, a shepherd and his pinprick flock, cringing hamlets, glass rivers – all appearing and vanishing like spirits within my view. And then, snaking across the fields below, a slow, silent beast, glinting with blade and musket, warty with carts and horses, flicking its tongue of thread-thin banners.

An army on the march.

I saw the soldiers, far below. I saw one face among them, turned upwards to trace my flight. I saw myself.

This was my new-found talent: to condense the world, to squeeze space and time into the little circles of my eyes.

I have never deluded myself. As a poet I was not one of the big boys. Never a Guto'r Glyn or a Dafydd ab bloody Edmwnd. I could walk the skin off my feet, kiss a hundred arses, flatter a thousand fools. But I would never be cwtched and moithered in sheep's wool, or stuffed with sweetmeats at the table of some preening friend of the King's. I could work a crowd, mind. I could sing of our Great Dead Leaders, of the Glories Yet to Come, of *Hiraeth* – spinning out the first syllable, biting off the last, wringing the tears from crab-faced soldiers and milky lordlings alike. I knew my business, and I knew my audience. I could sneer at the Mad Boar Richard, or swoon over the Avenging Tudor Angel as required for my patriotic host Dafydd ap Ednyfed ap Cadwaladr ap Einion ap Maredudd. And in the morning I could bow to the same respectable host, address him as David Meredith Esquire and wish him well in his bid for a decent English title. And believe me, my words were as genuine in sunlight as they were in torchlight.

I had my craft. It carried me from day to day, and that was all I demanded of it. But on that summer morning, at that nameless hall, I was given the glimpse of another life. I swear to you by all that's sacred: I had seen the rippling, scaly back of Tudor's army. And as I soared noiselessly over it, I had seen my own face, squinting up at the clouds.

A henchman's voice brought me spiralling back down to earth. He'd come clanking out to piss in the corner. He hunched his back, and swilled his phlegm around a bit, and then said, Had I heard the latest? Word was that Tudur had left his Breton nest and landed somewhere near Aberdaugleddau, and was on his way north to fight the King.

I tell you, my flesh sparkled: icy drops along my fingertips and up the back of my neck.

He said, From what he'd heard, it was a sorry showing – just a handful of poltroons who'd make poor meat for the King's dogs. (This from a man who, only hours before, had roared himself hoarse with esctasy, as I pleaded with Henry Tudor, Earl of Richmond, to release our land from slavery and our hearts from sorrow.) He said, Their heads may get to London, but only on stakes. On any other day I would have agreed with him. I'd done my battle-crying the previous night, and been fed and watered for it: there was no call for passion in the chilly dawn. But that day was different. I was no longer merely a poet. I was a seer. I knew where my future lay and I was going to claim it.

By the time dusk fell, I had walked as far as Cefn-y-Bont. The sun set. Great bards sang praises in the warmth of back-country palaces, and grew a bit fatter cooing for their Tudor saviour. Well, let them weave their verses. I'd done with that. I was beginning to taste life. I panted like a lover as I followed the route I'd mapped out, that morning, from the sky. I licked my scabby lips and ignored my churning stomach. I scrambled up a track, pausing to watch a hail of rubble clatter away from my feet and bounce with the stream over a ridge and into the darkening valley below.

1

Halfway down a steep crevice, James is clinging to the rock. A hard ribbon of water leaps past him. He presses his whole body against the rock, feeling its bite in his thighs and chest. He isn't sure where he is, but he knows this is the only route to the man's home. He must find the man and ask a question. Trouble is, the question keeps slipping from his mind, because water is washing over him and through him, leaving a creamy consistency on the roof of his mouth and behind his eyes. Petals are falling, too, from a tree on the lip of the ridge, far above him. If he lifts his head to see it he will flip over backwards and fall away with the water. He sees the petals, though: translucent, purple-grey. They patter on to his face and neck. Each petal that falls against the rock becomes bunched and tough as a hailstone and produces its own ringing note. The petals rain faster and thicker around him. The notes follow in quicker succession and melt into a stream of sound, ascending and descending, curling around him, easing him back from his lockhold on the rock, pulling him into the air and back into his bed in Terrace Street, where 'Song without Words' is flowing through the wall.

James opens his eyes to a blur of colour and splayed light. He puts his hand out, immediately touches his glasses and hooks them on. The colours resolve into a bland arrangement of furniture; his dream retreats. The piano music separates itself into individual notes. Whoever's playing stumbles over a phrase and corrects it, several times.

Downstairs the piano music is louder, clanging through the wall into his hallway. James stands in front of the long mirror and gives himself a false smile, checking for new lines. He pulls in his stomach briefly, then lets it rebound. He picks coins from the neat pile on the shelf in the hall and decides to run – gently, more of a jog, maybe – to the newsagents, and buy a paper before driving to work. The pianist stops in mid-phrase, leaving a dense silence. A car passes. James is taking his jacket from the hatrack: he pauses and listens. Nobody lives next door; it's been empty since old Mrs Farrell died, three or four months ago. The music starts again. Chopin, this time. A nocturne, he thinks, pleased with himself. He shuts the front door as quietly as he can.

'Was Henry VII a "middle-class king"?'

Low groans; heads bow and biros bob over the notepads. James watches Brenda Moore's circling fist, as she embellishes the title with little loops and swirls.

'Oh, stop moaning,' sighs James. 'You all know it's good for the soul. I've prepared a supplement to your reading list. Anything with an asterisk is *required reading*.'

Deggy Baker stretches his arms high above his shaggy head and a shower of loose pages flops from his lap on to the floor.

'Long hard one, last night, was it, Deg?' asks Cerys Emmanuel in an undertone meant for everyone to hear.

'Before you go, here are your last essays back. Off you go and peruse them over your coffee.'

Papers are passed from hand to hand. Cerys Emmanuel studies her essay with a smirk.

'Teaching by numbers again, Dr Powell. Point One . . . Point Two . . .'

'That's better than some of 'em,' pipes up little Barry Drew. 'I reckon some of 'em just bungs in a mark, dun bother reading 'em at all.'

'"Fair effort",' says Cerys, miming a flourish of words on the page. 'For which read, "Usual load of crap".' The consonants snap with defiance.

'Yeah, *very* likely,' mutters shy Brenda Moore, with resentment. They're all aware that Cerys is one of the best students of her year.

James feeds papers into his briefcase, pretending not to hear.

'If anyone wants to discuss my comments, feel free to pop in . . . Not this afternoon, though – I won't be here.'

Deggy shoves part of his shirt into his waistband. 'Going home to swot up on that old poet, are you? How's it coming?'

James grunts. He regrets starting his latest research project at all, let alone mentioning it to this crew.

'Not good? Bummer. Sorry to hear that. See ya then, Jim.'

Deggy drops and gathers up a couple of pens and stray papers, and shambles out, closely followed by Brenda and her timid gaze. In the corridor outside, Cerys is talking loudly to a group of friends. They weave in and out of Welsh and English, blending and inventing words as they hurtle from explosions of laughter to sudden secretive dips. James lurks in his office and steels himself for the afternoon's encounter with 'that old poet', tired already at the prospect of trawling through those florid lines that fatten his tongue and make his jaw ache. James acquired his Welsh late; he speaks it with careful, guilty precision. He listens enviously to Cerys and her clique as they chatter on. 'Point One . . . Point Two . . .' Another flash of laughter. James shuts the door on them, and waits behind it until the coast is clear.

2

We are all in search of a story. If none presents itself, we invent our own. The past has shut its doors to us. It is impossible to gain real insight into the beliefs and language, the characters and sub-plots of another era. Yet we are compelled to push against the doors, to peer through the keyhole. We simply refuse to accept that the past will not be revived. We cannot stop chasing the dead. We study portraits, puzzle over inventories, read between the lines of letters and memoirs. We even rebuild faces from air and bone, with computers and clay, seeking help from forensic scientists and artists, as though the passage of centuries was a crime to be solved. We hope for the impossible: that, some day, one of these death-masks will blink, and smile, and tell us its tale.

In terms of historical evidence, there is little to learn about Ieuan Gloff. Three fragments of a life remain. The earliest consists of two passing mentions in a family chronicle, of the poet Ieuan or Ioan ap Gruffudd, who 'was become a soldier for the bande of Sir Rice ap Thomas in the right godly and worthie cause of Henri Tydder, earl of Richmonde and did a grete jornay i-take.' The next is a letter to Humphrey Meyrick of Penfynydd, written in 1494 by John Griphiths, servant of the Crown, to ask for the hand of his daughter, Anne. Finally, a few last scraps of anti-English verse, all dated after c. 1507, all unearthed (as was the letter) from the 18th-century archives of a local Penfynydd historian.

What does this evidence tell us? It may relate to three different men: three contemporaries, all with the same name (albeit in translation), all hailing from or connected with a small and (at the time) isolated area of south Wales. More probably, these are the sole surviving records of one man's life, glimpsed at three stages of his progress from ambitious youth to sour old age. We will call him by the name put to the post-1507 verse: Ieuan Gloff ('Lame John'). We will examine his world and his time and, in his absence, we will presume to tell his story. This will be the story of a man who threw in his lot with the Tudor cause; of a man who helped put a Welshman on the throne, and whose reward was a place in the English establishment; of a man who lost his faith in the new regime and who ended his days writing venomous verse from a hovel in the Welsh hills. This is our account of the 'grete jornay' of Ieuan Gloff, whose patriotic fervour, political ambition and subsequent disillusion mirrored the journey of his nation.

James checks his watch. A motor bike revs up outside. He wanders to the window and leans back to peer as far as possible into next door's front yard. The 'For Sale' sign is still up. Wisps of brown leaves and soggy stalks fringe the narrow paved area, victims of the winter that also claimed Mrs Farrell. James remembers her dark, creased face at the front room window, staring out, as he glanced in. She always sat at the very edge, drawn back with the curtain, monitoring; she never acknowledged his awkward half-waves.

James turns back to his desk, where several shallow stacks of paper, dealt into ranks, fight for space with his computer. He lays a friendly hand on the machine. It's a cast-off from the department, already out of its depth with young technology and covered with a thin layer of grime. It purrs and grinds, waiting for his return. James picks his nose half-heartedly and sifts through the articles and translations on his desk.

> Hen frad, yn ôl eu harfer,
> *Their old, old treachery!*
> Lle bo lladron, bydd llywodraeth.
> *Where there are thieves, there is government!*

All in search of a story. You can say that again. Months of poring through sheafs of court records, battle orders, barely readable parish histories and this is what he gets for his trouble: three fragments of a life. Not enough to construct a believable biography, not by anyone's standards. He had considered backing out and leaving Ieuan to rest in peace, until receiving a sharp sermon from Gail Fenwick, the head of department, about his meagre publication record.

'I don't want to be harsh,' she had said. 'You're a solid historian of the old school – and I value that. I really do. It's an essential part of our departmental profile. But publication is the name of the game. Without it, you will be assessed and found wanting-ah.'

Gail Fenwick has a habit of jumping off the last consonant of every phrase, expelling an extra syllable with the remaining air. James's project still had scope-ah, she insisted. Potential-ah.

James was transfixed; everything converged on that last word and the audible full stop. He lost track of what she was saying.

'You know, several people could be watching this space with interest-ah. *Media* people, James. It could be a *great pitch-ah*. Think about it. Unknown Welsh poet, hero of Bosworth, finds his fame and fortune in New-Era Tudor England-ah; then gives it all up, crying Home is where the Heart is and *Cymru am Byth*-ah. Fades into oblivion – until he's unearthed half a millennium later – *by you*. Marvellous. Just the job for a post-Assembly period drama-doc, don't you think-ah?'

The past has many points of access, she reminded him, steering him towards the door. Recorded fact is all very well, but . . .

'Take a *risk*-ah. There's a move back to narrative style – exploit it. Have *fun* with it. *You* know how to avoid overstepping the mark-ah.'

So James has permission to free-fall into history. He must invent a life. Height. Hair-colour. Favourite food, personal habits, friends and superstitions. He must do all this, without further reference to the documented dates, decrees, receipts and letters of warranty that have come up with nothing. The thought of it makes him dizzy. The thought of working by instinct, without the solid historical evidence to break his fall, keeps him in a state of almost permanent, low-level anxiety.

What if he's utterly, hopelessly wrong about Ieuan Gloff? 'What if' (as one of his students has mused), 'What if there *were* three different blokes?'

Too late. Ieuan Gloff has already formed in his head. James has seen the stubble grow, flourish into beard, wither. He has seen the flesh stretch and tan and pucker and crinkle away in a fast-forward journey to the battlefield, to London, and back to the hut in Penfynydd. The old bastard's there, limping around in James's head all day, like an aged relative. On bad days, James pleads with him. Please. Please, Ieuan, give me a clue. Fill in your lost years. Give me a flavour of your days. Sometimes, he even toys with the idea of holding a seance.

Nowadays we are hardened to the relentless assault of information. The tawdry, the trivial, the obscure, the dramatic . . . Sounds and pictures batter us from all directions. Screens, radios, headphones, videos – a chaos of rags and patches, a dissonant babble and blare.

In Ieuan Gloff's day, it was the poet who still, to a large extent, assumed the task of absorbing life's confusions, events and impressions. He observed; he understood; he provided a beginning and an end; he condensed it all into a fable, a verse, a single, clear voice. The medieval poet was a spin-doctor, a search-engine, a prophet, an entertainer. He was critic, humorist, historian, onomast, broadcaster of news. He interpreted the supernatural; he guided his listeners through tragedy and sorcery to the tale's triumphant end. His was an age-old role in a global culture. The French had their jongleurs *and* trouvères; *the Germans their* minnesingers *and* Meistersingers. *In Ireland he was the* fili, *in Hindu lands the* suta; *in Wales he was the* bardd *or the* prydydd. *He was a story-teller, rigorously trained in the rules of grammar and verse, thoroughly proficient in the old unwritten histories and traditions. A member of the oldest profession but one.*

The piano music has stopped. Mrs Farrell's front door slams and the whole house cringes. James starts from his chair, cracks his knee on the desk and sends a column of books sprawling. He slithers on one of the shiny covers and staggers to the window. His shoulder meets the glass with a mortifying thunk and he crouches and squints up and down the street. Nobody there.

Livvy hurries round the corner into Perry Street and stops short. She's forgotten where the bus stop is. Just another road, lined with terraced houses, almost a copy of Terrace Street, except that this one is narrower and undulating with new speed bumps. She remembers a break in the street where the bus stopped, with a newsagents and a chippie. Maybe it's the next left.

She's trying to compensate for the flaws of memory. That walk from the house to the stop had seemed so long and barren to a seven-year-old, buffeted between Mum and Nan as they talked about tedious things far above her head. Livvy retraces her steps to Terrace Street and walks on to the next turning. Maybe her judgement had been accurate, even at seven. She rehearses the bus route in her mind, and at the same time she sorts through the likeliest colours for the downstairs walls (neutral, clean), and plans her fortnight's schedule of tasks. And in another corner of her head she's opening a door, searching the half-lit room and smiling towards a movement, greeting her grandmother's frayed gesture with weary pity.

Maybe the bus doesn't even run here now; nearly every house has a gleaming little car posted outside. Livvy turns down George Street. This looks more hopeful – wider; a van is squeezing carefully between hedges of empty cars. And she can see the stop, and the break opposite with the newsagents and, now, a Tex-Mex takeaway. God knows what the bus fare is now; she feels for her purse in the shoulder-bag. It's a long time since she skipped along these roads beside Nan. For so many years, during Nan's decline, she used trains and taxis, timed to get her in and out without a pause. But she still remembers Nan's comforting recital, from the days of their expeditions together to the shops: quarter to and quarter past, ten minutes to get there, five to get ready, let's be off. Livvy checks her watch: quarter past eleven on the dot. Nan would be triumphant. A familiar, throaty growl makes Livvy look up. Unbelievably, it's the bus – not the old double-decker, but a stunted little 'city-hopper' in gaudy yellow and green – but there it is, struggling round the corner and missing the parked cars' headlights and wing mirrors by a hair.

3

By the time Gal arrives, the piano music has started up again. As James opens the door it switches abruptly from 'Over the Rainbow' to 'Music of the Night'. On the doorstep, Gal is holding his head to one side, listening, smiling, and James suffers his usual catch of breath at the first sight of his friend.

'I think Mrs Farrell's come back from the dead,' he says.

'Doomed to play *Phantom of the Opera* forever,' says Gal. 'She must have been a very wicked woman.'

James isn't troubled by his infatuation with Ellis Galloway. Gal has this effect on everyone. He has his father's height and pale green eyes. His mother is Malaysian, not beautiful but small, straight-backed and crackling with energy, and from her Gal has inherited the dense black hair with a bluish, gas-like sheen. At school the girls confided in Gal; the rugby players told him jokes; the teachers softened their eyes when they reached his name on the register. He and James sat at a double desk. James would watch him lope into the classroom every morning with painful gratitude.

Years later, Gal came to visit James at university. James's girlfriend at the time was an English student called Cat Simner. She watched Gal arrive from the window of James's room. 'Well, I know I'm beat now,' she said. 'You'll never find *anyone* that lovely to look at.'

James still keeps in touch with Cat Simner, although they drifted apart after he went to do his postgrad in London. Cat found herself a flat in Aberystwyth, where she's lived ever since. She spends her days at a window overlooking the sea, bashing out product features for trade magazines. James congratulates himself, from time to time, on their smooth drift from Relationship to Friendship.

Gal flops along James's sofa, legs dangling over one end, head and shoulders overshooting the other, like a big fish on a small plate. He crosses his arms to form a nest for his head.

'What's the recipe today, Jim?'

'Risotto. OK?'

Gal circles thumb and forefinger, and kisses them apart.

'So,' says James. 'How was your glamorous designer/photographer? Any . . . developments?'

Gal gives him a scornful, slow-motion blink.

'Plenty, actually, but not in your lewd sense. We talked about my Fresh Starters idea. She's going to give me a hand with the display boards. How's Sonia?'

James reddens. 'Oh, you know. Busy.'

Sonia is working in Italy. She's been away three months, and he's on the verge of forgetting the details of her face and personality.

'Long-distance relationships. Bound to be difficult,' says Gal, sagely. 'All part of the global community. Ironic, huh?'

James escapes to the kitchen, and Gal raises his voice after him.

'Watch *Neighbours*, if you can; they deal with long-distance relationships a lot. Discussed it with my fourth-formers the other day, in fact. Soaps as contemporary drama. Do they reflect or dictate the issues of the day . . . ?'

James hammocks a pile of vegetable peelings into a sheet of newspaper and carries it out to the bin. The light is deepening around his garden's scalloped beds and conifers. To the right, the high hedge between his lawn and Mrs Farrell's ripples and shifts. James hurries back to the house, where Gal is now propped into the kitchen doorway.

'So!' says James. 'What's this Fresh Starters idea, then?'

Gal springs into life, pacing around, tripping over James's heels, making emphatic gestures, cupping and slicing his words, while James is dishing out food and pouring drinks. When they sit down to eat Gal still hasn't taken off his jacket.

'Madge Probert's latest bright idea. *Past and Present*, she wants to call it. 'Sfair enough. Tells it like it is. We're having a vote on it. That's just the name – not a problem.'

Madge Probert is one of the original 'Fresh Starters' – members of Gal's creative writing forum for the over-60s. She used to run a newsagents in Riverside Terrace; in her retirement she writes stories about repressed Victorian love. Then there's Harry Bakewell, a retired dock-worker, who writes good, spare poems about his father and brothers and the farm where he grew up. Mervyn Jarman, ex-labourer, delivery man, postman, pub landlord. Rene Dawes, the joker. Rose Lewis, the oldest in the group. Elen Rabbaiotti, Jaswat Singh, Meinir Griffiths, Greta Mason . . . Twelve loyal members in all, who spend their Monday evenings reading, dissecting and encouraging each other's work. During the tea break, they chat. Some of them have lived in this city – in the same house, some of them – for half a century and more. They swap notes. Gal is afraid they're wasting good material.

'I'm always telling them to *use* it, *use* all this stuff about, I dunno, carpet-beaters, carbolic soap, the old Kardoma, whatever. *This* is your fodder, I tell them. *These* are your ingredients. Get them *cooking*.'

Mrs Probert said they should have a Community History Day. Rose Lewis said they should all sell themselves to the National Museum. Gal wants to *mine* their reminiscences, to *recollect* and *reconnect*.

'Remember when I did that Pavement Poetry Day? – it struck me then, the *gulf* between writer and reader. The poet prostrated, the reader looking down from an impersonal height . . . No *immediacy*. That's what I want to aim for with this. *Immediacy*.'

He's shovelling in forkfuls of risotto, talking through it, washing it down with quick gulps of wine. After clearing his plate he gives it a slight, satisfied shove and balances back on the hind legs of his chair, with his arms hooked over the back. He scans the air, and James knows he is already furnishing the hall for his *Past and Present* event. Huge dates painted at random points around the walls, challenging our chronological perspective. Vast, grainy prints of photographs – members of the group, past and present: grotesque close-ups of folded flesh set against wistful, sepia youth. A low background accompaniment of world events – news commentaries, air-raid sirens, horses' hooves. School parties and pensioners shuffling round between different lives, different voices, on continuous loops of tape.

'We could have a "memories and metaphors" section, to introduce their poetry and stories.' Gal sweeps a hand across an imaginary display. 'And then a "speak up!" section, where you can add your own recollections. Or write your own poetry. As it comes. You go round, hear the Fresh Starters' anecdotes, maybe read an edited version, see their creative work – and see what it sparks off in *you*. Interaction. See?'

James nods. 'Sounds good. And oral history is very sexy at the moment.'

Gal tips his chair forward with a thud and touches James's arm.

'Yes, that's what I thought. You can give us a hand.'

James's heart sinks. He begins to stack the plates, but Gal has got hold of his sleeve.

'You'd enjoy it! They're a great bunch. Plenty to say for themselves . . .'

'It's not my period,' mumbles James, backing away and dropping a fork. Gal retrieves it and swings out of his chair in one movement, and follows James into the kitchen.

'James! This is grist to your mill! Getting back to your grass roots! The people's history – come on, you'd *love* it, and you'd be doing me a *real* favour...'

James serves up the apple crumble.

'You can give us the wider picture,' Gal insists, grabbing a carton of cream. James sighs. 'Just drop it for a minute, sit down and eat.' But already he can feel the little conciliatory, retracting phrases working in his mind, and he knows he's slithering towards a commitment.

Gal downs a spoonful of crumble and manages to continue, half-choking:

'*Real* history, James. Not yer book-larnin'. You'll *love* it.'

James munches thoughtfully. Behind Gal's ducking head, in an alcove by the fire, photograph albums, tapes, books and files are arranged chronologically or alphabetically along floor-to-ceiling shelves. Tomorrow he must fish out an article – 'The Bardic Tradition: Popular Mandate or Propaganda Tool'. His eye travels straight to the right shelf and the right volume. Then, not for the first time, James visualises another book, a crisp new hardback cover, gleaming from the centre of the shelf. It floats from its place and presents its dust-jacket for his inspection: a computer-generated medieval close-up of Ieuan Gloff's raddled face, glowering under James's vast name, and resting its chin on the title: *Portrait of a Poet*.

'So, you'll give me a hand with this then, James?' says Gal, wiping the cream from his bowl with his finger.

James rolls his eyes.

'Thanks, honey,' says Gal. 'I'll nip round with the details in the morning.'

4

It's late, but he can tell she's on her way out.

'Are you there?'

James presses the receiver harder against his ear. Sonia's voice returns, faintly:

'If you want to play games with your little friend, it's up to you. If you haven't got enough work of your own . . . But then it wouldn't occur to Ellis Galloway, would it, that you've got your own life to lead, and it might not involve doing favours for *him* . . .'

'Oh, come on, Sonia . . .' He sounds reedy and self-pitying. 'It's not like that.'

'Isn't it? I'm sorry, I thought it *was* like that. I thought that's *exactly* how it was. You trailing along in Ellis Galloway's wake, basking in reflected glory . . .'

'Can't you call him Gal, like everyone else?'

'I'm not interested in your playground pet-names.'

Didn't used to mind it, thinks James, remembering her too-white smile and dazzle of blue eyes, the first time she met Gal. Sonia had been setting up the department's computer system, and James had asked her to join him and Gal in the pub for lunch. She sat between them, at a corner table. James wrestled with the crust on his steak-and-kidney pie, while Sonia turned her back on him and raised her voice against the pub noise. It was Gal this, Gal that, do you know what I mean, Gal, and James why don't you get some more drinks in, then. She told Gal all about the new extensive database and ease of access to international resources, and James made occasional supportive noises. Gal laid on the charm for a while, as always, but then his attention wandered. Sonia's searchlight beam lost track and faltered. She tucked her hair behind her ears in an unexpectedly gauche gesture. James felt fractious and foolish on her behalf. Damn Gal, he'd thought, the supercilious bastard. And that afternoon James had asked Sonia out to dinner.

'It's ridiculous,' she's saying, now, 'the way people prostrate themselves before him and do his bidding.'

'Well, whatever,' James says. 'I've said I'll do it. It's just taping some interviews, keying in a transcript, that's all.'

'Which, of course, *he*'s too busy to do.' Sonia tuts. 'I hate all that oral history blather. Endlessly recycling the past, at the expense of the present.'

Silence. James imagines her, framed in a rectangular room, inclining her head towards a red-and-gold city sunset. Clay-coloured walls, terracotta floor, Sonia's henna-tipped, earth-brown hair and her tanned legs at a sharp angle to their shadow. He can almost detect the smell of her skin: clean and wild – wet shrubbery; and he almost misses her.

'Listen,' says Sonia, 'I've got to go. My friends are waiting. We're going to a . . . club, or something.'

'How's work?' he asks, feebly.

'Oh, you know,' she says. 'Busy.'

When she's gone, James sits pouting at the phone, and wonders how long it will be before she confesses that she's not coming back.

5

It's pouring with rain, and James is having trouble getting into his car. He fumbles at the lock, swears at it, gives the key a final shove and feels his glasses lose their grip and plunge. He catches them and drops three folders.

'Oh, fuck!'

'Hup! Language!' says a voice behind him and he turns to see Vernon Lightfoot, from three doors down, lifting a vast umbrella to include him.

'Locked yourself out? Tried the old double twister trick?'

Still holding his brolly aloft with one hand, Vernon Lightfoot gives the key a dexterous tweak with the other and the lock clunks open.

'You're a genius,' says James, peeling his folders off the wet pavement.

'Comes to me natural.' Vernon Lightfoot is small and slim and perfectly bald – smooth above the obsolete hairline, corrugated below – and always smiles a cartoon smile. James feels obliged to chat.

'By the way, I've got this list of people to visit, and there's a Mr Lightfoot in Albert Road – any relation?'

'Aye, my brother Charles, the poet'. He pronounces it *poy-ett*, with a sarcastic arching of the eyebrows.

'It's just that – a friend of mine, Ellis Galloway, runs a writing group—'

'Aye, that's right, he does all that stuff, our Charles. Writing group one night, life-drawing the next. It'll be ballet-dancing before you know it. Always were a bit of a queer. *You are too wonderful . . . to be what you seem . . .*'

James realises with a jolt that Vernon Lightfoot is singing. Piano music is drifting through the rain from Mrs Farrell's open window.

'Don't hear that one much these days . . . *Honest and tru-lee, You stepped out of a dream . . .*'

Vernon's voice is tinny and tremulous, but he sings with great energy. The music stops. A pale-eyed, mournful face appears, and the window is clapped shut. Vernon Lightfoot jerks his head towards the house.

'Mrs F's granddaughter, come to do up the place and sell it on. She'll get herself a pretty price for it an' all – these old houses goes like 'ot cakes now. So there'll be more strangers here, again. Only thing keeping your property prices down is us old 'uns 'anging about.'

His smile expands, pushing his cheeks up into tight, pink crescents. 'Never mind, eh. We'll be out of it, soon enough.'

'Poor Perkin Warbeck,' says Brenda Moore, with a ferocious blush.

Cerys Emmanuel snorts. 'What about poor Perkin Warbeck's followers? Abandoned on the coast to have their heads cut off? *Bastard.*'

James looks at his students tetchily, over the top of his glasses – a pose he's assumed in recent years; a kind of tribute to his old history teacher, Mr Healey.

'To get back to the point, please – would we say, then, that Henry is playing a tricky game at this stage in his reign? Having to secure his position against—'

'A tricky game,' mutters Cerys, bitterly.

'All those lives,' breathes Brenda. 'Gone.'

'Yeah, but it's not like they're innocent bystanders, is it?' chips in Barry Drew. 'They're all out to get the king, innay? If he doesn't get them first.'

'But they're not just doing it for a *laugh*, Barry,' says Cerys. 'They believe in their *cause*. They really *believe* he's usurped the throne – like, like . . . a military coup, or something. Isn't it, Dr Powell? And *they* get off their bums and do something about it, instead of shooting their mouths off in the Union bar . . .'

A wave of 'Oooh' from the others. James draws a long, deep sigh, closes his eyes and surrenders. Only ten minutes to go till lunchtime. Then he can escape to the library and the soothing whirr of the microfiche.

'Trouble with activists,' Deggy is saying, 'All for changing the world, but when the going gets tough . . . it's other people gets killed.'

'Mm, great world we'd be living in if Deggy had his way. Serfdom, slavery, oppression – hey man, hang loose' (Cerys waggles her head and blesses them all with a peace sign), 'let's not get heavy about this, people, someone might get hurt . . .'

It's a surprisingly good impression of Deggy's sleepy accent, and even James laughs.

'I bet *you* were an activist, Dr Powell,' says Brenda, 'in your younger days.'

'Nah, he's a historian,' says Deggy. 'He knows all about activists and what they do. Revolution, war, genocide . . . that's action for you, mate. That's what the brave new world always comes to. Blood on the streets.'

Brenda nods vehemently.

'Blood and guts,' grins Barry. 'Human nature, that is. I bet you couldn't pick out *one year* in history, when some bunch of people isn't beating the crap out of some other bunch of people, somewhere or other. Innat right, Dr Powell? Not *one week*. You could do a book on that. "A History of Atrocities". Bet you it'd sell *millions*.'

'For Christ's sake,' breathes Cerys.

'Well, it would, *any* money on that. Why d'you reckon people buys the papers? Good browse over breakfast – who's been tortured or raped or chopped to bits. Same thing.'

'That's not *history*,' says Brenda. 'That's *news*.'

It was about 1974. In a classroom on the second floor, James had found a seat near the window-ledge, and was concentrating his vision on a splattering of pigeon-shit on the window. Small domestic sounds came from other classes along the corridor; the motorway purred beyond the playing fields. James's flesh was crawling. He was desperate not to cry. Maximilien Robespierre was about to sign the death warrant for his dearest friend.

'Did his hand tremble?' asked Mr Healey. 'Did the Incorruptible hesitate? This was his most cherished friend – some said his lover. Did he nearly change his mind?'

James was bundled onto the death cart with Camille Desmoulins; struggled to keep his balance without the use of his bound hands, as it rolled and jumped towards the guillotine. Felt, for Camille, the pressure of the frame against his throat, the businesslike grip keeping him in position. Glanced up at the spectators' bored catcalls, and met Mr Healey's eye, blinking over his half-moons. When the executioner hoisted the dripping head before the crowd, the rest of James's history class cheered.

'I should have done Politics,' Cerys Emmanuel is saying, to hoots of derision. 'At least politicians make a difference. You can't make a difference about what's already happened.'

James shuffles his notes on his desk with a snap.

'Well, Cerys, if you do decide to change subjects, be so good as to let me know.'

She smiles awkwardly down at her writing pad, doubling her chin and suddenly looking like a child. James wants to bite off his tongue.

It's late in the afternoon when James grows conscious of the ache in his wrist and lower back. He takes his glasses off to rub his smarting eyes. He's been working in the library for hours, caught up in the debris of the past: quills and sealing wax, sabatons, tassets and pouldrons, names from a medieval elf-world: Throgmorton, Coetlogon, Poyntz. Searching through all this clutter, on the look-out for more familiar names: John Griphiths, Ieuan Gloff, Ioan ap Gruffudd, Johan, Jan . . . No sign of him. No clues.

James begins to pack his notes and index cards with a mixture of relief and despair. A five-hour search for an absence. He's still free to do as he likes with Ieuan's life. James pushes his seat away from the screen and kneads his back. He realises, as his stomach muscles relax, that they've been rigid with tension all day, and that Mr Healey is still hovering at the back of his mind. He must be in his sixties now – or his seventies? – if he's alive. James shakes his head at the idea that Mr Healey could die.

He can hear the voice now – nasal, a little pompous, always compelling: 'Imagine it if you can, motley crew' (pacing between the desks, tapping his palm with a plastic ruler), 'Imagine Great Queen Bess herself, the Virgin Queen, moving her scabby troops to tears: "I know I have the body of a weak and feeble woman, but I have the heart and stomach of a King". And teeth like rats' droppings, I shouldn't wonder. And what do you suppose she *smelled* like?'

James always suspected that Mr Healey could commune with the dead. That he could call up the sounds of history, the taste of the air, the touch of cloth and furniture. James had longed to learn that skill. He longed to open the past like a book.

When he pulls up in Terrace Street, Gal is on his doorstep, bending down to peer through the letterbox. He turns at the sound of James's car.

'*There* you are. I've brought you the tape recorder, for your Fresh Starters gigs. Did you get the list of names? You'll like them, honestly; they're a friendly bunch, and they only bite when they've got their teeth in.'

He follows James into the cold house. James switches on lights and squats in front of the gas fire. He says,

'Remember old Healey?'

'Healey?' Gal is fiddling with the tape recorder, jabbing at buttons. 'Denis Healey?'

'*Neville* Healey. History teacher. Oh, for God's sake . . .' James strikes a match against the box several times, with unaccountable fury.

'Oh, yes, Nev Healey, I'm with you. What about him? Is he dead?'

James aims the match at the base of the fire and recoils as it pops into life. He's suddenly lost all inclination to reminisce. Gal says,

'I've brought you something on oral history, too. Might be worth flicking through. Main thing is to get them on to the old days. Don't let them wander off on to crime rates, or the Euro.'

James, still on his haunches, takes a scroll of printed sheets from Gal and unrolls it. He skims across bold subheadings and italicised phrases: narrative-pure and narrative-episodic . . . generative questions . . . . non-obstructive, supportive affirmation . . . martialling fragmentary data . . .

Gal sets the tape recorder decisively on to the dining table.

'Neat little thing,' he says, patting the machine fondly. 'Not too intimidating.'

James rolls up the paper again and gets to his feet.

'Want some food, then?'

'Well, if you're offering – Thanks, doll . . . Nev Healey!' Gal buckles on to the sofa. 'He was one of the bad guys, wasn't he? Made you say that verse in Welsh, in front of everyone.'

James had forgotten the Welsh verse incident. Tuesday morning assembly, and Miss Gravelle's grim contralto vibrating over the cross-legged ranks:

'O Death, where is thy sting? O Grave, where is thy victory?'

Gal, next to him, head bowed, lips nearly closed: 'Well, come on, where is it? I know you've put it somewhere.'

James bursting with 11-year-old hilarity, taking his cut of the joke: 'Yeah, come on Death, don't mess about . . .' and his skin contracting as Healey's pinched tones sliced across Miss Gravelle's performance. 'James Powell!' – his own name, intimate and terrible – 'James Powell! On your feet!' Turning heads, delighted smirks, and Healey, traitor, holding up an apologetic hand to disgruntled Miss Gravelle. 'James Powell. You obviously have little time for our reading from the scriptures this morning. Maybe you have something more diverting for us to hear?'

James, trapped in his own hammering brain, far above the rest of the world, terrified that if he lost concentration his hand would flick across his flies as a security check – a habit that had only recently set in.

'You do attend Miss Gravelle's Welsh classes, I take it?'

'Yes, sir.' A hiccough of laughter from somewhere, as James's face screwed itself into a brief contortion (another new habit).

'Then I'm sure you'd like to show us what you've learned. A verse from The Bible perhaps? *Yn Gymraeg*?'

James is opening cupboards in the kitchen. I am thirty-six years old, he reminds himself, and I am in my own house, preparing my own supper. There is nothing to be afraid of. He takes out a packet of dry spaghetti, a pot of mixed herbs, a tin of tomatoes.

'He didn't make me say it, in the end,' he says, comforting the panic-stricken boy he's left stranded in the silent assembly hall. Then, louder,

'Healey wasn't that bad. He didn't make me *say* the verse. Just threatened.' But Gal doesn't hear, or doesn't answer. James hurries the memory on, ends the silence: it's OK. He tells you to sit down, that's all – keep your comments to yourself, James Powell, and sit down. And then there's the pressure of Gal's foot against your own, conveying guilt and apology and support.

6

Livvy moves from room to room. Most of the furniture has been taken, and she's used one of her sporadic episodes of energy to roll back the carpet and scrub down the walls of the front room. She's opened a tin of paint: Hint of Mint. Safe and clean; the sort of thing that will appeal to a wholesome young family, say, or a professional single. A smell of dust hangs around the walls, and under it an older, deeper smell, a den-like smell of age, and tired flesh. Livvy opens the window to the spring rain, and turns her back on it. Strange how this room is reduced and darkened by bareness. It had been crammed to the hilt with her grandmother's lumpy furniture: the green, straight-backed armchair, the three-legged side-table, the gilt mirror with its knobs and curls, the hideous fudge-coloured hearthrug. Just the piano, now, and a standard lamp.

Livvy's worried about the wiring. It must be at least thirty years old, probably nearer sixty. In the evenings these rooms are edged with smoky yellow rings. The light itself seems as old as the rattling fitments. She wanders to the lamp and reaches for the light switch – a small, brown handgrenade, hanging on by a sinewy twist of wire. Livvy switches it – on, off. On, off. Then she leans against the piano and shapes a chord, changes her mind and wanders to the back room. This was the comfortable room once, where she was let loose to tumble on the sofa and cut out faces from her nan's magazines on the floor, while Mum and Nan drank tea and spoke in little packages of words, spaced apart, taking turns. Then, at some later stage, Nan abandoned this room, let it grow damp and chilly while she sat in the fuggy 'parlour', watching the street. That move had marked a change – the shift from secure, infinite old age to fragility. Disintegration.

There are still a few ornaments on the back-room mantelpiece, and two framed photographs: one of Mum holding Livvy; the other of Nan and Frank on their wedding day. He was always known as 'Frank' among the women. Never 'Grandad', never 'Dad', just Frank. Livvy had longed to call him Grandad, and did, in school, casually throwing the term around as though he was just another part of her family. In fact, she never met Frank. She knew him only through her grandmother's anecdotes and her mother's sharp disclaimers: 'He was never around much. Didn't make much impression.' Said in a way that discouraged further questions.

Livvy picks up the wedding photograph and studies it. When she was little, her nan used to take the picture from the frame and hand it to her, by the powdery edges, and Livvy would bring it up close against her face, trying to force her way into their unfocused, happy world. There's her nan, with stray strands of hair blowing across her cheek. Laughing, surprised, at the camera. There's Frank, wrapping Nan's arm around his, smiling with closed lips. He had a thin moustache – 'just like David Niven,' Nan used to say.

Livvy replaces the photograph and takes up the picture of her mother and herself. This is a shiny, black-and-white shot. Her mother stands in a doorway, rucking up her oval face against the light; she's hoisting baby Livvy up, showing her off, almost defiantly. Livvy can inspect this, now, as if it's a photograph of a stranger. It still triggers memories, but flickering in isolation, out of sequence, they're harmless enough. She knows how to control memories: it's like opening and closing a valve. She can shut them off just as they pick up momentum. It's a kind of dare.

Anyway, she must get on with the painting. Livvy trails back into the front room.

Crouching over the can of paint, Livvy considers the ragged boundary on the wall, between her tide of fresh colour and the retreating sprigs and blobs of Nan's old wallpaper. She dips a ruler into the paint and shifts it, enjoying its slow, viscous lapping from one side of the can to the other. She's unable to stop herself sinking a finger into the middle, and only just resists the temptation to plunge it into her mouth. Hard to believe that something so dense and creamy and new could do her any harm. At Christmas she and her mother used to set out to the Heath Park woods and collect fir cones, cold air smacking their faces, and then they would stop off at Thomas's shop and buy two military little bottles of glittery paint. One silver, one gold. Back home, they would spread newspaper over the table and paint the cones – she remembers the smell, metallic and headachey, like alcohol, and her mother's surprisingly delicate dabs with the brush, gilding each layer of scales, turning the cone as she worked. Bubbles of gold and silver quivering on the paper, glittering and moving on her fingers, and her mother's sudden screech as she snatched

Livvy's hand away from her tongue. So she never did get to know the taste.

Would Hint of Mint taste of peppermint creams? Livvy is back at work now, heaving the brush up and down, advancing towards the last patch of Nan's bruised walls. This wallpaper, dreary and familiar, has soaked in the conversations and silences of over 40 years. Frank put it up during one of his settled phases. Feathering the nest, showing willing. Staking his claim. Nan used to reminisce to Livvy's mother, with a gratitude that survived Frank's lapses and prolonged absences,

'Frank loved this wallpaper. Went out and chose it himself. Put it all up, never a word. Remember, Peg? When Father Papered the Parlour?'

Little Livvy enjoyed these recollections, even when she had come to understand how selective they were. She would turn to her mother, hoping to witness a flash of affection and shared memory.

'Remember, Peg?' Nan would prompt, ignoring Peg's closed expression. 'We came home one day and it was all done! Thought we'd got the wrong house. Didn't we, Peg?'

'Yes,' said Livvy's mother. 'Frank was there, for a start.'

Livvy, twirling her brush in the can, wrapping it in paint, lifting it to let the excess slither away, is still cursing her mother. Why couldn't you just play the game, just for once? All Nan wanted was to play the game. Happy Families. Why not pretend, for Nan's sake, why not laugh and shake your head and gasp all over again at Frank's wonderful surprise?

Livvy glares at the doorway, at the spectres of her mother and grandmother, home from the shops, goggling at the walls. There's Peg, granite-faced, ten-year-old Peg, blocking every challenge and appeal as Frank wipes paste and slivers of paper onto his workshirt.

'Frank! What have you done!' There's Nan behind her, all shining eyes and gratitude, taking off her rainproof hat. 'Look, Peg! What do you think of this!' – and there's Peg turning away from the whole performance, mulish, accusing, keeping her thoughts to herself: what right has *he* got to change *our* home?

Yes, but that was then. That was over half a century ago. Livvy lets the brush slap against the wall. You grew up, says Livvy to her mother's ghost. You had a child of your own. You knew how it was to explain away an absence. You could have played along. For Nan's sake.

Livvy pulls a broad stream of paint across the last corner of sprigs and blobs. There you are then, she says to the air. All gone now. I hope you're satisfied.

PART TWO

You wouldn't think it to look at me, but I'm a hardy creature. Of course I am. You don't cover that many miles a day, most days of your life, without building a certain amount of endurance and a pair of sturdy legs. But I made a slow journey upcountry that summer. At times I thought I would never catch up with the Tudor march. The main trouble was that every two or three miles I could feel my new gift burning behind my eyes, lifting my soul. The urge was so strong to rest where I was, and let my mind take flight. Sometimes I succumbed, sat on a rock, shut my eyes and gave myself up to the soaring bird-vision. But I had not learned to take control. I rose higher each time. The life beneath me unravelled too fast. Specks of humanity, whole generations, seemed to flourish and die in an instant, like insects, before my eyes. When I came to myself again I would be shaking and sweating. I have to admit, I offered as many curses as thanks to the Lord for my new talent. Still, as I said, I'm a thick-ribbed, strong-legged man, and by setting off before dawn and bedding down after dark, I made progress. I slept where I could. Occasionally at an inn – though I was trying to spare my costs. Under a hawthorn hedge. In a farmer's barn. In a haystack. The nights were easier than the days, which were hot and dusty. At Llanfoist I heard rumours that Rhys ap Thomas was not far off, leading an army of his own upcountry to join Tudor's band. I decided to take up this trail and throw in my lot with him. Near Castell y Paun I was given milk by a ploughman's daughter, and told her I was off to put a new king on the throne. She was mightily impressed, and lay with me in a ditch – though she couldn't quite recall the present king's name, and only knew that he was 'a devil', but wasn't sure why. When we'd done I was suddenly gripped with panic. I held her fast to me, while she wriggled and pulled at her skirts, whining that her father might come by. I tried to tell her about my visions.

I can see the life ahead, I whispered at my stout-buttocked confessor. 'I swear to you,' I hissed, 'I can fly above the world, above time, and see life unfold beneath me. I can see the future.'

'Very clever,' she said. 'And can you see me rocking a child with beady eyes like yours?'

Ignorant slut. I don't know why I bothered.

After five days I passed through a hamlet where the women were still at their doors, clucking to each other across a trail of slush and horse shit, left only a couple of hours before by Rhys ap Thomas's retinue. I pressed on and came to the brow of a hill, where I could see the last of his company disappearing around the edge of the wood below. I could hear the gentle rustle and stir of men and horses beyond the trees; I seemed to hear the pounding of their hearts. I took a short cut, slithering down the bank. The noise grew louder, wilder. Drumbeats punctuated the crash, clatter, flash and thunder that now began to throb about my ears. I caught up with the camp-followers – a group of large, dull-eyed women, laden with packs, chewing like cattle and walking with a slow, steady roll. That henchman was right, I told myself. They must be a sorry crew, if this lot is for whoring as well as carrying.

I said 'Do you follow Y Bonheddig Rhys?'

One of them nodded without interest, making her jowls shudder, and I quickened my step to overtake them and reach the main march. The swelling beat of that drum, the drone of movement and grinding of dust – I thought my skull would crack. Suddenly I was struck by my tiredness. The base of my spine had been groaning since the episode in the ditch. My hunger was a dead weight, dragging at my stomach. Ahead of me were the stragglers, some of them opportunists, like me, with only their daggers and country clothes; some of them were pikemen, who had fallen behind to chat. Further on was the rumble of heavy carts, and beyond them, I guessed, a more experienced body of soldiers, carrying their weapons with arrogant ease. As the track swung away from the woods and began to climb the next hill, I could just make out the rumps of horses and a flutter of banners, all in a haze towards the head of the army.

One of the countrymen turned and winked, and passed me a hanch of stale bread. He had a square, freckled head and orange-pink hair, and he grinned to reveal a row of white but irregular teeth. I thanked him, but my heart had frozen. All over this stranger's face, under his skin, dark red blotches of blood opened and spread. As I watched, their edges met and merged. The flesh glowed, blackened, melted away, until there was only a crooked-toothed skull leering at me under his ginger mop. I squeezed my eyes shut to cancel the vision, and staggered slightly. The freckled man reached out and took my elbow to keep me on my feet. He said,

'All right then, friend? Sure you want to join us? It's a long march ahead, and who knows how many days in this sun, eh?'

I shook my head, and said I was fine, and rediscovered the rhythm of my stride and the balance of my body. Behind us there was an eruption of footsteps and shouts. Two youths had come running from a farm behind that hamlet, laughing and daring each other, flushed with the glamour of the battle to come, and with their escape from an eternity of toil and boredom.

1

Mrs Rose Lewis is a birdlike, blanched-out woman. She and James sit in a small, cramped room with olive-green paisley wallpaper. Mrs Lewis manoeuvres herself and her two sticks round a low table heaped with Nice biscuits, Mr Kipling cakes and a brown teapot with a crocheted cover. James bashes his legs against the table and stumbles backwards into his chair; Mrs Lewis settles like silk into hers.

The tape begins to run. James coughs too loudly. Mrs Lewis's frail voice points out to him how the machine works ('It'll run back the other way no trouble. My grandson's got one just the same.')

'Perhaps if you could introduce yourself . . .'

She leans forwards and enunciates each word roundly.

'Mrs Rose Lewis, born in Trefelin, in nineteen-hundred-and-eleven. Good bit older than you.'

James laughs politely. Rose scrutinises his sweaty face and the smudge of Mr Kipling icing on his trousers.

'How old *are* you?' she asks. 'I can't tell these days.'

'I'm thirty-six.'

'Oh, thirty-six. You probably think I'm from Mars, then, do you? One of the little green men. I remember that – thinking old age was nothing to do with me. Even when you notice the changes in yourself – grey hairs, little lines and wrinkles, all that – doesn't worry you much, does it? Aye, we all think it's different for us. I used to see myself in the mirror and think: oh, well, I'm tired, I'm busy, see – it won't last forever. When I've got time I'll put that right. I'll get back to normal. My first husband Freddie, he used to say I was like a china doll, when we first met. I thought, When I get some time to myself, I'll be like that again. A china doll. And then, one day, you stop being busy, and your husband's dead, and you're 88, and no one looks at you the same'.

James is taken aback. He has the impression that she has rehearsed this little speech. He is losing the initiative already. He takes a folded piece of paper from his pocket; it rustles in the silence. He checks his notes, coughs again, and asks Mrs Lewis about her childhood.

'Bread and dripping. Ham – good, thick ham, sliced off the bone. And my mother made apple pie with three little leaves and an apple, made from the pastry shavings, stuck on with milk. All good and fresh, mind. Even when we lived in Trefelin, there was always a good spread come tea-time. Don't know how she did it. She worked miracles.

'She hated Trefelin, my mam. Hated sharing. We had the upstairs, if you can imagine it, and Mr and Mrs Lloyd and Violet lived downstairs. Well! Mam came from the country, but she said that lot made more *stwr* than the farmyard – snoring, grunting, calling each other names . . . I remember when they heard about their son, out in France, you know. I was only little – tiny – but I remember that: how the sounds changed. It was quiet for days on end. Such a relief.'

The gas fire hisses in the background. The room is stifling. Rose Lewis, her skin and bones transparent in the morning light, pulls her cardigan closer round her shoulders.

'There was this song. Violet used to sing it. If Mam had to go out, Violet used to keep an eye on me. She used to stomp up those stairs singing it: *Hold the fort, for I am coming, Sure to keep the – something – hot! Baked potato in the oven, Coffee in the pot!* – or was it mashed potato? Well, she always sang that, even after losing her brother.'

A clink and gush of tea being poured – rich, muscular, red-brick tea.

'It was a funny old time, that. Lot of men coming back with bits missing. I remember going up the hill to pick sheep's wool off the fences. To stuff into Uncle Johnny's shoes. He lost his toes, you see.'

James's voice, gentle but distinct, guides her back to the point:

'Did *you* like Trefelin, Mrs Lewis?'

'Well . . . it was cold. And damp. And Mam was always cross. There were slugs, too, behind the sink in the scullery. And cockroaches at night, Violet said, by the range. Warm, see. Me and Violet were a bit like cockroaches – always trying to get near the range. But there were awful rows, oh, terrible carry-ons, about that range. We were all meant to share it, see, us and the Lloyds – split the cost of the fuel. Mrs Lloyd accused my mam of all sorts – following the coal-merchant's wagon, she said, picking up the bits that fell off, picking them out of the horse-doings, chucking in useless old clinkers, instead of buying proper stuff and giving the miners their due.

'But me and Violet were all right. We used to shuffle close as we could, try and reach the warm patch with our bottoms. I used to think it was like a big old duck, that range, sitting on its nest, watching us.

'I tell you who *was* hurt in the War, now. Up on that hill, behind the houses – there was this old soldier used to hang about there. Smelled terrible. Said he'd give me a penny if I held his hand.'

She pauses for effect, observing James's reaction. Mocking him, while James prickles with dread.

'And then he swung his arm round and there was just a knot, an empty sleeve, and then he laughed, and his teeth were all black and yellow. He was *filthy*.'

She spits the word with all the shock and venom of a perplexed six-year-old.

'When I told Mam she said, "That's just Cakey Bob, he emptied that sleeve for King and Country". But I hated the soldiers after that . . . And by the way, they should have cut off that other hand, too.'

She is daring James to ask what she means. The dense heat, the heavy, stale smell of vegetables and lavender, and her sly, suggestive smile all close around him. He can't meet her watery gaze. He asks her when they left Trefelin.

'Da and Uncle Johnny got a grocer's shop in town. Just a little shop. We lived behind it. But it was our little empire. The grocery emporium. Had a proper pantry and a gas stove. The shop front was like our little stage. Drums of fruit, we had, and biscuit tins on the counter, and pats of butter and cheese . . . And Mam was a gam about the place – running it *her* way, none of your Lloyds now – shaking out the rugs, sweeping the floors, sieving the ashes, blacking the grate, polishing the fenders . . . A right little palace, that was. And we ate like kings, too. Surplus stock from the shop, fish from Draycott's, meat from Hatchett's the butchers. But even with the pantry, hot days were a trouble. Sometimes Da used to bring the bacon in, slice off a hanch and –ych! – maggots! Squeezing out from the fat.'

A hiccoughing sound from James, as he replaces a Nice biscuit.

'"Our little friends are back," Da would say, and he'd lap off the bad bits and serve up the rest. Anyway, Mam went off Hatchetts in the end. Said they sold bad meat – dragged me down there once, to get her money back because we'd been ill with it. Kicked up a real fuss. I was *so* ashamed, but she was pleased as punch, getting her refund. Bought me a sugar-stick on the way home, to celebrate. Mind, in those days she thought nothing of popping across town to the market. In her later years she wouldn't even go to the end of the road. Stopped going outside the house. I had to do the shopping for her and Da, as well as my own family. She just wouldn't set foot out the door any more. Stayed put like a queen in her castle. Even when it all changed.

'Uncle Johnny . . . well, he went to the drink a bit. People couldn't spend so much, see. Customers coming in after broken biscuits or pecked fruit. Stock went down. Da wanted to sell up, but Mam wouldn't hear of it. "This is my home," she says, "And I'm not budging." Took us a while to notice something was up.

'Mondays, when I was first married, I used to take our wash over, and me and Mam would do the lot together, in the wash-house. Having a natter while we stoked the copper and all that – thrashing away at the sheets and smalls in the dolly tub. Then she starts refusing to go into the wash-house. Afraid there might be spooks in there, she says. Made out like she was joshing, but she meant it.

'When Da died I said, "Come to us, Mam, don't be soft. I can take care of you." But she wouldn't have it. Someone else took on the shop, and Mam moved upstairs.

'Wouldn't come to my first husband Freddie's funeral. That upset me. And she *liked* Freddie, really fond of him. He used to call her "old girl" – she loved it. But she wouldn't come. "I'll say a prayer from here," she says. I ask you. Prayers for the dead at the grocery emporium. "Aye," I says, "and I'll ask the vicar for a pound of spuds."

'Wouldn't come to see me married the second time, to Len. I went to see her, I says, "Please, Mam, come and see me wed, it'll mean the world to me." She give me a hug and you know what she said? "Now you go on and get married," she says, "But watch you don't ever forget poor old Freddie. Don't do anything to hurt his memory," she says. "He'll only come back and haunt you." Well, we'd not long since buried Da. That probably tipped her over.

'Poor old Mam. Living in a grocer's shop, and couldn't go out to get the provisions, by the end. There was me, with a family of my own to feed, keeping back some *cawl* or a bit of pie to take it over to her, like she was a pet cat. And her such a wonderful cook, too. My food was never good enough, mind, even then. Oh, the meat was rotten, it wasn't done right – where did you buy it? Why are you bringing us poison meat? she'd say. She even blamed me for Da passing on. Said I must have given him bad beef. And he hadn't even been eating beef. Went out like a light over a fish pie, he did, in 1950 . . .'

Rose pauses for breath and James regains control.

'When you think back, though, Mrs Lewis . . . would you say it was a hard life? Or a happy one?'

She shrugs, testily. 'It's not finished yet, you know.'

'No, I didn't mean . . .' (Shit, thinks James. Don't retract – respond. Don't argue – ask.)

'What sort of question is it, anyway? Was it a happy life? How should I know? There were happy times. Everyone has some happy times.'

Ask, don't argue, thinks James, and presses on.

'Can you think of any *particularly* happy times?'

A long silence. Then she takes pity on him, and gives a conclusive nod.

'Every Saturday, me and my friend Gwenan used to go to this sweetshop on the corner. Aniseed balls, two a ha'penny. They had this brass scoop. They used to scoop them all out, and twist them into a tidy little paper cone. And Gwenan always took first suck. Then she passed it to me, mouth to mouth, so as not to get sticky fingers.'

2

The historian is a gambler, dealing in probabilities. In describing and analysing a past event, he or she does no more than place a bet. Even in the case of recorded events – even in the case of events that occurred within living memory – even so, the odds must be weighed up. What are the chances of an account being full, accurate and objective? What are the chances that a contemporary interpreter will understand the narrator's intentions and nuances? Then again, when there is barely any information at all, barely any form to study, the stakes are so much the higher.

James takes off his glasses, rests his elbows on the desk and digs his knuckles into his eyes. Through two walls, he can hear the muffled lilt of the piano: *As Time Goes By*. For a moment he seems to be asleep. Then he sits up straight, highlights the whole paragraph, and deletes it.

The historian is a detective: examining evidence, tracing behaviour patterns, calculating outcomes. The medieval historian is a detective who can never close a case. There are no witnesses; there is no one left to question, no one to clarify statements, no one to confess or to deny. The case of Ieuan Gloff is more elusive than most. In tracking down our man, we have little to go on – only a handful of clues; a good deal of circumstantial evidence and hunch.

Our first glimpse of Ieuan is fleeting: a casual reference by the Llwyd family historian, who notes that the bard Ieuan ap Gruffudd did come from Penfynydd to sing verses at a daughter's wedding. The year is 1483, over half a century before parish records were introduced to pin down souls. Two years later, the anonymous scribe remarks that Ioan [sic] ap Gruffudd, bard of Penfynydd, took his grete jornay, joining the ranks of Rhys ap Thomas, heir to the Dinefwr estates and erstwhile Yorkist, to fight for Tudor and the Lancastrian cause on Bosworth Field. After this, our subject vanishes for nine years.

We begin with what we know. Penfynydd exists today as a hilltop estate, on the edge of a dying colliery town. In the 15th century it would have been little more than a scattering of farms. This may have been Ieuan's place of birth, or his home in later life, or the home of his patron.

For many hundreds of years, the Welsh bard was a traveller. Poets-in-residence were not unknown: a privileged few were kept in the permanent service of a particular court or manor. In the main, though, these were wandering minstrels. Some tramped the whole length and breadth of Wales as they composed the lines required for religious holidays, special festivals or nights of unspecified revelry. Others roamed from house to house within a limited patch of territory, and supplemented their literary earnings with additional work – such as farming. Perhaps Ieuan was one of these.

Poetry was his vocation, nevertheless. As an aspiring young bard, maybe the younger son of a wealthy farming family, he was taken into tutelage, along with a few other apprentices, by one of the old hands. From this retired master of the craft, he learned the complexities of form and vocabulary, of ancient Celtic myths, and of the family trees of potential benefactors. The little of his verse that remains to us was written down during his lifetime. This suggests that Ieuan occupied a reasonably high rung of the bardic ladder. Below him were the people's poets – the balladeers who entertained the market crowds – whose names have disappeared along with their work. Above him were the stars – the Dafydd Nanmors, and Lewis Glyn Cothis and Guto'r Glyns – creators of some of the richest and most elegant lines in the language, who fraternised with, and arguably influenced the most powerful players on the political scene. Judging from his few legacies, Ieuan was not in their league.

When he undertook his journey to battle, Ieuan ap Gruffudd was presumably young and fit enough to march, but experienced enough to have established himself in his trade. We have only probables and possibles. We must make an educated guess. Let us suppose that in 1485 Ieuan was twenty-one. The year of his birth, then, was 1464: the same year that Jasper Earl of Richmond, Henry Tudor's uncle, sneaked on to a ship with a bale of straw on his back and sailed to Brittany to plan the restoration of Lancastrian power.

James groans and takes off his glasses again. He's so tired. He rests his head on his arms. There's the Rose Lewis interview to transcribe yet, and then the next one to arrange . . . Sonia has told him again to back out of the whole business.

('Just say *no*. Why is everyone so desperate to be Ellis Galloway's slave? Don't be such a *wimp*, James.')

But Gal was right. James does know how to do this. He knows how to listen to the Rose Lewises, how to hear the significance, to draw the larger picture from her accounts of washing and eating and cooking and cleaning. He has faith in her memories; he receives them, and shapes them into a coherent testament. He respects them.

Once, in a bedsit in Archway, he lay in the crook of Cat Simner's plump arm and told her she had no respect for other people's lives. She had been describing her secret hobby. 'I look round houses,' she said. 'I go to estate agencies, and pretend to be buying a house, and they show me round people's homes.'

James was horrified.

'That's like burglary,' he said.

'Don't be daft. I don't *take* anything. I just poke around in cupboards, and look at the photos on the piano. You'd be *amazed* how many people buy flowery furniture, even for the tiniest rooms.'

James pictured her breathing in the air of a stranger's bedroom.

'You *are* taking something,' he said, piously. 'Just crashing in there and nosing about . . . It's so *selfish*.'

She was laughing at him. 'What's selfish about it? They don't know I'm not a potential buyer. What do they care?'

He was annoyed. He shifted away from her in the thin bed. He said, 'Sometimes, it's as if you don't know *how* to consider other people's feelings. They're all part of a big performance to you, laid on for your personal entertainment.'

She stopped laughing. 'Well, I'm sorry I'm such a hard bitch. It must be a great disappointment to you.'

Not long after that, she stopped staying with him on her trips to London. She had an aunt in New Cross, and stayed the night there, instead. ('I don't want to distract you,' she said. 'I know you postgrads. You need the small hours for referencing.')

James clenches his teeth as a question begins to form involving Sonia. He moves his hand to wipe the question away, and touches the rim of a hat, tipped over his eyebrow. He lifts his head to watch the dust sparkling in the beam from a high window. Slender silhouettes loom against opaque glass. Lettering repeated in shadow across the floorboards – *J. Powell, Private Eye* – quivers and disappears as the door opens. She's dark against the sunlight. But her outline is enough to stir his attention.

'Mr Powell?' A voice that slides round his neck and licks his ear. She steps into the light. 'I'm Sonia Dawes.'

A woman with one-way legs to paradise. A woman with eyes that burn cold like electric light.

'There's something I need to tell you.' The purr of an Italian cat. A wildcat, with a scent like the forbidden land.

She drifts across and finds a mooring on the desk. She scoops off her hat and releases a waterfall of blue-black hair.

'Aniseed ball?' She makes an 'O' of her pink mouth and her

tongue emerges, tipped with a wet, glistening jewel. This dame keeps her fingers clean. But her face is changing – growing thinner, shrinking around the bones. James turns to the window, where the choking peaks of the skyscrapers have become rocks, emerging from a wide plain that suddenly plunges, hurtles into a tangle of trees and then deeper, to the river, which clangs and crashes against the bank so that the gathered crowds can barely hear the man who stands before them, balancing on a rock, yelling:

'Get off your bums!'

The crowd mumbles, builds its own momentum, calls, jostles. They're screaming now, moving towards the man, carrying James with them, and then a new voice thunders over the babble:

'On your feet! *Yn Gymraeg*!'

They turn like children to the towering figure of Neville Healey – who metamorphoses into Melvyn Bragg before their eyes. He's wrapped in a monk's cowl, which flaps wildly around his only arm as it hoists and drops, hoists and drops the great bell of truth, with tranquil rhythm: da-ding . . . da-ding . . . da-ding . . .

Shit! How long has the phone been ringing? James jerks his head from the desk and wipes away the stream of saliva that's already spreading a blot across his shirt sleeve. He stumbles into the hall.

'Hello? Sonia?'

'Sorry, it's only Cat. Are you OK? You sound like someone's just hit you with a sledge-hammer'.

James reels. Black specks are floating across his eyes.

'No – it's . . . I forgot my specs . . .'

'How's old Ieu coming along? Getting you down?'

James grunts.

'Keep having these *dreams* . . . I was just thinking about you, as a matter of fact—' ·He trails off, changing his mind.

'You saucy devil. Tell me all about it when I get there.'

'Get where?'

'I'm taking over your spare room for a few days, if that's OK. Got a few people to meet for company profiles. I won't be in your way . . .'

James thinks of Cat's last visit. Sonia was there at the time, and James was tense and wary from the moment Cat arrived. He worried that Sonia might be grazed by Cat's exuberance; he watched her maintaining a careful distance, and wished Cat would leave. Cat is untidy, chaotic. She broke a mug, and got biro marks on the spare room curtains. She left a book on the floor and trod on it, breaking the spine. Sonia fell over Cat's bag and jarred her knee against the door. James fretted over the best way to ask Cat to go. Cat thundered up the stairs, bellowing 'Gangway, bladder about to burst!' and James noted Sonia's controlled detachment, her narrow, averted face and languid eyelids (and wondered, in passing, whether he would grow to dislike her in due course). Thank God, thinks James, she's not here now.

'Of course you won't be in the way,' he says. 'As long as you pick up your toys after you. When are you coming down?'

3

Cat is sitting on the kitchen floor, biting her nails, while James makes coffee. She's left a way-marked trail from front door to kitchen door: backpack, jacket, left trainer, right trainer. She's knackered. She stretches her legs and braces her feet against the washing machine. 'The trains were crap – bring back British Rail! – the buffet was shut ... I'm gasping. Any biscuits?'

'How long are you here for?' asks James, stepping over her legs to get to the mugs.

'Couple of weeks, if that's OK? I've got to see some bloke in Pontcanna who sells adhesives, and then a week Friday there's a woman who makes sports bras down the docks. Yes, I'll tidy it up now, just let me sit for a bit.'

She leans her head back and shuts her eyes, and James eventually asks: 'How's ... things?'

Without opening her eyes Cat says, 'That's all finished.' When he doesn't answer, she looks at him and adds, 'There were complications.'

James nods shortly, discouraging further revelations, but Cat offers them anyway.

'The divorce wasn't as pending as he made out. But the wife got more and more pending every day, and in the end I thought, sod him. If he can't make up his mind I'll make it up for him.'

'Shift,' says James, giving her a muted kick on the thigh. He's balancing a tray with milk, mugs and chocolate Hob-nobs.

'You know, sometimes,' – Cat is heaving herself to her feet – 'I think you and Sonia have got the right idea. I mean, it's very civilized, really, isn't it? Six months together to release all your pent-up passions and six months apart to get on with proper life'.

She follows him into the back room.

'Tempting fate, though, maybe,' she says, reaching past him to snatch a Hob-nob. 'The half-yearly break. Ever felt the urge to stray?'

'Not particularly, so far.'

'Mm ... I suppose Sonia would be a tough act to follow, slim-brown-bitch. And there's always self-help, I suppose – oh, don't be so *prissy*, Jamie. It serves a purpose.'

'Did I say anything?'

'You made that face. Anyway, I've made an executive decision. From now on I'm only prepared to consider relationships on a part-time basis. Strictly recreational. I'm going to have fourteen cats and wear a straw hat to prune my windowbox.'

Her face loses all animation and she sits chewing her thumbnail, glassy-eyed. James recognises this sudden drop of mood.

'Drink your coffee,' he says. 'I'll go and get more biscuits.'

In the kitchen he moves about quietly, waiting for her spirits to pick up.

There was a time when these dips and surges drove him mad. Never knowing how she'd react, or what would set her off. It could be tears or chair-throwing frustration or laughter; it could be a rejection letter, or world famine, or nothing. Eventually he developed strategies. When she wept, or sank into morose silence, he occupied himself, and waited. When she flew into a rage, he left the room. He learned not to argue or defend himself. That only left him bewildered and shipwrecked.

'What can I do?' he would moan to Gal. 'You can't reason with a hurricane.'

James wonders whether her mood swings are less extreme these days. Or whether he's more understanding. Maybe it's all become less personal. He's more alarmed, now, by Sonia's relentless, placid logic than by Cat's furies.

After leaving London, just before getting his job at the college, James went to visit Cat in Aber. He had gone with some trepidation, conscious of their cooled relationship, unsure whether some kind of apology or explanation or row was in order. But she had seemed genuinely pleased to see him. They walked along the seafront towards Constitution Hill, leaning against the wind. They kicked the bar at the end of the road and turned back, letting the wind nudge their steps. Cat suddenly stopped, and flung her arms around him.

'We're better off like this, aren't we?' she called, and her voice was flung ahead of them. 'As mates.'

James is boiling the kettle for more coffee, biding his time. Up the hall comes the piano music again: *I saw you last night and got that ooold feeling* . . . He lets the steam from the kettle-spout warm his face. He's thinking about Cat's hugs. She's never changed the way she hugs. No need. Even in bed, her hugs weren't erotic. Engulfing, enveloping, bordering on aggression. But not sexy.

'Matthew,' she has said of her latest, 'Matthew says I'm like a polar bear. He's afraid I'm going to crack his bones one day.'

Sonia doesn't really hug at all. She embraces. Thin arms balanced around his shoulders and neck, hovering. Her hip bones jut forward, holding her crotch at a finger's-width distance from his. He can't hold her without wanting to crush her, find contact with all that contracted skinniness. James places his hands briefly against the hot plastic of the kettle to change the direction of his thoughts.

In the other room, Cat is having trouble getting the gas fire to ignite. She flicks and clicks, flicks and clicks the dial.

'You need a match,' he says, coming in. 'It's broken.'

'Never mind. It's not that cold.'

James sets out a second helping of biscuits. Cat sits, and pats her palms on the table: decisive.

'Anyway. I've come down to work, not to cry on your shoulder.' She picks up her mug of coffee and rests her lips for a moment on its rim.

'You never liked Matthew, though, did you?'

'Oh, come on. I only met him once.'

'But you thought it wouldn't last. Didn't you. I could tell.'

James starts a reply, then shuts his mouth. This is always her way: making out that he's damned her relationships from the start. Well, he thinks, you shouldn't pick such weird ones, if you want them to last. The dog-walker who slept with his labrador. The pretty lecturer with tired eyes and swollen lips, who rang his parents every evening and shouted obscenities at them. Matthew, a wine bar manager, Bearded Leo, a writer, both estranged from their families; Leo also battling with a drink problem.

('Is she determined to get hurt, or just remarkably slow on the uptake?' asked Sonia with mock innocence, after Bearded Leo had returned to wife and bottle.)

James watches Cat stir her coffee, recognises the misery and humiliation settling around her, and tries not to acknowledge his own sense of relief. He hadn't taken to Matthew, as a matter of fact. Bit too pleased with himself, James had thought.

Cat taps her spoon against the mug.

'So! What's Gal's new scheme about, then? Trust you to get roped in. I'll give you a hand with it, shall I? While I'm here?'

She cuts the surface of the coffee with her spoon and watches the spiral of froth gather against it. She says, mainly to herself:

'I'm going to be a sugar-mummy. A kind of Gloria Swanson,

lounging around in flowing stuff, having toy-boys sent up to relieve my seclusion.' She licks the spoon and takes three large gulps from the mug. 'Sod him.'

4

Rose Lewis stands in her kitchen, transfixed. Something – maybe the smell of tea-leaves, or the light draped across a corner of the cooker – has brought her to a halt. This has happened a few times in recent months: the feeling that she's heard a phrase or seen a face before, in an enclosed, private part of her mind. But it's gone, and Rose gets back to her task, passing one of her sticks to her left hand and pouring into the pot with her right. She then balances both sticks against the cupboard and transfers the tray – untroubled by the slide and rattle of the crockery – on to a small trolley. Taking the sticks up again, both in one lumpy hand, she shuffles sideways into the sitting room, pulling the trolley behind her in short, noisy bursts.

Before letting herself down on to the armchair, Rose pauses for breath and has another think. She's revising her memory, correcting her own mistakes.

She was wrong about the range. Violet rarely came to sit in front of it with her; usually it was just Rose, amusing herself with her distorted reflection in the oven-door handle. Thin, pale, with wavy fair hair scribbling around the forehead and cheeks; making daft shapes with her mouth. Unconsciously, Rose imitates her younger self, rearranging her rucked-up, see-through old skin. Then she starts her descent, lowering herself with the help of the sticks, hand under hand, until she reaches the safety of the armchair. She checks her surroundings: remote control for the telly on one arm; portable phone on the other. Tea trolley at an angle to her knees, within reach (with a bit of shifting around, which she'll get to in a minute).

Rose aims the remote. A line stretches across the TV screen and then springs into life. A spectacled face looms up, talking. A jerky old film of horses and carriages and women in large hats and skirts flash in and out of his sentences. Rose switches channels. Three young men arranged on a stage are being pointed and railed at by members of the audience, and a line of text appears: *'Slept with their best friend's parent.'* Rose nods at the screen, relieved to be immersed in strangers' lives.

Sometimes Rose forgets the weakness in her legs and makes a false start, expecting to spring out of her chair. This was something she tried to explain to that drip with the tape recorder: the conviction that all these discomforts, pains, inconveniences are as temporary as a head-cold, and will get better. Still, on the whole, Rose is easy enough with this routine of old age. The morning cuppa. The morning movement – still pretty regular, thankfully. The washing and dressing. The morning TV. Three days a week Ffion, the home help, comes, and Rose does some writing ready for her class, feeling that it would be inconsiderate to sit there watching the telly while someone else cleans away her dirt.

'What rhymes with "river"?' Rose will yell over the noise of the hoover, tapping her cheek with her biro.

Ffion switches off the hoover and stares into the middle distance. '"Clever?" "Deliver?" No . . . "Give 'er . . . one!"' and they'll both cackle as Ffion resumes her cleaning.

There are other visitors, too: the health visitor once a fortnight, the chiropodist once a month. All cheerful people, and all mercifully uninvolved, with that detachment in the eye that qualifies their caring questions. Rose likes the detachment. The professionalism. That's what she saw lacking in that boy, the interviewer. He was too disturbed, too touched by her memories. Like someone fingering your clothes with too much interest.

Rose takes an unsteady slurp of tea and switches channels. The phone rings, and she swears at it. This portable phone, this bloody ball-and-chain, was a present from her daughter, Irene. And like Irene, who was the most awkward of her babies, it cries and cries until she picks it up. Rose jabs at the 'talk' button and shouts, over the telly:

'Hello, love.' Irene always calls in the early mornings. Now that all *her* children are adults, Irene finds the hours long and empty. She isn't as self-contained as her mother.

'All right, Mum? How's the legs?'

Rose takes a mouthful of Nice biscuit before answering. She's never really been comfortable talking to Irene, only child of the second marriage.

'Ffion coming today?' says her daughter.

'Not today. Got to go in a mo,' says Rose, turning up the volume on the telly. 'The adverts are finishing and I want to watch the film.'

Family is important to Irene. She spends so much energy keeping in touch, remembering birthdays and anniversaries, ringing to see that everyone's OK – not just Rose but her three half-brothers and their families, her children, all the various offshoot families of spouses and partners. As for Rose, she's lost count of her grandchildren and gets their names mixed up. She has three great-grandchildren, who are nothing but round, indistinct faces dribbling and gurgling in shiny colour photographs. The only name she remembers among them is Rosalind, known to everyone else as Lindy. (Rose made up the other names for James's benefit, and added, for effect: 'I love them all, the little devils.') She knows she *ought* to love them all: children, grandchildren, great-grandchildren – and thinks she probably does. But on the whole she prefers life without moorings. Weightless. It's easier, and funnier, that way.

But she does feel a spasm of guilt when her daughter rings, and she has to steel herself for another conversation. It was so different with the boys, her and Freddie's sons. They just came and went, part of the bustle and toil of her first marriage. They all looked like their father, Freddie Evans: all ears and teeth and thick, dark, wiry hair. And like him they buzzed around on the edges of her life, landing for food, shelter, a bit of businesslike affection, before taking off again to the outside world.

Freddie Evans.

Rose only has to repeat the name to start laughing. That was the effect he had on her, always. Made her laugh. '*What a lucky man I am*,' he'd sing, '*The luckiest in the world! Always full of beans, Because I love the grocer's girl!*' He used to take her hand with care, in the early days, cradling it like a butterfly in his, frightened of tearing the wings. Then he would murmur some nonsense, hood his eyes like Valentino, kiss her wrist, and her arm, and Rose could never keep a straight face.

Freddie Evans.

'When I retire,' he used to say – and him only twenty-two or so – 'When I retire, Rosie, we'll have a proper garden, by the sea, and we'll go to the seafront and watch the ships.'

That was his ambition: to sit with her on a bench in a sea breeze, and watch other people sail away.

Rose considers that young nitwit's question: Was it a hard life, or a happy life? As if you could look at it, and turn it about and mull over it, like a biscuit. Sweet or sour? Plain or jammy? Rose doesn't know what her life has been. It crept around her, and merged into the steam and scrub-water of the kitchen, and the heavy smell of soapy wet laundry and the faintly toilet-pan smell of chicken carcasses, waiting to be boiled. Even her three boys, her lovely, Freddie-faced boys, ceased to be individual characters.

She was always in such a rush with them, doling out their food, clipping their ears, sending them off to school, washing and washing their sheets and underwear until her hands were blood red and hard as gravel. And then the war was over, and they were all alive, and the boys were taller than their parents and on the prowl among the local girls, and she remembered what Freddie had said about having a proper garden by the sea, and for a time Rose believed she'd already grown old at thirty-eight.

One evening in 1949 Freddie stumbled, in a drunken haze, under a doctor's Morris Coupé. A policeman came to the door to let her know. She grasped the facts, understood what he said and accepted his condolences. She thought, I must tell the boys. She went into the kitchen and prepared tea for five, as usual.

She had to break the news to her parents. She took some sausages for them at the same time, to save herself two trips. Da said, 'Oh, Rosie, oh, my Rosie,' and put his fists into his eyes. Rose said to him,

'How can I tell Mam? She can't manage as it is. She'll be living in the cupboard, next thing.'

Da choked with a sob that was a half-reluctant laugh, and Rose was pleased with herself for that.

In the event, her mother didn't have hysterics or shut herself further away. She sat at the back of the shop, ashen, preoccupied, and Rose knew she was thinking about the funeral, and how to get out of going. Rose hated her mother that day.

Trouble comes in threes, they say. In the space of a year, Freddie was knocked down, Da snuffed it into the fish pie, and Rose married again.

But that's not fair: Len was no trouble. That was the point of Len: no trouble. He never upset her, and he never made her laugh. Len had worked next to Freddie in the baking factory. After the funeral he made regular calls, and sat in the kitchen, saying nothing. Rose was strangely relieved by his presence. Someone to watch that she didn't turn out like her mother.

People may have thought it was too soon, but for Rose her second marriage was simply the next step. The next task to be undertaken. Besides, her boys had all left home or were about to leave, and they had no objections. She'd be taken care of. So there they all were in the wedding photo – three grinning Freddies, towering over Rose and her bald, overweight new husband, who had grown a beard that didn't suit him, for the occasion.

By the time Irene was born, life had slowed down. There was still Rose's mother to cater for, cringeing behind doors in her own home, but Rose's boys had vanished into their own lives, and Len was merely there. Irene's childhood was an unsettling novelty for Rose. Instead of wolfing down her food and rushing off, Irene picked at everything, helped clear away, sat wanting more tea and a chat. Rose never knew what to say. Len would come in and stand with his hands in his pockets, and he and the girl would talk, directing their comments at Rose's back as Rose rolled out pastry or peeled potatoes.

Over forty years later, Rose still lets her daughter lead the conversation.

'Well, we'll be down soon to see you,' Irene says, every time. No doubt they will: responsible Irene will surely decide it's for the best, and they'll move back from Bristol, to be near her aged mother. Then there'll be impulsive visits, offers of 'nipping round to fix your supper'. Rose dreads the day.

Then it's: 'What have you got in for tonight? Anything tasty?' Irene feels that Rose should be eating more healthily. Fresh vegetables, fruit, that sort of thing.

'Make sure you have something hot. And don't do without. If you can't face it, call Ffion, she'll knock something up for you.'

For tonight, Rose has planned bacon, liver and onions, all neatly packaged into a frozen meal-for-one, the greatest miracle of the modern age. The microwave was the only halfway useful Christmas present ever bought for her by her children. They clubbed together (despite Irene's misgivings about microwaved food). Rose waits for it to ping every evening, balanced on her sticks, and sings to herself: *Hurrah for Beetox, What a delightful smell! The stuff that every self-respecting grocer likes to sell . . .*

She takes the plastic dishes out with one hand wrapped in a teacloth, and lets the food slide onto her plate in one steaming mush.

The price is right, the cook's delight, how easily it's made!

Then on to the trolley goes the lap tray, next to the lemon barley water (prepared in a jug by Ffion and put aside for the week). And Rose shuffles to her place, timing her arrival for *The Bill* or *Peak Practice*.

So join the happy members of the Bee–tox brigade!

If the phone rings during supper Rose turns the TV volume to maximum until it stops. She needs solitude to savour every mouthful, closing her eyes briefly, gloating over recollections of mouldering pies and soft vegetables and long, sweaty hours over the stove.

Was it a hard life, or a happy one?

It's not finished yet!

That told him. That brought him up short. Every time she thinks of it, Rose blows an insipid raspberry, and her flimsy shoulders jiggle with mirth. It has occurred to her, of course – this business of the future. The certainty of death. She has wondered whether she's supposed to know what to do, and how to contemplate it. Is it a gift that's meant to come with age? Well, it hasn't come to her. Rose has no more idea how to confront the inevitable now than she did in 1949, when she laid a fifth place at the table for her dead husband.

After saying goodbye to Irene Rose switches off the phone, flicks channels and settles on a trail for *Stage Door*, which she thinks she saw with Freddie once at the Odeon. Never mind families, never mind death – this is what's real: *Stage Door*, starting in half an hour. This, and the scent of flour on her mother's hands; and the bounce in Violet's song with every tread on the stair; and the warmth of the floor by the range, seeping in through her buttocks. The rest of it – the men she married, the children she bore, the endless trudge through illness and recovery, illness and death, accident and tedium; all that, which was supposed to be the construction of her own life, her own self, it all flits past as an afterthought. Real life, the real Rose, leapt straight from the range in Trefelin to her armchair in front of the telly in Pritchard Street. Rose dunks another biscuit and holds it up, letting the tremor in her hand send droplets of tea back into the cup.

5

Pen-y-Wenallt Hill sweeps round into Albert Road. Every house has a bay window and an area at the front the width of a large flower pot. As they pass, James and Cat glance through the windows: a woman adjusting her wig in the mantelpiece mirror; a man asleep in the glow of daytime TV; a cat watching them from its sill; two children fighting on bare floorboards in a knocked-through, street-to-garden room. Meat is Murder stickers. Some houses have low walls at the front, with dumpy hedges; some still have little stumps of rusty iron, where the railings were taken to be melted down during the war.

James checks his list and slows his pace.

'Number 33,' he says. 'You don't have to come in.'

'No, I want to. I like getting people to talk about themselves. It's my job.'

Like every other house, number 33 has a small porch, decorated on each side with floral ceramic tiles. Some residents have polished theirs up to a stained-glass sheen, but Mr Lightfoot's tiles are rough with dust and grease. Behind the railings, instead of a flowerpot, there's a folded-up trestle table covered with a sun-bleached rug.

The door opens a couple of inches before snagging on its chain. The narrow space is filled with Mr Lightfoot's glare. No, he's not expecting a James Powell. No, he doesn't remember talking on the phone last night. He shifts, and one eye blinks at them through the crack. It swivels around, up and down, with blatant suspicion.

'The project,' prompts James. 'Fresh Starters. Ellis Galloway's class – you know, Mrs Probert's project—'

The door shuts, rattles and opens wide. Seen whole, Mr Lightfoot seems diminished and harmless.

'Oh, aye, I've got you. This remembering thing. That Probert woman's daft as a henhouse.'

He turns from the door but leaves it open, so they follow. He indicates the front room with a subdued, defensive wave. James and Cat sit on the sofa, which is shabby and mottled and smells of dead cigarettes. Their host stands with shoulders hunched; he scowls at the tape recorder, which James has produced from his pocket. Charles Lightfoot is his brother in reverse: an upside-down version of the crescent smile, and eyebrows that dip instead of arching, giving him a permanently melancholy look. He has slightly more hair, but plasters it snug against his head.

'Your brother's a neighbour of mine,' says James.

'Vernon, aye.' Charles Lightfoot throws a nervous glance towards the door. 'I expect you'll be wanting a cuppa.'

PART THREE

We passed through Llanidloes and word got back that Tudor's troops were not far ahead. We were marching well. On 12 August we reached Y Drenewydd and there was a great commotion. A detachment of Tudor's own army had come to meet us. I had never seen so many people: townsfolk milling around, cavalrymen manoeuvring their steeds with studied nonchalance, infantrymen chatting like women. I'd never known such an atmosphere of excitement and fear. We slowed to a shuffle in the town, and there were children bounding around our legs, guffawing up at us with their snotty noses and hysterical hatch-door mouths. I wasn't close enough to get a good look at Tudor's men – just the sidling and nudging of horses far into the crowd, and the impression of colour and foreignness. My pink-haired friend was laughing a high, boy's laugh, and had tears in his eyes. 'Well, *bachgen*, we're on our way!' he kept bawling into my ear. 'We're on our way!'

His name was Gwilym. Gwilym Cwm Teg – refused to take a surname, not from pride but from practice. 'Still hold to the older ways, where I come from,' he said, with an embarrassed eagerness that made me like him. He came from a village in a fold of hills, mid-country. He'd been a smithy. He'd have been the village smithy all his life, too – that was his lot. Until his brother came back from a fair, one day, full of some cock-and-bull tale about a pilgrimage to the Holy Land. So they both set off. Left their poor old father to shoulder the business he thought they'd taken over, and walked twenty-four miles to Carmarthen to join the march. When they got there they realised it was a march to war, not to God, and the brother took fright and turned back for home.

'I wasn't much troubled,' said Gwilym with an amiable shrug. 'Come that far, might as well stick with it. My brother always had more interest in the forge than I did, anyway. Bit of a runt, he is, but he'll soon build his strength for it.'

Gwilym wore a large sword, which battered awkwardly against his leg. He wasn't used to carrying them, he explained. He had 'borrowed' this one, which he had been finishing off for a visitor at the local manor. He also had an axe, which he passed to me. On his second night with the army he'd been woken by a deserter picking his way across the camp. In return for his silence, Gwilym acquired the axe.

'Must be a damn fool,' Gwilym said, 'to give this up. Food, company and see the world. I never thought life could be like this.'

When I told him my profession he quoted some verse at me:

Y mae hiraeth am Harri,
Y mae gobaith i'n hiaith ni.

One of Robin Ddu's – God knows where he picked that up. And not one of his best – 'We long for Henry, There is hope for our language.' All the fervour of a dead fish.

'I'd wager old Robin's sword never left its sheath,' I said, sourly.

A baffled look crossed Gwilym's face and he wittered on,

'Poet, eh? Don't see so many of your lot around these days. My father, now, he loved a decent verse. When he was a boy, he told us, there'd often be some versifier on the scrounge for a drink, trying out his stuff on the villagers before going up to the Big House.'

'Well,' I said, 'times have changed. It's all *reading* nowadays. If it isn't *printed* it's not worth their favour.'

He nodded slowly. 'Pity. I like a verse, too. A good song. There's nothing to beat the human voice. And what good is reading for the likes of me?'

He grinned and clipped the back of my head. 'Best thing for us, *bachgen*, is to go where the action is. Food and company. See the world. That'll do for us.'

After Y Drenewydd, a new urgency eddied through the ranks. We gabbled and joked like maniacs as we marched. And then fell completely silent for hours at a time. My visions, which had left me in peace for a few days, began to waver at the edge of my thoughts again. I clenched my teeth, concentrated on my blistered feet, on the dryness of my mouth and the rhythmic swing of my arms. A shower of rain left us bedraggled, steaming and scuffing against wet wool and leather. Discomfort was a useful distraction. I didn't want to look ahead. Let life unfold as God willed – I didn't want to see it until it happened. I couldn't remember why it had been so important for me to take this adventure. I tried not to think about anything at all.

We joined the main army at Amwythig and camped near the Hafren that night. Thousands of men and boys, followers, grooms, archers, knights and squires, all busying themselves with their own tasks, cleaning their weapons and armour, tending to the horses, laying the fires, ladling out ale and stew. All spread across the hillside, like a vast city with buildings of air. Among the knots of movement, the fires began to glitter, livid against the deepening sky. Gwilym stood up and stretched his great knotted arms and said,

'It's like living in the heavens, aye.'

He tried to squint into the dusk and make out the dragon on Richmond's standard, but it was lost in the distant white wisp of the commanders' tents. Gwilym suddenly grabbed my arm, 'What's the trouble, boy?'

I felt dizzy; my knees softened and he helped me to the ground. I was so tired of resisting the pull of prophecy, the force that threatened to draw me away, over the camp, up into a stiller world.

'Gwilym,' I muttered, and he yelled again, 'What's the trouble?'

'Gwilym, I have a gift.'

'For me?' He was genuinely surprised at first, like a child, but laughed quickly when he realised his mistake.

'I can see . . . I am a seer,' I said. I was clawing at his sleeve now, trying to anchor myself to the present with his squat strength.

A steward came kicking around to check the fire. He got into an argument with one of the old hands, Cochin, who was barking at him, 'I've lit fires in camps all over Christendom and beyond, good boy, and I've never let one run free yet.'

They both looked up as I fell forward onto my hands and Gwilym shouted, 'God's balls!' I was aware of people crouching over me; I heard someone say, 'Go on, then, give us a show.'

I was off the leash.

Rising too fast, hurtling up, as time screams past below, a seething, bubbling torrent of days, years, deaths. Gradually my flight steadies, the vision begins to settle. But it makes no sense. I am struggling like a sparrow in a net. A tangle of something plucks and pinches at my limbs. I see no people. I am blinded by a writhing, screeching mass of . . . of what? Of words. Words and forms. A cataract of babbling sounds and shapes. (Miles away, worlds away, I hear Cochin and Gwilym mumble encouragement: 'Go on, go on, then what?') Eventually, perhaps by my own bidding and despair, a spirit appears beyond the torrent. A child, naked, runs towards me, terror in her distorted mouth and flame at her back. And then another ghoul: a fleshless face with lightless eyes, a shuffling body which is hardly more than air. Now armies of spirits. They shuffle blindly, bowed almost to the ground, and fall, one after the other, silently, into black, fathomless pits. They begin to merge, to become a pulsating ghostly mass, with only the suggestion of human features, insubstantial mockeries of man; they reach out and withdraw, reach out and withdraw, in a strange, dumb dance. I can make no sense of it. They hover between life and oblivion. They can no longer penetrate the downpour of words to touch me. They shrink away from the words, and yet they are soaked in them, drowning in them. Drowning in words.

They fade, spin into the distance, and Gwilym's puzzled face is close up against mine.

Steward and Cochin were balanced on their haunches, watching. As I emerged from my trance, Cochin squeezed his lips into a disappointed pout and fiddled with his beard.

I heard my own voice slithering out of delirium: 'Words . . . drowning in words . . .'

Gwilym turned and gobbed into the ground.

'Sounds like the bloody poets will be taking over, after all.' He clapped me on the back and my elbows buckled.

'He would say that, though, wouldn't he,' growled Cochin, heaving himself to his feet and feeding the fire. His face took on a sinister glow over the flames.

'See any wondrous beasts?' he asked casually.

I moved my head, still feeling a little sick. 'Just words,' I quavered. 'And forms.'

'Beast of two backs was in there somewhere, I'll warrant,' said Steward, trying to be matey. Behind us, a group of camp whores burst into laughter.

'That'll never change, *cariad*,' cawed one. The steward swung a hand at them in a filthy gesture and mused, 'What does he mean, then, "forms"? What sort of "forms"?'

'Men with the bodies of wart-hogs, that sort of thing,' suggested Cochin. 'I seen pictures of that. In Bruges. Made me ill for a week. Horrible.'

'Or wolves,' said Gwilym, who was sitting beside me, rubbing my back, up and down, up and down, as I shivered on all fours. I let his heavy hand and his voice soothe me back into the real world.

'Never mind your pictures,' said Gwilym. 'My grandmother knew a woman who met a man with a wolf's body, on my life she did. Up in Glastir woods. Grabbed her by the arm and demanded a fuck – said he'd been put under a curse by the devil, and that would lift it. She spit in his eye and ran like wildfire, and they found her all in a sweat, sitting in a ditch half-crazy.'

(Under my breath I was still delivering my testimony: 'They have no substance. They moved faster than I could follow.')

But they'd all lost interest, now. They were arguing and laughing about Gwilym's grandmother's friend, and whether she should have risked a fuck to save a soul, or whether it was all a trick by the devil himself, waiting to get her in his arms and pull her into the bowels of hell.

Under the weight of Gwilym's kind hand I eventually lay on the ground and dozed to the murmur of their voices and the diminishing noise of the camp: a clank of armour, the whistle of a dagger being sharpened. Every so often I floated into consciousness and caught a sentence, which sank back with me, clear and meaningless.

'Without my say-so, no fire is allowed to burn.'

'Them dogs never tires of it, do they?'

'I'm sure it was him. I heard him speaking French.'

'I seen him myself, when I was in Brittany.'

'Well, when I was in France I seen men and women without a stitch. All sitting in a pool of water. Eating and drinking. Cavorting. Horrible.'

Next time I woke, the fires were dying and most of the camp was huddled in sleep. I peed on the last of our fire and stood blinking, damp and trembling. Trying, still, to understand the omen I'd been granted, and wondering – if truth be told – whether fear and fatigue had invented the whole lot. I suppose I should have been worrying about the battle to come. But my mind nagged and lingered around those spirits, retreating and advancing with them, calling to them: who are you? Are you like us? Are you afraid? Do you have eyes, and souls? Do you have names?

I picked my way back to Gwilym's side. I needed his broad back against mine. Maybe this was no gift, after all. Maybe it was madness. At any rate, I reasoned, I'd better come up with something more entertaining next time, if I was to keep these men as my comrades.

1

Charles Lightfoot was named after his Uncle Charlie, his father's elder brother. They had all inherited the names of the dead. Vernon after one grandfather, George after another; Emlyn after a great-great uncle. Mary Ethel had taken two of her grandmother's four names. Hand-me-down names that outlived their owners. Uncle Charlie wasn't supposed to be dead; but maybe by the time Charles came along, they'd finally, secretly, given him up.

Charles never felt right about taking Uncle Charlie's name. For one thing, he didn't look right. He grew up thinking of Uncle Charlie as a real-life music hall turn, with a clownish grin and a fag-end floating from its corner. There were no photographs of Charlie, but they all knew about his round gnome-face and his sticky-out ears and the hats he wore at silly angles. Good old Charlie, laff-a-minute, right old card, sauntering round the pubs with his hands in his pockets, a lifetime's wisdom crinkling the corners of his twenty-one-year-old eyes. That's how old he was when he joined up – twenty-one, and already a ladies' man with a full-trousered, cocksure swagger.

When Charles Lightfoot was a child, he thought of the Great War as a grand party, a glorious outing, rattling with jokes and rakish army caps and men's knowing laughter. He begged for more tales from his father, of the front line his father had never reached. And these tales were all about Uncle Charlie. The War was no more than a backdrop for Uncle Charlie's stunts. Charlie – organising cockroach races and lice-clicking competitions; Charlie – parading behind the lines, rolling up his trousers and waving a leg – *Mademoiselle from Ar-me-tiers, Paaaarlez vous?*; Charlie – writing to his mother not to worry, calling her Ma, telling her about their 'high old time (apart from the racket)'.

Charles Lightfoot used to study himself in his father's shaving mirror. He would let his muscles relax, turn and catch himself unawares, try and catch a sudden, lurking spark of Charlieness. But Charles Lightfoot's mouth was a small, downturned bow. His eyes were anxious and pensive. At eight years old he already had a fine comma at the end of each eyebrow, waiting to harden into a puzzled frown.

His brother Vernon should have been Uncle Charlie's namesake.

Vernon would stand facing the window, in the light, so that their father could inspect him, and Vernon's broad smile would stretch to its limits as his father shook his head and said, 'I dunno. He's the very spit of 'im, he is. It's like old Charlie's come back again . . .' (He never completed the sentence, never added '. . . from the dead.' Never openly lost faith in Uncle Charlie's existence.)

No. Come to think of it, Vernon wasn't the right one to take that name. He was no variety hall comic. He was no buffoon. Vernon's smile carried the ghost of something worse. Even when they were boys.

Uncle Charlie and Uncle Albert had been the only ones to make it to the front. There were other boys in the family – Charles and Vernon's father, and Uncle Eddie, and a confusion of other uncles. But they were too young to go, and anyway their mother started locking them in the house after Charlie disappeared. In case they got ideas. They *could* have sneaked out – there were ways. Charles's father was tall for his age. He could have retrieved the key from behind the mantel clock, he could have drawn back the bolt and nipped across town to the recruitment centre at the Neptune Inn.

('Young Men! *Wŷr Ieuainc*! THIS WAY TO THE FRONT! Why are you stopping HERE, when your pals are out THERE?')

Some of their pals *were* out there, too, at fourteen, fifteen, sixteen. But Charles Lightfoot's father didn't go. Uncle Albert came back from Italy with half an arm missing, and funny in the head. Their mother found a new hiding place for the key. If the war had lasted another six months, Charles Lightfoot's father would have *had* to go. They'd have come for him, the authorities; they'd have broken down that door, bolt or no. He could have been out there with Charlie, laughing at his jokes and winking, keeping track of his big brother, keeping a tight grip on his sleeve until the guns stopped. Or at least he could have seen exactly when and where Uncle Charlie performed his final magic trick, and vanished forever into the mud and smoke. But anyway. The war ended, and Uncle Charlie didn't come home, and eventually their mother stopped mentioning his name. And Charles Lightfoot's father never set foot on foreign land. He took the names of the dead for his children, because he couldn't bear to pass on his own.

Sometimes, at night, young Charles Lightfoot would lie like a board, trying not to feel Vernon's piston feet and pointed elbows. He'd watch the hairline of light at the edge of the bedroom door, wait for it to snap into darkness with a slight 'ping!', wait for the unthinkable grunts and creaks from his parents' room to fade away. And still he'd lie there, watching the door, waiting. One night, he knew, the door would glide open and a deeper shadow would fill the darkness, and he would recognise the gentle glint of smile and merry eyes, and Uncle Charlie would give one brief, catarrhal laugh and say:

'You, boy. Give me back my name.'

When Charles Lightfoot's grandmother finally unlocked the doors and released the flock of uncles, they scattered. All but two: Charles's father, who was going to learn about electricity, and Uncle Eddie. He did well, Uncle Eddie. Hung round the docks at first, selling ribbons to the Norwegian sailors to give to their girls. Ended up with a milliner's shop in Castle Street. He had an eye for business and a way with words, and he got Charles's father to fit the electrics in the shop at a knock-down price. He took to his quiet nephew Charles, who crept along walls and hid in corners, while the others rampaged and roared. Uncle Ed would let Charles sit in the shop and roll lengths of ribbon and stack hatboxes. He had a house, Uncle Ed, and a young wife, but she was run down by a tram. So Ed wrote a will and left the house and the business to Charles. At the time, of course, he had no inkling – why should he? – that fashions would turn upside-down and inside-out, that women would start smirking at their mothers' hats, and wearing their long hair loose and knotting scarves carelessly round their heads against the autumn wind. The shop went downhill. Eventually it was sold off for next to nothing, and stocked with souvenir dragons and miniature lovespoons. Uncle Eddie lingered on into senility, drooling in his house, calling Charles 'dear old Albert'. Charles didn't want a hatshop, anyway; he had practised his father's trade since the age of 14, made a decent living at it, and was settled enough in his rented rooms near the Arms Park. But when Uncle Eddie finally dribbled to a halt, Charles accepted what was given, and moved into the house. The room where James and Cat sit to conduct their interview is still furnished with Uncle Eddie's things. The carpets are frayed at the edges and balding in the middle. The stairs are spongey underfoot. Charles Lightfoot lives in another man's house, under another man's name.

2

'There was Uncle Charlie, Uncle Albert, my dad, Uncle Eddie, and Stan, Clifford, Tom, er . . . er . . .' Charles pauses and scowls at the fingers he's been checking off as if he might recognise another one.

'All those uncles!' Cat exclaims, to fill the pause. 'Your poor grandmother.'

James stifles a yawn. He's finding it hard to keep track.

'Well. Different generation, innit. There wasn't so many of *us*,' says Charles, a little defensively. 'Just me and Mary Ethel and George, and – and . . .' his hand wavers slightly over his mouth but his face registers none of the alarm that has flickered through his body. Surely he can't have forgotten his own brother's name? Is he going to die doolally here, just like Uncle Ed?

'. . . Oh, and Emlyn!' he shouts. 'Emlyn. And Vernon of course.'

James tries to get a grip and leans forward. 'And were you the only writer in the family?'

Charles sucks in his cheeks primly, suspecting sarcasm. He says, 'We never had time for all that. None of us. *I* never had time for all that, most of my working life.'

James nods earnestly. 'At school? Did you enjoy writing at school?'

'Left at fourteen. We all did. You did, then.' Charles shifts in his chair, embarrassed. 'Would have been sooner if my mother had her way. Used to drive her up the wall, all that schooling. Waste of time, to her, the three Rs. Never get you anywhere, she used to say. And we were always coming home, see, wanting a book for this, a book for that. Spend good money on books, when your trouser-seats is down to the threads? Well you can't have it both ways, she says. You can have it on your bums or in your heads, choose which.'

Cat and James laugh, and Charles gives them a sly, pleased look, and carries on, though he knows he's rambling.

'Well, at that age an empty head is better than a frozen bum. And she just wanted us fit, and fed, and out in one piece. Same in the war – just wanted to *get on*. Used to flap round like a blue-arsed fly during the air raids. Siren goes off and she's there saying "Oh, leave me *alone*" – like as if Hitler just wanted to mess up her wash day.'

Charles swallows. He's ashamed of using that phrase, 'blue-arsed fly'. He remembers how shocked he was to hear his father using it about his mother. And now here he is, pulling out the same words to try and hold the interest of two youngsters he's never met in his life. Making his poor, frazzled, barely sane mother into a comedy character, just for something to say.

Charles's mother wound up tighter and tighter, like a crazy clockwork toy, while his father sank into silence and guilt. Charles remembers their home as a vibrating box, pulsing with waves of panic, resentment and provocation. It was full of noise and mood, then, that house. Vernon went on living there for years, even when the others had moved out, or died. Charles never understood how Vernon could carry on there, with all those inimical spirits fizzing and hissing round his head. He only finally upped sticks when a house came on the market in Terrace Street. Sometimes Charles wonders whether Vernon does these things just to torment him. But of course that's nonsense.

For some reason James keeps asking him about food.

Charles has remembered about the muffin man and his bell, and that seems to be keeping them happy. And now that he thinks of it, there are other things: chunks of slimy bread, lifted from bowls of hot milk and eaten with extravagant slurps. Or saucers of broad beans, *ffa* his mother called them, with a dab of butter as a weekend treat. He stores each dish ready to serve, knowing this will do the trick.

Charles is beginning to enjoy himself. He has realised that he can deal out memories as he chooses. He feels safer, now. He begins to show off. That's why, later, he lets his guard slip and talks about Noreen. But never mind. No harm in that. At least he doesn't start prattling on about Vernon. You never know what might get back to Vernon's flapping ears.

Bloody Vernon has always been there. That's half the trouble. Charles can reel off facts about the others – George, with his divorce and his bankruptcy and his sudden departure for New Zealand. Emlyn and his gambling. Mary Ethel, poor old girl, lumbered with that half-wit husband and her horrible moaning kids. He can carry on like a fishwife about them, and isn't much bothered. He even finds a link with food, for James's sake, and tells them about George writing to them, finally, from the other side of the world, and complaining that he can't get laver bread for love nor money.

But Charles is not going to talk about Vernon. This young feller with the tape recorder is a neighbour of Vernon's. No doubt he'll call round to play him the tape, and they'll listen to it together, laughing at Charles's dreary recollections. Always there, Vernon. No getting away from it. And there he'll be until they're laid down together in the same hole, like as not. Who'd have thought. The one brother Charles would gladly see the back of, still hanging around. The one member of the family Charles never could abide.

3

In bed, while Vernon squirmed and farted next to him and George tried to bribe Emlyn to sleep on the floor, Charles would repeat to himself like a prayer: 'I hate Vernon. I *hate* Vernon . . .'

He never could detach himself, never managed to form new alliances within the family. George was too old, and was already claimed by Emlyn, with his ingenious games and bets. Mary Ethel tutted at them all with sisterly contempt. Only their father held out one brief episode of hope.

It was such a different order of things, those rows between Charles and his father. Cheek-flushing, throat-straining, life-or-death stuff. It started after Charles left school and became his father's apprentice. There were few words between them at first, as Charles watched his father twist and snap wires, and they stood together in narrow trenches of earth, heads touching as they bent over the cables. There was another war, a new war, and Charles's father had missed out for the second time. He turned 40 just as it all stopped being a 'B' picture and got serious. Too young for the first show, too old for the second. He *could* have found a way to get round it . . . people did. But Charles never asked his father about such things. He just learned, and worked, and endured his father's simmering guilt.

They'd come home one evening, and his father had taken his usual place, by the little table with his wireless and accumulator, mumbling behind his newspaper. That evening they'd run out of tanners and the wireless was cold, so Charles could hear what his father muttered. 'Bloody Stalin,' Charles heard. 'Bloody Reds and their Second Bloody Front.'

Charles thought he would finish his cup of tea and slip out of the kitchen, but it was this same problem that would beset him again half a century later. One minute the words were sailing harmlessly through his head, and the next thing he knew he was saying them aloud:

'Stalin knows what he's on about, and where would we be without him? Up a bloody gum tree, that's where.'

His father folded the paper down and stared. Charles thought he was going to laugh. Then his father's eyes widened and his mouth set and he leaned forward, putting the weight of his arms on the paper and making it crackle on his lap.

'Our Mr Stalin,' he said, slowly and carefully, 'is a slippery little bugger. Can't trust 'im, shouldn't be trusted. And don't swear in front of your father.'

That was just the beginning. Night after night they'd be there, voices rising, faces reddening, fingers jabbing at the wireless or the headlines, while Charles's mother grimaced in mock despair and clattered in the kitchen, and Mary Ethel stood pointedly around in her Civil Defence uniform and talked about Going Off to Do Something Useful.

And Vernon lolled in the doorway, and watched, and grinned.

Vernon thought Charles had blown it. He thought there was advantage to be taken. He tried lobbing in a few comments about sabotage, and troublemakers, and never being too sure whose side some people were on.

But Charles had scored his victory, and he knew it. When he and his father stood face to face, showering spittle and accusations, they shared something Vernon would never understand. Their father yelled at Charles to get a move on in the mornings, stood in the hallway shaking the newspaper at him and bundled him through the door with a sparkle in his eye.

'What d'you think of this then? Strikes! – with a war on? Come on, let's hear you speak up for your comrades!'

It was Charles who was summoned to the back room to listen to *The Brains Trust*. Charles who was called down to admire – or (with a bit of luck) sneer at – his father's ARP warden helmet and armband. Vernon did what he could to reclaim attention. He joined the Home Guard. He lounged around in his uniform, smoking Craven As, and knocked the back of Charles's knees with his rifle butt. Charles didn't care. He had brought their father back to life.

4

Charles is at the window with James and Cat. He's pointing out the block of flats on the horizon, where two streets were blown away in 1941. (James is eyeing the tape, which he thinks may have finished.) That was just rubble and wires, Charles is saying. He recalls going to watch his father make it safe, and feeling the wires like hell's webs brushing the top of his head. He tells them about learning his father's trade, even while he was still a schoolboy, and later, going as his apprentice to work on the docks, on the battleships, re-connecting fire control systems and stringing degaussing cables.

Charles talks and talks, even when James starts to tap his watch and make leaving noises. Charles tells them about the way he would try and walk like a man, like a soldier, with a heavy tread, as he trudged home in the blackout after work. He tells them about the night the Students' Union was bombed. He tells them about the time his father was called out to a house that was hit, and saw a young woman standing at the end of the hallway, smiling at him. 'Nice to see a cheery face,' said Charles's father, before noticing the shard of glass that had flown out of her front door and speared her through the throat against the wall . . . Charles blathers on and on, trying to drown things out. Just as he used to try and drown out Vernon's whispers in bed, at night, pulling his body in tight under the blanket, trying to create a sliver of space between them. Vernon shuffling even closer. Pressing himself against his brother's back. Craning over Charles's hunched shoulder and breathing his confessions into his ear.

What he'd been up to.
After blackout.
Back to my old tricks, Chimpface.
Poor Esther Bell.

5

Esther Bell was small and light and had black hair that spread into a dense, springy hedge just below her ears. She had tiny, lighter hairs on her brown neck. Charles could see them when he walked behind her down the lane to school, and he could smell her intimate, sour-sweet, warm-milk smell. Her socks lost their grip and were forever crumpling round her ankles. She would lift a weightless knee to pull one up, first the left sock, then the right, barely losing the rhythm of her walk. She had perfectly round, pebble-black eyes. She and her brother Sidney, who was even smaller and pudgey, had gone to school with the Lightfoot brothers. They had walked in front of Charles and Vernon all the way from their front gate to the school gate every day, and never said a word. Vernon made sure he and Charles were behind them: if the Bells tried to leave a little later he would wait, clutching Charles's arm and watching, until he saw them emerge from their house, and he could catch up and fall into step. In the early days Vernon would step on the back of Esther's shoes, or knee Sidney up the bum, and in those days she would turn and tell him where to go. Which made Vernon fling back his head and laugh a whinnying schoolboy laugh. When Esther (and Sidney, under her instructions) took to ignoring him, he tried words, instead.

Esther, your slip's showing.

Esther, fancy a pork pie? Bit of skinned sausage then?

Esther, what's that pong? Is that your brother? Is that you making that pong, *Yidney*?

One October Vernon was kept home for two weeks with a chesty cough. Charles avoided the Bells altogether on Monday and Tuesday. On Wednesday he fell in alongside them, as they filed hand-in-hand through the gate. Halfway to school he said, casually,

'We've got a test today.'

'Yes,' she said, without looking at him. 'Spelling.'

'Can't spell to save my life,' lied Charles. Esther's mouth twitched. Sidney, at her side, said in a stage whisper,

'Is the other one dead?' and Esther said sharply, 'Shut up.'

By the Friday, Esther was looking directly at Charles when she spoke. On the second Monday, when he rounded the corner and the Bells' gate came into view, Esther was fussing about with Sidney's muffler. Sidney was wriggling and pulling, and broke away as Charles approached, taunting,

'You can stop now, he's here!'

As they walked, Sidney skipped and dragged ahead of them. Esther began the conversation, saying,

'Do you think I'm a morbid person?'

Charles, who'd never come across the word, said he didn't know.

'My mother says I'm a morbid child,' said Esther.

'Oh,' said Charles. He tried to gauge from her expression whether this was a good or a bad thing to be. Esther studied the pavement, lost in thought, and then said,

'Are you ever scared you'll die in the night?'

Charles thought, If I did, I wouldn't be able to feel Vernon kicking any more. But to Esther, he said:

'Sort of. Sometimes.'

'*I* do. I pray that I won't, every night. Only, it's not really praying. More like . . . lists.'

Sidney was trying to prise something out of the gutter. Esther yelled at him,

'Stop that, or I'll tell Miss Hughes.' Then continued, in her normal voice, to Charles:

'I make lists. Names – family and such, and then God-save-the-King-and-protect-the-Empire. Then, I do capital cities. Then times tables. Only bad ones – nine, eleven, twelve. And that's it. Has to be in the right order. That means I'll wake up again in the morning. Do you ever do things like that?'

'Yes,' lied Charles. 'Sometimes.' He was light-headed. He'd never heard her say so much to anyone.

Vernon's chest cleared; he was sent back to school. He slowed his brother's pace with a warning thump as they neared the Bells' house. Esther came out first. Charles caught a flash of pleased recognition across her face before she spotted Vernon and settled into practised neutrality.

'Where's Yidney?' Vernon brayed. 'Oh, here he is! All right, Yidney?'

Vernon and Charles marched behind them. Vernon was growing fast now, towering above the other three. He fell into silence, and satisfied himself with the faint movement of Esther's hair under his breath.

In 1940 Esther and Sidney were sent to stay with their aunt in Shropshire.

'Oh, well, Charlie boy,' said Vernon, laying a hand across his brother's shoulders. 'Your little pals have hopped it to the promised land.'

There was an alley behind their backyard, where the neighbourhood boys skimmed cigarette cards or had a kickaround after tea. Charles was sometimes hauled in to give up his pullover as a goalpost and, if they were short of numbers, to stand in goal. Charles thought he might like football, if he could play with boys his own size. But when the pummelling, snorting, bellowing mass edged up the alley towards his goal Charles found his grubby hands opening and shutting, opening and shutting, and he would be crab-hopping from post to post, trying to keep his mind off his aching bladder. And inevitably the ball would cannon past, giving his leg or shoulder a malevolent shove, and Vernon would lead the general outrage.

'Ah, Charlie, you nance! Queer boy! Go back to your knitting, Charlotte!'

Always Vernon's holler, above all the rest.

(That was the alley where, later, Vernon went back to his tricks. Back to my old tricks.

Poor Esther Bell.)

Esther Bell came back from Shropshire with hips and an embarrassed stoop to hide her new breasts. A young woman – still in socks and girlish dresses, still walking to school in the mornings, home in the afternoons. Charles saw her occasionally, as he followed his father to work, and lingered. In his overalls, carrying his toolbox, he was awkward, under the burden of a new character.

'You're back!' he said.

'I'm back,' she said.

'Going to school?' he said, with only a hint of condescension.

Her parents thought it best. And she had wanted to come home. And besides, she insisted, she was going to join the Civil Defence. And not only that – if she could talk her parents round, she'd leave school and get work in the armaments factory.

'Come on, what's up?' called Charles's father, who was kicking his heels at the corner of the road, anxious to continue their latest debate.

Yes, all right, she would meet Charles on Saturday.

Charles galloped after his father, the toolbox clanking painfully at his side.

They met at the Silver Kettle Café. Charles managed to find

them a table, ducking past the hovering servicemen and dithering old ladies. Esther knew one of the waitresses.

'Hello, Esther,' said the woman clearing their table. Esther said, 'Hello, how are you?'

Charles was impressed by her casually adult manner. When the waitress had gone, Esther leaned towards him and whispered something about her father having 'done business' with the woman's husband – 'but he's a bit of a scoundrel, by all accounts.'

That impressed him even more.

Esther's aunt had been kind to her and Sidney, she said, but too nervous to cope. Weepy. Worrying all the time about their cousins abroad, and wondering what had become of them. It was Esther who had to get Sidney dressed, who made sure he went to bed at a decent time.

'It's odd to be back,' she said, pouring tea. 'But I wanted to come. I want to be in the thick of things.' She seemed to be trying out a new accent, more curved and brittle, as though they were acting a scene in a film. 'People are funny in the country. They talk about the War as if it's a cricket match. They want us to win, but it doesn't really seem that important to them.'

Charles didn't think this was likely to be true. If this had come from his father, he would have given it short shrift. But he gulped, and said,

'That's people for you.'

'Even my auntie,' said Esther. 'Worrying herself to a frazzle, because she hasn't heard from cousin Sim. But she doesn't take a newspaper. Doesn't follow the War. Hopes everything will just sort itself out.'

She pinioned him with her black eyes. '*It won't,*' she said. '*We've got to sort it out.*' And then she repeated, 'I'm going to leave school. Soon as I can talk my parents round.'

On an impulse, Charles said, 'Do you still pray in lists?'

She gave him such a thunderstruck look that he immediately regretted it. He couldn't tell whether she remembered telling him, or not. She lifted the lid of the teapot, and agitated the leaves with her teaspoon.

'I don't pray at all,' she said. 'I don't see the point. You sound like my auntie. She's always saying, If you pray hard enough, God will hear.'

Charles twisted his mouth, hoping she'd interpret it as an apt response. He wasn't sure how politic it would be to condemn her aunt's opinions, even if Esther disagreed with them.

'What I say is,' she went on, letting the lid clop shut and wagging her spoon at him, 'Why does He hear some people, some of the time, and not everybody else? Other people must be praying hard, too. Everyone must be. Cousin Sim must have been praying hard. And where is he now?'

For a few months, Charles was buoyed up. Serious Esther, his argumentative father, even the bomb sites and gashed streets – it all made him feel keenly alive. He was conscious of the boundaries of his body, as though he had water all around him. He felt he could be free of Vernon; one day Vernon wouldn't matter at all. This, he told himself, this is how life should be. He enjoyed worrying about the War and hating the Nazis. He considered the prospect of joining up with a mixture of dread and relish. He felt that he could see them off himself. He was invincible.

It all lasted until George came home. He'd been injured in Sicily, and came back with a stutter and a bandage wrapped diagonally around the top of his head. They said he'd recover but he needed rest, and the double vision might last. A bed was made up for him in the front room. Their mother had to lead him to it; their father stood in the hall and watched their progress, opening his mouth without a word, opening it and closing it again, like a fish. Charles thought of his stints in goal down the alley, of the terrible approach of players and ball, of his hands opening and shutting in despair.

Their father started getting up in the middle of the night to go and watch George breathing. They had to be quiet. No wireless. Another strike broke out, but Charles's father skimmed the story without comment. He was distracted and melancholy; he brooded now about Uncle Albert, and sneaked looks at Vernon again, searching for Uncle Charlie in his profile.

George's vision did right itself, and he regained a voracious appetite. He moved back to his old bed; Mary Ethel had to go and share with her mother again. Charles, of course, had been stuck with Vernon all along. The war was hurtling to a close; in the heaving ratings' quarters on an Atlantic supply ship, Emlyn was busy running a book on the number of weeks to go. Charles began to fantasise about leaving home.

He thought he might tell Esther about his plans. He wasn't sure why, or what response he hoped for. He just wanted to show her that he considered the future, a future apart from his home and siblings. He started to tell her one late afternoon, as they were walking back together from town. Vernon passed them, on his way to parade at the Citizens Hall. He gave Esther a jokey half-salute, and said, 'All right then?'

She turned to follow his progress, and remarked that she hadn't realised *he* was in uniform, these days. Something in her tone told Charles that she had crossed into a different territory, where old schoolyard cruelties and betrayals could be set aside and forgotten.

'Might be in uniform, but as for knowing what it's all about . . .' he started, but Esther wasn't listening. Lank-limbed Charles, with his boy's frame and his overalls tied at the ankles to stop them dragging, noted the straightening of Esther's back and the swinging rhythm of her stride, and understood that he had been left behind.

'Got a new friend?' Vernon's voice whirred against his ear that night. 'Little Esther Bell, eh. Only she's a big girl, now.'

Uncle Eddie came to see their father. The two men sat in the kitchen staring into their cigarette smoke. Charles heard Uncle Eddie rebuking his father:

'It don't do no good, see, chewing it over and over. He've long gone, and there's an end to it. Leave him be, now, in peace.'

Catching sight of Charles as he skulked in the doorway, Uncle Eddie extended an arm and adopted his affected, buttery public voice:

'Ah, let's have a look at you, then, sunny jim. There you are' (to Charles's father), 'Here's the lad you want to look to. Growing fast – my word. Young lady on the arm, next thing you know.'

Charles sniffed in disdain. He knew better. He had been wrong about the way life would be. He had been naïve. But he was past all that. His father's burst of animation had been a one-off, a passing fluke. And Esther no longer dropped in at the Silver Kettle.

He had waited there on two occasions, and he would not wait again. The waitress, the woman who had known Esther's name, had smiled at him as he sat there alone but, much to his relief, made no comment. He accepted her smile as a consolation. He took in the elegance of her face; he took in a calmness, too, and a clarity, despite her busyness and the perspiration on her forehead and chin, and the strands of hair that flopped loose from her cap. Charles resolved to speak to the waitress, if he should see her again.

At night, he clamped his hands over his ears.

(Esther, I says, fancy a bit of pork sausage?
Try a bit, Esther. Go on.)

In his nightmares, Vernon advanced, slowly, with his Home Guard uniform and his grin, as she walked backwards, into the shadows, matching her pace to his.

(Go on, Esther, try a bit of this. Better than the skinless variety.)

6

Charles realises, suddenly, that he is talking at the top of his voice. James and Cat are looking doubtfully at each other. Charles coughs and stops and a silence stuns them all for a moment. Then James is moving towards the tape recorder, and Charles knows that they will leave, that the door will shut and shudder and echo around Uncle Eddie's cold house, and that he will be left here, with Vernon's whisperings, left here shouting to himself like a bloody lunatic. He makes one last bid, desperate and hoarse:

'Did I tell you about Noreen?'

James sighs, but Cat shows a glimmer of new interest.

'Noreen . . .'

Charles ignores James and concentrates on the girl, holds her attention and even finds that he is gripping her wrist.

'She was . . . a special friend. You asked about why I started writing. That was it. Noreen.'

'Your wife?' ventures Cat. James drops hopelessly on to the sofa.

'No, more's the pity. She wasn't . . . it weren't on the cards. She were older than me. Much older.' Charles tries a coy smile. 'People didn't used to like that, see.'

So he tells these two strangers, the kind girl and the bored boy, about his affair with Noreen; how he fell for her the first time he saw her, how he was a kid, then, and she was in her 30s, and lovely, a lovely lady; how he came back from National Service in 1951 and went looking for her straight away; and he was 22 then, he was a man, and Noreen could see he was serious, not just a mooning young kid. She knew he meant it then. And she was beautiful. But it wasn't easy for her. People didn't like it – the age gap. And finally, she said it would have to end.

He tells them all this. He tells them she was the love of his life. Charles Lightfoot actually uses those words: 'She was the love of my life.' Squeezing Cat's wrist, letting his eyes swim. And, he says, when it was over, he would go back to his digs after work and he wouldn't know what to do. So he started writing poems. That's what he says, and for all he knows that might even be true. Anyway, it keeps them here, it keeps the whispering at bay, for another 50 minutes.

7

James is slumped on the sofa, brooding about Anne Meyrick, and John Griphiths' written request for her hand. He thinks he may have tracked her family to a land dispute in 1348.

Meurig ap Meurig applies for the return of his three hectares of land, his two oxen, eight sheep, three pigs and chickens, having mortgaged it out for 12 years to his cousin, Hywel Wynn Meurig ap Ednyfed, during a time of adversity. Hywel Wynn Meurig ap Ednyfed claims that the lease has been renewed for a further four years, giving him full ownership rights. The cousin wins his case, and the homeless Meurig ap Meurig slinks back into history.

Is this a forefather of Anne's? Do Meurig's fortunes change for the better? They can change so abruptly. The flourish of a tax-collector's quill; the bite of a flea; and whole generations, whole families, vanish from sight.

On the armchair opposite, Cat empties the contents of a file on to her lap: several sheets of paper, each one with a handwritten poem in tiny, immaculate copper-plate.

'You should say something about social conventions,' she says. She takes a swig from a bottle of beer and scrutinises a poem.

'I'm just saying, when you write up this interview with Mr Lightfoot, you should say something about changing conventions. The age gap. Peer pressure. How much it's changed. Or hasn't, come to that.' She waits to gain his attention. 'James. I'm saying – Mr Lightfoot and his older woman. Noreen.'

'It's not an interview,' says James. 'It's not my place to say anything about anything. He's not being judged. He's just telling his story. That's what Gal's after – immediacy.'

Cat tuts. 'Oh, *Gal* . . .' She returns to the poem, and James returns to his thoughts, which soon expand into a daydream. He's in a basement ringing with cold, sitting at a table, brushing dead cobwebs off heavy volumes: *The Land of Morgan, its Manorial Particulars*; *Hanes Plwyf Penfynydd*; *Limbus patrum Morganiae et Glamorganiae*. His nostrils flare at the scent of bound registers, 19th-century 'gleanings', annals and antiquities. A smell like dust and digestive biscuits. A smell that comes off the pages onto your fingers in a yellowish smear.

Cat reads from the first sheet: 'This Street.' She looks up, expectantly. 'It's so awful, though. All alone in that house, raking over his past. The wasted life.'

'There's probably a lot more to his life than one failed affair,' says James, irritably. 'I think he was showing off. To you. Trying to prove something.'

Cat gives an exasperated gasp and goes back to the poem. After a while she starts giving little hums of appreciation and interest, glancing up to invite a reaction. James is tucked into a corner of his sofa with his eyes closed, dimly calculating, under his daydream, how many times he's rung Sonia, and she's rung him, over the past week.

Eventually Cat clears her throat, snaps a piece of paper straight and reads, just louder than necessary:

> *'This street is dusty any time of year.*
> *Cars cut through too fast.*
> *But neighbours still take their time here,*
> *Some faces I know from the past.'*

'You don't have to trawl through his poems, you know,' murmurs James from his half-sleep. 'He was only trying to impress you.'

> *'One ugly weed has found the sun.*
> *It pushes through a crack in the yard.*
> *There used to be flowers here, now they've gone.*
> *Keeping them alive was too hard.*
>
> *There's lots of houses like that in this town.*
> *One loose brick in the wall*
> *Could bring the whole lot falling down*
> *Leaving nothing at all.'*

Cat's voice trips and she fishes up her sleeve for a tissue.

> *'The trees on the pavement don't look too good*
> *Nothing much round here grows.*
> *My hands are old and rotten like that wood.*
> *Nothing lives for ever, I suppose.'*

Cat busies herself with her tissue and glares at James.

'That poor bloke,' she snaps, accusingly. 'Sitting in that ugly old house, with nothing but his past to think about . . . and what might have been . . .'

James tries to think of something appropriate to say, but his mind is pulled back to the archive, where Sonia has just emerged from behind a column of cracked books. Her hair and body are caked with dust: dust sketching the wrinkles around her eyes and the fine lines at each end of her mouth; nestling in the little niche between her collarbones, skittering down into her cleavage.

James longs to submerge himself completely and wallow in sleepy arousal. He's aware of Cat's frosty attention, keeping him on the boundary of consciousness. Next door, Livvy strikes up the opening bars of 'A Nightingale Sang in Berkeley Square'.

Cat gives her nose a thunderous blow. James's fantasy evaporates.

8

The door rattles open and a stocky woman with a squashed face enters, thuds across the floorboards and heads for the grey plastic chairs stacked around the edges of the room. She wrestles one chair free, takes it to the centre of the hall and sits.

More people arrive. Two women, talking noisily. A man with a military walk. Three more women, turning back with nursery voices to the last and oldest woman, Rose Lewis, as she moves forward in time with her two sticks. They fetch their chairs – Mrs Probert carrying an extra for Rose – and set them in a tidy crescent facing the wall. Mrs Probert returns for a third chair, which is placed alone, with reverence, facing the class.

'Anyone been "done" by this history feller yet? For this exhibition-watchamacallit?' asks Rene Dawes, leaning round to address everyone else in the row.

'I have,' announces Rose Lewis, braced against her sticks like a medieval monarch.

'What's he like, good-looking? Bit of all right, is he?'

'He's a drip,' says Rose.

More people are arriving, setting their chairs in a second row. A tangle of voices hangs round the centre of the hall. In comes a barrel-bellied, grinning man with wisps of white hair waving like smoke around his ears.

'Here he comes...'

'Late as usual...'

'We'll tell teacher...'

'In the corner, Harry!'

Harry waggles his head and holds up his hands and says in a cracked, high pitch, 'Got here before wonderboy, though, didn't I? Where's our lord and master then, eh?'

After a few minutes the conversation sinks, broken only by Rose, who is giving out orders to her neighbour: 'Hold that stick while I find my Extra Strong Mints.'

Greta Mason sniffs expressively and looks at her watch.

'I hope he's not going to be too late. I have to leave at eight prompt this evening.'

Harry shifts in his seat to beam at the back row.

'Everyone done their homework?'

Charles Lightfoot rolls his eyes and folds his arms.

'You had your visit then, Charlie? From this whatsisname? Down Memory Lane? Get anything out of you did he? All your sordid past?'

'Aye, mun, you want to watch what you say,' Mervyn Jarman chimes in. 'Leave them skeletons where they are.'

Elen Rabbaiotti starts up her infectious, bronchial laugh and gets a wink from Mervyn.

'Waste of bloody time,' says Charles Lightfoot.

The door flings open.

'It's that man again!'

'Later than Harry tonight.'

'Just so that you know, Mr Galloway, I must leave at eight prompt this evening'.

Gal lopes to his seat and sits, making a triangle of his long legs, balancing ankle on thigh.

'Sorry I'm late, people. Hope you've made the most of it by planning your readings for tonight. Now then! Let's hear what you've got to say!'

One by one, members of the group don glasses, clear throats, thumb through notebooks and read.

Mrs Probert, whose daughter slammed the phone down on her an hour ago, gives an extract of her historical novel. *Tilly thought London was the most filthy, noisy and exciting place she had ever seen . . .*

Greta Mason, whose husband is gradually disappearing into Alzheimer's Disease, reads a new poem.

> *'If I could paint a picture clear*
> *I'd show the song that I can hear*
> *From blackbird, finch and mottled thrush*
> *When sunrise makes the grey sky blush . . .'*

Gal rests his head on his hand and pouts at a grubby corner of the ceiling.

'Very strong use of rhyme and rhythm by Greta, there. What do we think about that? Does it move the piece along? Or does it hold us back?'

They wave their notebooks at him like order papers. Mervyn hollers.

'Poem's not a poem without a rhyme. It's just notes.'

'Nonononono,' blares Mrs Probert. Jaswat Singh elbows Charles in the ribs and they exchange a weary look.

Gal puts a finger to his lips. Silence falls. They lean forward to listen.

'I want you to think about where we hear rhyme and rhythm in our daily lives. Sayings. Proverbs. Adverts. *Why* they're used. Do they *work*.'

His gaze sweeps along the row, lighting cheeks and eyes as it goes, never settling on one face.

A shutter in the wall rasps open and a nicotine-stained voice calls: 'Urn's hot!'

During the tea break, the Fresh Starters hurl slogans at each other.

'You'll wonder where the yellow went, When you brush your teeth with Pepsodent!'

'They come as a boon and a blessing to men – The Pickwick, the Owl and the Waverley pen!'

Meinir Griffiths, whose husband left her three days after her 60th, is balancing her teacup against her chest and telling Gal about her Auntie Dora, who in moments of crisis would cry: 'Jambuckrubberdean!'

'I always thought it was a very rude word indeed,' she breathes. 'But it turned out to be an advertisement—'

'Zambuck, rub it in!' yells Mervyn Jarman triumphantly.

Gal smiles blankly at the top of Meinir's head. A few moments later he calls across the general chat:

'Interesting point raised by Meinir here – about euphemisms and swear words. Might be worth a discussion next week – are there any words we find unacceptable? Are we offended by some words in conversation, but OK with them in literature? Have a think.'

Resentful looks are lobbed at Meinir, who smirks back.

During the second half of the class, Meinir reads a poem about her house.

> 'My house is quiet. My house is wise.
> It watches the world with its window-pane eyes.
> It holds by the corners its apron of herbs,
> Contented and still, till it brings down the birds . . .'

'Well done, Meinir,' says Gal, 'That's really *shit*!' He flings his head over the back of the chair and pinches his nose, too late to stop the blood from streaming over his mouth and down his chin.

Gal's disciples bustle from their seats and crowd round him.

'Put your head back further if you can,' says Mrs Probert, yanking it helpfully, 'and count to sixty.'

'No, it's *down*, not up, it should be between his knees . . .'

'That's for fainting, mun.'

'Look, you should be holding it *here*,' says Greta Mason, wedging her own finger and thumb over the bridge of Gal's nose.

'Blood pressure, that is.'

'He'll have to have it done, you know – they'll have to stick the poker up.'

'*Iestyn*, whassamatter with you all?' barks Mervyn from his seat, 'It's a nosebleed, not a ruddy brain haemorrhage.'

The class breaks up early.

'Coming for a drink?' Mervyn asks Charles Lightfoot, but Charles has a thumping headache and goes straight home.

'Sight of all that blood, I 'spect,' Mervyn tells Harry.

They escort Gal to his car. The women fuss: Can he drive? Is he feeling weak? Mrs Probert insists that she will bring him a bottle of Floridix next week to build him up. Rose Lewis tells him to eat more spinach. Harry grasps his arm as Gal struggles to get into the car, and has to be prised away. Gal wedges tissue up his nostril and drives away, mulling over a plan to bring his Over 60s to meet his English pupils in a 'Poetry Bridges the Gap' day. The women wave him off and fret to each other as the group breaks and drifts. They finally head home nursing sweet, sad visions of helplessness: tender shadows under green eyes, dark hair falling across a pale forehead, waiting for a capable hand to brush it away. So young, and so much more fragile than he thinks.

9

It's one o'clock in the morning. Gal is sitting up in bed, absently stuffing his nose with fresh tissue. A notebook is propped against his knees. With his free hand he flips through the pages, skimming through ideas. Poetry on the Net (website for kids and Fresh Starters?). Changing City – making poetry on city life for the kids and city memories for F.S. Expectations. Old age: what it brings, what the kids fear/hope it will bring.

His hand freezes in the action of turning a page – a loosening, a melting in the back of his head; he's set it off again. He leans back on the pillow, tastes the dark trickle down his throat, and shuts his eyes. The tinny flavour, a slight suggestion of dizziness, cold braille travelling down his back and electric hieroglyphs jigging across his eyelids – a cocktail of sensations that hoist him back into childhood. He was more prone to nosebleeds, then. 'It's your high altitude,' his mother would say, trying to mask her anxiety. It's not unpleasant, though, this feeling – never was. If it happened when he was alone he would sneak into his bedroom and lie on the floor, jamming his head back so that his neck arched, and he would wait, enjoying the pressure of the carpet against his scalp. He would lie there, breathing steadily, waiting for the wash of excitement that always followed. It comes to him again, now – a cleaning, lifting wave of anticipation.

Gal remembers how he used to open his eyes and see the world framed, upside-down in his bedroom window. Roofs and chimneys hanging from the sky; a splinter of aeroplane humming across the cloudy floor. His mind would be fluttering with the edges of ideas. He would long to get to work, to try and form them into poems, smooth and tangible as stones, each one a slightly different, unnameable shade. He would be ready to find a pen and paper, suspend his thoughts until words came of their own accord. But he would wait, afraid of triggering a fresh gush of blood; he would promise himself ten more minutes, and before they were up he would doze off, or his mother would call, or he would have thought of some urgent new manoeuvre he must try on his bike before it got dark.

One-fifteen. Gal's neck is aching. The bleeding must have stopped by now. He opens his eyes and sees nothing but the bedroom ceiling.

Across the city, Cat's sleep jangles with children's voices. Five of them. Five children. She has no doubt about the number, but she keeps repeating it to herself as though she might forget. She tries to count, but they move and merge and disappear and reappear. She starts again and again – one, two, three – aware of their names but unable to articulate them. The children watch her. Their eyes are stretched open, oval, afraid and knowing, the whites wide and luminous – one, two, three – they have skull-noses, sheared off short, and their faces fall away beneath the cheekbones into narrow, slack-jawed shadows. She thinks one is missing, but can't quite tell. Should there be five? Or has she only imagined the fifth? Then her arm touches something, a fidgeting warmth. Cat finds that she is carrying her smallest child, who is covered in fur, like a kitten. It rests cool paw-pads on her neck, occasionally pricking her flesh with the very tips of its claws.

It begins to rain. James's house stretches and contracts like a ship, but nobody hears it, or sees the shadows of its furniture twitch in the wind. James is flying at speed, twisting and turning low over contours of land, without understanding how: if he thinks about it, he will fall. He nosedives over a ridge, trees, a wide river, darkness, and then he's standing absolutely still, at the side of another man, of his own age and stature. Together they regard an endless plain of mud. Clumps of mud-coloured shrubbery. Here and there, a vague, mud-sculpted cross, stabbing the earth, leaning towards it. The muddy skeleton of a garden, and, beyond it, a row of slippery steps. James asks, 'What is this?'

'A homecoming,' says Ieuan. Then he says something else, but the wind is building up, beginning to box their cheeks and ears, and the rain is battering their bodies and the ground, smudging the few landmarks, driving every form and every colour together. James stirs, hears the rain sizzling on the window, feels and acknowledges the solidity of his bed and his room and his house in Terrace Street, and turns over into another dream.

At half past four Cat wakes up, snapping straight into full consciousness, and lies listening to the last drips of rain, and to the memories that have assembled themselves while she was asleep. Her mind is absolutely clear. She's replaying an incident at school. She was nearly eighteen, helping out at the school-leavers' party. Sliding pineapple chunks and cheese on to skewers, handing round plates of Ritz biscuits and fish pâté, flashing her most capable smile at parents and teachers. Mr Dodd, her geography teacher and idol, was topping up the white wine. Cat was given a glass. She held it casually, just another adult having a drink at a party. Mr Dodd tried to pour some wine into it. Her hand shook so violently that the neck of the bottle rattled against the rim of her glass like a high-hat, and cheap white wine sloshed down her arm and over her sleeve. Cat groans in her bed, reliving the shame and thinking up plausible lines – 'It's my weak exam arm'; 'I've caught a nerve'; conjuring up an indifferent laugh, seventeen years too late. Cat lets her arm drop across her eyes, but other scenes flap mercilessly into her mind.

The time she got drunk at one of her father's parties, threw a tantrum on the patio and threw up in the kitchen sink.

The evening she spent blinking at Bearded Leo's friends, taking their ironies literally and wilting under their pity and kindness.

That lunch at the pub with a group of freelance sports journalists. The way she flirted and postured and tried to tell a dirty joke but got the punchline wrong. The way she half-smiled and rummaged in her bag, when one of them mimicked the Asian barman's accent.

Cat appears before herself, a charlatan, a coward, but not enough of a charlatan or a coward to matter. A bit player, all overdone attitudes, without the mitigation of good intentions or doubts. Her life amounts to no more than this: a collection of minor failures. Soon she will be thirty-six. Then thirty-seven. Then she will be in her forties, and then her fifties, and it will still be the same. Some days she will busy herself and forget; some nights she will lie paralysed by her past botcheries and retreats. She has avoided everything, all her life.

A bird begins its song, looping and weaving and popping. Cat moves a hand under the duvet and lays it timidly on her stomach.

10

When the rain begins, thrumming against the roof, clattering down the skylight, Livvy shifts herself on the attic floor, rubs her eyes and sits up. Her hair is heavy with dust. She shouldn't have come up here so late. She should have gone straight to bed and left this until tomorrow. But the urge to get everything done is threatening to rise into panic. She's only got another week to make the house fit to sell, and then she must get back home, back to work. She leans away from the dim light fanning out from one bare bulb. Something touches her cheek; she starts and moves in a low, furtive crouch towards another box. This is the trouble: she can't stop searching. As soon as she unfolded the ladder and toiled up its wheezing steps, two, maybe three hours ago, she knew she'd be stuck here. She always did get marooned in Nan's attic, imprisoned for whole afternoons by its secrecy and gothic sloping ceiling. It never fulfilled its mysterious promise. A couple of mossy hatboxes, an ancient tin chest with a broken lock and a few buttons inside, a cracked porcelain washbowl. It was enough, in those days, that she could pull up the trapdoor and disappear, engulfed by stifling, ancient air. None of her nan's old rubbish is here, now. All thrown away when Nan was still fit enough for her periodic clear-outs. Now Livvy has real treasure chests to explore. Now there are boxes and boxes of dying newspapers; handwritten shop receipts; bills, stained with rust from the paperclips; documents about the house, in archaic print on thick official sheets. Her mother and her grandmother and anyone else who could have cared about this stuff are all dead, but Livvy still enjoys an illicit thrill as she hauls out congealed stacks of folded paper. Where had it been hidden all those years? Certainly not in her mother's flat – no nooks and crannies there: everything taken in at a glance. But someone must have hoisted all these boxes up here, some time after Livvy had left to make her own home. Maybe it had all been stashed away in this house, all the time – under the stairs, under Nan's mountainous bed – plenty of places that would have been out of bounds to an inquisitive child.

She's halfway through the latest box. Birth certificates – Margaret Ann, 1936. (Livvy catches her breath, before recognising her mother's full name.) Olivia May, 1961. Father unknown. Marriage certificate – Nan and Frank's, 1935. Livvy claws down to the bottom of the box, down to its globules of fluff and dead flies, but finds nothing else. No answers. (She grits her teeth at the memory of her own nagging: 'Why are *we* called Farrell, Mum?' 'Nothing wrong with it, is there? Well stop asking daft questions, then.')

Another document – Margaret Ann again – died this 18th day . . . A life neatly rounded off, certificate to certificate. Livvy assaults a new box, tugging at the corner of a thin waft of paper. She tears it and has to lift out a file full of cut-out cookery recipes and readers' tips before retrieving it, then finds it's just another receipt. From Hawke & Son, Licensed Dealers, Paid to Mrs Farrell, for one brooch, mother-of-pearl, £1.6/-; one pair amber earrings, £2.1/6. So that's what happened to those earrings. Livvy's mother, sitting in front of the dressing table, peering into the mirror, making a lipstick face; fussily clapping the lid back over the thick red crayon with its elegant little slope; clipping the little amber circles on to her ears. A cousin's wedding, a Saturday bus ride into town, a visit to Nan's . . . they all used to qualify for the lipstick and earrings. Livvy loved those peaceful five minutes, watching her mother's reflection from the bedroom door, before normal life resumed with 'Get cracking, girl, I'm not waiting for you.'

She doesn't remember when the earrings disappeared, but she's known for a long time that her mother pawned and sold things. She's known all along how much was sacrificed for her sake – she was never allowed to forget it. All the efforts put in, to set her on her way, to give her *proper, professional* piano lessons, to *make the most* of her talents. Mustn't forget that – mustn't change her course, once it was set. Was the lipstick another luxury that fell by the wayside? Or maybe it went out of fashion. Or maybe her mother just grew too tired to bother.

What time is it? Must be late. Livvy's wide awake now and still unloading papers. She doesn't know what she'll do with them, or what she's hunting for. A note, an apology, an explanation . . . she finds a cheap brooch, crescent-shaped, with the pin bent double; a picture, drawn by herself: Nan and Mum having tea – generous loops for Nan's hair, and astonished round eyes, or glasses, maybe. Furious zig-zags for her mother. No mouth – odd, that. Wishful thinking? Come to think of it, Peg's mouth never gave much away. If she thought something was funny – something on the telly (never something Livvy said) – her mouth would turn down, and her nose would move, working from side to side as though she might sneeze, and then her eyes would water and she'd say, 'Oh, dear,' as if it was all an unfortunate lapse.

Livvy looks again at her mother's death certificate. Checking. Nan didn't ring her until two days after it happened. Didn't know what to say, probably. Or wanted to get everything straight, tidy, before Livvy arrived on the scene. What *did* she say, in fact? Livvy can't really remember, but it was something like 'Your mother's heart's broken down' – no, that can't have been it. 'Given out.' That's more likely. Anyway, it made Livvy think of a car rattling to a halt. Pretty accurate, in a way. Her mother came home from her shift at the Spar, put the kettle on, took her shoes off, sat on the couch and stopped living. Didn't even take her mack off, said Nan, as though it had an eerie significance. Didn't phone to see if Nan was all right, as she always did on Tuesdays and Thursdays (visits on Saturdays and Mondays). So Nan called the neighbour, 'Auntie Jen,' who had a key. 'Just nip round and check on Peg, will you, Jen? And mind you don't say it's for me.'

Livvy sifts through disintegrating sheet music, bought second-hand by Nan for her to practise: 'Fairy Lightfoot'; 'Two Little Tunes'; some music-hall songs – where did they come from? 'Ginger, You're Balmy!'

She remembers Auntie Jen's voice, hushed with shock – 'I thought she was sleeping. Honest to God. I thought she was sleeping, poor old Peg. Only her eyes wasn't quite shut.'

Watching to make sure you wiped your feet, Livvy had thought, patting Jen's arm. Watching to see if I'd come.

The rain's easing off. Livvy is suddenly sick with tiredness. She's aware of the skin dragging under her eyes. She starts her cautious descent down the attic ladder, pausing, before switching off the light, to survey the new chaos she's created. So she'll have to come up again tomorrow, after all, and put all these papers back. And decide what to do with them. Burn them, probably. They're only papers. She could have found anything, a photograph, a letter from him, some words for his baby girl, complete with 'love from Daddy, kiss-kiss-kiss' and his name in brackets. But it would only be paper.

When dawn breaks, Livvy dreams about her mother. She can't help it, of course. It's no good just deciding not to. The strange thing is that she can never quite forget, even in the depths of the dream itself, that this is all wrong – that her mother should be dead. So when Livvy's mother turns to her in the back of a taxi and gives her that long, resigned stare, Livvy is thinking: What's happened? Did we make a mistake? Has she got better, after all? And with that question comes a lunge of dread – so we'll have to go through with it all *again*. Her mother is directing the cab driver now, resting a hand on his resentful shoulder and flicking her forefinger to left and right, yapping:

'Up here, no, it's quicker if you turn there.'

Then the word 'scurrilous' booms from the featureless driver in a deep, muffled vibrato, and her mother sits back, profoundly shocked. Livvy will remember the precise sound of that word for two days.

'Come on, Mum,' Livvy is nagging, out in the street. They're on the edge of a milling, mumbling crowd, and Livvy is plunging into it:

'He's there! Come *on*' – and she looks back to see her mother's round, pale face, which is also her nan's face, withered and liver-spotted. She knows she's going too quickly, leaving her mother-nan behind. Mother-nan is waddling grimly on, trying to keep up (after all, she's been ill, she's been dead). But Livvy can't afford to wait – she'll lose him in this crowd. In fact she only just glimpses his back sliding between two strangers.

She's there! At the head of this clamouring queue, at the flap of the tent, she's as high as a bridge; she pulls the flap to one side and looks down on an endless, dark sea of people, people in dinner jackets and jewelled dresses, chattering in the half-light around their tables, clinking glasses, glinting and winking as they turn to watch her fly over their heads towards the light. The brazen, golden light of a stage. She understands, now, where he is – there he is! In his white jacket and kingfisher bow-tie, smiling up at her, while he takes his place among banks and tiers of musicians who are already swaying and tapping to the music. Thick, swooning, swooping harmonies sent to lift Livvy even higher; her father's music, instead of his arms, lifting her right up to the point of the roof. She turns easily in the air and lets it carry her up, up, until her eyelids and hands are pressing against the canvas and her back is arched against the glorious swell of music from the bigger, biggest best big band in the world.

Livvy wakes with the music still in her head. Her topsheet has worked its way over her face but she doesn't dare move, afraid of dislodging that creamy, multicoloured sound. The whine of the milk cart drives it away and slowly, Livvy disentangles herself from the bedclothes.

11

Livvy's been wondering whether to take up all the carpets and have done with it. So far, she's taken it up from the hall and landing, the stairs and the front room, where Nan had left a threadbare trail as she shuffled from bed to armchair and, sixteen hours later, from armchair to bed.

Why was she still getting up at six every morning? Livvy thinks it might be something to do with old age. She doesn't guess that the morning air and the early light, falling through the house in cool, complex waves, used to make her nan feel connected with life, as if something might *happen* today.

So half the house is carpetless and hollow, but there are still the better rooms, left to themselves for so many years: the back room (orange and buff, in small geometric patterns); Nan's own bedroom, where she had a small, oval rug to save the carpet (plain and pink); the spare room – Peg's old room, small and narrow (sky blue with darker blue swirls). Livvy feels she should probably leave them, as they're in good shape and she doesn't like waste. But there's the faint trace of humanity about them – that smell, like old tights, too familiar and too alien at the same time.

Livvy pulls on her dungarees and goes heavily downstairs to make coffee. She's fed up with this, now. She wants to be in her own home, with its clean, green spaces and simple lines and the light touch of her neat Kemble keyboard. Playing Nan's ivories is like breaking rocks. The keys remind her of bad teeth. Too soft a touch and they give up altogether, hitting the deck with an empty thunk. Livvy's tempted, though, as always: she leans in the doorway, drinking her coffee and glaring at the piano, resisting the urge to sit and play and play, just for the mindless ease of it, just to let the hours slip.

She can remember the exact moment when playing the piano stopped being a chore. She was six years old, nudged, tugged and bullied as usual, every step of the way. From lying on her tummy in the flat, watching *The Monkees* or *Marine Boy*, her whole body taut with the effort to will away the dreaded moment. From the slam of the flat door, down the two disinfected flights of steps, during the infinite wait for the bus and all the way across town, pleading, promising, raging against her immovable mother. Changing her tactic with every slap on the leg, hissed threat or swordlike finger thrust into her face. All the way along George Street, Perry Street and into Terrace Street and then, at Nan's door, her mother's final, reined-in demand, with awful spaces between the words:

'Are-you-going-to-behave?'

Then the shame of tear-marked cheeks as Nan, trusting and vulnerable, opened the door – 'Here she is: Miss Music!' – and Livvy rushing to the piano, trying to hide her misery, to save Nan the terrible blow of knowing Miss Music didn't want to be there at all.

(She never saw the look exchanged between the two women. Or her nan's private relief when the hour of Livvy's dogged playing, of her own exaggerated praise and Peg's intense concentration was over.)

Melody in G. Fingers curled, wrists up, as Miss Craig had taught her. Using her whole upper body to press down those iron keys. B-G-D-B, the terrible, looming F sharp, the thumb-under-finger manoeuvre waiting to trip her up and set off another livid, desperate outburst.

'Oh, go on, chicken, you're doing *very well*.' (Nan)

'It's no use stremping and stranking, you're not going home till you've done your practice, I'm not paying for you to lie around doing nothing from lesson to lesson.' (Peg)

'I don't care *I can't do it* I HATE MELODY IN GEEEEEE!' (Miss Music)

Then came the day.

No different from the others – same rows, same threats, same tears. No reason for a change, no sudden comprehension or trick of the trade. But this time, her thumb slid smoothly into position, her hand adjusted itself with easy logic, and the F sharp disappeared into a loop of sound, tied into a perfect bow. A Melody in G. That's when Peg sat back with solemn triumph. That's when Livvy, aged six, caught a breath of something, a flicker of something – a future. Something she could do. That's when her course was set.

Livvy doesn't go to the piano this morning – she can't think of anything to play. Usually she plays whatever occurs to her, or whatever happens to be on top of the pile in the old piano stool;

she plays it only because she can. There's satisfaction in it – as her fingers rise and fall, in place, in time, and the notes canter on calmly towards the double bar. But the music never really moves her, barely touches her in fact, except in her big-band dreams.

She turns away and clatters down the hall to the stairs. A violet and red tulip glows on the freshly painted bannister, a reflection of the stained glass in the front door panel. Livvy is a six-year-old genius, standing on the doorstep, clutching her music importantly to her chest. Behind her, Nan ushers them out and says to Peg, in the adult voice that's supposed to be inaudible to six-year-olds,

'There we are, see. All worth it. Must be in her blood.'

And the air is palpitating around her head, disturbed by her mother's silent, guarded exasperation.

PART FOUR

The land was changing. The hills were lowering their heads, dropping their shoulders: we felt exposed. We hankered for the fussy, motherly, inquisitively close hills of Wales. At Newport we were joined by Gilbert Talbot's troops, and our spirits rose for a while. But with every advancing mile, remnants of our confidence were left with the horse-dung and footprints. The names grew flatter with the land: Shut Heath. Milford. Longdon. Farewell. Nervous rumours shivered back through the ranks. As we approached Tamworth, word got back that we had lost our leader. 'Vanished. Gone. The Earl of Richmond and fifty of his most experienced knights. Gone without a trace.'

We marched into the dusk, and the stories grew more fanciful – and more credible.

Henry and his guard, on their way to meet with Stanley's army, had been ambushed and slain by King Richard's spies.

They had been swallowed up by a sudden mist and transported into another world.

They had stopped to drink at an enchanted stream and, in their delusion, had taken each other for hideous demons, and fallen upon each other, and now lay in a bloody heap on some bleak hillside.

We were all feeling the strain. A couple of attempts were made to start up a ballad, but they trailed away after a verse or two. Cochin grabbed one of the small boys who had been skipping alongside us since Lichfield, and sent him running to the forward ranks to pick up any gossip. The *crwt* returned, shining-eyed from his glimpse of the cavalry's dazzle of armour. He was also smarting from a smack on the ear, and he knew nothing.

As the light failed we marched past the stink and whine of a swaying gibbet. A piece of grey something flopped from it on to the road and immediately four dogs came panting among legs and cartwheels to squabble over it.

'When I was in the Levant,' Cochin piped up ahead of us, 'I saw men eating each other. Well – *I* didn't see it. This merchant told me. But *he'd* seen it, with his own eyes. God's truth. That's how the Infidel punish their slaves, see. Making them eat each other.

Bit by bit. Start by peeling the skin in little pieces and chewing. Made me ill, when he told me. Horrible.'

There was a wretched silence, divided by the plodding of our feet, the rumble of wheels, the distant clicking of hooves.

We made camp. Our little scout was still with us: apparently his mother was a follower (or so he claimed). He called himself Hekyn. Nobody but Cochin could understand him. Gwilym spoke no English at all. Mine was a far sight better than Cochin's garbled attempts (which included measures of a dozen other tongues), but he seemed better able to unpick the child's dialect. As we fed the fire, Cochin gave Hekyn fresh instructions to keep him amused, and the boy slipped off, darting between men and horses.

'I told him to go and find Harry Tudor,' laughed Cochin. 'Ask him where the devil he's been.'

We ate salt mutton, mouldy cheese and maslin. Even Gwilym had stopped eulogising about the food, but he gnawed on his crust with some relish. He caught my eye and winked:

'Any more predictions for us, boy?'

I shook my head, though I knew the night would be full of them. They no longer struck me breathless and knocked me out of conscious life, but they trickled into my days and dreams like water. Even now, Gwilym's jovial face was collapsing into a death-mask, a dark gash opening lengthways down his throat; my soul echoed with fear and resignation. I shut my eyes tight and hung my head. It hadn't escaped me that this gift of prophesy – true and terrible prophesy, unlike the sophistry of my profession – that this had come from God. And why? Why me? If I could rise high above workaday life, if I could know what was to come, see time unwind so carelessly before me, who was I? What was I? In my weaker and hungrier moments I admit the question scampered across my mind before I could stop it: was I something more than a mortal?

I embraced my knees and huddled into the warmth of the camp fire, appalled by my blasphemy. I muttered a prayer.

'Christ Alive!' bellowed Gwilym.

He was holding his left hand up, examining it with astonishment. A long, clean curve of red gradually expanded across his knuckles.

'Did you see that? Damned devil's-arse cat! Where did it come from, anyway?'

None of us had seen a cat. We exchanged uneasy looks. One of the camp followers came, chewing a leaf, and spat the sappy mess with expertise over Gwilym's cut. She was young and plump, and Gwilym sat quite happily making eyes at her, while the rest of us discussed the issue grimly.

'Doesn't look good,' said a man known only as Llwynog. 'I've never seen an omen clear as that before battle.'

Cochin began expounding his theory about Satanic familiars and their ability to disappear in the vicinity of flame. He was interrupted by the return of Hekyn, who slapped down on to his knees and looked at us all importantly.

'Well!' he announced. 'I seen the lords. Real lords. I know cos they was speaking foreign.'

Llwynog lay back on the ground, unimpressed.

'And I heard,' said the boy, more loudly, 'I heard one of them archers talking, saying Richmond and twenty men, he says, is lost and gone for good.'

Cochin translated; a shudder passed around the fire and along the neighbouring groups.

'That's it, then,' said Llwynog dully, from his prone position. 'Soon as the fires settle I'm off. They can hang me if they like. But I'm not throwing myself on the King's sword in the name of a leader we haven't got.'

Ten minutes later Llwynog fell asleep. He had to be kicked awake at first light, and as he was grumbling to his feet there was some kind of commotion elsewhere in the camp, and word came round that Henry was only a mile off, safe and sound.

I heard the news with a dip of disappointment. That night had been free of visions. I had woken with a relieved sense that my adventure was about to peter to an end. But before the sun had warmed away the dawn we were forming into ranks again, and ready to march.

Rhys ap Thomas himself rode past before we set off: tall in his saddle, with a thick, black moustache. He shouted encouragement – I didn't catch the words, but the mood was obvious enough. It made me suspicious. Sure enough, before the morning was out, a new tale had filtered through. The triumphant arrival of Stanley's army, which was to have swollen our ranks that very day, was not going to happen.

'Three thousand more, it would have been,' said Cochin over his shoulder, with the assurance of a knight-in-command. 'But they say Stanley's a filthy traitor, after all.'

At his side, Llwynog muttered: 'Doesn't look good. Doesn't look good at all.'

'Ah, don't listen to him, boy,' Gwilym's cheerful voice boomed in my ear. 'What does he know? What does anyone know?'

He grappled with the hilt of his sword to ease its pounding against his leg. A raw scar, knitted up by the follower's leaf-sap, ran across the back of his hand.

'How's your wound, Gwilym?' I asked.

He looked at it briefly and shrugged.

'Damned devil's-arse hellcat. Didn't even see where it went.'

We reached Merevale Abbey and made camp. It was a beautiful evening, full of the last light's birdsong. We stripped to the waist and refreshed ourselves in a stream. Gwilym laughed at my scrawny arms and pigeon chest.

'Your verses don't give you strength, boy, however hard you go at 'em!'

He was like a tree, broad and solid and almost hampered by the branch-width of his arms. He suddenly clutched me round the back of my neck and plunged me head-first into the water, pulling me out again and shaking me as if he'd pulled up a trout by the tail.

'Don't worry, wordsmith,' he said as we clambered out, cheered and applauded by a small audience of soldiers. 'I won't let them scratch your maiden skin!'

I wanted to believe him. I wanted to believe he would survive, and protect us all. How could that tough, scorched flesh and that open smile be ripped and flung across a battlefield? I nearly succeeded in forgetting my bloodsoaked premonitions.

The following day we marched across open land.

'Not long now, lads,' said Cochin. 'Trust me. Not long now.'

We did trust him, too. The nervousness that had dogged us for days had set into a clenched resignation. My visions had become one long, hard scream that vibrated behind my thoughts. We reached Whitemoors and, sure enough, the commanders made their rounds, telling us the day would be ours, God and Righteousness were on our side, and we must fight like furies for the sake of liberty, peace and the rightful king, Henry the Seventh.

After they'd finished, and we were collecting our food, there was a coughing and bumping about our legs and Hekyn was among us.

'I seen him,' he insisted (according to Cochin's translation). 'The new king, I seen him riding out. Horses were like *that*,' reaching up and out to illustrate, with an amazed look. 'Gone to find more friends, I heard them say.'

Cochin gave the boy some cheese.

'Best scout an army ever had,' he declared.

While we were eating, more troops arrived – some of them, we gathered, having deserted from King Richard's camp. Then we saw a fine sight. A knot of riders at the distant edge of the field, led by a figure who was just a glint of light ('That's him, that's Tudor,' said Cochin through his food). Behind them, a sea of white. Hundred upon hundred of white-hooded, white-cloaked spectres, their horses walking and nodding their necks as one.

'*Iesu*,' said Gwilym. 'Death himself has sent an army.'

Cochin started up a song and suddenly, inexplicably, we all became light-hearted and merry, swapping tales, jokes and threats as though we were at a cattle-fair. Hekyn giggled manically at every bawdy comment and pinched Gwilym's arm until he was cuffed, chortling, to the ground. I gave them some heartening stories of Arthur and Llywelyn Fawr and Lludd and Llefelys, and I must say I was on good form.

'Now, then,' said Gwilym, after draining his ale-pot. 'We'll have a fortune-telling from our prophet here.'

'Aye,' yelled Cochin, 'And make sure you see victory and long life for us all!'

I began to sway where I sat, to and fro, to and fro. I shut my eyes and tipped my head back and moaned, quietly at first but gradually louder and higher, louder and higher until – 'AAAAA!' – I sent them backwards with a piercing shriek.

There was a murmur and a barked reprimand from elsewhere in the camp. I let my head drop, then lifted it, opened blank eyes and spoke.

'Blood and gore, blood and bile, the splinter of bone, the tearing of tongues . . .'

And so on, and so on. When I sensed they were losing their nerve, I brought it to a glorious close:

> 'Blood and bile, blood and gore,
> The spear splits the mad white boar,
> He twists and jerks in Death's embrace;
> The victors bow to God's own grace,

The dragon spreads its fiery wing,
And Tudor! Tudor! is our King!'

It went down well, of course, and the cheers rippled out towards the boundaries of the camp.

We said Mass. The sun was low and the shadows stretching as we knelt with a sound like a long wave lapping the shore. As we prayed I felt the gentlest, briefest touch of Gwilym's hand against mine, fleeting as an insect.

'What do you think it's like?' I whispered as we all finally lay down our heads. 'In battle?'

Gwilym rested his head on his arms and thought for a moment.

'Better than waiting,' he said, in the end.

Apart from Cochin, who snored like a sow, I don't know how many of us found rest that night. My mind was awash with strange scenes. Fortress towers too high to remember the ground. Satanic creatures thundering through grey, barren lands. I seemed to be underwater, gazing up through cloud to a circle of light above: I could not reach it, and I could not bear the cries of anguish that bubbled down to my captivity. Perhaps I slept, fitfully: it was hard to tell, now, where visions ended and dreams began. Occasionally I would be aware again of the oddly soothing night-noises, the coughing and rustling and faint mumbling of the camp.

It was a relief when the stirrings of the night became the purposeful clatterings of the day. Long before the sun appeared the grooms were at work preparing the horses, and we could hear the cautious clink of armour being fitted. When the call came most of us were already on our feet. We were drawn into ranks. Before us were the archers, shifting from foot to foot and flexing their free hands. I felt comforted by their presence, like a child hiding in the woods. Gwilym and I stood side by side, near the front, with pikemen behind us. To the left and to the right, an endless wall of men, shoulder to shoulder. We could hear the snorting of horses and the low, restraining words of their riders. We could see the commanders trotting past their divisions. Rhys ap Thomas rode back and fore, occasionally dropping a comment to some soldier in the vanguard. I turned and craned my neck to see that the spectres of the previous night were still with us, a sepulchral company of white, seated silently on their patient mounts to our left. I was afraid to look at Gwilym. Afraid to be tormented with another glance at his future, another splash of his blood. My bladder was throbbing. A muffled, emphatic declaration from somewhere to my right prompted a gasp of interest and a scattering of hissed questions and comments. Apparently our leader was exhorting us to fight with courage and . . . well, I can only guess. I began to sink into a comfortable torpor, and to think about my sore feet, and then suddenly there was a shout and a scurry of hooves and we were off to battle.

As we marched some know-all behind me said,
'Still no Stanley, then. God have mercy on us.'

A broad, open stretch of ground. Dismal marshland to the right, quivering with soggy grasses. I pictured myself wading into that bog, sucked back at every step, arrows splashing at my feet. We stopped. I could see nothing, no one, beyond the heads of our front line. Perhaps King Richard had decided not to fight, after all. I stood with the sun warm on the side of my head and speculated that, should no one feel inclined to act, we could stay in that moment forever.

Another order. I didn't understand it: I didn't need to. I had become one part of a large and lumbering creature, moving without thought or volition. We went forward with small, shuffling steps, jostling against each other, while the commanders on their horses side-stepped and directed. A stamping, ringing, sweating, beating dance into position. Gold-and-green fields wheeled slowly about before us. The sun moved its comforting hand to our backs. As we turned, the land swooped and dipped, then resolved itself into a high rise of ground, directly ahead. Gwilym's arm pressed urgently against mine. I blinked upwards, squinting at the hilltop, and a dribble of piss escaped to warm my breeches. Facing us, a forest of weaponry extended the whole length of the ridge; behind it hung a haze of silver and bronze. My heart lurched in and out of its rhythm.

'Look at them,' murmured Gwilym. 'It's the whole world. The whole world up there, watching us. And wanting to kill us.' I thought of his brother, hobbling back to Cwm Teg, embracing their tired father, taking up the hammer again, taking Gwilym's place at the anvil.

Let's begin, then. In God's name, let's begin.

To our left there was still movement, as the hooded retainers and infantrymen turned to face the foe. We waited, breathing each other's rancid air, listening to the slow tread of the men and the horses' tranquil clop, clop.

The barking and baying of commanders began: goading us, hounding us. Were we men? Did we have pride, did we have red blood in our veins? Would we lie down with our faces in the mud, to be trampled and kicked by Richard's rabble? By that murderer king? That filthy, arrogant scum? Or would we show them what we could do? For our rightful leader! For our nation's glory! For TUDOR!

A dutiful shout drifted back from the ranks. For Tudor . . .

The barks grew more insistent. Were we *cowards? Girls?* Were we—

My heart exploded.

A squeal, a giant fist denting the ground, a splintering, a squelching, and the patter of earth-clods about our shoulders and heads. And then, in the after-shock, a high, unearthly keening, like the call of some satanic bird.

The archers got to work. Unfathomable commands flew through the summer air and, as the noise died, we heard that trudge, trudge, clip-clop of the battalion lining up to our left. My hands shook, darted everywhere, fumbled for my dagger, my axe, unable to close around them. I had no idea at all what to do. Another squeal – thud – splinter; beside me Gwilym let out a howl and I turned towards him – not yet, dear Lord, not yet! – but was blinded by a maze of arms and weapons.

One clear command: 'Stand fast!'

I repeated it aloud, in a quavering, woman's voice.

'Stand fast! Stand fast!'

I clung to those words for safety.

Something fell heavily against my back, and I crashed forward onto a cursing archer. Staggering to regain my balance, I became aware of a soft rain, spitting into sudden, vindictive screeches, close against my ear. I hunched down, afraid to look up, afraid that the very act of looking would draw the spinning barb into my eye. Hiss, hiss, screech . . .

Two archers fell at my legs together, entangled in their bows and shoving me several paces back. I fell but was propped almost upright against a wall of bodies. One desperate hand emerged from the complexity of corpses and clutched at my hair. I pulled away as an arrow, two, three arrows, thudded into the lifeless flesh where I had been leaning.

I was on my hands and knees. I had not yet managed to draw my dagger. A man fell face-upward at my fingers, staring up at me as if to share his surprise. An arrow embedded itself needlessly into his cheek and his face dissolved towards it like water into a pit. Straining to control my retching belly, I finally wrenched my dagger from its sheath and – what now? Manically, I thrust it into my dead companion's shoulder, then withdrew it and tried to gain courage from the blood that slithered down its blade.

Get up! Get up!

A ripe taste of vomit at the back of my mouth. Hiss, hiss, screech. Thud and splinter. A muted, businesslike din of men firing, falling, firing, falling.

Then a new noise.

A rumble – a summer storm? I lifted my head and saw, through the mesh of men and bows, a torrent of hooves and open mouths hurtling down the hill towards us.

The intoxication of battle has little to do with the warrior's cry, or with bloodlust, or even with the fury of unutterable fear. That tempest of horses, bellowing men, braced lances and hatred came ploughing into our ranks and I was lifted, somehow, lifted and carried like a pup, with my feet in the air, a full half-mile. I had lost all control, all will: I was abandoned to fate in that charge, expecting at any moment to see my stomach pierced by wood and iron, to watch the first gush of my innards . . . and I was elated. Let the will of God prevail.

I landed on my back with an impact that rattled my teeth in their sockets. Having discarded me the charge passed on – a deafening crunch of hooves, one of which grazed my forehead. Weeping Jesus, it hurt. I could have curled up there, among the cooling bodies, pressing away the pain with the palms of my hands. But my mind was kept sharp by a rich stench of blood and shit, and by the other survivors, now scrabbling to their feet. I went with them, brandishing the dagger that had failed to touch a living soul. We ran, stumbled, hopped and sprawled back towards the front line as the pounding of hooves faded, turned and swelled again behind us. I fell against my own blade, saw a black cloud of blood open across my breeches and only then felt a stinging pain. As I limped and lolloped on, a call was passed back in cracked voices:

'Stand fast! Fast to the standards!'

The horses that had seemed on top of us had disappeared. To

left and right, the silver ripple of our own knights, miraculously still drawn up in battle rank. A lull.

Perhaps, I thought, perhaps we have lost the day. Perhaps it's all over and I can lie down here, safe among the dying and the dead, until night falls and I can crawl away.

Still, I searched the crop of upturned faces, searching for my poor doomed friend. Some of the features had been torn back to reveal jutting bone or thick, brown ooze. I had forgotten the urge to vomit.

A jarring between my shoulder blades.

'Get *up*! You cowardly shits, get *on*! To the standards! To the death!'

His horse nudged past, crackling through broken arrows and ribs.

With a vague sense of shame, I realised that my axe was still bound to my side. May I be granted one more vision, I prayed. One more vision of blackness and death, even of hellfire licking the edges. Then I shall know, I shall accept my fate, and I shall lie here and rest until it comes.

A gasping pikeman grabbed my arm and dragged me to my feet, leading me on with the others. We seemed to advance for hours; the pikeman had me firmly in his grasp, whether to pull me on or to keep himself upright it was hard to tell.

A great, thickset, bearded man was before us. He made a deft movement, and the pikeman's head hung off its neck. His hand stayed locked around my arm, and I fell with him. I landed against his chest, and heard the lapping and bubbling of blood leaving his body. Behind the bearded killer came more. Dozens, hundreds more, hacking their way through the ranks. Perhaps I should join them, I thought, and raised my eyes. They met the wild gaze of a young, clean-shaven boy. He held a halberd high over his shoulder, but seemed to have frozen on the spot. His tunic was embroidered with the smeared, once-white boar of Richard. He crumpled on top of me: one more life finished. Some other young boy must have driven him through the back.

An eternity of fighting, above and around me, as I lay with my face buried in the pikeman's bloodied chest and the Yorkist boy limp and heavy across my spine. Again that curiously quieted sound of labour and effort: grunts and cracks and the blacksmith's clang, clang. No prophecies, now: I could only recall the past revelation, of Gwilym and his red, slit throat.

Time passed. Is it possible that I *slept*?

There was silence. Except that a new wave of noise had broken far, far away, and swept into the valley and out beyond my world.

I began to understand that I was still alive. I levered myself with difficulty off the pikeman, and the Yorkist boy rolled to the ground. I stood, shaking, and peered at the dried blood on my leg. My head throbbed where the hoof had brushed it. I was surprised to find my fist tight around the hilt of my dagger.

Here and there, other figures rose from the dead. I began to pick my way – where? God knows where. One creature was wedged at an angle among the fallen, his head and shoulders stiff, his arms set hard above him. As I passed I recognised his face, which was dirty but unharmed: his eyes were open and incredulous in death. It was Hekyn. He must have sneaked on to the battlefield. For an adventure.

The sun was lower. How long had it been since we stood with the sun on our cheeks, waiting for the day to commence? Years?

Another burst of sound: fragmentary yells and the growing violence of running feet.

Up the hillside and across the dead came a flood of men, almost flying over the ground, some of them shedding their weapons as they went. Hesitantly at first, then with increasing panic, I cantered, galloped, tore along with them, forgetting my injured leg, my pounding head. All was lost. Henry was killed, the day was done. And who cared, after all? Who cared which tyrant occupied the throne? I ran for my life, ran across hands and bellies and faces, ran like a witch on the wind. The marshy ground approached and, ahead of me, the latest of my visions came alive, as soldiers were pulled to a halt, their feet imprisoned in the sucking earth, or flung themselves headfirst into the bog with the force of their momentum. On their heels came the enemy, swinging, scything, with a long, hoarse cry.

My belt was yanked back, doubling me in breathless agony, and I went down in a heap. My assailant splayed across the grass near by.

'Tudor is King!' he croaked, turning on to his side. 'Tudor is King, boy! Your prophesies came right!'

Gwilym laughed like a madman.

I could not restore my breath and only wheezed:

'Tudor? . . . King?'

Getting to his feet, Gwilym reached forward to seize my hand, and blood spattered across his brow.

A red-bearded soldier keeled over on to his back between us. Cochin's throat had been slit cleanly, lengthwise, with a dagger. Some retreating Yorkist's final, desperate lunge.

'Horrible,' said Gwilym. I laughed so hard, I almost threw up.

We followed the army to Stoke Golding, whooped like children at every commander who strutted up to be knighted by the new king; wept like children as the diadem was fitted clumsily on Henry's bared head.

'We'll never forget this,' Gwilym yelled above the racket, tears staining his wide face. 'And we'll never be forgot!'

I was suddenly aware of the pain and weakness in my leg. Gwilym carried me to the followers' encampment, where field surgeons were hard at work. They treated the gash on my leg with comfrey, gave me leopard's-bane for my head, and I settled back against a bank to rest. The night was closing in. Gwilym sat himself beside me.

I wanted to ask him whether he would start back for Cwm Teg the next morning, but was afraid of the answer I would receive. He saved me the trouble.

'Good night's rest, boy,' he whispered as darkness slid over the soldiers' moans and sobs. 'Then we'll be fit to march to London.'

1

'Designers do it. Carpenters do it. *Blue Peter* fans have been at it for thirty odd years. Sticking things together. Along with therapy and the combustion engine, it's made us the civilized society we are today.'

Cat is motionless except for her fingers, which are sculpting words, sharing the letters between them in waves, to and fro, with a fluid sound like simmering water.

'It certainly is a sticky business. The £22m adhesives market is gummed up to the hilt with awkward issues. Health and safety; the environment; industrial pollution – all leave a taste as nasty as that glossy bit on the flap of the envelope.'

She taught herself to type during a summer holiday, when she and James were students. She had come to stay at James's parents' house for three weeks. 'I'm not being a nuisance?' she pleaded, swamping James's mother in one of her hugs. She didn't want to outstay her welcome, she said. Only, it was a minefield at home these days. Sulks from her father, because Cat *still* hadn't met his new girlfriend. Nerves and guilt-trips and hyperactivity from her mother, who kept insisting that she fix Cat a chorus part in her local G&S Society production, so that they could spend their evenings together. 'I'll pay rent,' she offered James's mother. 'I'll take a bar job. How much do you want?'

James's mother wouldn't hear of it.

'You get on and learn that typing. That's the best fall-back you can have. There's *always* work for a typist, no matter what.'

In the mornings Cat shut herself in the spare room, which was painted in light yellows and greens, and was always full of sun. She sat at the old sewing table and practised, tapping out exercises from the manual –

> *Yonder youth put your yellow yacht in the yard yesterday*
> *Bobby is buying a box of bizarre big books*
> *Quick and pretty tough and skinny Quick and pretty tough and skinny* . . .

Getting her fingers caught and bitten as they slipped between the old-fashioned keys.

'It's an elegant machine, though,' she said, when James's mother came up with scones and lemonade. 'Better than these electric typewriters – they're so stubby. Like little tanks.'

She stayed an extra week, and reached sixty words per minute.

It was a hot summer. In the afternoons, James's mother put out the deckchairs and called up the stairs: 'You *need* fresh air. All work and no play . . .' So they sat in the garden drinking lemonade, and James's mother told Cat anecdotes about her years as a school secretary, and about Mr Harman the PE teacher, who took a bit of a shine to her and brought her buttercups. 'If things had taken a different turn . . .' she confided. But James's father, who taught Maths, had been quicker off the mark. 'And that suited me fine, really. You just think, sometimes, don't you? – What if. Just curiosity, nothing more.'

When James wandered out to join them, they stopped talking, and beamed at him, shielding their eyes from the sun.

'We're just chopsing,' said Cat. 'Girls' talk. Me and Mum.'

James looked at his mother, expecting to see a trace of discomfort, but she only laughed and gave Cat's arm a push.

James went to see Gal. They lay on the cool floor in Gal's room with their arms flung across their faces, and listened to The Cure. Later, Cat arrived with James's mother to pick James up. When James came down they were standing in the conservatory, admiring the garden. Gal's mother wore a silk, embroidered white vest-top and deep pink trousers. He heard her actor's voice, and saw his mother, looking tall and awkward beside her, and too hot in her flowery waisted dress.

'It's an attitude I can't fathom, Siân,' Gal's mother was saying. 'It's a constant source of reproach to me that I've lost touch with my own cultural heritage. I know damn well that if I hadn't, I'd be passing it on. A language, any language, is a gift. You don't withold it. You just don't. You pass it on.'

James's mother plucked at the collar of her dress and said,

'Well, you're probably right . . .'

Then Cat moved behind and between them, put her arms around James's mother's waist and Gal's mother's shoulders.

'It's all very well,' she said, in her joke-sermon way. 'But some sisters had enough on their plates feeding and raising their sons, without passing on cultural thingummyjigs too.'

Gal's mother gave Cat a slap on the rump.

'Diplomat,' she said, and let her hand rest in the small of Cat's back. James stood in the room, unnoticed, while Gal's music continued its muffled course upstairs.

'Dry transfers herald a new adhesive dawn, a brazen challenge to industry giants Stickit, with their whopping 75% penetration in pastes and sprays.'

James stands behind Cat reading her article. He's got a damp towel over his arm and an empty loo-roll in one hand. He's come in to lecture her about the state of the bathroom: talc cascading across the floor, discarded dental floss on the rim of the basin, straight hairs and squiggley hairs all over the bloody place. But he says nothing. He can see the weighted curve of her cheek, quivering slightly as she works, and the smaller, looser, swollen curve of flesh below her eye. He knows she's been crying. He says,

'Coffee?'

'Please,' says Cat, without stopping. 'Thick and bitter, like my men.' She looks up, showing him her puffy eyes like a confession, smiles, and turns back to the screen.

James waits, then puts his free hand on her shoulder. She moves, just enough to make him take it away again.

2

The exact position of Rhys ap Thomas's contingent on the battlefield – with Ieuan, of course, in its midst – is uncertain. Henry Tudor placed himself at the centre of his troops. To his left, the hooded retainers of John Savage. To the right, Gilbert Talbot's men. Commanding the centre and the vanguard, the Earl of Oxford. Richard III's army of 12,000 was arrayed along the slopes of Ambion Hill. Sir William Stanley halted his own 4,000 mounted retainers, in red tunics bearing white harts, at a non-commital distance from the action.

The attack began. Richard's gunners fired their serpentines, sending four-pound cannonballs into the Tudor lines. The Duke of Norfolk's long-bowmen began their work. Then Norfolk's 8,000-strong battalion charged downhill. The Earl of Oxford compressed his thinly spread front line, planted his standards in the ground and forbade his men from moving more than ten paces beyond them. His cool head and clever tactics had the desired effect: the disciplined troops formed a wedge, fending off the Norfolk charge and a subsequent hand-to-hand encounter, in which Norfolk himself was killed.

So far the skilful strategies and manoeuvres of both armies had been equally matched; but Henry could not afford further confrontation without the help of Stanley, who was still observing events from his position north of the battlefield. In a last bid to secure his help, Henry and his bodyguard rode out from the ranks and galloped across open ground towards the Stanley force. Seeing the Tudor standard flying, Richard III and a contingent of knights (there is some debate as to the actual number involved) rode at full tilt down the hill. No doubt Ieuan and his fellow soldiers watched with awe, as this last chivalric battle-charge marked the passing of an age. Richard led the way on his white mount and struck Henry's standard-bearer, Sir William Brandon. At this crucial point Stanley finally gave his retainers the battle-cry – 'A Stanley!' – and rode into action, promptly turning the course of events in Tudor's favour. Richard's horse sank into marshy ground, and the king was cut down. As news of his death spread his troops fled, and shouts of 'God Save King Henry!' filled the air.

One source has it that Richard III was killed by a Welsh soldier wielding a halbard. Could the man who despatched the last of the Yorkist kings have been Ieuan Gloff himself?

James is spooling idly through an article from the *Cambrian Archivists' Society Journal*: 'Seclusion, Disease and Social Deviancy in the Medieval Economy'. There's a stillness in his office, balanced on its symmetry and order. He could go home, but the prospect of discarded tissues and socks and Cat bearing up exhausts him. He glances at the picture on his desk of Sonia, with her unblinking, sky-blue eyes. He wishes Cat would leave.

He reads about isolated spasms of plague in south and west Wales. A current of death, pulsing from hamlet to farmhouse over the damp, scrubby uplands before fading away in the mist, five hundred years ago. A cloud darkens the room, sharpening the glow of the screen. The room's tranquillity is reduced into something dull and cold. James wheels his chair backwards, to the window, and watches a draggle of students emerge from the library across the square and disappear into the Union. He sighs, and fishes for his car keys.

As James is unlocking his front door, Livvy is crossing Terrace Street behind him, heading towards her grandmother's house. She's been shopping for provisions, and is weighed down by two bulky plastic bags. As she hurries from the pavement, judging the distance of an approaching car, the bag in her right hand takes on a life of its own. Its insides shift, a long gash travels down its side, and half its contents spill onto the road. Livvy begins to squat down, then hops back awkwardly, as a blue Volvo swerves round her, horn blaring, and catches the edge of a packet of sugar, which fans its contents impressively across the tarmac. The squeal of tyres, the thump and blare and their promise of an incident, bring a few passers-by running. James, hesitating on his doorstep, is shouldered aside by Cat, who dives out of the house to get involved. A woman is already trying to help Livvy bail the shopping into the remains of the bag, while a man stands over them giving directions. The man is Vernon Lightfoot.

Cat, Livvy and the other helper disappear into the late Mrs Farrell's house, arms full of loose packets and tins.

James and Vernon Lightfoot follow as far as the front door and stop at an invisible boundary. Vernon grasps James's arm.

'Heard about Charlie did you? Keeled over on his doorstep last night. Heart, they reckon.'

James feels a scoop of shock in his chest. 'Oh, I'm so sorry . . .'

'Aye, off up to see him now, at the hospital.' Vernon is still smiling. 'He's a tough old bastard, mind. He'll pull through.'

'You're hopeless. *Hopeless.*'

Cat rustles angrily through the phone directory.

'Did you bother to ask which hospital? Penmount, I suppose it'll be. That *poor* old man.' She sounds hard and righteous. 'He must be so lonely and frightened.'

'I told you. His brother was on his way there. I told you—'

'Oh, yes,' the volume swells alarmingly, 'oh yes, a duty visit from his brother. Big deal.'

James says cautiously, 'He's not necessarily the only—'

'Fine. So *you* don't need to bother. Very nice, James. Very community-minded and considerate.'

She's pushing her lower lip up, now, keeping her chin steady, looking over his head. He hasn't seen her this bad for a long time.

'In-patients please,' says Cat sternly to the phone, then covers the receiver.

'I'll go and see him tomorrow afternoon,' she says, with control, then, half-turning away from him, 'And by the way, I've asked your next-door neighbour to supper.'

3

Charles Lightfoot has changed colour. His face has turned from dreary yellow to doleful blue-grey. He's been hoisted into a half-sitting position against the pillows; his loose skin tries to slither back down.

He and Cat exchange a brief look of quizzical alarm. His eyes are filmy and fluid. He's dissolving, thinks Cat. Bit by bit, he'll be slurped up that tube in his arm like lemonade up a straw.

She sits by his bed, holding his file of poems, unsure what to do with them.

'These are *very* good,' she says.

Charles Lightfoot lifts an arm a couple of inches from the bed and lets it fall again. It could mean 'Thank you'. It could mean 'Who cares'.

'How are you feeling?' Cat asks, in a lower voice. One of the other patients in the side-ward, asleep or unconscious, crackles and scrapes through his open mouth. His neighbour, who is trying to read, fires outraged looks across the top of her glasses.

'Ah, well,' says Mr Lightfoot hopelessly. 'That's it, then, innit.'

He speaks in a crumbling whine. Cat puts her hand on his: she has an instinct for hospital choreography. His hand is long, corrugated and dry – not unpleasant to touch.

'James – you know, Dr Powell, who interviewed you – he sends his *very* best . . . his love.' She produces a card, takes it out of the envelope, flashes the message (in her writing) at Mr Lightfoot and props it on his bedside table.

'He had hoped to come along, but he's under so much . . . you know, his work is so . . .'

She picks up another card which is already on display. 'Get Well Soon', in lanky, spiralling print; then, in capitals underneath: 'VERN'.

'Oh, your brother's been to see you – well, that's good.'

'Aye. Aye, Vernon's been.'

A nurse comes in and talks loudly to the unconscious man, without result, then shrugs and leaves.

'Mr Galloway sends his best wishes too,' lies Cat.

Mr Lightfoot gestures vaguely towards the file. 'Aye, well, you can give him them. He might be interested, might not.'

Cat leans forward, with an eager, tragic look.

'I think – the poem about, you know, about the crack in the wall . . . all good things coming to an end . . . I just wondered, is that one of the ones about your . . .' – she casts about for the historically correct word – 'your *sweetheart*? It's very touching. Nora, was it?'

Mr Lightfoot regards her with moist and baffled eyes. His chest rumbles; his head tilts at an uncomfortable angle.

'You remember, you told us, when we came . . . but, well, it's none of my business, I know . . . I just wondered . . .'

At last, Mr Lightfoot puts his head back and closes his eyes. Cat listens to his breathing. She decides to wait until he's asleep; she'll put the poems on the end of his bed and leave. Suddenly he says:

'Poor kid. Poor little mare.'

He struggles through phlegm and exhaustion. Cat isn't sure that he's fully awake.

Another pause, marked by the snoring man and the rustling pages of his neighbour's book. Then Charles Lightfoot talks again,

'Always turning up. Just when you thought he'd finally buggered off for good.' He takes a long, laboured breath.

Cat is taut with attention, her face round and bright. She's afraid of trampling over his thoughts, but eventually offers a careful prompt: 'Nora?'

'Oh, Noreen, aye.' Up goes the arm, and drops. Charles Lightfoot opens his eyes and sets about entertaining his visitor. 'Lovely lady, Noreen. Classy, sort of a look of Loretta Young, I always thought. I were a kid when I met her. Surprised she give me the time of day. She were twice my age.'

'It's so difficult, isn't it.' Cat rests her arms on the edge of his bed. 'It's all very well to say age doesn't matter, but when people all around you are saying it's wrong . . .'

'Aye,' Charles nods politely. 'And she were married, and all, mind. Wife and mother. Should have kept my distance, reelly. But there you are.' He glances at Cat from the corner of his eyes, enjoying the impact of his disclosure.

'Actually . . .' Cat begins, on an impulse, but he interrupts.

'Nineteen-fifties.' He looks at her, testing her. 'Before your time.'

Cat smiles apologetically, and dips into a mental stock of assorted images. Black-and-white streets, urban drizzle, Alec Guinness shiny in a college scarf, wide, red mouths, knobbly-hubbed police cars, American saloons, Elvis, Rock around the Clock, Suez, Korea, Hungary . . . She struggles to place Charles Lightfoot, young Charles Lightfoot, somewhere among the jumble.

'Well, it were before that, the first time, like – just after the war. But it were the nineteen-fifties, reelly. That were our time.'

Noreen, dabbing rain with a hanky off her long, oval face. Strands of wet hair clinging to her forehead, pushed back hurriedly under the rim of her hat. Noreen, with the smattering of lines around her eyes, already beginning to reach along her cheeks, where they would deepen into crevices as she grew old. Noreen nipping off the bus two stops early, or dashing up the market stairs to the first-floor coffee bar, or waiting at the station for a train she wasn't going to catch, just to be with him. Just to spend another ten minutes, half an hour, with Charles Lightfoot.

He tells Cat for the second time that he was only a boy when he met Noreen. But he reckoned he was a man. A working man, earning a proper wage, and set up for life. The thing that impressed him about Noreen, he says, was the *go* in her: always getting on, always in a rush, going to her shift at the Silver Kettle, or setting the pumps at the Tudor Arms, or dragging that lumpish daughter of hers to school. She never let it bring her down, though. Noreen had fight in her. She was on a quest. Even when she stopped to chat, she was edging away, itching to busy herself. Her husband was never around. 'It's his work,' she would say, vaguely, 'takes him off.' And she would give her daughter's arm a shake – 'Did a grand job on the house, though, didn't he? Made it pretty for us?'

She was always making excuses for him, on the defensive. But her husband's absences didn't merit too much comment, in those early days. Lots of women's husbands weren't around. Noreen was battling through, along with all the rest of them.

Charles talks about 'coming back for Noreen' after his National Service. He likes the phrase, with its hints of fate and passion. 'It were like starting life all over again,' he says. 'About 1951, must've been. Coming home, ready for anything. Like everything were possible.'

Noreen was still rushing about as usual, still chivvying her sulky girl along and bustling from shift to shift. But even she was beginning to slide towards defeat. She was up against a stronger enemy, it seemed – something that was picking on her, *just* her, pulling at her humour, drawing blood from her face. Frank had been back for a while, God knows from where; then he'd disappeared again. And now Charles had come home.

Cat is still there, at his bedside. Charles says, 'I 'spect you're shocked now, aren't you?'
  Cat starts an exaggerated denial.
  'Aye, people think all that's something new, playing around, doing the dirty. But there's nothing older than love and sin.'
  Cat waits a little longer, but Charles has drifted off again. She wonders whether it's the drugs making him wander like this. She feels suddenly bored and detached, and aware that this man is a virtual stranger to her. When his eyes glaze over again, Cat gets up quietly and leaves.

4

Cat has gone, and Charles Lightfoot has forgotten she was ever there. He sits in a private silence, letting his heavy breath rock and lull his body. He will need the pan soon, and the prospect of that humiliation keeps him from sleep. But not yet, not urgent yet. The man opposite continues his rattling. From the corridors and from the wards beyond comes the cheerful percussion of hospital routine. A woman trots past and calls a name. Further away, a child cries. Half dozing in his bed, Charles is cut to the quick by a sudden vision: Noreen, with an expression he hasn't thought of in forty years. A suspended expression, eyes wide, eyebrows meeting in an indignant point, mouth pressed against the irresistible tide of laughter and – oh, yes! the tip of her nose! It used to twitch like a rabbit's before she laughed – he'd forgotten that. He sees it as though she's there. He used to know, when her nose started twitching, that he'd won her round, and it would win him round, too – because it looked so daft and so funny. Twitch, twitch, and then the loud, rickety laugh and streaming eyes.

A phone rings. The man opposite has a coughing fit, then resumes his snoring without regaining consciousness.

Noreen's back room. When? 1952? or 53? Tasting the powdery sweetness of her make-up. Pressing his hands against her back to stop them trembling, feeling the coarse material of her blouse and the warmth of her, underneath, and the startling complication of her bra-strap. Trying not to stare at the wedding photo, Noreen and Frank's happiness framed and centred on the mantelpiece.

Reckoned he was a man, did he? What a joke. What a fib. Knew nothing. Done nothing. Bit of fumbling in doorways with nameless women who thought they looked like Veronica Lake. Pawing between their thighs, tweaking their suspenders because he didn't know what he was supposed to do. Modelling his kisses on the flicks, jamming his mouth on theirs in a rigid clinch. He hadn't known you could *move* your lips. Noreen showed him that – moistening his lips with her tongue, flexing her mouth against his, as if she was telling him secrets. She used to reach up and push away Charles's hair, smooth it back. (He used to oil his hair, he remembers now, every morning.) What did she see when she cradled Charles Lightfoot's face in her hand and gazed at it? What did *he* see, when he looked in the mirror and prepared for their next clandestine meeting? Can't remember.

'Tea!' a voice explodes by his head. Charles switches easily into the present, only slightly taken aback by the rumpled old hand that reaches shakily for a mug, and that turns out to be his own.

There was the time – quite early on, he thinks, in their relationship – when the daughter, poor dumpy, ungainly Peg, came slamming through the front door an hour earlier than expected. Noreen pulling back, slapping him away, her face lengthening in dismay, her voice unnatural as she called out to her girl. Did Peg ever know about them, about Charles and her mother? Did she suspect? She never would meet his eye, would she? Used to shy behind her matted hair. But that didn't mean a thing.

Charles puts his mug of tea on the bed-tray. He's weak, but he doesn't want to relax now. The undertow of memory is growing too strong. He lets himself be carried by it, though he knows very well where it will lead. He watches the tea-lady as she trundles out into the corridor.

He never came face to face with Frank. They were like two figures in a weather-house: when Frank went off on his travels, Charles was allowed through the door (as long as nobody saw, no curtains twitched). Then, *he* was her husband: he knew the soapy scent of her sheets, the weight of her mustard-coloured eiderdown, the precise routes and dips and crannies of her body. It might last a few days, a fortnight, three months – but as long as it did last, as long as Frank stayed away, Charles was himself again. And once again he found himself thinking, This is how life should be.

When Frank took it into his head to return home, Charles would leave. Then Charles withdrew into a pretend, interim life – the life everyone else took to be real. He became Charles the drab bachelor, in his ten-shilling digs at Mrs Keating's, doing his humdrum job, visiting his mother at weekends, enduring her hints about Nice Young Girls and Getting Him Settled, enduring Vernon's constant, knowing grin.

He never knew how long that pretend life would go on – before Frank nipped out for a pint or a pound of baccy, and didn't come back. He never knew whether this time Frank might decide to stay put for good.

It was hard to tell how long these periods lasted, with their wall-staring, pillow-biting, Noreen-less nights. They slipped out of focus, out of colour. Only one grainy, fatigue-blurred episode stays with him – one which has a date attached: 1953.

Mrs Keating knocked to ask if Charles fancied going across to her sister's to watch the Coronation. He said, No, thank you; he wasn't much interested in all that. She said 'Ho!', taking it as a personal affront, and flounced off. Charles stood in his room, at the narrow window, behind the stand with the earthenware bowl and jug, and listened to the whoops and chatter of a street party somewhere out of sight.

Two days later, Charles's father fell into a coma. Charles and the others were summoned home. At some point during the walk from his digs to his parents' house, as Charles was picking his way over trampled bunting and flattened cigarette packets, his father slithered out of existence in a darkened bedroom. When Charles got home, his mother was busy mopping his father's mouth, straightening his head on the pillow, tidying up, getting organised.

She wanted a proper church funeral, though their father had been chapel if anything, probably not even that. Mary Ethel said it wouldn't be allowed, the vicar wouldn't let them, but there didn't seem to be a problem, as it turned out. They filed into the church behind the coffin – Mrs Lightfoot, dry-eyed, worrying about the funeral tea, Emlyn, Vernon and Charles, Mary Ethel and her horrible brood. George had sent his condolences from Auckland. The vicar said a few words, and Charles heard none of them. He was thinking about Noreen, picturing her in a black dress and veil, picturing Frank Farrell's funeral. Afterwards, they all shuffled out and stood awkwardly round the grave, peering in. Their mother kept an eye on the time.

'Come on,' she said, impatient. 'We'll catch our own death at this rate, and the sandwiches want cutting.'

They made for the back gate. A few mourners, old workmates of Charles and his father mostly, stood chatting to the vicar or inspecting the wreaths and headstones. As the family tried to keep up with Mrs Lightfoot, Vernon gave Charles's thigh a surreptitious pinch and jerked his thumb towards a dark-haired woman, slightly overweight, who was stepping self-consciously between the plots.

'See our old friend there?' he whispered. 'Can't get enough of me, see, our Esther. Always coming back for more.'

During these intervals, when Frank was back at home with Noreen,

Charles had nightmares. They punched him awake at four every morning. Newsreel images. Phantoms. Gutted and fleshless. Arms and legs and heads, wrung out and woven into contorted heaps. Teeth. Spectacles. Tottering death-walks, faces with sockets for eyes, black pits for mouths. Sometimes, among the tangle, a movement: a face turning, making the limbs shift and click. His mother's face. Or Emlyn's. Or Esther's.

Bellowing, half out of his bed, Charles was stunned back to sense by the twilit bareness of his room. He straightened the bedclothes, climbed back into bed, tried to lull his heart. Maybe today. Maybe Frank will leave today.

The nightmares sketched themselves around everything else. Seeing his mother work her jaw around her ill-fitting dentures, seeing a colleague at work hooking spidery specs around his ears, seeing Mrs Keating crack her knuckles, before fitting a cosy over the teapot with a neat tug . . . encroaching on it all, drawing outlines around it, was the horror of piled possessions, and arms, and legs, and heads.

He had to wait. One day, out of the blue, Noreen would appear again. Standing at a bus stop, strolling across the park, passing his digs, just by chance, she would stop and greet him, and comment on the weather, and happen to mention that Frank had popped out last night and hasn't been back.

Then it was Charles's turn. He came back to her, and brought with him armfuls of nightmares, dumped them at her feet to be swept away. She laughed at him, sweetly, petted him like a child. She held him, pressed his arms against his sides, comforted him, told him things that weren't true. He felt Noreen's wedding ring, embedded into her finger, cool on the back of his neck.

Charles would try to lose himself in her indifference, to be transformed by it. They had seen them together, these newsreels, in the smoky stalls of a fleapit on the other side of town. They risked these outings sometimes, arriving separately and sitting as far towards the back as possible. Noreen had watched the horrors on the screen, shaken her head, grabbed his hand, worn the same mask of incredulity as everyone else in that cinema. And yet, when she left five minutes before him, and climbed the steps to daylight, she had shed it all, like an old coat. For Charles, those scenes had altered the future; they would form a backdrop to everything he did, as he grew old. Some part of him despised Noreen for her callous, imperishable good humour. A greater part of him envied her its freedom, and needed to share it. So he let her nurse and cradle him; he let her tell him his nightmares weren't real, were nothing to worry about; he asked her impossible questions—

'How can we ever be happy, after that? How can we be happy, when people have done that?'

And Noreen would place her steady hand against his cheek, while he accepted her answers, without believing them—

'Happiness is a gift,' she would say. 'You can learn it. Like mending cars or wires. Might as well use it as waste it.'

Happiness, for Noreen, was nothing to do with goodness. That was why Charles loved her, and why he would never understand her. Charles longed to shake off his notions of reward and retribution. He longed to be like Noreen.

5

A snapshot. A moment observed, catalogued, defined. Cat stands in the hall, frozen in the action of hanging Livvy's denim jacket on the hatstand. Her arms raised, her head twisted to the left, watching. Noting.

Livvy, with her faint halo-tang of white spirit and paint, with her pallid hair tied back into a long pony-tail, with the stiff, stricken attitude of someone who has just this instant suffered an accident, or experienced a mystical event.

Facing her, masking the kitchen door, Gal: serene, detached, long hand extended in assurance and reassurance.

From the kitchen, James's calls of greeting – an unreal echo from some other world.

It might be nothing. It might be an interlude, amounting to nothing, shared by no one, an awkward pause before the dinner party begins. Just a banal sequence of introductions, superficial questions, taking of seats and drinks, serving of food. No comment, no acknowledgement to prove that there's anything unique or significant here. No evidence to transform these few hours into a particular cluster of time, when decisions are taken, choices formulated, directions changed. If anyone does testify that this is an evening when futures are marked out, who's to say they're right?

Cat hovers between the kitchen, where James and his saucepans mumble and bubble together, and the back room. In her head she's describing the scene and the conversation, editing and summarising. The back room oscillates in candlelight. Livvy sits in taut right-angles on the sofa; Gal is folded into the armchair, all knees and wrists and eyelashes. Cat pours their wine, moves among the strands of sentences.

'. . . and do you compose your own music?'

'Oh, sometimes... when I get the chance . . .'

(Cat recognises the lie and files it away.)

'Well, you know, if you're moving down here, we should think about doing some work together – words and music – it's something I . . .'

In the harsh light of the kitchen, Cat hisses at James,

'Is she buying that house herself?'

'Not as far as I know.' James kisses at a spoonful of spicy liquid, then passes it to Cat. He frowns, taking in the question. 'If she is, I'll have to have a diplomatic word about that piano.'

In the back room, Gal's eyes blaze relentlessly at Livvy. She becomes conscious of herself looking back at him and her head jerks with the effort of maintaining contact. She can almost taste the coal-blue swing of his fringe.

'It's a great gift,' Gal is saying. 'Music. A great gift.'

He is captivated – by this new idea: harmonies and dissonance, melody and counterpoint, syllables, rhythms, the lift and drop of mood, all waiting to break into words. Lyrics. Expressing the inexpressible. Gal is smitten.

He is also mistily aware of a more immediate sense of power. He's experienced it before: he knows the signs. He looks into the centre of Livvy's eyes, and smiles, and nods. He's in control. He's enjoying himself, much as he might enjoy driving a smart car. It's all part of the event: something transient, something to fill the time.

As they eat, Gal tells them about his nosebleeds. He laughs it off, modestly, with a lingering dip of his eyes that suggests tragedy and forbearance. He once ruined two new jumpers, one after the other, by bleeding all down them, he says.

Cat protests through a mouthful of chicken, 'Can we save the details until *after* digestion, please?'

James remembers the occasion. Gal's mother had sent her credit card through the post, so that Gal could buy another jumper.

Cat swallows hard and stares.

'You mean, she told you to forge her signature?'

'Yes, well,' says Gal, 'she's got a funny foreign name, hasn't she. Nobody knew it was a woman's name. It wasn't a problem.' He crinkles his eyes at Livvy.

'Gal, it's the *principle*! You don't forge someone's signature to get money!'

Gal shrugs. 'Why not? I wasn't stealing – she was giving. What's wrong with that?'

'It's . . . it's, it undermines the whole basis of . . . *trust*, that's what . . .'

Gal's shoulders begin to shake. He purses his lips against his laughter and rolls his eyes at Cat in mock outrage.

'. . . of honesty! Of identity!' blurts Cat. 'It's . . . it's . . .'

'It's breaking the rules,' Gal interrupts. 'That's what's knotting *your* knickers. Not finer ethical feelings. Fear of getting caught. Rules minus reason.'

'Oh, rules minus reason! Argument by soundbite!'

James stands up. 'Pudding anyone?'

'I never realised she was so tight-arsed, did you, James?' says Gal, smoothly fending off a side-swipe from Cat.

Livvy watches them, watches the invisible link between them, like spider's silk, and is queasy with jealousy.

It isn't that Livvy tells lies. She doesn't. Other people *hear* lies. They *provide* them, when she's said next to nothing. She's not even trying to mislead. She goes so far as to correct them, makes a point of saying that, actually, teaching is her bread-and-butter work, she can't really, truthfully, call herself a pianist as such at the moment. She explains quite clearly that, well, she *has* put her grandmother's house on the market, and she *hadn't really* considered moving down here – hadn't given it much thought at all.

But they lift the conversation away from her and turn it into something entirely different, and say things like,

'It must be very hard, breaking on to the recital circuit, let alone staying on it,' and 'Well, quite, why go through all the palaver of selling if you can just pack up and move here yourself . . .'

They alter her life, and Livvy lets them do it.

Gal asks about her family:

'No one here to help you get everything in order?'

'No, nobody. Just me. No brothers or sisters, or cousins, or anything. Mum died a few years ago. And . . . well, I never really knew my father.'

Gal cocks his head with interest; the black hair shimmers.

'I never really knew my father.' How did a phrase that for years was clamped shut by anger and embarrassment suddenly take off with such dramatic potential? Livvy grins and talks on a rush of adrenaline.

'It's all a bit of a mystery. My mum would never talk about it. Well, her dad was a wanderer too, and I reckon she'd just had it with men altogether. My nan did tell me once he was something to do with a dance band.'

'That's where you get your musical talent from, then,' says Gal, conclusively.

Livvy has nothing else to say. That's the truth – that great, empty cavern in her head – and, this time, no one has offered any speculation to help her out of it. There's a pause that swells into a silence and is about to paralyse them all when Cat asks whether anyone saw that article about the average life span reaching two hundred before the next century's out.

'You'd have your mid-life crisis at a hundred,' says James, cheerful with relief.

'But just think if you reached two hundred and you *still* hadn't sorted yourself out. You'd be *really* pissed off then, wouldn't you?' says Cat.

'Yes,' says Gal, 'and *really* ugly too.'

And then the phone rings, and James hurtles into the hall and shuts the door behind him, and Cat raises her eyebrows knowingly at Gal and says 'Sonia'.

Gal turns to Livvy. 'James has got an extremely glamorous girlfriend who lives in Italy.'

Livvy mimes 'Ooooh' in an eager, curious way, but Gal says nothing else, and she's too daunted to speak by the gloom that seems to have seeped into the space between him and Cat.

When James comes back, Gal murmurs, 'Everything OK?'

James makes some slight movement, lost to everyone else in the dim room; Gal changes the subject and starts fussing about stacking bowls and making coffee.

Hours later, James is leaning back in the armchair, mouth half-open. Cat sits with her back against his legs. Dirty glasses and cups catch the pink candlelight. Cat says,

'So, what about Gal and women? Or men? What's it all about?'

James barely moves his lips to reply: 'You know 'swell as I do.'

They've toyed at this exchange, from time to time, for fifteen years, without getting much further than that.

After a while, Cat says,

'He's right, though. I am rule-bound. Fear of getting caught – that's me all over.'

Feeling that a response is required, James says,

'We have nothing to fear except fear itself.'

'I know that. But I *do* fear fear itself. So that's no help.'

They hear the faint thuds and creaks of Livvy going upstairs in her grandmother's disembowelled house. James lifts his head with an effort, and takes a deep breath. He begins,

'Sonia . . .'

But Cat has spoken across him, firmly and clearly –

'James. I'm pregnant.'

James's breath escapes in a sigh and he lets his head drop back against the chair.

6

This has never happened before.

Livvy stands in Nan's cold kitchen, holding a mug of coffee, looking out at the overgrown garden. Part of her mind is harrying her, making lists:
– Do something about that hedge.
– Tackle those weeds.
– At least cut the lawn.
But it's not at the centre of her attention.
This has never happened before. Never. Never like this.

Of course, if Livvy could stop and think about it, objectively, rationally, she would have to admit that it *has* happened before. Many times. This *is* what happens, exactly this. Every time.

But the chant drones on, insistent, rooting her to the spot. Never. Never like this.

She didn't dream about Gal last night. She didn't have to: the notion of him layered everything; it was there, behind her eyes, in the pressure of her head on the pillow, before she woke. Last night, in fact, she dreamed she was in a chorus line, a crescent of chubby-legged high-kickers. Ruby Keeler, Ginger Rogers, Livvy and her nan, all arm-in-arm, under the stage lights: stomp-kick, stomp-kick; with the bandleader springing up and down on his toes, flapping his chicken-elbows, smiling up at her. He had a smooth, egg-shaped face, luminous over the dark orchestra pit. Not Gal's face at all, nothing like. But Gal was there, nevertheless – wrapped around her fantasies like a sky, moulding himself to the inner curve of her skull.

She stands in the kitchen in an early-morning slant of light and breathes in some gesture of his: the way his hands swam around his sentences, the way he said her name, precisely, as if pronouncing a strange or difficult word.

Of course it's happened before.

The man who lived in the flat two floors down. Her English teacher at school. The theory lecturer at college. One of her older piano pupils. It always began like this, didn't it? – their features blotting out the future, their names hanging just behind everything she said. And further back, much further – when she was a small skinny girl, no more than five, irritating everyone with her moon face and her slouch back and her open, triangular mouth. There was Denise Harris on the next table, always bright and sharp, with her perky blonde bunches and round chin and funny laugh. Livvy brought home two class photographs at the end of term – one black-and-white, one in artificial colour. She gave one to her mother but kept the colour photo, drew a neat circle in felt-tip green around Denise, and hid it in her room. In school, they sat back to back as they worked, drawing in the hands of a clock, or sticking cotton wool on to pieces of card. Livvy would round her shoulders, trying to disappear into Denise Harris's high, husky exclamations and fidgeting arms and legs. Later, she would sit in the school bus, face squashed against the window, semi-conscious with desire and hope – hope that one day she might be sucked into the energy and laugh and sweet-sticky smell of Denise Harris, and lose her own Livviness altogether.

Today, though, in Nan's kitchen, under the faint pressure of a hangover, Livvy finally decides that this has never happened, never this badly before. She thinks of past boyfriends, but knows this is cheating – they were a wholly different matter. None of them was imprinted on the back of her eye, or listening to her everyday thoughts and conversations. Boyfriends were separate people, delineated and confined. Just other people, who happened to have asked her out. She can barely summon their names.

It's clouding over. The kitchen darkens and Livvy shivers. Well, if it rains she won't have to tackle the garden. She remembers that some bloke used to call round once a fortnight when Nan couldn't manage any more, to rein in the bushes and keep the grass down. Ted. Terry. Something like that. Maybe she'll pop round and see if James knows who it was.

She wanders into the hall and lays one hand on the bannister, rephrasing the things she said last night, tidying comments and touching up responses. At the same time, she's reliving a Saturday afternoon, years ago: Livvy crouching on these stairs, scowling down at her mother, who was here – on this spot – grasping the bannister and giving as good as she got. The two of them (she recalls, packing the scene into sentences to narrate to Gal) – the two of them, mouthing anger, straining and spitting and squeaking as they tried to keep their voices beyond reach of the back room and Nan's hearing. Livvy, red in the face,

'I've got a *right* to know.'

'Oh, you've got a *right*, now? Just drop it. This is other people's business, not yours. What difference can—'

'I *want* to know. And Nan thinks you should tell me, too.'

'Don't you go moithering your nan about this. She's not as fit as she was, and she's got nothing to do with it.'

'Yes, she has, she's—'

'Leave your nan alone. She doesn't know *anything*.'

'Don't you *dare* make Nan sound *senile* just to keep your *grubby* little secret safe'.

'Shut your mouth!' and then, curbing her temper, Peg pushed her face between the bars of the bannister, 'I'm telling you, stop picking at it. There's no point. Get on with your life.'

Livvy was afraid of her mother. Not that she would lash out, or rage, or lock her in her room. When Peg glared at her with that despairing impatience, verging on contempt, Livvy was afraid that it would all start to crack, and come crashing down, all the brick-wall defences. All the stony, sour determination. Livvy was afraid her mother might give in.

But Peg wasn't a quitter. Even when Livvy gambled on one last taunt:

'I must take after him. He was a musician, wasn't he? Don't you *want* me to thank him for that? For giving me something to be proud of?'

Even then, Peg could set her lips and stand for a moment, considering her daughter, and then ease away from the bannister and say,

'He wasn't anything. He wasn't anyone. Forget him.'

Livvy goes into the front room and cranes her neck at the window, looking out for signs of life next door. She knows Gal isn't there – but every impulse, every movement has become a thread, woven in with other threads, growing into a great, bulky, multicoloured strategy. She will go round and thank James for the dinner. She really ought to repay them, with a meal . . . not here, obviously. A restaurant perhaps . . . but Livvy's funds are running low, and she needs to go back and resume her teaching. Very soon.

She turns and props herself against the narrow window-ledge, admiring the freshly painted walls. It's a decent-sized house. It's a wonder her nan kept the rent paid all those years – the rent, the meters, the coal . . . never mind finding the funds to buy it, eventually, outright. But buy it she did – in 1954, for £900: an event recounted to little Livvy with the ritual of a nursery rhyme. There was always a suggestion – never made explicit – that Nan's family had known better days. The piano was something to do with it – a revered symbol of some past gentility. We would have gone onto the streets, Nan would insist with theatrical pride, sooner than give up the piano for the means-test. But it never came to that. Possibly she'd had a nest-egg. She can't have managed it on her earnings alone. Old Frank must have paid his way at least part of the time – even when he was off on his jaunts. That was another untold story: what Frank did during his absences to keep body and soul together. Livvy has recently assumed it was something dodgy; as a child she never bothered to ask. Frank was already a fictional character by then – as unremarkable and unreal to Livvy as, well, as David Niven.

'Why don't we go and live with Nan?' she would whine to Peg. 'She's all on her own, we could keep her company.'

'Nan doesn't want *you* under her feet all day, madam.'

'Yes, she does. *I* could go and live with Nan, and *you* could stay here. Then Nan wouldn't be lonely any more.'

After leaving for college, Livvy took it for granted that she would make her own home in some other part of the country. Not necessarily London – though in the event that's where she ended up. As long as it was crowded and anonymous and an off-putting journey away from her mother's. Livvy got into the habit of regarding herself as a refugee. Now, as she muses about the state of Nan's floorboards, and frets again about getting the place rewired, she begins to reassess. She's still a young woman. There's no one left to avoid here. No one left to measure distances. Who's to say she's 'ended up' at all?

Livvy's been meaning to phone the estate agents and chase them up. They've only found one prospective viewer so far, and he didn't turn up . . .

A door slams next door, in James's house. The threads interlock; the pattern builds. Livvy winces as a knot in her belly tightens. She thinks, I will give the estate agents a ring. Talk things over. Ask them to take that 'For Sale' sign down.

7

'It doesn't matter,' Cat said. She got to her feet and stretched her lips in one of those playing-at-stoical smiles. James was pinned back by a wave of expectation. He must say something. Not just something – the right thing. He was baffled, petrified by indecision. She gave him his opportunity, and he failed to live up to her crisis.

'Makes no difference,' she said, with infuriating breeziness. 'I just need to deal with it.'

James knew he mustn't let her leave the room without any response at all. He garbled his words.

'What does he – I mean, is, does Matthew know?'

The wrong thing.

She was at the door; she swung round and would have hit him, he guessed, if he'd been near enough.

'*Fucking* typical! Does *Matthew* know! This is the Matthew who's treated me like *shit*, who doesn't give a *toss* whether I live or die – but, hey, fruit of his loins, heir to the estate, so does *Matthew* know? He's got a family of his *own*. What should I do, go and throw this in through the window, like a stick of fucking dynamite? What for? For his macho pride? No, OK, Matthew *doesn't* know, and don't you *dare* make me feel like some kind of heartless bitch just because I'm not—'

James was squeaking from his chair in self-defence.

She snapped off her sentence and spread both hands in front of her, palms out in a stop sign.

'Matthew,' she resumed, quietly, 'is not the issue here. I just need to deal with it. That's all.'

She went up to bed. James sat clutching the arms of his chair for another hour.

In the morning she was brisk, grabbing toast, gathering notebooks for an interview in Butetown. She said,

'I'm sorry if I embarrassed you last night. I should have kept it to myself.'

'*No—* ' James wanted to throttle her.

'Do you mind if I stay a few more days? I need to finish this off, and then—'

'Of *course* you can stay . . .'

'—and then I want to look up some information. I don't want to do it up there . . . Too many networks . . . Word gets around . . .'

He waited for the front door to slam before dropping his head and fists on to the table. He moaned. His voice was flat against the table top.

'This is *nothing* to do with me!'

'You must remember: Parliament then was not the Parliament we see on the news or in the papers today. When we speak of the Commons, we're not talking about Prime Minister's Question Time. When you think of the Lords, don't picture rumbling old peers, half-asleep and on the brink of redundancy.'

He pauses, waiting for one of their wisecracks, but they're keeping their heads down this afternoon. James is tired and edgy, and knows his attempts to stimulate interest are coming across as rebukes.

'And *don't*' – he slaps the back of his hand against an essay – '*don't* make pat assumptions. Think it all through. Henry regularly summoned about ninety-odd lords to sit in parliament – yes. But did they all attend? Did he summon *more* than that, without leaving any record? Did he ask some of them, face to face? We weren't there. We don't know. But we can ask the questions. Read your evidence. Weigh up the probabilities. Imagine the possibilities. No examiner will expect you to come up with *answers*. Just use your *sense*.'

Barry clears his throat. Brenda's stomach grumbles.

Even Cerys is more subdued than usual.

'Sense isn't much help,' she ventures, 'if you're not studying sensible people.'

Deggy picks his ear and examines his finger.

'Yeah,' he mutters. 'That's the trouble with human beings, uh, Cerys? Never know what they'll be up to next. Need someone to whip 'em into line, tell 'em what's good for 'em.'

Cerys opens her mouth to reply, but glances at James's grim face and lets the argument fizzle out.

He can hear her: a creak on the stairs, a shuffle. He lies in bed, surveying the ceiling, until he knows sleep has evaporated, and then with an effort he sits up.

She's crouching on a stair, halfway down. He can't tell whether she's crying. Knotting his dressing gown around him, he sits on the step above.

'I've never really felt grown-up,' she says. 'Isn't that . . . disgraceful?'

He puts a hand on the back of her neck. She's more thoughtful than distressed.

'I think we're different like that. Do you? From people before us. Parents.'

A suggestion of light is lifting the shadows in the glass panel at the top of the front door. James's voice is hoarse.

'Every generation thinks it's different.'

'No, but it's true, I think. We haven't had war, have we? – to make us grow up. We didn't have to get into the corsets, or get married, or start a family, as soon as we hit twenty. We had choices.'

James shifts round to lean against the bannister.

'Depends who we're talking about, I'd say. Some people have more choices than others. In *every* generation.'

'Well. You're the historian. You'd know better than me.'

They sit in silence. James clenches his teeth to stop them chattering.

'*Look* at us all,' she says. 'All galloping into middle age, and never . . . I don't know . . . never *burdened*. Never taken on a *burden*. Not *real* burdens. We have to make up little disasters, to convince ourselves we're adults.'

James thinks, Shall I ask her about the pregnancy? Or are we talking about something else altogether? As if he already has asked, she says,

'Lots of people think it's irresponsible, don't they, to have a child. Not wanting to bring children into such a vile world, and so on.'

'It's not *all* vile,' says James. 'Anyway . . . I've always thought of you as an optimist.'

'Mmm . . .' She's biting her thumbnail again. 'But not stupid. I know it can all go wrong. I prefer to think about the best outcomes. But I can still imagine the worst.'

'Well . . . Most lives fall somewhere in between, I suppose.'

'But what kind of a gift is that for a child? – "Here you are, I've given you a life. It'll probably turn out somewhere between the best and the worst. With a bit of luck you might *not* get ill, get murdered, get run over, get depressed, hate your job, feel a failure, or die alone." It's not much of a deal, is it?' She mimes pinching a fag from between her lips, and puts on a gravelly, salesman voice. 'Best I can offer you, my darlin'. Mediocre life and not a lot in the way of catastrophe.'

Another silence. Presently she lays her head on James's lap, and may have fallen asleep. James may have nodded off himself, for a few seconds. Suddenly Cat says,

'Do you reckon our parents went through all this? I can't imagine it, can you? They just got on with it.'

With a sudden burst of energy, she levers herself to her feet.

'Look! – it's getting light. Shall I go and put the kettle on?'

8

We move on to our next clue: the letter to Humphrey Meyrick of Penfynydd, signed by John Griphith, Servant of the Crown.

How do we know that, at this point, we are dealing with the right man? Could this not be an entirely different man – a case of mistaken identity? After all, it may be sheer coincidence that this battle veteran, bearing an Anglicised form of Ieuan's name, is writing to a family on the poet's home patch. More than coincidence, though, surely, that he urges Meyrick to 'call unto mind the tales that I was wonte to tell of divers wondrous thynges.' That was then, he seems to say, but look at me now: a Servant of the Crown.

This, in itself, tells us relatively little, though it presumably impressed Humphrey Meyrick. 'Servant of the Crown' could mean anything from an official of the King's Council, at the heart of government administration, to a humble Chancery clerk. We know the names of 227 members of Henry's council, gleaned from lists, registers and extracts compiled in the 16th and 17th centuries. Some names appear repeatedly, some only once; John Griffiths is not among them, but this tells us only that his name was not among the fragmentary records that survive. We are none the wiser about our Servant of the Crown. But the likelihood is that, as a young man from a respectable though minor landowning family, having acquitted himself well in battle, Ieuan was given a reasonably remunerative appointment – perhaps as an accountant in the increasingly important Chamber of Receipt.

Not a particularly glamorous role, then – but the contrast in fortunes must have been striking, nonetheless. Before Bosworth, Ieuan's prospects had been restricted by penal laws that barred Welshmen from holding Crown office, buying land in or near the boroughs, marrying into English families or serving on juries. Men on the make were known to have shrugged these laws aside, especially during the chaos of civil war – but, as we have seen, Ieuan had not been among those men. He had been getting by, as a minor wandering bard, with limited expectations.

Now all things were possible. Welshmen were swanning around the court, running the councils, taking up trades and professions. Charters were issued giving the Welsh rights to lands, titles, castles and offices. The floodgates opened to a generation of budding entrepreneurs and political careerists. Ieuan himself had a new name, a new language and a new way of life.

James reads over the last paragraph. He will, of course, have to scrap the whole thing. If only he could catch up with that train of thought that sets off in his mind whenever he's in the bath, or in the car, or about to fall asleep. Not a train of thought, exactly. More a cloud of thought, accumulating and dispersing to no apparent scheme. But glorious, certain – revelatory. When that cloud gathers, James knows precisely what to do with Ieuan Gloff: how to edge around his life, painting this and that section of his landscape, until the man himself is revealed as a blank but discernible form among the colours. He knows *why* he's doing it, too. He feels the poignancy of comparing this two-bit poet with his high-powered contemporaries, of tracking down one individual's route through national change and historical event. Today James has the conditions he's hankered after: peace and quiet. No piano music from next door. No classes or lectures to give. Cat is out – at the library, swotting up company figures for her next profile. (That's what she said.) He listens hard, but can't detect any radios, hi-fis or screeching children from anywhere in the vicinity. He should have a clear run. He should be able to follow that cloud. The only interference is from his own brain. Shards of irrelevant conversation, trivia, cropped and sketchy sentences, all milling about, blocking his path to coherence. I must upgrade this computer, he thinks. I wonder how you do that. And tomorrow, or the day after, I'd better fix up another of Gal's blessed oral history sessions. Get it over with. I should expand on the peculiarities of pre-Tudor Welsh administration. Or is that labouring the point? Make it televisual . . . Make it accessible . . . He notices that he's peckish. Were there any Pringles left in the cupboard, or did he and Cat finish them all in the early hours, after her latest dawn crisis?

He can't work with all this row in his head. He might as well be at a party. In fact, thinks James, maybe it would help to have external noise. To sort of draw the detritus away, into itself.

Let us set John Griphith in his new home, and take a look around. Not a luxurious house, perhaps, but sturdy; three stone storeys, on the rural edges of the city. He eats well – plenty of fresh fish and meat: haddock with garlic, plaice boiled in ale, oysters in vinegar, lamb, pork, small game. He may stroll in his knot-garden now and again, but he no longer keeps fit tramping up and down the countryside to ply his trade. We can safely assume that Ieuan has put on weight.

Does he think often of his old world – the dark green, dark brown world of his youth – as he sits at a table laid with silver? Is it conceivable that he would give all this up and return to third-rate poetry and utter isolation in a hillside hovel? Can a man's loyalties and priorities change so swiftly and completely – and back again?

All these are questions that must, in due course, be tackled. For the time being, however, John Griphith is settling into his new position as pillar of the establishment, and we may safely turn to his daily tasks and responsibilities as a member of the Chamber of Receipt.

All this text, all churned out, hour by hour, just to be wiped away and started again. The trouble is (James starts drumming a samba against the arms of his chair), the trouble is that nothing seems to *connect*. Ieuan Gloff, Anne Meyrick, the Tudor accounting system, James Powell's mind – all separating into hard, individual kernels. Entirely independent of each other. But maybe that's it: nothing *does* connect. Sitting here, trying to join up a life, trying to link past and present, he's just filling time, playing a fool's game. Like stapling water.

James decides to try that extraneous sound theory. He gets up, turns the radio on, and stands with his head bowed over it for nearly a quarter of an hour, listening to the afternoon play.

9

At midnight, Cat knocks on the study door and looks in.

'I'm going to bed. Shall I switch everything off in there?'

'Might as well. I'll be in here for a while yet.'

She saunters in and stands at his desk, aimlessly sliding his papers to and fro, repeating titles and phrases from them, under her breath. James tries to focus on his task.

'What are you doing?'

She comes round to look over his shoulder.

'Checking back through Ieuan's later poetry.'

She stands behind him, watching the screen. He can feel her breath on the top of his head. She says,

'What does all that mean?'

'I thought you were going to bed.' But James scrolls back up to the first stanza, and begins to read it out in his most theatrical Welsh, stretching wide around the vowels and drilling the 'r's.

'Lovely. But what does it *mean*?'

'Hang about – well, that bit is: "Leaving your land, leaving purity, leaving wealth and the safety of the hearth..."' He races through the words carelessly, and her face twists with incomprehension. '"Sorry the branch without its bird, sorry the rootless oak." Something like that. Pretty awful stuff, it has to be said... Good night, then.'

'Tell me the rest of it, and then I'll go up.'

James sighs.

'Er... well, roughly – "A man's... den... protects him – he's blameless in his own home. A naked soul may fly from its nest, to be, er, clothed by God and His blessing."'

'Is he dying, then?'

'Hard to tell. Or is it about someone else dying? Or about something else entirely – alienation? Spiritual or political? Answers on a postcard. He does manage not to take a pop at the Saxons here, which makes a change. The rest of what we've got is fairly venomous. This one's more...'

'Regretful?'

'I suppose so. Regrets, futility... maybe it's his swansong, who knows.'

Cat props herself against the desk, next to him, with her back to the screen.

'Say it in Welsh.'

James tuts, but he launches into it again willingly enough.

She's holding her head to one side, considering the sound of the words. James can see a tuft of white hairs at her temple. She begins to speak, and he catches a lightning glimpse of the way she will look in twenty, thirty years: a mask of her older self, waiting to emerge.

'Your Welsh is impressive,' she comments. 'I mean, as far as I can tell. It sounds good.'

'It's rusting fast. I don't practise enough. Most people don't come asking for readings of Ieuan Gloff.'

'Oh . . . why don't you practise on your mother?' asks Cat, wide-eyed. She knows all about the awkwardness involved. James's mother treated his late enthusiasm for the language with confusion and embarrassment. As if he might be accusing her, the way Gal's mother had, of negligence, or worse. James ignores the sarcasm in Cat's question.

'I've given up trying. I used to try out the odd phrase on the phone, but she got all flustered and chirrupy. As if I'd tried to talk about sex, or something. I just leave it now.'

His sentence ends decisively, and he turns his full attention to the computer, pretending to study the screen. Go, he thinks, go away and leave me in peace. Give me a few hours to myself before the night-wanderings start.

Cat is examining the ginger hairs and freckles on the back of his hand, as it guides the mouse unnecessarily around its mat. She says,

'You've got your mother's colouring, haven't you. She used to have red hair, didn't she? You can still see that patch of marmalade in among the white. Very striking. Or at least, it was still there when I last saw her.'

'Mm. Still there.'

Cat watches him pretend to work for a moment.

'Funny how these things work out, though. D'you think you'll go bald, like your father?'

'Probably'. Here we go, he thinks. At least it's not four o'clock in the morning, this time.

'Do you think you're more like your mother than your father? They're both quite similar characters, though, aren't they? Quiet. Nice people.'

Poor Dad, thinks James, for no particular reason – only that he always thinks 'poor Dad' whenever his father's mentioned. Tidied into the corner with his newspaper, tidied out of the house with his golf clubs, to play a game that didn't much interest him with people he vaguely disliked. James pictures them both, stationed at the kitchen sink; his mother washing, rinsing, handing plates, spoons, glasses, his father wiping delicately, as instructed, and placing them correctly on the draining board. Going through their paces, side-by-side, singing their little snatches of songs and sayings, every evening, for the best part of forty years.

'Ever-so, ever-so, Thank-you-ta!' (taking a dish from her soapy hand).

'And there we have it, my lords, ladies and gentlemen!' (as she empties the washing-up water), 'and we shall have no other.'

What did they say to each other before their code of fossilised jokes and reassurances had been developed? James tries to imagine their first bagging of a catchphrase – laughing at it, dropping it into conversation, storing it up for the future.

Cat yawns.

'You're very lucky, to have your parents. *Nice* parents. That's what you need. Mine were such a *mess*. "They fuck you up, your Mum and Dad . . ."'

James sits back in his chair and removes his glasses to wipe them on his shirt.

'You're exaggerating. You didn't have such a bad time with them. You doted on your mother. Come on.'

(He remembers her at the funeral service, red-eyed but smiling, clasping his arm as he left the chapel. 'Everyone's *looking* at me,' she said. 'I don't know how to be a Bereaved Person. I'm going to hide behind you, for a while.' And she tugged him with her, away from her father, who was standing stiffly, looking grey and uneasy, his new wife gripping his wrist as if to stop him from floating away.)

James says,

'If you go round spreading these versions of your parents, people will start to believe you.'

'You're probably right. I wouldn't want that.'

She lets the flat of her hand pause momentarily against her stomach.

'Must be a terrifying thing,' she says, and James can hear the fall of mood. 'Going from being just any common-or-garden prat, to being a parent. Knowing everything you say is forming the basis of somebody else's hang-ups. Makes you wonder why *anyone* goes through with it.'

She bites her nail, gazing at a ring of lamplight on the edge of the curtain.

'So,' she says, suddenly. 'What do you make of this Ieuan geezer, then?'

James grits his teeth. There was a time when he was charmed by these conversational jolts and *non sequiturs*. Now he suspects they're done for effect.

'Got his biog all sorted, you reckon?' she says.

'Well . . . There's only so much I can do . . .'

'Bollocks! There's *everything* you can do! I thought you had a free hand on this one?' She swings a leg at him and he bats it away, then wishes he hadn't. If she senses impatience, she'll goad him all the more.

'What's the scenario?' she persists. 'Is he a sort of Tudor Don Juan, d'you think? Maybe he had a thing with some worthy's wife, and had to run for the hills when he got found out.'

'No, I think—'

'Or maybe he lost everything in a wild bet. Or gave it all up for lerv. Or maybe he was some kind of spy and had his cover blown – they had spies then, didn't they?'

'Yes, they had spies then, but the likelihood is—'

'*Likelihood*? Come *on*, James! This is your big moment! Who wants to know about some Tudor bore who lived by *likelihood*?'

She leans towards him, but he doesn't react.

'Anyway,' she says, her voice subsiding again. 'Nobody much *does* live by likelihood, do they? I mean, look at me. If you'd asked me fifteen years ago . . .'

James notes the hesitation. Fifteen years ago, they were still together. '. . . Well, if you'd asked me then, I'd have said, the likelihood is, by the time I'm thirty-five, I'll be an arts correspondent for *The Guardian*, working part-time until my fourth child is old enough to go to school.'

Getting no response, she resumes her attack. 'Nothing goes to plan. Your poet's life probably didn't go to plan.'

'I *know* all this,' says James. 'It's what I tell my students – "Weigh up the probabilities, imagine the possibilities" . . .'

Cat nods, crestfallen.

'Yeah, well. I say bugger the probabilities, go to town with the possibilities. What we want is Ieuan the Hero, or Ieuan the Villain.

Or the genius. Or the tragic victim. Not some run-of-the-mill 16th-century geek who always does the expected.'

'Unfortunately,' says James, 'that may be just what he was.'

She's loosened a ridge of skin along her fingernail, and fiddles with it diligently. James looks at his watch.

She says,

'I've fixed an appointment.'

'Ah.'

'At the clinic. Just for a chat.'

'I see.' James doesn't really see at all. He would like to ask, from sheer curiosity, who chats, what about, and what happens then. Perhaps she would *like* him to ask. He says,

'Are you OK?'

'Of course I am!' – with a yelp of impatience. 'Why shouldn't I be?'

'Sorry. Just asking.'

'Anyway. I'm going to bed. Just thought you'd want to know.'

'Yes. Right. Well . . . Sonia should be back from her concert by now. I'd better give her a quick ring.'

10

'What's that noise?'

'Can you hear her? It's Carla. She's trying to say hello – aren't you, sweetheart? Oh, she's such a beauty, *yes she is* . . .'

'Sonia, who the hell is Carla? And what's wrong with her sinuses?'

'She's a little *rat-face*, aren't you? A little *rat-face*.' Sonia drops the cosseting tone abruptly. 'She's Francesca's chihuahua. I'm dog-sitting for a couple of hours.'

'Francesca? Is she the one who lives below?'

'She's my boss. James, stop interrogating me. It's especially galling when you don't retain a single thing I tell you.'

This deliberate, self-conscious bossiness, not without warmth, is a surprise to James. Their last conversation was strained and terse, and he was half-expecting this call to be an earnest re-appraisal of their relationship.

'Anyway,' he says, 'at least it shows you're trusted. If your boss is prepared to hand her dog into your care . . .'

Kissing noises explode in his ear.

'Oh, she's a little *love*! Aren't you? It's quite alarming how besotted you can be with an animal. And it's definitely physical . . . I just want to *squeeze* her and *bite her ears* . . .'

'All to do with power, I expect.'

'Disturbing, really. But I'm *definitely* going to get a dog, when everything's . . . settled.'

Now it comes, thinks James. She's been softening me up. He helps her along.

'When you say "settled" – is anything decided yet?'

'The contract's up in six weeks. I'm just going to sit it out. See which way the wind blows. Nothing's been said, formally. I've got no intention of making decisions on the basis of half-promises and flattery.'

'And what if they offer renewal?'

'We'll have to discuss that as and when it happens.'

We? James is taken aback. Is this the kindness before the kill? Or has he been misreading it all? For the first time, it occurs to him that she may be quite happy with arrangements as they are. That they may carry on, as a couple, week after week, phone calls, reunions, plans, decisions, friends automatically pairing their names. He feels dented – either with relief or disappointment, he's not sure which.

'I've got a long weekend coming up,' she says. 'I could nip over, if you like. Or are you up to your eyes in Ellis Galloway's work?'

'No . . . no, but—'

Sonia and the dog are involved in a brief commotion. James tries to rally his thoughts.

'I'd love you to come,' he blurts, when she returns. 'The only problem is—'

'Oh, God. Hasn't she gone *yet*? For pity's sake, James, are you absolutely intent on being a doormat?'

'Well, it's not quite that—'

'I mean, all right, there's a bond between you. Fair enough. I *do* understand that – look, I'm not some jealous teenager. I don't expect you to cut off your past and renounce all friendships. But, James, she *is* a grown woman. She can't cling to your shirt tails for the rest of her days. You can't let her trample all over your life, whenever she's been ditched by another disastrous man.'

'It's not really that—'

'I choose my words quite deliberately, James. You know I never say things for show. She may be very sweet and well-meaning – she *is* – and I know you're very fond of her – but this *dependency* . . . Emotionally – I'm serious – she's *walking all over* you . . . All right, Carla, just a minute, baby.'

James can hear a crescendo of yapping in the background.

'You're a considerate guy, James. You're not about to turn her away, and that puts you in a very difficult position.'

'Sonia, listen. It's not that easy—'

'It's *never* that easy, darling, establishing your boundaries in a friendship.'

Darling? That's a new one, and it jars. Somehow it adds to the distance between them. (Unless she's talking to the dog . . .)

'Come here, Carla, come up here, sweetheart, *that's right* . . . She's happy, now. She just wanted a cuddle.'

James presses the receiver nearer his mouth, as if to keep it away from the chihuahua.

'You could still come over,' he insists. 'Just because—'

'Oh, God *no*, I don't think so, James. I didn't even like to phone, knowing she was there. I purposely held out until the other evening – I thought she was *bound* to have gone by then. Listen, I don't mean that to sound unkind. But the two of you – I'm not really *involved*, you know? It's all rather . . . *exclusive*.'

James looks bemused at the phone. He's never known Sonia be so vulnerable. She's waiting for his response. He begins,

'The only reason—' he lowers his voice conspiratorially, 'the *only* reason Cat's still here . . . Well, the real problem is, she's . . .'

Sonia waits. Carla pants and snuffles like a new baby. Sonia says,

'Is she there?'

'She's gone to bed.'

'Go on, then.'

'The problem is,' says James, 'The problem is . . . Cat's got work to do. I said she could stay until it's finished.'

PART FIVE

You might suppose it would be worse for Gwilym. After all, I'd been around, met all manner of people, slept under every kind of roof and none, accustomed myself to the stink of men (which is far worse than the pure, hot air of the dungheap). Before joining the march to Bosworth, Gwilym had hardly strayed beyond Cwm Teg, except to walk to market or up to the Big House for the Nos Calan fair. And yet he took to London like a hound to the hunt. He liked everything about it – from the river like a country all of its own, carrying its buildings on the current, to the trickle and slush of the lanes, the squawk of urchins, the scream of pigs and sellers by day, the murderers and roaring torches by night. He even liked the bells that nagged and nagged, hour after hour after hour, all day and all night. Gwilym took all this under his belt, with the same easy delight. I was the one half out of my senses with the press of people – in the streets, on the river, in the rooms below us, next to us, across the alley (where the roofs almost kissed, and you could have stepped out through one window and in through the other and barely feel the breeze at your feet).

It wasn't the kind of life I'd had in mind. Not that I'd expected very much. I wasn't such an idiot as to expect riches, high office, profound thanks or a pension from our grateful king. But I had thought there might be better work and welcome for two battle-scarred veterans, who had hobbled and hitched their way along 140 miles to the royal capital. Far from it. Some of the oafs we met in the city hadn't even been aware of the coronation. 'Oh, I knew there was some to-do,' they said, 'but I didn't know what it was.' To be captive here, in two murky rooms, listening to the arguments and love-grunts of unseen strangers beneath our feet – it was more than I could bear. To make matters worse, Gwilym seemed to have no notion of earning his keep. It was left to me to find work – which I did, thanks to my literacy and fluent English. Oh, yes, a grand situation *I* secured for myself: advertising other people's second-rate verse – much of it obscene – for a Westminster printer. Gwilym seemed to think our problems were over. I trudged the streets, singing random lines of smut, tailed by mimicking beggar-children and hawkers; Gwilym spent his days in aimless exploration. I scraped together enough to pay our rent; Gwilym diverted the landlord with tales of his nightly prowls from alehouse to theatre to stew.

His English was paltry. Many of his new friends took him for a Fleming at first, or a Bavarian. But never mind – they all loved Gwilym. All slapped his big back and kissed his wet mouth and swore eternal friendship after an hour over the jug. I, who tried so hard to tighten my pronunciation, who practised my clipped consonants and narrowed vowels – I was 'Scurvy Taff', 'Tavy the Thief', 'Leek-breath'. Even the printer mocked my limp.

Gwilym was becoming a leech. A burden. And yet, I found it hard to rest without him. The din outside our lodgings was different after sunset, but no less intrusive or alarming. Curfew meant nothing to these city rogues. And I had come to depend on Gwilym's inert bulk beside me. It chased away my visions.

While he pursued his pleasures at night, I fended off sleep, and the horrors it brought with it, by planning our escape from this dismal place. I rehearsed the arguments I would use to convince Gwilym to leave with me. I resolved to talk him into striking out again for Cwm Teg. I imagined going back to my old way of life, plodding around the manors and halls again, with a batch of new verse: 'The Glorious Victory of The Brave Bull of Anglesey'. Gwilym would come with me, as my protector; I in turn would be his guide.

This was how I plotted, turning in my bed as the bells struck up again, and some drunk howled below my window. I even considered leaving the country altogether: obtaining passage for the two of us to Hamburg or Ghent. I was sure it could be done. I only needed to hang around the portside, drop a whispered word into the ear of some friendly cloth-exporter. Anything. Just to get away.

Most nights, Gwilym did eventually creep home. But sometimes he was enticed away until morning. He might fall into a game of Gleke, or make a specially generous new friend; or some underworked whore or lustful young rake might have offered a good price for his company. Then, my panic would mount as the night progressed. Without Gwilym I knew that I would lose my grasp on earthly thoughts, drift away from my own body, see the earth spin away beneath me once again.

One such night I flew into a vision of such clarity that, when the wretched London light squeezed its way into our attic and opened my eyes, I took my bed and the damp walls and the street-cries to be an illusion. My night's journey seemed to be the real life I had left.

There was a ditch – a long, narrow ditch – running from edge to edge of my vision. It was half full of putrid water and gliding with corpses and rats. There were men, drawn up against the wall of this ditch, pressed up against each other, and I was one of those men. My legs were warm and shrivelled where they were planted in water, numb with cold above. Beside me, his bristled cheek scuffing mine, was one man whose merry eyes and weak lips stung my heart, as if with the love of a brother or a son. I understood, but not for some while, that the violence around my temples was noise. The whole sky, the grey earth that gripped us was all noise. Noise that I had not thought possible. Throaty commands were scratching against the noise. Jokes and ballads and sobs evaporated into the noise. I knew this place well. I turned my head with difficulty, fighting the pressure of noise. I turned towards my brother, or my father, or my son. Our faces almost touched. He spoke. The words were swallowed by noise.

The noise stopped.

A terrible silence engulfed us. Suffocated us. Silence stopped our ears. Believing we had lost our hearing, we said nothing.

Time passed.

Under the smothering shroud of silence, one by one, with the tentative, fragile motion of invalids, we climbed to the lip of the ditch. One by one, we picked our winding paths across a devastated field, pausing to consider an upturned, loose-jawed face; or to test with a light kick a protruding arm, preserved by mud and death in a casual farewell.

Chinks of sound broke into the silence. The hacking death throes of a lost boy. The murmur of a soldier asking for help.

I stood, sinking into a featureless land, waiting, while the future gathered itself.

I saw the diminishing shadow of my brother, my brother caging his head with his hands, receding into drifts of smoke.

Four descending bells tore into my room with the feeble sunlight.

The door wrenched open and Gwilym, bulging with drink, pitched forward onto the bed and passed out at my side, wedging me flat against the wall.

I wriggled free and put on his coat – a good, heavy, green woollen coat – a present, would you believe, from one of his new admirers, a dyer's widow. I had not asked what favours had deserved such a gift, nor why he had bothered, since he never wore it and didn't feel the cold.

As I blundered down the lane, clutching my bowl, gathering up the Gwilym-sized sleeves and skirts – the hem dragging in the muck behind me – that dream-vision blocked my eyes and mouth, and I was seized with a doubly urgent need to escape this city. I found the water-carrier, who treated me and the coat to a smirk of disdain as he palmed my money. (We had to pay for God's water in this unnatural place! Would they levy a charge on the air we breathed? When I protested to Gwilym, whose mother had brought his water from the hill or the well nearly every day of her life, he simply shrugged and cuffed my ear and said, 'O, *bachgen*, it's just the way of the world.' He was quite happy to use the free public water, for all its nightsoil and offal.)

After washing I set a cup of clean water by the bed. Gwilym would be mad with thirst when he woke. I left him sprawled on his back and made my quaking way towards the printer's office. The coming winter filled me with dread. Could I keep myself alive, never mind Gwilym, if the snow fell? I tell you, I could have wept that day, even to one of my own vapid songs. The memory of a gratified host's blazing fire, and the immediate prospect of five hours' work before breakfast, made me sore with *hiraeth*. I reached a crossing. Ahead was the route to Westminster and the printer's shop. To my right, a side-street led towards the docks. I remembered my fantasy of persuading a merchant to take us abroad. I thought of the drivel I would be required to advertise that day. I turned to the right, and began the long walk to the river.

There I stood, wrapped in a coat several sizes too big, while the rest of the world busied itself with trade. Sun-darkened men, half-dressed even in this weather, shoved me aside as they heaved crates and barrels along the dockside. Seagulls cried in dismay at the masts and banners that speared their sky. Great walls of wood sighed and purred in the water, slimy with the smell of oceans. Men in fur-rimmed hats and cloaks gesticulated and argued. Men with scrolls and charts eyed the cargo with suspicion. I had walked all the way here, without a sane idea of what to do. I had walked away from our only regular source of income. I considered keeling over into the water.

Among the clamour of profanity and strange languages, my ears picked up a familiar, upturned inflexion. A big, burly fellow was harrassing a merchant, swelling with indignation at every innocent shrug. He was speaking Welsh. Only the words were English. I approached, and greeted him. He turned, flushed with exasperation: it was Llwynog.

Llwynog had stayed with the march, unlike us. He had ingratiated himself with the commanders, and made sure it paid off. He was kept on by one of the King's men, who had 'interests' in imports and exports; he was a useful, daunting presence when matters of trade came to a dispute. He raised his eyebrows at my sunken cheeks and strange clothes. He said, 'Leave it to me, *gyfaill*.' He was sure his master would be pleased to help out an old soldier.

Llwynog was true to his word. Before Christmas I had new employment, slithering around on shipdecks, ankle-deep in sludge, tallying barrels and calculating dues. By All Saints, Gwilym and I were sitting down to smoked bacon, by the light of a crackling fire and half-a-dozen candles. By Candlemas of the following year we had moved into a custumer's house behind the port, and our supper was brought to the table by Mrs Mytton.

I was diligent in my work, polite and thorough in my business with the merchants. Their angry resentment at the tunnage and poundage to pay, my impatience to get the job done and tot up the duties in one piece, and the close scrutiny of the surveyor's clerks, all encouraged me to be quick and honest. I knew full well, of course, that among other custumers hushed bargains were made, coins slipped into quick hands, packages concealed and spirited away. I later learned that I had gained my own post by replacing an official who'd been dismissed for embezzlement. But I hadn't the courage or the confidence to try my luck.

Then Gwilym disappeared. For a week there was no word of him. After a long day's work, I had to venture out to his squalid haunts to search for him. I made a nuisance of myself, accosting drunks and prostitutes to ask for news of the Welsh blacksmith. After four days I decided he had been stabbed in some backalley altercation. My prediction had come true, after all.

I returned from work on the seventh night and he was kneeling at the bed, apparently unable to climb in. Where had he been? I demanded. Oh, he'd been living the fine life. He'd met people who knew what good food was, what fashionable clothes were. He'd thrown a new, velvet short cloak on to the floor. It was already stained and fingered, but new nonetheless, and expensive too. I never discovered who it was who'd taken Gwilym under their wing for a week's enjoyment. I left him retching on the floor and slept on a chair, in my clean but simple parlour.

The following day, I worked like a dullard. I blinked over my tally, looked stupefied at the fat, foreign merchant before me, and failed to find my tongue or finish the business. Presently the merchant stopped abusing me and began to mutter sharply under his breath. This was no threat – it was a proposition. My guard was down. His request was straightforward: he wanted his sealed cocket, his certificate claiming that he'd paid the duties on his wool and silk, fair and square. A little extra for me, a bargain for him. I did not turn a deaf ear this time; I did not slink away, or draw myself up and issue a haughty rebuke. I thought of the chill that hardened my bed a little more each day. I thought of the coins, the pretty gold angels, chuckling in that merchant's purse. And I showed him my palm.

I became a master at this unnamed trade. The merchants liked my style. Unlike my custumer colleagues, the merchants could hear no particular folly or deception in my accent: I was just another foreigner to them. I was careful to keep my transactions strictly secret. I never overstepped the mark – never grew too greedy, never flaunted any fashionable garb or ate more heartily than usual when we stopped to break our fast. I learned to recognise potential conspirers among the tradesmen; I had an eye for the high tippers.

I bought better clothes for Gwilym, a plumed hat and a jewelled ring, but it didn't curb his restlessness. We ate good beef twice a week; afterwards, he would tap his fingers on the board and then, suddenly, snatch up the trencher bread, mop up the pools of gravy and claret and dash out, saying he was 'just taking this for the beggarwoman on the corner'. That was the last I'd see of him before sunrise.

My secret business continued to do well. The authorities, who were so wary of fraud, so willing to see bribery and corruption at every turn, never thought to suspect me. My bony, ascetic features and subdued manner seemed to convince the surveyors that I could be trusted. Since nobody had ever visited my home or dined at my table, nobody noticed my increasing comforts.

Gwilym drank his way through the spring months. I tried telling him that he must set himself to finding work, pay his share – or go. He would listen, nod blearily, and lose consciousness. At Rogationtide I extracted a promise that he would come to hear a public sermon on sobriety and remorse. But the day came and Gwilym could not be shifted from his bed. All my efforts were useless. I could hardly throw the man out. Despite his idle months he still had ten times the strength of a lame versifier with a wheezing chest. I was no match for him.

I bought plates and forbade trencher bread at table. I fed him double portions, hoping his gluttony would tire him out at home. I hid my little hoard of angels under the floorboards – but he had no need of those. Gwilym had friends with full purses in every alehouse in London.

I began to curse the day I had fallen into step with this wretch.

1

Madge Probert is a good couple of inches taller than James, not counting the extra six inches of glaring white, pillowed hair. She ushers him and Cat into the lounge with a balletic sweep of her arm, blinking at them through large, square glasses. They pick their way with caution past small porcelain figures on shelves, coloured glass animals behind glass cupboard doors, and a perfectly groomed fluffy hearthrug. The three-piece suite is pale gold, with white cushions to match Mrs Probert's hair. James casts around for somewhere to rest his tape recorder without causing stains or breakages.

Mrs Probert perches opposite them and smooths her dress over her stomach with manicured hands.

'Very nice to meet you at last.'

It's a projected, clipped voice, used to giving orders.

'We'll try not to take too long,' says Cat hastily. 'I know you must have other things to get on with . . .'

'Do you?' Mrs Probert shoots her a look that almost cracks her glasses. 'Which other things would they be?'

James decides to establish control at once and begins to formulate his generative question:

'Well, Mrs Probert, what I'd like to ask you about is your—'

'At this stage in life,' raps Mrs Probert, raising a hand to him, while keeping Cat in her sights, 'you have to *look* for things to do. *You're* the people with too much to do. That's why you make last-minute appointments, and arrive *late*.'

Cat mumbles something and her mouth droops with resentment.

'So we can only assume,' concludes Mrs Probert, 'that *I'm* the one with time to waste.' She turns her attention to James. 'Now. What do you want to know?'

James feels the heat rising in his face and rebukes himself: I am an adult. I am not going to be bullied by this woman.

Madge Probert grew up with the market. There's a picture on her mantelpiece of her parents, Florrie and Sid, and her grandfather – all in their round-rimmed hats and striped aprons, standing behind their butchers' stall. Florrie is a thick-set woman with a laugh that trebles her chin. Sid is shorter, round and bald, and eyes the camera suspiciously. Florrie's father stands with his hands spread on the counter in front of him: defiant. In charge. Madge Probert looks at that picture, and immediately the smell of the market surrounds her – sawdust and meat and fish, all folded in with the noise of the stallkeepers and customers, and the puppies in their cages upstairs, and her grandfather's cleaver following its long arc into a dull thwack in dead flesh. Madge would be taken to the stall every weekend and holiday, but as soon as it got busy – and it always did – she would wriggle away, between the huge shopping bags and baskets, and make her way up to the top floor, to crouch in front of the puppies and rabbits and share their misery through the cage bars. When she was older she had to lend a hand on the stall – wrapping off-cuts and weighing sausages. But Florrie noted the turn of her mouth and whispered to Sid,

'It don't come natural to her. Handles the meat like it'll bite her.'

Although Sid said nothing, Madge knew that her father sympathised. He had come to butchery by strategy, not nature. It was her mother who loved the life.

As for her grandfather, Madge has two memories of him. One is sturdy and red-faced and loud, bellowing *'Nice* bit of pork, now, *juicy* pork belly,' and teasing the women who tap their half-crowns on the counter for attention. The other shifts and turns in his chair, by the fireside in her parents' house, pawing at his knees, stroking his sleeves in an endless, compulsive dance. His great balloon-face has deflated around a shrunken skull. His mouth yawns and snaps shut, or skids from side to side. This is the grandfather who told Madge his story, to frighten her, and to gain some passing relief. Not a story that Madge would relate to strangers, even sixty years later. Not a story she bothered to relate even to her own family. It's not a significant story: it may not even be true. She doesn't waste time on it in her interview with James and Cat.

Instead, Madge tells them about the market, about the little packets kept behind the counter for special customers during the war. She tells them about her husband Arthur, who ran the newsagents on the corner opposite her parents' house, and about the relief of leaving butchery for the clean stacks of magazines and cigarette packs, and about being rushed to hospital in the paper-van to have their baby.

'Forty years we ran that shop. Forty-five years we were married. A good business, and a good marriage. I put that down to routine.

It's very underrated, routine. Gets you through a lot. Sorting the papers, ordering supplies, serving the regulars, doing the books, going to the bank. Same with being a wife. Knowing what he eats, how he likes his shirts ironed, when he goes to bed, what he's going to say . . . I looked after him, he looked after me, and I'm not ashamed of that, no matter what people might think today. Have you two got children? No? You're leaving it a bit late, but then people do these days. They expect to have forty years of fun before getting round to all that . . .'

On an impulse of sympathy, James squeezes Cat's hand. Mrs Probert notices – he can tell from the subtle change in the angle of her head.

She says, 'I don't suppose you two are even married yet.'

'Oh, no – we're not . . .'

'Well, times change, and *I* can't hold back the tide. It's a pity. Making vows is nothing to be ashamed of. My marriage was one of the greatest achievements of my life. According to my daughter I was no better than a servant. But I was *proud* to make my husband happy. I was *proud* to do my best for my daughter. I don't call that a waste: I call it a life. No one's life is a waste.'

Mrs Probert was a fussy, anxious mother – she's prepared to admit that. Clutching her daughter's wriggling hand in the park, hauling her past the boating lake, and past the other children's delirious screams and full-pelt races down the grass banks. She used to send notes to the teacher, inventing allergies and chest troubles so that her daughter would be kept safely incarcerated in the classroom, looming head and shoulders above the younger pupils, while the rest of her year trooped off to the Empire Baths for swimming lessons.

'But there we are,' says Madge Probert. 'It's a dangerous world to bring up children. Even worse, nowadays; *I* wouldn't want to be raising a child in *this* world. Anyway, better safe than sorry, I always thought. And it can't have done her any harm. She's a solicitor in Birmingham now.'

Madge and Arthur Probert retired and sold the newsagency, and three years later Arthur fell down the stairs.

'There I was, climbing the stairs ahead of him as usual, and I asked him if he'd remembered to put the empties out. He always needed reminding, head like a sieve. He didn't answer, so I turn round and there he is, crumpled in a heap at the bottom of the stairs.' Mrs Probert's voice soars with indignation. 'How could he have fallen down all those stairs without a sound? And then this young man comes round asking me questions about it, taking notes, as if I'd done something terrible. I've never seen the like.'

As James and Cat are leaving, Mrs Probert produces a folded piece of paper.

'Read that,' she says. *'That's* what an old lady does with her time. Shut the door behind you please, and post it through the letterbox when you've finished. I don't want to wait in the draught.'

They stand in the porch while Cat reads the letter, which is from a publisher of historical romance, expressing interest in Madge Probert's manuscript, *Tilly Comes to Town*.

'Blimey,' says Cat. 'People can make a fortune writing those. The old bat's cracked it.'

James feeds the letter back through the slot and calls 'Congratulations!' after it, making the page wince as it floats down to the ivory carpet.

Mrs Probert doesn't hear. She's back in the lounge, sitting with her hands on her lap, telling herself she's a fool. (A tightening of her interlaced fingers emphasises the word. *Fool.*) Making her little speeches; waving her publisher's letter around. Pathetic old fool.

Despite what Ellis Galloway might think, this project *was* Madge's idea. Its purpose and its shape were quite clear to her. Just like the poetry workshops, just like the letters she writes to the *Daily Telegraph* and the *Western Mail*, these interviews, the whole *Past and Present* event are there to provide a finish. A frame. Closing things off, loading them with validity. This is what counts, as far as Madge Probert is concerned; this is what gives opinions and scrambled emotions their appropriate place in the world: hard, clean-edged formality. So that they can be laid out, exhibited before the sneering younger generations, stopping them in their tracks. Look, here. Listen to this. This matters.

Now, though, she wants to run to the door, call after that couple – Wait! Wait a minute, that wasn't right. That isn't what I wanted to say.

There are too many other stories. That's what Madge Probert realises, now that they've gone. Too many stories that were not her own, that were handed down to her and stuffed into her head and around her hopes and worries, whether she wanted them there or not. Though not many would believe it – not even her own husband and daughter would believe it – Madge was always a listener. She knew what it was to grow up with other people's stories plucking at her clothes and tangling about her legs. That's why she never passed them on in her turn. That's why, even though they're as much a part of her as her own reflection, Madge Probert keeps these stories to herself.

2

From Nan's bedroom, Livvy sees James's car arrive. She sees Cat getting out and James driving off. The grime on the window adds a foreign-film grain to the scene. Livvy drags her finger down the glass. How long did Nan have to put up with the slow obscuring of her view? Window cleaning had been on Saturday mornings. Nan would stand on her fold-down step-and-stool, with her skirt drawn to a point just above the knees, and an old scarf tied round her head, and her arm would move across the glass in measured circles, from the left-hand corner of the pane to the right, from the top to the bottom. To do the outsides she sat on the sill, facing the room, high above the street, and circling, circling. In later years she moaned as she worked from the pain in her hardened knee-joints. Don't *bother* with it, Mum, Peg would snap, We'll get someone round, it won't cost much. Nan wouldn't hear of it. They use dirty flannels, she said, they leave smears. And Peg would mutter, Well, if you think I'm doing it, think again. I've got my own home to keep clean.

Livvy opens the window and leans out, twisting about to inspect the outer panes. Down below, Cat is fumbling with the spare doorkey. The squeak of the sash makes her look up.

'Careful!' she calls. 'It's bad enough scraping your shopping off the road. We don't want you splattered all over it too!'

She's about to let herself into James's house. She's looking forward to a few hours alone, while he's at the library. She wants to think. Or not to think. Livvy is still leaning out of the window, her hair hanging like a spaniel's ears.

Cat steps back again.

'Coffee?'

'She was a bit of an old bag, to tell the truth.' Cat eases off her shoes and tucks her feet under her on the sofa. 'But here she is with a thundering great publishing deal on her hands. Fair play to her.'

Livvy sips at her coffee. It tastes of brown paper. She assesses the room for the second time.

The bookshelves, in one alcove, exactly filled, with no volumes shoved in on their sides, no gaps, no frizzy edges. In the alcove on the far side of the chimney breast, two racks of CDs, also full. The table, opposite, stripped and stressed, with a solid square boot of extra wood on each leg. There's a framed 18th-century political cartoon on one wall, showing a pot-bellied soldier apparently about to moon at a ringleted maid. On the opposite wall, over the table, an abstract painting, all vivid yellows and swirls of cream. Livvy had been conscious of its glow and points of light, behind Gal's head, as they ate. Today it reminds her of lemon-meringue pie. On the table, on the seats of the chairs under it, on the floor – loose sheets of paper, biros, notebooks, used envelopes, chocolate wrappers, two unwashed mugs, a pair of bunched-up socks.

'That's me, I'm afraid,' says Cat, following Livvy's eyes. 'I've sort of hijacked this room. I was working in here this morning, as you can see . . . I'd better tidy it up, I suppose. It drives James nuts. He's so methodical.'

'What sign are you?' asks Livvy.

'Sign?'

'Of the horoscope.'

Livvy is serious. Cat checks her impulse to smile.

'Er . . . Leo? Something like that. August the 23rd.'

'What about James?'

'No idea. The sign that's totally incompatible with Leo, possibly.'

Livvy's eyes are on her, weighing up her sincerity. Cat finds herself babbling to fill the gap.

'I don't mean that, really. We get along very well. Considering his anal retention, and my . . . havoc. We muddle . . . along . . .'

Cat curses herself. This is my own fault. I *invited* her in. She looks guilty, as if Livvy can read the thought.

'What about . . . the woman, the one in Italy?' asks Livvy.

'Sonia? Oh, that's not really . . . oh, I see what you mean – no, this isn't – I mean – James and I are old friends. We go back years. Yonks. Anyway. How's the decorating going? Are you definitely moving in for good? How will that affect things, with your performing, you know, does it make a difference? I don't suppose it does, does it? Except that it's further to travel, maybe? To concert venues and . . . whatever?'

Livvy swallows some luke-warm coffee.

'I'll have to take on some pupils. I might look into peripatetic work. Approach the local schools.'

'You'd need to ask Gal about that,' says Cat, slyly. 'He knows about all that.'

'He seems to be very busy.'

'Gal? He's always busy. And he's always got a whole battalion of little helpers being busy on his behalf. Look at me – I wasn't here five minutes before I was involved in all this oral doo-dah. And he's got you working on a musical for him, hasn't he? – after only one meeting . . .'

'I don't think he meant that seriously,' says Livvy, showing no signs of warming up. Cat thinks, Why am I bothering? But she presses on.

'Don't bank on it. Hey – you could set some of these oral histories to music, how about that? C'mon kids, let's put on a show!'

Livvy sits rigid with incomprehension. Cat begins to lean back on the sofa, then changes her mind and straightens up. She considers the possibility that Livvy doesn't know how to chat, or how to leave. I'll wait until she's finished her coffee, she decides, and then I'll give her a straight choice: another cup, or maybe you have to go. Wearily, she says,

'Mr Lightfoot's life, now. That would make a good musical.'

'Mr Lightfoot?'

'Another one of Gal's literary protégés. He had a good tale for a musical, I reckon. Young man falls in love with older woman, they're shunned by narrow-minded society, they part. Sad – *genuinely* sad. Hard to believe people were so judgemental.'

'The stigma,' says Livvy, suddenly.

'Yes . . . exactly . . .' Cat stretches her arms and neck with a subdued imitation of a yawn, but can't see how much coffee is left in Livvy's mug. 'Yes . . . stigma would be right up Gal's street, I imagine.'

'Well, I can tell him all about that.'

Livvy searches for a surface for her mug, and eventually sets it on the floor. Throwing down the gauntlet, thinks Cat. Livvy continues,

'People forget what a big deal it was then. It's not so important these days. But it mattered then.'

'Mm, I'm sure it did,' agrees Cat, who isn't sure what Livvy's talking about, and is waiting for the best moment to hand her the exit cue.

'There were ways and means of getting rid of it, even then,' Livvy goes on. 'I'm sure Nan could have found someone to fix things, even if Mum couldn't. There were people, you know – contacts. On the grapevine. The only thing I can think is, she didn't have the money.'

Cat's face clears, and slowly she registers the fact that Livvy is referring to herself as 'it'.

'Still, there's plenty of others found a way, plenty more hard up than Nan. Lots of unwanted creatures like me never saw the light of day.'

She sits with her hands in her lap; half her face in shadow, the other half caught by a low beam of sunlight from the French window behind her chair. She looks etched, self-aware, an illustration in a cheap Victorian novel. Cat says, cautiously,

'But – then, perhaps your mother *wasn't* ashamed. Perhaps she *wanted* to have it. You.'

Livvy bows her mouth into a sneer. Neither of them speaks for a moment; Cat wants to apologise, for not knowing her lines.

'Well,' says Livvy presently. 'Anyway, it's all changed now. None of that hypocrisy. That's something to be thankful for.'

'Mm,' says Cat.

And then Livvy's attention seems to fix on the air, like a dog sensing a thunderstorm. She marks something: a change, a shift of silence. Cat is nervous. Cornered. She begins to waffle again.

'And then they do say write about what you know, don't they? I don't know if that applies to composing too, does it? But I'm sure Gal *would* be interested – in what you . . . You can't assume he wasn't serious, anyway – next thing you know, he'll be handing you lyrics and fixing up the *première*, he's like that – probably something to do with being Sagittarius, or Mercury, or whatever . . .'

Her hands are shaking. Livvy observes her, until the words have petered out, then says,

'You must come and see the house, now that it's more or less done. I can show you a photo of my mother and me, when I was a baby. If you're interested.'

Cat's polite interest comes out as a manic guffaw. She says,

'More coffee? Or do you have to go?'

3

Madge Probert's mother, Florrie Butterworth, had worked the market since she could walk. She and her father had a pitch in Castlebury, a small, dull town on the border. As soon as she had enough strength in her arms, young Florrie was skinning rabbits. Stood in the stinging wind and the drizzle, and whipped their outer selves off in one neat move, leaving a perfect, smooth, pink imitation of a rabbit hanging high in her hand. She would sing as she worked: *'I WANT to sing in opera . . .'* *'Oh, oh, Antoni-oh, He's gone awaaay . . .'*

Her father, Ernest Butterworth, master butcher, watched her and winked solemnly at his customers. He had brought her up alone; his wife (who was never mentioned) had simply gone one day, while he was at his stall, leaving Florrie securely bound into her cot next to their bed, with a torn corner of paper pinned to the bottom of the blanket, saying 'Sorry'. Until that day, Florrie was not Florrie at all. She was Ruby – named, her mother declared, for her ruby-red lips. But Florrie never knew this.

When her father returned that evening, his child was oven-hot and screaming fit to bust. Ernest cursed his wife and he cursed his daughter. He smashed the hideous little china ornaments his wife had kept on the mantel. He tore up every last reminder of her presence and threw the scraps away, and he threw Ruby's name away with them. Later, as he sat in the dark with his head in his hands, he repented a little, and decided to let his daughter keep Ruby as her second name. In case her mother should ever come back. One of Ernest Butterworth's neighbours had not long since had a child of her own, and she agreed to care for Florrie during the day, for a few coppers a time. Ernest considered offering the child up for good, but as she grew stronger and fitter he allowed himself to grow fond of her, and began to carry her with him to the stall and the slaughterhouse. When she was old enough to ask about her mother he simply said she'd 'gone to 'Merica with another man', and that he'd hear no more about it. Florence Ruby Butterworth accepted his answer, and put it aside forever. She was a single-minded, robust little girl who couldn't be bothered, even then, with loose ends.

Florrie was fourteen when the Great War broke out. As it progressed, her father thanked God for having no son to send to the trenches. He took to parading up and down in front of the butcher's stall, making a performance of his swivelling limp and built-up heel, to ward off dirty looks and white feathers. Florrie carried on with her peeling and singing: *'And UP would go Antonio, and his ice-cream – cart!'*

After work they would go home and sit opposite each other by the fire, feet touching, and Ernest Butterworth would pretend to concentrate on his pipe, casting guilty glances at his daughter's fast-developing chest and muscular arms. Not that his thoughts were impure: he never laid a finger on Florrie, not even in paternal affection. Just that her increasingly womanish spread and bulge put him in mind of his wife (although she had been a small woman), and that stirred up a muddle of misery and anger and murderous lust.

So when Ernest's sister Betty wrote from Cardiff after the Armistice with new plans for her niece, he didn't throw the letter straight into the fire. He hawked and spat at the grate, and sucked at his pipe, read through the letter again (tracing the lines with a square-tipped finger), and then put it behind the tea caddy while Florrie was busy with the supper.

Ernest's sister Betty was a cook for a doctor's household – nothing grand, but, as she said, it was a decent living, with bed and board and all in the warm. What about that girl of yours, Ernie? she wrote. Out there in all weathers. Can't be doing her any good, with all these fevers around and the like. She should be under a roof, with good clean clothes on her back.

Ernest watched Florrie as she hoisted a pan onto the stove. She was built like a heifer, but she did have a hacking, mannish cough. After supper, when she fell asleep in her chair, Ernest stared at her open, childish mouth and the glow on her cheeks.

A week later Ernest retrieved the letter, showed it to Florrie, and told her she ought to go.

Florrie didn't make a fuss. She was the same height as her father now, and would soon overshoot him. She saw his agitation as he thumbed the tobacco in his pipe, avoiding her eyes. She said,

'Right you are, Dad, I'll go. But I'll send for you as soon as I've put a bit by, and we'll go back to what we do best.'

Her father stooped slightly, as if he was already retreating into lonely old age. He was battling against the urge to embrace her – not tenderly, but fiercely, in panic, so that they would both hurt. The way he used to hold his wife.

Florrie packed a small, square suitcase and caught the train to Shrewsbury and the connection to Cardiff. Her Auntie Betty met her at the station. Betty had arranged for Florrie to join her in the service of Dr and Mrs Parry, in their large but plain detached house on the outskirts of the city. Dr Parry was a dapper man with a black moustache and white hair. He had been quick-tempered, and his wife loud-voiced, before the war, but as Betty said,

'They won't give you any trouble now. Keep themselves to themselves, mostly, since losing the three boys.' They reserved their sarcasm for each other nowadays, and left the staff alone.

The 'staff' consisted of three: Auntie Betty, Mrs Tannery the housekeeper and now Florrie, as a maid of all works. There had been two maids before the war, 'two giggling ninnies' as Betty put it. When they both left to be married (and in one case almost immediately widowed), Dr Parry was not inclined to replace them. It was Betty who persuaded him to take on a third pair of hands.

Florrie did well. She was good at the early mornings, quick and thorough in her tasks, cleaning out and lighting the fires, beating rugs, folding sheets. Auntie Betty and Mrs Tannery watched approvingly as she scrubbed the pots and cut their bread-and-butter. They kept up a provocative commentary which Florrie ignored with good humour.

'She's a fine, strong girl,' Mrs Tannery would say. 'She'll make some lucky lad a wife and a half.'

'He'll have to be a strapping lad himself,' cackled Auntie Betty, 'to make the most of a big girl like Florrie.'

'Good luck to him!' Mrs Tannery would be heaving her bulky chest now, and licking her lips. 'All the very best of British to the boy, whoever he might be!'

Florrie had two half-days off a week, and was always in great haste to be off. Mrs Tannery suspected a beau. She would be waiting in the kitchen when Florrie returned, leering at her over her mending.

'Come on then, girl, let's hear about him. No war wounds, are there? All in working order?'

It was on one of Florrie's half-days that Mrs Parry's silver cardcase was found in Mrs Tannery's coat pocket. So Florrie wasn't there to hear Dr Parry's tirade, or Mrs Parry's tears of betrayal, or the lacklustre sympathies of Auntie Betty (who had found the case) as Mrs Tannery slammed her belongings into her Gladstone bag, still bleating that she was an innocent woman, that God would see justice done, and anyway she wouldn't stay in this house of thieves and liars for all the tea in China.

Auntie Betty had taken her place in Mrs Tannery's chair by the time Florrie came home.

'Well, the old sow has gone and good riddance,' she said, in a matter-of-fact way. 'So you can see your young man in peace from now on.'

'I haven't got a young man,' said Florrie. 'I just like to be out in the air.'

As soon as she was released from her duties every week, Florrie caught the tram into town, past the park and the strolling couples, past the queues to see *Pollyanna*, past the castle and into St Mary Street. Here she would get off the tram and stand like a supplicant at a church door. This was her temple: the indoor market. She entered gravelly, respectfully, through the pompous arched doorway; she gazed up at the high glass ceiling, while around her the prattle of the market vibrated in echoes towards the light. She would take her time, weaving around the stalls, examining crockery and haberdashery and fish-heads and *bara brith*. Finally, inevitably, ending up at M E Hatchetts, Purveyors of Best Quality Meats. Every week, twice a week, she would be there, nudged and cuffed by the passers-by, gazing at the Hatchett family as they trussed and cut and boned and rolled and threw out the occasional rallying cry to the crowd. Tom Hatchett, heir to the business, was a pimply young man with coarse, sandy hair. He noticed the well-built young woman who stood at some distance, twice a week, without buying. He wondered whether he was the attraction. One afternoon he risked calling,

'Can I help you, Miss?'

Before long they were spending Florrie's free hours chatting at the stall, so that Tom Hatchett's Uncle Meurig began to tell him off (in his mild, apologetic way), for idling with his sweetheart instead of earning his crust.

Tom took Florrie to see *Romance of the Redwoods*. He pecked her on the cheek, but was afraid to do anything more, in case she recoiled from his abrasive skin. So he was surprised when, after he'd seen her back to the doctor's house one evening, Florrie announced that it was high time they settled on a date. He suspected her of mocking him. He waited for her to laugh, but she just gave his chin an upward tap to shut his mouth, and said,

'And now that we're engaged, I suppose I'd better give my

notice. In the meantime, tell your uncle to clear some room for me in his house.'

Tom and Uncle Meurig had no notion how to contradict a woman like Florrie. They assumed that if she could arrange the future with such confidence, she must have some claim on it.

'I'm giving my notice in,' Florrie announced, standing at the kitchen door, unpinning her hat.

Auntie Betty had been sitting with her feet up, holding a glass of stout in one hand and picking her teeth with the other. She regarded her niece with astonishment, which almost immediately became spite.

'Well, that's a nice thank you, I must say. I go to all this trouble, pestering the poor Doctor, setting you up with a comfortable position . . .'

'Never mind,' said Florrie, unruffled. 'You'll find another helper, soon enough.'

She packed her small, square suitcase and moved into Uncle Meurig's house, on the corner where two terraced rows of houses met. Florrie settled herself into the box room, and by day took up her position behind Hatchett's stall. Tom and Meurig could only slip each other sidelong looks as she prepared the clod and the brisket, and the belly and the chops. Her authority seeped with the blood into the slabs and over the hooks and through the white coats and aprons of the two dazed men. To save any awkwardness, she told them, they might as well refer to her as Mrs Hatchett, straight off. Only for work, of course – just for decency's sake. It was only a matter of time, after all, before it would be the truth.

But somehow time slithered by and Florrie made no more mention of weddings and dates. On the rare occasions that Tom summoned up the courage to broach the subject, she was impatient. He suggested shopping for a ring; she waved away his nonsense.

'No point. I wouldn't wear it on the stall, would I? – with all this mess.'

Three years went by. Customers were asking particularly for Mrs Hatchett. Tom and Meurig spent a lot of their time mopping the tiles and bagging the offal, while Florrie greeted the cooks and housewives in her brusque, competent way, selected their cuts and handled their money.

One evening, when the market doors were shut and the air quivered with the clatter of stall shutters, Tom took several deep breaths and said it was about time they made their plans, one way or the other.

'Yes of course,' said Florrie, half-closing her bovine eyes, and Tom fluttered with relief. 'Of course we will,' she said. 'We'll go and see the minister next week and set a date.'

But before the week was out there had been a bit of a scene.

A customer had battled to the front of the crowd, dragging a pasty-faced girl behind her, to complain that the blade and chopped kidney she had bought there for a pie had nearly done her family to death. Look at my girl, she insisted, appealing to the shoppers around her. Been fetching up her innards all night. I thought I'd lose her, I really did. It was the young man who sold it to me, she added. Young Mr Hatchett. And him the son of the business! He should have known better – selling me rotten meat.

Eventually they appeased her with a refund, but the other shoppers dispersed before choosing their meat, and takings were right down for a couple of days.

After that, Florrie couldn't find a kind word to say to Tom. He skulked at the back, out of the customers' sight, while Florrie muttered darkly about falling standards and loss of precious business. There was no more said about seeing the minister. Eventually, Tom accepted defeat. Six months after the bad meat incident, in the summer of 1922, Tom Hatchett shook his Uncle Meurig's hand and went to work the ships.

At about the same time, Florrie struck up a friendship with the paper-seller, who manned a kiosk in the market entrance. She would take him mugs of tea, and stand staring out at the rain while he patted and rearranged his stock and fitted his cold knees into the open side of his kiosk, and blew his constantly running nose.

One morning, before the market doors had opened, he told her about the only time he'd ever been with a prostitute.

'A healthy girl,' he said, and he didn't avoid Florrie's eyes. 'I didn't so much want to *do* anything. Just wanted her to hold me, while I slept.'

Florrie wasn't the least bit shocked. She liked his honesty. She admired it.

Five weeks after Tom Hatchett had set sail on his first sea-voyage, Florrie moved Sid Gittins from the paper kiosk to the humid comfort of the Hatchett pitch. They married before the year was out, though Florrie never troubled to correct the customers who went on calling her 'Mrs Hatchett'. Sid learned to live with the rich smell of fresh meat. He did his best to follow Florrie's directions, and not to retch over the fat and gristle. He and Uncle Meurig developed a code of glances: when Sid was floundering and about to be ill, Uncle Meurig would step in without comment and take over his task.

Poor Uncle Meurig. His nephew had disappeared, maybe beneath the waves; they heard no word. But then, as Florrie pointed out, Uncle Meurig had gained a new family. He wasn't to worry. She and Sid were his kith and kin now, good as, and they would see him right in his old age. Uncle Meurig agreed that, in the circumstances, it would make sense for Sid to move in to his wife's adopted home. He couldn't argue with the practicality of giving them his more spacious bedroom, and moving his own bedding to the box room. He hesitated about the will, hoping perhaps that while he hesitated, Tom would come back, or that he himself would die – he did feel, some days, that he could pass away with the weariness of all this reasoning and concluding. Finally he let Florrie decide, as usual, and do the necessary. She told him what changes to make and how to word them. His one act of defiance was to keep the stall in his own name. But it was no defiance at all, really. Florrie didn't seem to care.

Florrie was irritated at Sid's persistence on their wedding night, but she let him have his way for courtesy's sake, and fell pregnant. She miscarried in her fifth month, and was infuriated by the pain that doubled her up, and the metallic reek of blood that – unlike the blood on her slabs – made her heave and howl. When it was all over she let Sid understand that it would not be discussed again.

The next time Florrie indulged her husband was soon after her thirtieth birthday. It was 1930. She and Sid were both slightly the worse for drink, having attended Uncle Meurig's funeral and wake. Florrie fell pregnant again, and it was while she was carrying Madge that she wrote to her father in Castlebury:

'All fixed and ready for you now. The pitch does a sound profit and is nice and warm. Join us as soon as you can, there will be plenty of room here, even with baby, and Sid is wanting to meet you.'

So by the time Madge Gittins was born, this was her family, and this was her home, and this was the only way life had ever been or ever could be. Florrie and Sid and Florrie's father Ernest, and little Madge, all living in their house on the corner, and purveying the best quality meats in the market; and occasional, puzzling visits from a large, stern woman called Betty. That was Madge's world: a world which had no knowledge of Uncle Meurig or Tom Hatchett. The house on the corner where two terraces met; the market; the impatient thump of Ernest Butterworth's oversized boot, and his swollen, flushed face and currant eyes looming across the cot or over the counter, and the indistinct flavour of dread that filled every day as naturally as sunlight. Madge Gittins was taken to the market stall on Saturdays and propped on to a stack of crates to watch the show. She had a grasp of the players and their roles, before she could say their names. Ernest, shrugging and winking and bellowing at the customers, slapping and slicing the meat like a swordsman, pausing at Florrie's side to soak up her warmth and strength. Florrie, his daughter, Madge's mother, remembering the customers' names, asking after their poor old mums or their hubbies, monitoring her father's work with quiet triumph, being called 'Mrs Hatchett' by the regulars (her professional name, young Madge assumed: her stage name). And Sid, out of the way at the back of the area, sweating and puffing over his mop and bucket. Madge would crane her neck from her perch to see her father in the wings, sometimes catching him in some private debate with himself, squeezing baffled eyebrows as he tried to understand what had happened to his life. Then he would notice Madge, serious little Madge, and twist his lips comically, in mischief, to make her smile. Thwack! would go Ernest's cleaver, and Madge and her father would both look away, instinctively knowing that it was best not be discovered, even in such innocent collusion.

The truth was that Florrie had misjudged Sid Gittins. When he related to her, so openly, his encounter with the prostitute, Florence had believed him to be bold and wilful. She had been struck by his directness, by the way he called her Florrie, not Miss Butterworth (or Mrs Hatchett); by the way he addressed her as an equal. As a friend. It had crossed her mind then that she might not summon her father from Castlebury after all. But Florrie was wrong about Sid. In Sid's world, prostitutes were tradespeople; his tale was not designed to shock or impress her – it was just one of the tales he had to tell. Like his first beer, or his first pay-packet. He told her the truth, because he hadn't the imagination to tell lies. Sid wasn't bold, or wilful. He wasn't a man to take charge.

On the whole though, Florrie came to the conclusion that it was all for the best. If Sid was repulsed by the business and cowed by her father, well at least she and Ernest could get on with things in their own way. Only Madge felt her father's timidity as a wound; as soon as she was old enough, she would clamber down from the crates and escape from his humiliation into the crowds.

Almost as soon as Ernest Butterworth arrived at his daughter's pitch, he became known as Mr Hatchett. It didn't bother Ernest and Florrie that they traded on a dead man's name; it didn't much matter that the real Mr Hatchett, Tom Hatchett, might sail back into Cardiff dock any day. Florrie had been thorough in her advice to Uncle Meurig; his will had left no caveats or loopholes. The sign remained above the stall, with its fading, curled lettering: 'M E Hatchett, Purveyors of Best Quality Meats'; and Ernest, the bluff senior butcher, was soon known to everyone in the market – including those who remembered Meurig and Tom – as Old Hatch.

In 1938 Old Hatch cut down his trading hours, complaining of a tremor in his left hand. Not long after that, he gave up altogether and became the quaking, drooling creature in the fireside seat who frightened his young granddaughter with stories.

4

'Shall I tell you something? Madge? Madgey? Shall I tell you a secret?'

Leaning towards her in a series of shudders; sucking and spitting the words that she already knew by heart.

'Hell isn't a hot place, Madgey. Hell is cold. Colder than death.'

Round-eyed Madge Gittins, kneeling on the hearthrug at her grandfather's feet, mouthed the words with him, thrilled and shivered as the fear he had taught her tickled her spine. Colder than death. She knew, before she was ten years old, how cold the water could be in a flooded quarry, and how dark, how unimaginably, eternally deep.

This was the story that Old Hatch passed to her as a legacy. The story that has clung to Madge through sixty years, like a second, clammy skin.

One summer day in 1888, a boy exploded into the wood; veered crazily as his stunted leg thrashed towards the ground; fell forward, clawed at the earth, tried to shout but could only yelp; tried to hear another boy's reply but heard only his own gulping breath.

Through the woods, beyond the trees, down the slope and over the quarry; Old Hatch directed his granddaughter's imagination across a map of his past. She noted the clean, calm lid of water and the clouds moving sleepily across it. She understood the force of its attraction. Old Hatch took her back, further back, unwound time by just another hour or so: an hour before the lame boy fell, and whimpered, and gave up the search for help.

Three boys, now, crashing out of the wood, chasing and mocking each other down the slope. One boy heaving off his boots, releasing the withered leg from its anchor. His two friends stop to examine the pale limb and he lets them study it, straightens it and points the malformed foot with pride, until their curiosity dies and they turn to see the water shine. Three boys hurl themselves down the slope, the third hopping nimbly at the rear. Three boys shatter the cold surface, laughing and screaming.

Madge Gittins never wanted the story to go on. She wanted it to stop there. She would think, If I concentrate hard enough, I can change the ending. Sometimes her mother, busy at the sink, would call to Old Hatch, 'Not again Dad. Let the girl alone.' But she didn't press the point. She would lose interest, and get back to her task, and presently the story would go on.

Scan the water. Peer through the spray. Madge Gittins and Old Hatch, compelled to re-examine the memory together. But they never do catch the moment when one boy dips under the surface; they never spot the waving arm or feel the sudden, frantic struggle.

'He sank so easily,' spluttered Old Hatch. (It was hard to distinguish the old man's expression from his condition. It could be consternation, or wonder, or relish.)

Time skipped a beat, and presented Madge with two puzzled boys, diving and surfacing, diving and surfacing, gaping at each other as the water regained its composure, listening to the ringing, cold silence.

Two boys out of the water, one sprinting across the wasteland and out of sight; the other floundering, kicking his weak leg across the twigs and undergrowth of the forest floor.

Madge Gittins' grandfather would reach out a flapping hand and snatch at her wrist.

'Maybe we could have found help from the town. Maybe it wasn't too late. But I was too slow, with my leg, and my friend just kept running. Just kept running away. And we neither of us ever told a soul.'

All these years, over half a century, Madge Probert has been the sole guardian of a poor drowned boy, returning to him in solitary corners of her mind, assuring him that she knows, she has not forgotten.

The story would end as Madge Gittins knelt there, absorbing the echoes, and her grandfather would fall asleep. Sometimes Madge would sense the presence of another troubled listener, out of sight, and she would look round and catch a movement at the door. But Sid generally kept out of his father-in-law's way. He referred to the story only once – in the market, while his wife was occupied with a customer. He bent his head to his daughter's ear and whispered:

'Never you mind Old Hatch.' (He never could call him 'Grandad'.) 'You don't have to believe what he says. It's just tales – they're all he's got.'

Eventually, Florrie Gittins took to locking her father in the house while the others were out at work and school. To stop him wandering, she said, though he was barely able to leave his chair by that time. Madge fretted. What if he was hungry? What if he hurt himself? But her mother swatted her anxiety away.

'He's got no appetite now, girl. All he wants is to sit.'

During air raids they half carried him into the cupboard under the stairs. Florrie didn't hold with hiding in shelters, and the rest of the family carried on as normal.

One day, Madge came home from school and knew from the quality of the silence that her grandfather had died. He was in his chair as usual, with his head at a clumsy angle; Madge stood in front of him and inspected him in his new stillness. She thought she recognised the other grandfather, the vigorous, overbearing master butcher, in his punctured features. She was still standing there when her parents arrived, and Florrie grasped her shoulders and shifted her out of the way.

'Well, that's over then,' was all Florrie said, but there was something unfamiliar in the tone that made Madge and Sid feel they should leave her for a while.

They went to sit on the doorstep. Sid lit up a fag, and they watched the clouds turn pink. They could hear the scuffles and calls of children playing in the next street; the lights were on in Proberts Newsagents, on the opposite corner, and young Arthur Probert and his father could just be seen moving about at the back of the shop. Sid took a long, long pull at his cigarette and pursed his lips to release the smoke. Then he said, for the sake of something to say,

'She'll fetch us in when she's ready.'

It was 1945, the war was over, and Madge was about to leave school and escape into another life.

5

Charles Lightfoot stands unsteadily by his hospital bed, buttoning and unbuttoning his cardigan, as his brother Vernon folds pyjamas and rolls socks – with surprising precision – and packs them into Charles's overnight bag. As Charles is allowing himself to be taken by the elbow and led out to the lift, Ellis Galloway is receiving a visitor on a ward one floor down.

Gal has had a mishap. It happened at three o'clock that afternoon, while he was teaching the last class of the day. He was padding out his slow, measured circuit of the classroom, offering occasional snippets of advice, encouraging his pupils to focus on the poet's imagery, to consider how *they* would describe being in love to, say, a visitor from Mars. He was relaxed, sinking into the sleepy Friday afternoon atmosphere. Through the window he could see the school playing field, and beyond that the motorway, pulsing gently. Around him, the comforting sounds of writing, paper-rustling, an isolated cough. He felt at home. It seemed to Gal that this was the real sum of his life, and that it had lasted forever, suspended over everything else: one long tranquil schoolroom afternoon, stretching from this particular hour, back to him and James at their twin desk, scraping surreptitious blotty doodles along the ridge at the top, and pressing old chewing gum into the redundant ink-wells.

The horizon shifted and a voice piped up, 'Mr Galloway . . .' He could taste watermelon and Marmite. He saw dark splashes on the back of his hand. A frightened face flew past, and a desk smacked him from forehead to chin and knocked him out cold.

James hates hospitals. He bounces on his toes and talks in an appallingly jovial way, a parody of his father.

'Don't tell me – Madge Probert went bonkers with a baseball bat.'

Gal grimaces. His nose is purple. A swathe of blue shadow across his face is beginning to flower into a bruise. One eye is half closed; the eyelid is pink and fleshy.

'Hit by an unexpected desktop,' he says, thickly.

James makes a performance of positioning the visitor's chair and sitting on it. He just can't seem to act normally.

'So! Are they sorting you out, then? Telling you what's what?'

He keeps looking round at the other patients, at the windows, towards the door.

Gal hardly moves his lips as he speaks.

'Not sure if I blacked out before or after impact. They're doing some tests. Don't think it's anything horrendous.'

'Horrendous! . . .' James clutches at the word in distress.

'No, *nothing* horr—' Gal pauses to wipe spittle from the corner of his mouth. 'The nosebleeds – same old thing. Delicate membranes.'

James sits helplessly, staring at Gal's face. His heart is racing. He feels as if he's the one who took the impact. By instinct he would take Gal's hand. He knits his fingers together to quell the instinct, and rests his arms on the edge of the bed. He looks like the chairman of a board meeting.

'Do you want me to fetch you anything? Call someone?'

'Mm . . . no. Thanks. Going home tomorrow. School knows . . .'

James checks the ward and the doors again. Where the hell is she? He examines the ceiling lights, and taps his feet under the bed. He should have brought something – he realises that now, and it's so bloody obvious. Grapes, a newspaper, *something*. Hit by sudden inspiration, he leans forward.

'By the way, I've got something to tell you. About Cat . . .'

At once, he has misgivings. Gal's face is turned towards him. Cat didn't actually *say* her pregnancy was a secret. And Gal wouldn't count, anyway, would he?

'Uh? Gossip?'

'You – you know, she and Matthew . . .'

'Oh? The wineo? Split up?'

'He's gone back to the wife . . . but . . .'

A maddening itch breaks out on James's neck. He rakes away at it, still throwing out glances towards the door. He wants to tell Gal, to engage his interest, and impress him with his confidante's role.

'So? . . . Zat it?' Tentatively, Gal touches his swollen lip. 'No surprises there. And Sonia?'

'Sonia? How d'you mean, "And Sonia?" She's fine, as far as I know . . . Well, I *do* know. She was going to come over for a few days . . .'

'Mm,' Gal is tiring, retreating into his cocoon of pain.

'She can't, though, as it happens – it's not – well, it's difficult of course, with Cat there – you know how they are – especially –'

Just to regain Gal's attention, James almost takes the plunge. 'Especially since – this news, I was telling you—'

'Bloody hell!' Cat's voice booms down the ward. 'Gal, man, you look like a monkey's backside.'

At the bed, she reaches past James and gently brushes the hair from Gal's eyes. Very swiftly, very softly, she strokes the unbruised edge of his cheek with her fingertips.

'You poor bugger,' she says. 'Are they keeping you in?'

'Not really . . .'

'Just long enough to come up with the Latin for "haven't got a clue" . . . Well. You want to be left alone. We won't stay long.'

Cat sets two paperbacks on his bedside table. James inspects them enviously: good choice. Cat props herself on the bed, sandwiches Gal's fingers between her palms and launches into an account of Madge Probert's interview.

'And she's going to be the Catherine Cookson of the new millennium. All thanks to Ellis Galloway, muse and guru of the mature creative writer.'

Gal's eyelids are drooping.

'We'll go, then, and leave you in peace.' Cat lifts Gal's hand and kisses it. James consoles himself with a wince of ridicule over her head.

'Want anything?' asks Cat, getting up. 'Clean knickers for tomorrow? James can lend you a pair. I'll make sure they're clean.'

'Mm. OK. Thanks.'

'I'll drop them round later on. I might consider taking up a bed myself – I'm in here often enough.'

James and Cat walk down the corridor, past signs to X-Ray and Maternity, past a newsagency with bottle-glass windows, past the coffee machine and the toilets.

'Wait here,' says James. 'Dodgy gut.'

Cat dawdles up and down, looks at the display of children's paintings along the wall, tacks towards the paper shop, and sees Livvy's distorted face regarding her from the other side of the glass.

'What are you doing in there?' asks Cat, amiably, peering round the door. (Lurking, she answers herself, noting that Livvy hasn't bought anything.)

'I did as you said, and phoned the school . . . To get Gal's advice about teaching work . . . They said there'd been a terrible accident . . .'

Cat moves forward, suddenly afraid that Livvy will start to cry, and puts a hand to her arm.

'It's not that bad,' she says, with an exasperated, maternal tone. 'Bruises, that's all. All he wants is a proper rest.'

Livvy is rooted to the spot. Cat begins to feel silly, and backs away again. 'Anyway. I'll leave you to it.'

Livvy isn't about to cry, but she is brimming. Elated. When they told her, on the phone, about Ellis Galloway passing out, Livvy felt her life propelled forward, cannoning into a new context. She had phoned, she had asked for Ellis Galloway, and this event had sucked her in. Her head and her body are buzzing with the adrenalin of fate and opportunity.

James is pale; his forehead is tight with worry.

'James,' says Cat, 'There's nothing to stress about. He's prone to nosebleeds, he lost blood, he fainted. That's all.'

All the same, she's affected by his mood. Her curled-up fear uncoils itself and sways inside her. What if it's *not* all right? What if, what if . . . Gal seems to her today to be so . . . breakable. How can they keep him in one piece? She looks at James's stricken face and wonders what they would do, if they had no Ellis Galloway. As they stride down the corridor, she takes James's hand in hers.

Livvy contemplates Gal's battered face without a smile or a greeting.

'Pretty, isn't it!' says Gal. His spirits sag at the sight of her.

She doesn't reply. Gal, who is usually so adept at maintaining eye contact, or ignoring it, flickers to and from her gaze.

'Lucky I didn't break my nose. Or crack my teeth . . .'

His eyes water with the effort of speaking; a dribble of saliva escapes over his unwieldy bottom lip. Livvy moves to the side of the bed, taking a tissue from her jacket pocket, and mops it up. Gal lifts a hand in vapid self-defence.

'What brought you . . . ?'

'I came to see you.' She's talking deliberately, like a drunk, to contain her zeal. 'I rang the school, and they told me—'

'Rang the school?' His manner has switched. He's suspicious.

'Cat told me to ring you . . . about work . . . Are you going home tomorrow?'

'Mm. Might go . . . to parents . . .' He stumbles over the lie. He's got no intention of going to his mother, who would exhaust him more than his aching face.

'Is that far?'

He shrugs. He feels under siege.

'Where do *you* live?' she asks, stubbornly.

Gal can't see any way not to answer.

'I . . . Wh–near Whitchurch.'

'Which street?'

'Off—not far from Pendraw Road . . .'

She nods, satisfied. The details she can find out for herself. Gal resolves to say nothing more until she leaves.

'I've been thinking,' Livvy says, sitting down, 'about what you said, the other evening. About collaborating. Words and music.'

Gal hesitates but manages not to respond. She appears to register the tactic and continues.

'Now that I've decided to stay here . . . I need to be involved. Not just teaching, not just the same old routine. I mean, I need to be involved in something . . . valuable. This probably doesn't make sense.'

Gal is struck by this intense determination that's driving her on through her diffidence.

'Cat was talking – we had coffee, and she was talking about the way we judge people. Or used to. We were discussing my . . . situation. My family – you know. My *father*.' She presents the word like a trophy. Gal's eyes are half closed. She can sense the long tilt of his eyelashes. He's listening.

'I've never thought before about . . . *using* that. I mean, creating something out of it.' Then a real disgust slips into her voice. 'I'm talking *total rubbish*.'

'No,' says Gal. 'You're not.'

'You see – the truth is—'

This part is important, Livvy knows. This is vital. This is the next surge forward.

'The truth is, I'm not . . . I'm a fraud, Gal. I've never *cared*, really, about music.'

He looks at her. His green eyes look at her.

'It's just my job,' she says. 'Not—not—'

'Not your vocation.'

'Yes! Except – when I started to think about *this* – about what you said, about . . .'

She stops. Her face is taut, insistent. Her hands are bunched into fists on her lap.

'About writing something?'

Gal is on surer ground now. He's flattered by her eagerness, but believes he can handle it. He feels kinder.

'It sounds silly,' she says. 'But – making it into music, turning it into music – and you putting it into words – it's, it's so – I think we *could* do it. I keep imagining it. Like making a dance, only you're directing the steps, and following them, all at the same time . . .'

Other visitors are leaving, waving and calling along the ward. Livvy's fists loosen. 'Sorry. You think I'm stupid. You probably weren't serious about it, you were just being polite.'

Gal hears the rattle of the medicine trolley from the corridor. Soon the nurse will come to usher out the stragglers. He's more or less safe.

'No,' he says. 'It's interesting. What you're saying, it's interesting. Don't dismiss it. It's worth pursuing.'

He genuinely wants to encourage her. He has no thought of doing anything else.

Livvy gets up as the nurse is approaching. She says,

'You could go and stay with James and Cat, couldn't you? Till you're feeling fit.'

The nurse hovers at the bed.

'I'm sure they'd make room for you. I saw them going out, just now. Hand in hand. Like Darby and Joan.'

She moves towards the nurse, whose arm is out, ready to scoop her off the ward.

'I really think,' says Livvy, as she leaves, 'we can work together.'

6

Vernon guides his brother out of the ambulance-car and waves it off.

'Aye, aye, step lively,' he says. His smile is fixed, but the eyes follow Charles's progress with apprehension. Charles is rehearsing the movements of old age. He feels for the kerb with his foot; he puts a hand out to the gatepost and leans for a while, breathing hard. He is no longer just Charles Lightfoot growing old; he has hollowed himself into anonymity.

'Come *on*, mun,' urges Vernon, who has gone ahead and is waiting at Charles's front door. He isn't taken in by all this. He reckons Charles could, if he wanted to, draw himself up and strut along the path like any youngster. He might be right – but it's not going to happen. That's not the kind of person Charles is, any more.

Charles takes his time.

'You could have some decent flowers here,' says Vernon conversationally, gesturing at the narrow front area. 'In pots, like. Suit you down to the ground, that would.'

Charles shuffles past him into the dark hall and Vernon stays leaning on the doorpost, surveying the street. Spindly trees, evenly spaced, struggle through their allotted spaces in the pavement. At the opposite house, a man in a vest with snake tattoos across his back and his head shaved to a bluish tinge is applying fresh mortar between the bricks with slow delicacy. A car passes, revving up fast, and sends a wave of dust rattling back down the road.

'Like Brands flamin' 'Atch,' Vernon says, to nobody in particular. 'Whipping up all that muck. If you did grow anything, it'd keel over soon enough.'

He shuts the door and goes to look into the sitting room. Charles has sunk into one of the brown armchairs and is resting his head in one hand, eyes shut, scowling. Outside, a small child gallops past, letting out a long, loud war-cry that hiccoughs at every step. Its mother comes clacking behind it, calling threats. Somewhere in the house a clock tuts.

Vernon sighs, waits, then says, 'Well, they said you might feel low for a bit. I'll go and brew up. Leave you to stew for a minute.'

Charles hears Vernon clanging around in the kitchen, and his jaw tightens. He should tell him to go, but he hasn't got the energy. Besides, the prospect of sitting here alone while the house grows cold with the dusk is more than Charles can handle. It seems to him that he's more likely to die when he's alone. So he wonders whether Vernon will stop over, while reminding himself that he doesn't *want* him there. It's just circumstances, that's all. Vernon's whistling 'There's a Rainbow Round my Shoulder . . .' with a dense vibrato. He comes back and hands Charles a mug of tea with exaggerated caution before settling himself on the sofa.

'Out there, in the alley,' he whispers. 'I says to her, get a taste of real meat while you can.'

No, no, of course he doesn't. Vernon isn't saying anything at all. Charles concentrates: Vernon is a seventy-four-year-old man, sitting on the sofa, sipping hot tea.

'I says to her, I won't tell. Put my hand on her mouth, and she never give a peep, boy.'

Well. It probably wasn't even true.

Charles shifts in his chair, and consolidates the thought. He probably made it all up, in the first place.

'What?' says Vernon. Charles coughs abruptly. Has he been thinking aloud again?

'Nothing,' he says.

Slinking into the damp shrubbery. Taking handfuls, mouthfuls, just for revenge. Stealing her child.

'What?' says Vernon. Charles gawps.

'Nothing,' he says.

It appears that Charles must be losing his mind, though nobody warned him about it. Vernon's whispers drizzling into his thoughts, the past melting into the present . . . He takes a gulp of tea and asks,

'Do you remember Esther Bell?'

Vernon casts about, as though searching for a physical presence.

'Jeez-uss! You don't half come out with 'em. That's going back to the Dark Ages, now, mun, and there's me, I can't hardly remember my own address these days.'

Charles nods.

'Aye, you're right there. My memory's been playing tricks on me, an' all. Can't remember things straight.'

'Well,' Vernon puts his mug on the floor and gets up. 'You want to live for today, boy, let the past alone. There's no changing it. I tell you what – I brought by some of them chocolate marshmallows yesterday. Want some?'

That's the trouble: everything gets mixed up. Everything gets into a mess. And how do you decide, who's there to tell you, what's right and what's wrong? What happened and what didn't happen? Vernon is the only witness. The only one who has always been there.

Vernon returns and offers Charles a plate of cakes. Charles half shakes his head and looks away. But before Vernon can retreat to the sofa Charles turns back towards him and, without meeting his eyes, says 'Go on then, just one.' He takes the chocolate marshmallow and gives his brother an irritable tap on the arm, letting his hand rest against the coarse woollen sleeve for barely an instant.

7

It's easy to forget, now, that Noreen is dead. There's nothing to indicate any momentous change. To Charles, she doesn't seem any less alive. But then, the real Noreen Farrell separated herself from the Noreen in Charles's head a long, long time ago. For years and years, while Noreen got on with things in that house in Terrace Street, not two miles away, being a mother, being a waitress, a barmaid, a grandmother, an old woman, a dying woman – all that time a different Noreen established herself in the mind of a man in his dingy room, and later in his uncle's old house in Albert Road, and led her own life there until she too had faded at the edges.

At first, it wasn't like that at all. Charles was all too welded to the flesh-and-blood Noreen, all too diminished by the distance between them. When it all ended, he spent nights in real, physical, rib-hugging pain. He had to work hard at detaching ideal from actual. He concentrated, during those nights, giving himself headaches as he slogged at his task, reassembling a new Noreen from individual components: her scent, her laughter, her skin. He forced her into his puerile poems, puzzled over phrases as if trying to break a code and release her essence. She ceased to be a person and became an atmosphere. She was in the sheets of paper, in his dowdy curtains, in the croaking door, in the food he fried at his two-ring cooker in the corner of the room.

Over the years, Charles Lightfoot, the electrician, would run into Noreen Farrell, the waitress, from time to time. In the newsagents, buying ciggies. At the bus stop. They would be genuinely glad to see each other: an oval-faced, ageing woman with a grown-up daughter and an errant husband; a quiet man with thinning hair and a melancholy mouth. He'd ask her about Peg; she'd ask him about his work, and they'd make mild small talk about the weather and how long these roadworks were going on. Banal, and easy, and quite a relief.

When had it ended? As far as Charles can recall, there was no defining event. Everything came in stages.

There was Noreen's pregnancy. She came to his digs, green-gilled, to tell him. She kept pulling in her breath, hard, so that Charles thought she might cry. But she didn't cry. She sat on his bed, and said,

'I wasn't going to let you know. I was just going to sort it out, and not tell you.'

Charles squatted in front of her, resting his hands on her knees to balance himself. He said,

'Oh, no. You couldn't have done that.'

She was looking past him. He began,

'Noreen—'

But her eyes locked suddenly on to his, warning him off. Don't start. Don't even suggest it. Frank Farrell still had first claim, and always would, as long as she believed he'd be back again.

So Noreen went off for a 'visit to her mother-in-law'. She told the lie openly, with confidence, as she left Peg in the care of the landlady of the Tudor Arms, trusting in Peg's peevish silence. The landlady put up a camp bed in the spare room. Peg went to sleep among empty boxes and broken chairs, listening to the drone and occasional outburst of the public bar, mulling over her mother's fib.

When Noreen returned she was laconic and preoccupied. Charles had never known her that way, and it made him slightly afraid of her. But that passed; that wasn't the end of it. In some ways, it even drew them closer together. Charles went to the house in Terrace Street every evening, late, after Peg had gone to bed. He and Noreen said little; had a drink, undressed, went to bed; Charles made sure he left the house at first light. Then one night he woke to hear her weeping, and when he touched her arm she turned immediately towards him. They cried together, wet faces pressed against each other on Noreen's damp pillow.

Then there was the second scare. A false alarm, as it turned out, but enough to change the way she embraced him. She became cautious. Tense. Holding him off.

That wasn't the end, either. They carried on. They became comfortable in each other's company. Frank's absences were, if anything, more protracted, his return visits briefer than before. When he did appear, he looked worn out and ill. He still had the pencil moustache, but nowadays it looked frayed and outdated and silly. When he disappeared again, even Noreen showed signs of losing hope. She was more reckless, less nervous, when Charles was there. She stopped glancing from the window, as she had used to, checking that Frank wasn't striding up the road. They made decisions, she and Charles. He broached the subject of their future a couple of times. She usually ignored him but one night, when Frank had been away many months, she heard him out, hardened her mouth and fists in a swift reflex, and then said,

'Right. Come on. Let's get on with it. To hell with everyone.'

Charles, still in his 10-shilling-a-week digs, was doing well at work, and saving. He helped her buy the house. It was a down-payment. An investment. It was for *their* home.

He came to the door in broad daylight. He embraced her before she had time to shut the door. He ambled from room to room with assurance, and a genial, proprietory interest. He examined the little silver pill box on the corner shelf, and the mirror over the fireplace, and the piano – lid down, as usual. He fingered the flowers carved into the dark wood above the keyboard.

'You've never played the piano for me,' he said, imagining this to be a new and significant point in their relationship. He saw himself leaning against the piano while she played something sentimental and personal.

Noreen, standing uneasily in the doorway behind him, said, 'I can't, love. Can't play a note. Wouldn't know where to start. I'll never get rid of it, though. It's my mother's, that. I'll always keep it.'

She sounded defensive, as if he might haul it away.

'My mother,' she added, 'was a proper piano-player – real playing. Classically trained.'

Charles was touched by her insistence. He tried, surreptitiously, to lift the lid, but it was locked. Noreen explained that her mother had started off playing for ballet classes, then went to work in the cinemas. All the big features. *Anna Karenina. Thief of Baghdad.* Matinées and evenings, dressed like a countess, with her hair piled in glossy, meringue swirls on top of her head, she'd sit gazing up at the giant characters, mapping out their fate, tracing their silvery expressions on the keys. Then the talkies came along and Noreen's mother was out of a job. Stayed at home, all afternoon, all evening, ruining her hands scrubbing at the grate and peeling potatoes, always in her drab old pinny, hair yanked back into a stringy bun. She hardly ever touched the piano again. If Noreen tried pawing at the keys she'd be shooed away like a cat.

This was the first time Noreen had mentioned anyone from her immediate family to Charles. He decided that this was a milestone. He had a twinge of that old self-confidence again, the same surge of conviction he'd felt in 1943: This is how life should be.

He wanted to give notice to Mrs Keating. He wanted to bundle up the curtains and the greyish bedding and the two-ring cooker and chuck them all out of the window and slam the door on his digs once and for all. Not yet, said Noreen. Wait a while. Let's just be sure. Give it till Christmas. If he hasn't come home by then, I'll *know* he's gone for good. She saw the suspicion in Charles's eyes, and hugged him, and said, 'I'm superstitious, that's all. Just till Christmas. Then to hell with him. You'll move in here with us, and I don't care who knows. It's no home of *his*.'

Charles wondered if she'd mentioned anything to Peg, but he didn't want to push his luck by asking. He barely saw the girl anyway. She was a fleeting presence, a sound of footsteps labouring upstairs to her room, a casual call to her mother, diplomatically avoiding any room where he might be.

December came. They went for long walks, through Waterloo Gardens, across the Heath, down to Roath Park and round the boating lake. Arm in arm, they paused to watch the ducks waddle on and off their islands. Noreen snuggled against his side.

'I don't care,' she said. 'I don't care who sees.' She looked up at him and her face was bright with cold. Charles said,

'Come on, Reen. It's nearly Christmas now. When we going to—'

'Just till Christmas, love. Then I'll be *sure*.'

Charles was sarcastic. 'Right, well, you let me know when I've got Frank's permission to get on with my life.'

Her mouth sagged; she looked old. He was sorry. He twisted his arm from her grip and put it round her shoulders, and said, 'Take no notice of me. Looking forward – that's all.'

'Not long now, love,' said Noreen.

Two weeks before Christmas, Charles was wrapping a gift he'd bought her. A brooch, in the shape of a half-moon. He wasn't good at choosing presents, but he knew Noreen would make a great show of delight, and be kind. Mrs Keating knocked twice on the door and opened it. There were no locks on the tenants' rooms. Mrs K liked to remind them whose house they were living in.

'Your *friend* called by,' she said, sour-faced, and handed him a note. It read: '*Don't come to the house. F. turned up this morning.*'

Don't come to the house. *My* house, she means, thought Charles, and sat down hard on the bed, tearing the gift paper. That bastard, he thought. I'll kill him. He bent double, squeezing the note in both hands, and rocking to and fro.

Maybe that was when it all ended, then. Except that Frank, as usual, didn't stay long. In fact, he left before Christmas Day.

'Before he had to bother about presents,' said Noreen. She'd come to let Charles know the coast was clear. It was Boxing Day evening, and she was on her way to her shift at the Arms. Charles was unnerved, opening the door and seeing her there, in her oyster-grey mack and rainhat. Only an hour ago he'd been sobbing: tearless, difficult sobs – all that Charles could produce. When she arrived, he'd been wrestling over a poem, mulling over the right word to describe the colour of her hair. He was caught off-guard, seeing her at close range again. She was exhausted, and less substantial than his poem-Noreen.

'Glad to see the back of him. Peg cheered up when he'd gone – said she'd been dreading Christmas Day with him there. What kind of a father brings a girl up to feel like that?'

'Well, he hasn't brung her up, has he,' said Charles. He moved to block the trestle table and his scribblings from her sight, as she sidled in and sat on his bed.

'He's not well, you can see that,' said Noreen. 'Smoking like a chimney. Looks like Death on a good day.'

Charles was awkward, unsure how long she'd stay. He said,

'Maybe he found a better nurse somewhere else.'

'Must keep an eye on the time,' said Noreen. 'It'll be busy tonight.' Charles stood with his hands in his pockets, waiting. Then she said,

'Look, I'm going to get some cash together, soon.'

'What for?'

'Start paying you back. It won't be much but . . .'

'Pay me back?'

'The loan. For the house.'

She had never referred to it as a loan before. Charles was angry.

'Forget it,' he said. 'It's a gift.'

She looked ridiculous, sitting on his bed, making no effort to remove her mack or her hat.

'A late wedding gift,' he added, 'for you and your husband.'

She didn't react. She sat back and leaned her head against the wall, and within a few moments had dozed off, snoring in her throat, the rainhat sliding comically over her eyes. Charles padded back to his poems.

8

So there are no final conclusions for Charles to recall. By 1960 – he is certain of this – the real Noreen did not exist: no more than any other acquaintance he might pass in the street. Once or twice he had seen Peg, serving at the Tudor Arms – her mother had wheedled her a job there. She was in her twenties by then, chubby and fair-haired and no less moody by the looks of it, with a small, wilting, poppy-red mouth. She and Charles barely acknowledged each other; Charles doubted whether she recognised him.

He can't understand how he came to be going to a dance, on a double date, and with Vernon, of all people. He does remember that, at thirty-one, he was worn out, and set in his habits. He also remembers Vernon's increasingly frantic gibes at him – at them both,

'Look at us, then, couple of old likely lads running wild. Can't tie us down, can they, boy?'

And there were girls. A drink at the Arms, a hurried grope and shudder in his room and goodnight, before Mrs Keating bolted the front door at midnight.

Vernon was working for a backroom bookies – 'Emlyn would be proud of me, boy' – and had his eye on the woman who ran the hairdressers' at the front. She had a sister, a redhead with an infectious but indiscriminate laugh. Charles couldn't dance. Why would he let himself be persuaded to steer this ginger-haired hyena round a sweaty hall all evening, while Vernon grinned at the hairdresser's cleavage? Loneliness, perhaps. There was that.

A band was playing – a scaled-down, poor-man's big band. It played out-of-date songs: 'Red Roses for a Blue Lady'; 'All or Nothing at All'. Most of the people there were Charles's age or older, and they sang to each other as they danced: *Long ago and far away, I dreamed a dream one day, and now that dream is here beside me . . . The stars at night are big and bright* (clap-clap-clap-clap!) *Deep in the heart of Texas!*

There was a bar; there were tables at one end of the dance floor; there were narrow rectangular windows set high in the walls – but Charles cannot put a name to the place. Some haunt of Vernon's, probably.

Charles was taking a drink to the redhead – something sweet

and viscous – dodging past animated groups on the margins of the floor. Peg Farrell was standing alone, arms folded awkwardly around a small red handbag. She wore a pale violet jacket over her dress – a short one, with three-quarter sleeves that rucked up into her elbows. Charles was surprised to recognise somebody in this place. He said, 'Hello!' without thinking.

Peg, straight-faced and startled, said 'Hello' back.

She may not have known who he was.

His memory trips there, and rushes him on – how long? A few minutes? A couple of hours?

Peg has taken her jacket off and is sitting at a chair with her back to the table. Who's sitting round that table? The redhead and the hairdresser? Or have they all been dismissed from the evening already? Is Vernon there?

Charles is squatting next to Peg, straining to hear her muted replies. He's probably a bit drunk. Her lipstick has smeared very slightly over the line of her upper lip, and he's fascinated by it. He *must* be drunk. She's telling him about someone called Dave. Dave is a member of that band – he's the drummer. Dave the drummer. Yes, they're local boys. Yes, they are very good. That's part of the problem. Always travelling, always doing the coast, the Midlands, here there and everywhere. He hardly ever seems to be with *her*. Peg Farrell is a bit drunk too. She shows him an engagement ring, stretches out her fingers and waggles them. The next moment she's picking the loose skin on her lip, and admitting that it's not *officially* an engagement ring, but it serves to keep her mother off her back.

Her mother.

In his cushioned, alcoholic haze, Charles notes a jitter of response in his chest and between his legs, but he doesn't give it much thought.

Flashes of movement, then: vignettes passing in and out of oblivion. Charles and Peg dancing. Peg's stomach and breasts against him, the heat of the hall and the press of dancers, the sweat inside his collar and running down the backs of his legs. Peg peering back among the heads and shoulders towards the band. Charles grasping her chin in his hand and turning her face to his, saying, Come on, girl, don't waste your time on him. Have some respect for your elders. Peg laughing at that – and it's uncanny, the way her nose twitches, and her eyebrows lift, as the laugh gathers pace.

He might be getting confused, though. It's too long ago, and he'd had too much to drink. Charles has difficulty knowing whether he feels her warmth, or imagines it. Whether Charles Lightfoot clutches Peg Farrell close against him, or watches her toiling round the dance floor in someone else's arms. Maybe Charles the spectator, who can't dance, is creating false memories for future use, as he sits at a sticky table, watching his brother grab at Peg's dress and buttocks.

And later, much later, falling into the damp, cold night – How does he know about that? Is it really Charles who pulls Peg down into the dripping shrubbery, fumbling and tugging, taking handfuls of her, mouthfuls of her, taking his revenge? Or is it Vernon who tells him about it, sharing every salacious detail, forcing his whispered secrets on him, as he did when they were boys?

'I says to her, I won't tell. She never give a peep.'

9

Nine years had passed sinced Henry VII's accession. The honeymoon period was over. Before his victory, the king had wooed the people and their poets with emotive soundbites. He would reclaim for the Welsh their 'erst liberties'; he would deliver them 'of such miserable servitudes as they have piteously long stand in.' The poets had welcomed him as their champion, their saviour; for many years they called him Owen – 'Owen the Deliverer', after his grandfather, the Queen's lover, and after their hero, Owen Glyndŵr.

Nine years on, what had been delivered?

To the ambitious, the gentry, 'Middle Wales', Henry had delivered unhindered access to the top jobs and titles. He had delivered efficient and profitable laws of inheritance. For this favoured section of society, Henry VII put his policies where his mouth was: sweeping away restrictions and native laws, handing out grants, gifts, annuities and appointments, allowing the Welsh to be 'as other loyal Englishmen'.

To the poets, with their dreams of old glories, political separation, freedom from the Saxon yolk, there was only spin: a new Prince of Wales, called Arthur.

In 1485 Ieuan ap Gruffudd was among those calling for independence. By 1494, he had felt the benefits of integration. He was John Griffiths, a man sufficiently secure in his financial and social standing to make plans for his own personal dynasty. His bride was selected and summoned to London – a decision based perhaps on financial negotiation, perhaps on social compatibility, perhaps on a past betrothal. The sole surviving correspondence, dated May 1494 and addressed to the girl's father, Humphrey Meyrick of Penfynydd, is essentially a business proposition. It deals with practical issues: Griffiths' income and status; the dower, and the travel arrangements. But there is a touching postscript, a note of reassurance for an anxious father: 'I swere on my faith and by the Grace of God that my good wyf will know non but prosperite and true faithfull love.' With that, all recorded trace of Anne Meyrick and her fate disappears.

She must have had an uncomfortable and perilous journey to her new home. There were no carriages – not even for the daughter of an affluent farmer – so Anne would have ridden, with her father and their small retinue, along the treacherous roads and tracks. But we may trust that she was gratified by her change in circumstances. She left a land *ravaged by centuries of poverty, lawlessness, blood feuds and social change. Having, perhaps, plighted her troth many years earlier to an idealistic poet with few prospects, she could now present her father with a favourable match to a respected court official.*

Whether or not the union was a happy one, we are never likely to know. It seems not to have been productive: no records exist to suggest the establishment of a Griffiths dynasty – none of the documents of bequest, claim and inheritance that we might have expected to find. If there were children, they may not have survived very long. Infant mortality was high, even among the rich. Over half of those born did not see out a full year.

In 1494, however, Anne Meyrick faced a prosperous and hopeful future. The wedding must surely have been a joyous occasion. The bride and groom, decked in their best satins, velvets and brocade, processed to church accompanied by musicians and maidens carrying bride-cakes. As a man of status, John Griffiths was permitted to marry inside the church, rather than outside the door, as was the custom for the lower orders. John promised to take his wedded wife, 'for bettere for worse, for richere for pourer, for fayrere for fowlere, in sycknesse and in hele'. Anne swore to be 'bonere and boxsom in bedde and atte bord'. Communion was taken. A veil was spread over the couple and blessed. Then it was home for the wedding feast: quail, venison, eels, peacock, salads and sweetmeats. Finally, John and Anne Griffiths retired to the bridal chamber, accompanied by their guests, who competed to catch the fair bride's lucky garter.

10

Livvy doesn't realise, as she stands outside the door to Gal's flat, how much she resembles her mother. It's Peg's single-mindedness, Peg's pig-headedness, that override Livvy's shyness, and blot out other people's response. Livvy won't be welcome here – far from it. She's under no delusions. Knocking at Gal's door at 9 o'clock on the morning after his discharge from hospital – it's an intrusion. He'll be annoyed – he might not even hide it. But Livvy won't let that hinder her progress. She has her goal and she's making for it. Livvy is her mother's daughter.

Ordinarily, Gal would have seen her off. He's had unwelcome attentions before – school pupils, colleagues – and he knows how to cope. He can be firm, brisk, but friendly; barring entry to his private world, without giving offence or making lame excuses. But Gal – as Livvy suspects – is not himself. He's tired. His head throbs. He's been badly shaken by this blacking-out episode; he hears and sees everything from the far end of a tunnel. He's in no state to shoo Livvy out. So she barges in, makes coffee, sits at the small, square table in his kitchen and begins her assault.

'I've been churning it all up lately,' she says, 'what I know, what I don't know. Coming back here, doing up Nan's house . . . Death seems to stir it all up, doesn't it? When my mum died, and when I lost my nan last winter – it was like people disappearing, but leaving this cloud of, of *stuff*, all swirling round my head before it settles.'

Livvy notes the fractional widening of Gal's bruised eyes. He's intrigued, despite himself.

She cooks him lunch – nursery food: sausage and mash. She ladles it out with her commentary, feeding him on her past, her mysteries. Frank, an enigmatic figure in a wedding photograph. Her father, faceless in her musical dreams. She says,

'There's so much, all tangled up. You're a writer – you can untangle it, make it into something. Give it sense.'

She won't stop; she talks on. 'In my family, men were just people in your head. They weren't real.'

She makes tea. 'This tale of my father being in a band. I don't even know if it's true. I used to think, That's why she pushed me so hard, with my music – to remind her of him. But that was stupid. She didn't want to think about him at all.'

Gal rests his forehead on the tips of his fingers. He tries not to hear. A modern opera, based on absence, she urges. A central character who never actually appears.

Gal says, 'It's all good stuff, Livvy. But I can't pretend I . . . I've got commitments of my own. This is *your* story, and you're quite capable of . . .'

'But you can tell it!' she half shouts. She fixes him with heavy earnestness. 'You're a writer. You show people how to write. You change their lives. It's *your* skill, it's your . . . *craft*. You can *help me*.'

Gal shakes his head, but he's lost track of his own argument. Why can't he do it, after all? Why shouldn't he apply himself to this idea? What reason can he find to run away from it? And besides, a shape is appearing, the outline of a sculpture or a sound. It doesn't seem so much: providing the structure. Filling in the words. Gal is always telling his classes and groups, always telling them – Start with one word. One line. Let it carry you to the next. Don't be afraid of your own voice. Time and again, he's told them that. How difficult can it be to practise what he preaches? The more she talks, the more possible it seems.

As Livvy waits for the bus home that evening, she lets herself shiver – not with fear, but with anticipation. She licks her dry lips, and considers the taste in her mouth. She thinks of Gal, crafting and polishing and paring her story into a work of art. A gift.

It's dark when Livvy leaves. Gal is wounded with exhaustion. He can't imagine surviving another day. Meshed into his fatigue is the background noise of Livvy's curtailed vowels, drooping around her two-note range. Livvy's mother, Livvy's grandfather, the imprecise grievances, the obscure indignation, whining and sliding through everything she says. Gal feels sodden; soaked in Livvy's past. In his concussed fug it occurs to him that this may now have become his own past, a forgotten past, uncoiling from her, coiling again around him, suffocatingly familiar.

He tries to revive himself, to set rational questions:

What exactly happened here today? Wasn't it just a visit? A nuisance? Why don't I simply brush her off? Why not flatter and encourage her, advise her to write the damn musical herself, while excusing myself and backing away . . . ? That's all I need to do, isn't it?

But an irrational phrase knocks persistently against his questions:

She has taken possession.

She arrives again the next morning, with a bag full of groceries, talks and unpacks the shopping, talks and drinks coffee, talks and cooks him lunch.

She says, 'My mother said playing the piano would be my way out. Out of her life, she meant, if you ask me.'

She says, 'I reckon my mother hated Frank. Hated her own father. So she got her own back on me, by not giving me a father at all.'

Gal finds himself wondering how her obsession will translate itself into her music. He wants to hear it. Another part of him says, Get out now. Get out of her past.

The following day, Gal decides to take refuge with James and Cat. He leaves the flat early, and reaches Terrace Street before James has gone to work. He rests there all day, avoiding the front room, where he might find Livvy spying through the window; and he stays for supper. He tells them about her visits, trying to mock her and entertain them, but he's not comfortable. Absurdly, he feels like a traitor.

'A pop opera!'

Cat flops on to the sofa next to Gal, holding her glass high to steady the wine.

'Not exactly . . .' he says. They've finished their meal, and he's succumbing again to his semi-concussed detachment.

'You could always introduce her to your Fresh Starters,' suggests James.

'That's right – leave her to the tender mercies of Madge Probert. She'll soon have her running for the hills, and her pop opera with her.' Cat takes a mouthful of wine. She's edgy this evening, and distracted. 'Who wants to know about *her* boring life, anyway? Mr Lightfoot, now – he's a *much* better subject. Bittersweet story of doomed love – couldn't do better, if she's after a hook for a musical.'

As if in reply, Livvy begins to play next door. Complex music, entangling with itself and pulling away.

'One of her compositions, do you think?' whispers Cat, wanting to laugh, on the brink of hysteria. No one answers.

'For God's sake, don't let Livvy wheedle you into something you don't want to do,' says James, suddenly.

Gal moulds himself into the corner of the sofa, away from Cat.

'I'm not.'

Livvy's music battles on, cutting across their conversation, until all they can do is sit and listen.

11

Two packing crates have been placed side by side in the middle of the floor. Livvy snaps out a white tablecloth and lets it drift over them. From the doorway, Gal watches her. His face is waxen yellow, one eyelid is pink and swollen, but the bruising is gradually fading away. Livvy smooths the cloth over the grain and ridges of the crates.

'It'll have to do until my real furniture comes.' She looks up, remembering. 'I asked James and Cat round later for a bite to eat. Since they're always looking after you.'

Gal ignores the accusation. Ignoring her won't do any good, though: he's established that. For a week since he left hospital, Livvy's kept up her visits to his flat, or summoned him to Nan's house, hammering out her themes, dogged in her conviction that they will create a piece of work together. Gal is overwhelmed – by her conviction, and by an alarming intimacy that infiltrates the air around them, whatever he does to ward it off. If he's sharp with her, it seems like the bickering of lovers; if he refuses to respond to her, it seems like petulance. Her stories are wound tight around him; the more he struggles to free himself, the more ensnared he becomes.

'So. Have you been writing?'

She's turning towards the piano, lifting the hair away from the back of her neck. It's not seductive – just a habit. She lifts her hair, and drops it; it's dry and prickly, like hay.

'Have you written anything?' she asks again, and Gal wants to hit her. No, he wants to wring her face, like a flannel.

'Not yet,' he lies. And I never will. You are nothing to do with my life.

He can't say that, though, because it's too late. She's here, padding round her home, in bare and rathery grubby feet. And he's already given in. There's a notepad to prove it, on his table at home, covered in his lazy italics, scored through with lines and crosses.

'Give it time,' she says. 'You're not yourself yet.' She sits at the piano and Gal, defeated, inches further into the room.

The problem is that he's made a start. If only he'd dismissed the whole scheme, refused to accept that he could or would write a libretto, and carried on with all his other projects, as before. But he's *considered* it now – the narrative, the characters; he's started to write, and he can't deny that even to himself. He sits, he writes – perfectly ordinary, functional words, logically arranged. He knows, as he writes, that it's not falling into place. It's not becoming anything – but that just makes him puzzle and pick over it all the more. He should be happy, intoxicated, at the fact that he's writing anything at all. Instead he's raging like a drunk, with a head full of coherent ideas and a mouth full of garbage. That's what it is: garbage. Waste. He scatters words around like empty packaging. They lie across pages waiting to be swept away. He reads over them. They reek of effort.

But this is his skill. This is his craft. It's what he teaches. What he's supposed to *know*. There must be some mistake.

Livvy's fingers are dawdling up and down the keys. Gal says, 'I can't spend too much time . . . I've got other priorities . . .'

'You'll manage,' she says; then, quickly, 'Listen to this.'

Her right hand paces out a 10-note phrase: E, up to C, down to G#, C, back to E, F#, G#, C, B, A . . .

She sits with her thumb on the A, brooding. Chords shift in her head, taking on their own characters. This will be Peg, then – a magnificent, monstrous Peg, lumbering through sinister chromatics. Semi-tones clash, and Livvy's bossy, ambitious mother is upgraded into a villain. Livvy listens to the harmonies, hoping to separate them into tangible notes. She plays the phrase again. Gal can't help hearing the music as an unfinished, raw sound that needs to be closed into consonants and sense. It must be possible to find the right words. They must exist. He doesn't have to invent them: just make his choice. It's what he's supposed to do.

'Do you know about the voice of the angel?' says Livvy. 'When you play some chords, you hear an extra note. Even though you're not playing it. Your brain provides the extra note, to complete the harmony. It happens with singing, too. People call it the voice of the angel.'

She says these things – she has a knack of throwing these notions at him. They irritate Gal, stay with him, hover over his notepad every evening.

Livvy lays her hands lengthways, wrist to wrist, along the keyboard, and presses out a low, poisonous dissonance that sounds like vengeance.

'We're going to do this,' she mutters, mostly to herself.

A large fly hurls itself under the slightly raised sash window, veers noisily around the room and bounces off Livvy's hair. She shakes her head once, tuts, and gets up. 'Shut the door,' she orders. She walks at the fly, gradually guiding it towards the window, reducing the circle of its flight; it comes to rest on the window-pane. Gal is seized with terror, sure that her moist hands will snap shut around it, that he'll hear it sizzle and cling to the paste-coloured palms.

'Don't kill it!' he cries. 'Let it out!'

She's already done it, scooping the fly downwards with one hand and lifting the window higher with the other. She looks at him with interest.

'Of course. What did you think I'd do? Eat it?'

James has brought cushions to put round the crates. Cat brings extra bowls and mugs.

'It's not very comfortable,' says Livvy, 'but I wanted you to be the first guests in my new home.'

She ladles out pasta. Cat lowers herself cautiously on to a cushion.

'Are you all right, Cat?' asks Livvy.

Cat laughs and colours deeply at the confidential tone.

'Yes, don't worry about me. Once I'm down, I stay down.'

The taste of pasta is tinged with paint fumes. Cat raises a beer bottle. 'Well! A toast to your new nest.' She twists about to appreciate the mint-white walls. 'You've done a sterling job.'

'Thanks.' Livvy kneels at the crate and pushes her food around with a fork. 'When I've moved all my stuff in,' she says, 'you'll have to come round for a *proper* meal. Won't they, Gal?'

Her fork taps against the bowl. Gal is sitting opposite her, his legs folded at an awkward angle. Since the accident his upper lip has tended to drag at his teeth, setting his face in a snarl. He ignores Cat and James and their quizzical eyebrows; his eyes scorch angry holes into Livvy's skull.

Eventually, Cat says,

'I shouldn't think I'll be here by then. I've got to let James have his house back, at some point.'

'Stay as long as you like,' says James, dutifully.

They all eat slowly. James wonders whether it's conceivable for a whole evening to pass without anyone breaking the silence. Livvy is indifferent, as far as he can tell. She tackles the pasta, which is on the rubbery side, spearing one piece at a time with her fork; she doesn't seem to expect anyone to talk. James's mind ricochets from one vacuous line to another. As usual, Cat gets there first.

'What about your musical, then, you two?' (passing James a disbelieving look on 'you two', which he gratefully accepts). 'How's it coming along?'

'It's not—' starts Gal, and simultaneously,

'Quite well,' says Livvy. She continues, 'We're not in a mad hurry. Better to get it right. Gal's got it all under control.'

'Come on, then,' Cat touches the back of Gal's hand, trying to break the spell. 'Give us a taster, gorgeous.'

He looks at her, sees the pleading humour in her eyes, and wants to grab her hand, share the joke, make a run for it.

'Just a snippet,' urges Cat.

'At least tell us what it's about,' says James.

Gal smiles, is about to answer, when Livvy interrupts:

'It's about the way people haunt us.'

Gal's smile evaporates. He corrects her:

'The way we're shaped by others. Even by their absence.'

'Mm . . .' Cat chews at her pasta. 'Bit like you, then, James. You're haunted, aren't you? By Ieuan Gloff.'

'Not exactly.'

'Yes, you are.' Cat turns to Livvy. 'I hear him sometimes from the other room, swearing at this dead poet. I think he's overworking.'

Livvy asks James, 'Do you dream about him?'

'Sometimes.'

'I dream about my father. Even though I never met him, I dream about him all the time.'

Here we go, thinks James. Cat is nodding in that infuriatingly concerned way.

He says, 'Odd things, dreams. Apparently most people dream about the royal family quite a lot. I dreamt about Melvyn Bragg the other day.'

Cat starts to stack the empty bowls.

'I think dreams have a purpose,' says Livvy. 'I think they're a way of communicating. Without being blocked off by space, and time . . .'

James juts his lips forward and pretends to consider the matter.

'Shall I help take out the bowls?' Cat starts to get up, but Livvy is already standing. 'No. Stay there. Gal will give me a hand.'

Cat and James sit glumly on either side of the packing crates, waiting for Livvy and Gal to return. They don't speak, or even make faces; they just watch each other, reassuring themselves and each other of their sanity, and their alliance.

Livvy has made coffee in a 1950s percolator that her nan had and never used. It has a long swoop of spout and a wooden handle. The coffee is thick and strong.

'I always remember my dreams,' she says, handing mugs to Gal to pass around. 'I think we should keep hold of them. We wouldn't have them, if they didn't have some purpose.'

'I don't know,' says Cat, 'What about the appendix? That's pretty useless, by all accounts.'

'We *must* have them for a reason,' says Livvy, stubbornly. 'If James is dreaming about his poet, he should take notice of it.'

'Recurrent congress with a 500-year-old hermit nationalist,' says James. 'Freud would have a field day.'

'Incidentally,' says Cat, 'what star sign are you, James?'

Livvy presses on. It's the only strategy she knows.

'If you wanted to understand about your poet, you'd have to know about *his* dreams.'

James is rattled. 'Not much chance of that, though, is there?' he snaps.

'You won't find out much about him, then,' says Livvy.

'But I'm not concerned with dreams. I can't be. Dreams aren't to do with . . . I mean, whatever they may tell us about ourselves, they don't have a past or a present: they're not reality. They're not part of our common experience, of history, and time. They're just . . . reflections.' He nods at the percolator, where a slice of Livvy's face wavers in the chrome.

'Look. That reflection might show you something about yourself. But it's not going to tell me much. Not as much as the *real* you does.'

Cat has transferred her attention to Gal, who's swaying slightly at her side. She says, in an undertone, 'Are you feeling all right?' but he doesn't notice. He's listening to James and Livvy, turning from one to the other as though he can't quite catch their words.

'The point is,' James says with kind finality. 'My business is the past, and the big snag about the past is that it's gone. All I can do is piece together what's left. Records. Relics. I fit them together, as best I can. That's what it takes – clues; common sense; rigour; detachment; and my best guess. That's the most useful and honest approach I can take – and it's got to be based, as far as possible, on facts. Things. Not fantasies. The past is not in my dreams. It's not anywhere. That's why I have to reconstruct it. Because it's gone.'

He yanks up his sleeve to reveal his wristwatch.

'Time marches on. That's my problem.'

Livvy pulls her mouth into a brief, frosty smile. 'You can't pack everything into past, present and future. If the past is finished, how come it's still in my head? Your watch can't measure what's in my head.'

Cat clears her throat. James says, lightly,

'Oh, don't go down that road, Livvy. You'll put me out of a job.'

He tugs his sleeve back over his watch, having established that it's only half-past nine. Can they decently leave at ten?

They drink the treacle-rich coffee. Livvy has taken down Nan's curtains; the windows darken, and the air grows cold.

'Personally,' comments Cat, 'I never remember my dreams. I'm not sure I dream at all. I know we're all supposed to, but . . .'

'We're all haunted,' says Livvy. Cat splutters gently into her mug. 'We've all got a . . . a No-Man's-Land.'

James stretches his face in disbelief. Cat says,

'Go on – what do you mean, exactly?'

'It's when you're not sure . . .' Livvy sees Gal lower his eyelids; she doesn't care that Cat and James think she's rambling. Gal will register her thoughts, and make something of them. 'It's when you're not sure if you're remembering a dream; or remembering something that really happened, or making it up. But it's . . . closer to you than anything else. More real than daily life. It's more important than dreaming.'

James feels a creeping of horror and excitement: is she actually insane?

'Being here, in Nan's house,' says Livvy, 'I get it all the time. It's full of ghosts, here.'

Gal sighs. He wants to laugh with James and Cat at Livvy's faery world. But it's entering his system like smoke, sapping his energy. At home, at night, he finds himself mulling over it, this nonsense. Testing its value, asking himself whether such lunacy has a merit of its own.

'Half-cock, half-digested New Agery.' James chucks his keys on to his desk; they splash onto a scattered pile of Cat's papers.

'The pasta wasn't much cop, either,' comments Cat, releasing her armful of warm cushions.

'I can't believe Gal is *actually*—'

'Oh, no. He *can't* be. That's just make-believe, on her part. Wishful thinking. *Must* be.'

James switches on the desk lamp and sweeps papers aside, searching for something.

'I don't know, though . . . You saw him, sitting there in a daze. He doesn't seem to know what's hit him. He's like some old boy watching Thatcher take over the Tories.'

Cat smiles. 'Maybe she's just *nice* to him. I mean, our Gal's not immune to a bit of unquestioning adoration, is he?'

James makes a spitting noise. 'Come *on*. Sleep with Lugubrious Liv, just for the sake of a little flattery? Never. Never, ever. That would be . . . that's like care in the community.'

James forgets his search and strolls to the window, hands in pockets.

An elderly woman, stooped and padded in several layers of clothes and an anorak, plods through the beam of a street lamp, with her shopping trolley full of bottles jingling behind her. Cat says,

'You look like one of those pensioners who watch the cars all day. Close the curtains.'

James follows the woman's laboured progress and tries to imagine where she's going.

Cat says, 'Anyway, Livvy's not so bad, I suppose.'

She switches on the main light and softens her voice. 'Why are you so cross?'

James is straightening the papers on his desk back into piles.

'Oh . . . just . . . some barking pseudo-buddhist, droning on about dreams, and . . . no such thing as the past . . .'

He abandons the papers, and starts picking up the cushions.

'I mean, what *use* is all that drivel? What *good* is it? How do you *deal* with life, if you refuse to put it all into some kind of . . . *order*?'

Cat follows him into the back room. He stumbles over one of her discarded shoes, kicks it into a corner and lets the cushions fall at his feet.

'James . . .'

'I tell you, if that woman thinks living next door is going to be all cosy popping-round-for-dinner . . .'

Cat, beside him, takes his hand.

'Listen. I want to tell you something.'

He turns towards her, and immediately she pulls her hand free again.

'Did you know . . .' She projects her voice self-consciously, away from him. 'Did you know that all a baby's bits and pieces are developed by twelve weeks? Amazing, isn't it? Well, nearly all, anyway.'

She steps across the cushions and on to the armchair, sitting with her knees to her chest and her heels on the edge of the seat. A pewter light glints through the French windows halfway into the room. 'The genitals don't form till nineteen weeks. Last to arrive, first to go, you might say.'

'You're going to have it?'

In his effort to be neutral, James makes the question flat and robotic. Cat hugs her knees, rocking slightly.

'Sounds easy, doesn't it? – "I'm having the baby." I'm having a bath; I'm having the soup of the day. It *is* easy, I suppose. You just don't *do* anything. The baby's in there, not going away, making the decision for you. One day, "I'm doing nothing" turns into "I'm having a baby", everyone breaks into a cheer, hang the bunting out, roll the credits.'

James doesn't know what to ask. There's a quick pulse drumming at his neck.

'What now?' he says. She leans into the shadow; he can't make out the expression on her face.

'Good question. What do I do now. Er . . . go home, I suppose, and wait around. Wait around for a few months, for this total stranger to come barging into my life and take it away. Bit like the bailiff, isn't it?'

She rests her forehead on her knees.

He says, 'Cat—'

The phone rings.

It rings four times. Then a click, and James's staccato voice on the answerphone. Cat looks up.

'Isn't that Sonia?'

A hum, another click, and the machine turns itself off.

'Look, Cat,' says James, 'You can stay as long as you like.'

'Thanks. I must get shifted soon, though. Places to go, people to see, money to earn.'

She worries at her thumbnail. She's realising that making her announcement hasn't helped; she still hasn't made her decision. She says,

'Thing is, I keep thinking I know what to do, and then . . .'

These past few days, every time she's tried to argue a clear case, for one course of action or another, her thoughts have been frazzled by the crazy notion that Livvy Farrell's gimlet eyes are upon them.

James settles on his knees on one of the cushions. He feels close to Cat this evening. He wants to be helpful and valuable to her. He wants to talk to her about comfort and security, make her feel easier in her mind. He wants to share his reflections about his parents, describe them swapping their daft sayings over the sink, tell her about their ossified rituals, about the way they console James, and frighten him, and hurt him. He's relieved that he didn't tell Gal about her situation; this evening, he revels in the privilege of keeping her confidence.

'I've been thinking about my parents,' he says. 'About the indignities of old age.'

Cat snorts. 'James! They're not *old*.'

Seized with guilt, James drops his theme. (Besides, he assures himself, their age was only an indignity when *he* was there to witness it.)

Cat's head snaps up, as she takes in his words.

'Were you going to say I should have a child as some kind of insurance policy? To look after me when I'm senile?'

'Of course not.' James is clutching at the seam of another cushion, rubbing the material and squeezing it with his fingers and thumb. He sees again the three women, with their backs to him: his mother, Gal's mother, Cat linking the two. He sees himself, looking at them – smaller and further away in his memory: small and harmless, and unnecessary.

'Another thing,' says Cat. '*I'm* quite old. In pregnancy terms. There's always the risk . . . you know . . . it won't necessarily be a healthy, bouncing bundle of joy.'

James can make out the glitter of book spines behind her chair. As her resolve slips this way and that, he fixes on the neat line of titles, until they expand and loom across his vision. His territory. He's startled by a vision of himself, tugging out books, paddling at them with alternate hands, flinging them into a heap on the floor.

Cat eases her legs into a stretch, preparing to get up.

'Scary,' she says. 'Too scary to think about. Maybe it's *completely* the wrong thing to do. And you have to say, life's pretty reasonable as it is. Why upset the applecart?'

James is up on one knee, still clutching the cushion.

'Is that enough, though? Pretty reasonable . . . ?'

Cat's on her feet now, arching her back, with her hands at the base of her spine.

'Well, you don't need to worry about that,' she says. 'You're not an irresponsible slut like me. You can just potter along as you are.'

'Potter along! Yes . . . thanks.'

'No, you know what I—'

'You're right, though. Even Lugubrious Liv is right. It's all bollocks, isn't it? Pottering along, looking for . . . well, I don't know – facts? events? Dead people's histories. That's my life sorted: that's what I do. I sniff around dead people. I speculate wildly about them, tell barefaced lies about them sometimes, so that another generation can come along after me, and go sniffing around themselves.'

'Sniffing around themselves?'

'That's it. That's my life.'

Cat stands with her hands supporting her back, her featureless face towards him.

'I didn't think we were talking about *your* life. One crisis at a time, please. I'm the one who's meant to be hormonal at the moment.'

'No, I mean – I mean, that's what I *am* talking about.' Stop now, James tells himself. Take a step back. Switch the bloody light on. But he wants to tell her. 'Do I want to spend all my life scrabbling about in the past? You know – what about the future? There should be a future. There *could* be. It doesn't have to be just . . . *me*. You see?'

He can hear her breathing.

'Oh,' she says. 'Oh. I see.' She lets her arms drop to her sides. 'And you reckon . . . *I* could provide you with a future. Yes? Me and Baby. How convenient! And, hey – you didn't even have to do the tawdry stuff! Just wait for Matthew to do the biz, dump her; let her dither about for a bit – then, when she's ready, step in with the home-assembly family kit, and away you go. What a brick you are, James. What an honourable thing to do. Gee thanks, Mister.'

James sinks slowly back down as she picks her way across the room to the door.

'And how jolly decent of Sonia to clear the way like that! I take it she *has* cleared the way? Was that her calling, just now, to congratulate the happy family?'

Cat slams the door behind her. James, kneeling in the dark, hears her shout from the stairs:

'Fuck you, James Powell. You already blew your chance.'

'Did you hear that?' Livvy pauses with her hands in the washing-up bowl. 'That shouting? Nextdoor?'

Gal carries on wiping cutlery. 'Just the usual, I expect. Cat letting fly about something.'

Livvy shakes soapy water off her hands, and dries them with the other end of the tea towel, which Gal immediately lets go.

'It must be good,' says Livvy, 'to be off the leash, like that, with someone. They're very close, aren't they.'

Gal says, 'I'd better be off.'

'But they're very exclusive, too. Not with you, of course. With me. They think I'm stupid.'

'No, they don't.' Gal is putting on his jacket, patting the pockets for his keys.

'Not stupid, then. But they don't think I *count*. They don't think I . . . *qualify*.'

'Of course they do,' he mutters, absently.

'No, Gal.' He cringes at the use of his name. 'You don't know. It's different for you. People *want* to know what you think. With me . . . sometimes it's like I'm invisible. I say things, but nobody takes any notice. Why *not*? They can't have all gone deaf. But that's how it is – they don't hear me.'

She stands nursing the stacked bowls in her arms, demanding a reply.

Gal flicks a hand at her.

'Forget it. It's not you. James can be a pompous arsehole sometimes.'

He doesn't look at her, in case she's smiling. He shuffles into the hall. So now he's slagging off his best friend, to keep Livvy sweet.

'Oh, James is all right,' she says, indulging him. 'And he's very fond of you, that's obvious.'

Gal says, sternly, 'I'm going home.'

'Right. Let me just put these away . . .'

He hears the rhythmic clink of plates from the kitchen. She catches him up as he reaches the front door.

'Go home and rest. I'll call you.'

Fighting the next wave of lethargy, Gal faces her, determined to make one last bid to take matters in hand.

'Look. Livvy.'

She narrows her eyes. 'We'll arrange to meet. Bring your first draft, and we'll . . .'

'Livvy, you know, I've got a lot on my plate . . .'

'Yes. But I know you can do it. You *will* do it.'

Gal searches for a formula. He wants to be gracious; friendly, dispassionate, conclusive. The silence mounts. Anxious to shatter its significance, he blurts out,

'Livvy, look. This past week you've been *wonderful* . . .'

He sees the smug rapture on her face. He sees her tip her head back, eyes closed. He can't think of anything to say.

Livvy almost forgets that Gal is there; that he might contradict, deny, open the door, walk away in spite of her. But eventually she recalls herself, opens her eyes again and regards him with a conviction and trust that make Gal feel physically sick.

He could pretend not to notice. He could start again, just say goodbye, casually, as if nothing has happened. But he's gripped with fear – of using the wrong words, of triggering the wrong reaction . . . He's lost faith.

Livvy steps forward and reaches out, watching him but not reading – or not accepting – his resistance. Her long, cold fingers extend towards the palm of his hand.

Oh, for Christ's sake – Why doesn't she *grab* my hand? Gal thinks in disgust. Why does it have to be a *test*?

He doesn't know what else to do. In an angry stupour, he closes his hand around hers.

PART SIX

i

'Satan's arse, Gwilym! Are you snivelling again?'

Gwilym pressed the fat heel of his hand against his eye, then took a draught of the claret he held in his other hand.

'You have no soul,' he drawled.

He was slumped in his chair by the window, spying with little interest on the passers-by below. Squares of light fell through the glass and framed the stains and bare threads of his shirt. I stood in the doorway and curled my fingers hard into my palms.

'Listen.' I tried to be calm. 'Why don't you go back? Go home. Comfort your brother. Weep over your father's grave. It may ease your grief.'

He shook his head, and was shaken by another sob.

'My poor father . . . never knowing if I'd lived or died . . .'

'Well, give thanks for that, at any rate. At least he could hold fast to the hope that his son met an honourable end in battle. Better than seeing him slide to hell with Gluttony and Sloth for companions.'

Gwilym's habits had not changed. In nine years he had grown bloated and sluggish. He was seldom approached for 'favours' now; the few coins he did earn were from a day's labour here and there – lifting barrels, or delivering messages. Bolsters of flesh had closed around his bloodshot eyes. When distracted he would tremble gently, head and arms and hands, sending showers of droplets over the rim of his tankard.

He gave a sniff, ripe and resonant as a fart.

'Let me be. Let me mourn in peace.'

I realised, as I watched him blub into his drink, that there was nothing left of our bond. Nine years of watchfulness and clever dealing at work had worn down my fear of lonely nights and my hatred of the city. My visions had faded, along with my verse. Gwilym had a room of his own, at the opposite end of the house. Everything about the man was without purpose, including this great act of sorrow. It was seven years since his father's death. He'd never spoken of his family after Bosworth, and if he hadn't shared a drink with that drover he'd have gone to his grave without giving them another thought. But Gwilym had fallen to prattling with this cattleman, who, as luck would have it, had walked through Trefin on his way to London, and had met a man who'd married a sister I never knew Gwilym had. The drover's gossip brought the old world surging back, and Gwilym learned with a shock that he had been an orphan since 1487.

'Go home,' I snapped again. 'Find your brother, get yourself a wife and go back to the anvil.'

It was a tired joke. He wouldn't have the strength to walk back to Wales, even if he was inclined to try. His jowls rippled as he turned towards me.

'What good am I to a wife these days? What man who loved his daughter would give her to *me*?'

I say that we had no bond of friendship left, but I wasn't unmoved by his despair. I approached his chair, fighting the urge to recoil from his stinking clothes and breath. I patted his dank shoulder.

'Come on, Gwilym. Rally yourself. Go and light a candle for your father, make your confession and bring your friend the priest home to supper.'

Gwilym would confess his sins only to Father Sebastian. I had tolerated their friendship in the hope that it would influence Gwilym for the better. As it turned out, the priest gave penance freely before suggesting new and more interesting sins to recount the next time. I could hardly complain; I went to him myself, to confess to my own daily deceptions at the dockside. He knew they were necessary to keep Gwilym clothed and fed, and was always indulgent.

That night, though, Father Sebastian was no help at all. Gwilym was worse than ever. Abusing Mrs Mytton, spitting at the candles, while the priest pleated himself into his seat, sniggering and dribbling wine down his chin. There was little I could do; after all, the supper had been my reckless idea. I drank to keep them company. When they snorted and guffawed over some puerile anecdote I smirked as best I could.

Gwilym thumped me across the shoulders.

'My good old Johnny Lame! My ugly bard!'

I sat there, poker-backed, waiting for them to set off for the stews, or pass out on the spot. I could bear it a little while longer, as long as I knew it would end.

Gwilym handed Sebastian the pisspot under the table. The priest fumbled under his robes. Steam rose from the shadows and the air was filled with an acrid smell.

'Hey! – You know what?'

Gwilym lurched forward from his chair, crashed against the table, scattered plates and saltmaiden and almost set the place on fire.

'You know what we should do? Johnny, here – sorry, the great *bonheddig* Mistar Griffiths here – he should tell us a story!'

I should have walked out and left them to their roistering. Instead I kept to my place and said, in a moderate tone,

'No, Gwilym. Never mind that.'

'Oh, yes, yes, Gwilym, mind it!' He stood shakily, then wheeled about in the excitement of his idea. 'You're a poet, aren't you! Come on – play your part! Tell us a tale!'

'He's not a poet,' slurred the priest. 'He's a thieving snatcher of duties and bribes . . .' He leaned towards me, set the brimming pisspot on the floor and nodded with grave piety. '*Sed ego te absolvo, portitor furas.*'

'Come on!' Gwilym was lumbering round the table. His cheeks and forehead shone crimson. I recalled my first sight of him, all those years and miles away, and the apparition of his future self.

'Come on, poet.' He was growling, now. Threatening. In recent years he had been known to plunge into sudden violence. Mrs Mytton had a scar on her temple to show for it. The genial, childlike Gwilym of the past was as dead as his dear old father.

Two shovel hands landed on my shoulders and crept towards my throat. He brought his fierce face up to mine.

'Tell us a poxing story.'

The trouble was that my stories had gone. Ieuan Gloff, who could conjure a legend for every boulder and lake in the land, who could shape a verse for every Christian occasion, who remembered every name, fate, tree and sheeptrack on his patch – Ieuan Gloff had forgotten the lot. The priest was right. I was Johnny Lame, now, Mistar John Griffiths, whose head was full of rates and duties, tunnage and poundage, rules and how to break them.

Gwilym's paws pressed around my neck. Father Sebastian, giggling in his corner, suggested:

'Tell us about your angels.'

Gwilym had boasted about my 'secret' hoard of coins. They had even spent a couple of evenings, the two of them, snuffling like pigs around the floorboards, and rummaging through my bedclothes, in a half-hearted attempt to find my treasure.

But the priest's taunt summoned another angel to save my skin.

'The angel!' I rasped. 'Yes, that's it – I'll tell you about the angel . . .'

Gwilym's hands loosened. While I coughed and caught my breath his fury dropped away and he began to whimper.

'An angel . . . to watch over my poor father's spirit . . .'

I stoked the fire and persuaded them to leave the table. I sat them in the traditional way, at my feet, below my words, so that they would listen, and believe.

I began.

I was out of practice, and the story formed reluctantly, shapelessly, in English. I lost my rhythm and tripped over phrases – but they were too drunk to know. Gradually I gained in confidence, mastered the words, and my skills came back to me. They had been in my blood all along, flowing under too many layers of frozen flesh.

I told them the tale of a young bard, in his first beard, striding across field and hill, fording rivers, braving forests to sing his songs wherever anyone would hear them. I told them of the storm sent by the devil to silence his song, the most terrible storm ever seen by man. A whirlwind of thorns to lacerate his skin. A downpour of rats to gnaw at his bones. A flood of bile to wash him to Hell. I described the light that shone weakly through the tempest, guiding the young bard to a meadow, and beyond that to a stream, and beyond that to a hillside, and into a cave in that hillside, and up through a tunnel in that cave – a tunnel that emerged on the high moors, where a cottage stood alone with an open door. I described the bard's trepidation as he crept into that cottage. I described the dark room that he entered, as wide as seven palaces, as tall as three church towers. I described the voice – a beautiful, ethereal voice – that called his name. I told them about the young bard's struggle to reach that voice; how he longed to find the lips that formed his name; how, despite all his efforts, his feet would not carry him into the centre of the room. How he edged his way along first one wall and then another until he found a giant hearth, filled with pebbles, and, among those pebbles, one sparkling gem. How he threw that sparkling gem into the centre of the dark room and was dazzled by an explosion of light. How he looked up, and up, and saw the angel-child, with her fair, soft limbs, and her copperflame hair, hovering high above him, entreating the young bard with her ocean-coloured eyes. I sang her song for them, 'O, bard of the simple heart, prove your love and loyalty and set me free . . .'

They were spellbound, those lackwits, the blacksmith and the priest. For the first time in many years I revelled in my power.

Where to take them?

What to do with that angel?

For three hours I led them through enchanted woods, fashioned magic swords, turned lovely damsels into slavering wolves and talking deer into ancient crones. Under my tuition the young bard met every challenge and passed every test, returned to release the angel and saw her transformed into a fairy princess.

We sat in the fire's dying warmth and contemplated her charms. Gwilym and Sebastian leaned against each other, almost asleep.

And then, like a fool, I told them her name.

A thousand London bells howled one o'clock and my companions were wide awake.

'She's real? A real angel?'

'Of course not. He's lying. Trying to impress . . .'

'Where are you keeping this angel then, Johnny? Tell us how to set her free!'

I explained that it was in another age, another land, but they would have none of it. They wanted to see her: a real, flame-haired angel; to touch her and own her and kiss her hem. It was Father Sebastian who tugged at Gwilym's sleeve and oozed,

'You've always said our poet should find himself a wife, haven't you, Will?'

I swear, I wrote the letter to protect myself. Gwilym had already shown his temper once that evening and I wanted to keep them sweet. I agreed to everything. I chuckled with them as we bent over the page, invented demands and conditions, riches and vows. The priest was the most devious of us all. He reasoned that I was, after all, an officer of the king, collecting cash for the royal coffers. A good catch, he mused. He even thought up a pretty line at the end, to smooth the way.

I would have put it on to the fire as soon as they had gone, but Sebastian insisted that I roll and seal it, and then tucked it into his robe, and the two of them, sober enough to need more drink, slunk out to visit a friend who brewed his own ale.

Even then, I wasn't seriously worried. I went to my bed. I had no thought that they would keep the letter. I certainly didn't credit them with the wit to track down Gwilym's friendly drover, hand him the letter and ask him to deliver it on his long walk back through Wales.

ii

She was shivering and wet. She stepped out of nowhere and addressed me in uneasy English.

I ignored her. One of Gwilym's whores, I thought. I kept a tight hold under my cloak on the day's private takings, and searched for the doorkey tied to my belt. Then she said, in Welsh,

'I remember your stories, Ieuan ap Gruffudd.'

I studied her face, but it was in the shadow of a hood, and the light was failing. She was an old woman, skinny, drawn, weary. She took down her hood to reveal dull, auburn hair. She stepped towards me, dropped into a deep curtsey, sank to her knees and fell against my legs.

Mrs Mytton helped her up the stairs. I followed, carrying the two small packs she'd left propped against the wall. We sat her by the fire; Mrs Mytton fed her some broth and gave her metheglin to drink. I still suspected some prank – a clever trick of the priest's, no doubt, at my expense.

She had come part of the way from Penfynydd on her father's horse, the woman claimed. Most of her belongings were lost when her servant made off with them in the night. I listened, stony-faced. She was not a convincing liar. Had Sebastian taken me for so willing a dupe?

Her own horse had become lame later on the journey, she said. A passing clothier took pity on her, and brought her the last 60 miles on his cart. They had reached London at first light that day. She knew where I lived – had it by heart, since the parish priest had read my letter to her father and herself. After the clothier had finished his own day's business, he had brought her here. That was her story.

She straightened herself then, and frowned at her surroundings. She said,

'My father thanks you most gracious, and begs to settle the matter of dowry when he hears I am happy and proper wed.'

I smiled, and replied, 'A rather unusual arrangement, don't you think?'

She turned at the cynicism in my voice – and there was something about the flash of trepidation in her eyes . . . Sea-green eyes . . . I glared at her haggard features. Could this really be the angel-child who'd enchanted me in a hundred dreams? Could a dozen years have turned my angel into this wizened old crow? Surely not. *Surely* not. Not her.

But I didn't throw her into the street. I let her talk on. I told myself I was playing along, seeing how far she was willing to take this game.

She apologised for her abrupt arrival.

Her father would, of course, have responded to my letter as was fit, she said. He would have arranged an appropriate meeting, done it all 'right'. She used the Welsh word, *addas*. But her father was not used to writing letters, she explained. And besides, there had been sickness in Penfynydd these last few summers. Four of her younger sisters taken. Her mother carried off with the Sweat, two years since. Her father was weak, too weak for proprieties. All he wanted was to see his daughter safe, and alive.

A feeble yarn. It crossed my mind to offer the woman to one of my merchant friends. She wouldn't fetch much of a price. She clearly was crushed by the effort of survival, whether on the streets or as one of a diminishing family. Four sisters . . . I thought of the farmer's wife, on the stormy night all those years ago, cooing and soothing her children, while I sat by the fire casting my spell on little Anne.

Eventually the woman stopped talking and leaned back, waiting for my verdict. I searched for something to say.

Then Gwilym appeared. He was sober for once. He hovered in the doorway, and his confounded expression told me that he, for one, knew nothing of our mysterious visitor.

I had to sleep beside Gwilym again that night, while the woman took my bed. The following day I announced my intention of sending her back to wherever she'd come from. I half expected her to spit in my face, call me a fool, and demand payment for playing her part. Instead she wept.

Yes, she had lied. She admitted that. Her father had been dead and buried two months before my letter arrived. And there was no one else. No thieving servant, no belongings to steal, no horse to go lame. No dowry. Only Anne, six graves and six wooden crosses. A few starving animals in a couple of weed-choked fields. A crumbling farmhouse, where she wandered around hand-in-hand with Death, waiting to moulder away into the Penfynydd earth. And then my letter had arrived. She took it to the priest, and he told her it was a miracle. An offer of hope. God clearly wanted her to live.

At this point, Gwilym pulled me aside. He grasped my arm and twisted it until I gasped. He said,

'I'll fetch Father Sebastian. He has marriage rites to perform.'

Wherever she came from, Anne brought peace to our household for a while. I wondered, from time to time, whether Gwilym had taken my story of the bard and the angel as plain fact. He treated Anne with exaggerated respect, if not a little fear, as if she might use her magic against him, or fly away. And maybe there *was* magic at work. The change in him began almost immediately. He found Father Sebastian and some approximation of a wedding ceremony took place in the dining room. When the priest blessed us he swivelled his lascivious eyes, flicked his tongue across his lips and winked at Gwilym. As soon as the last Amen was sung, Gwilym hauled him out of the room by the scruff of the neck and all but kicked him downstairs.

Gwilym drank only small beer with his supper that night, and every night that followed. He sat with us at every meal, passed Anne her food and watched her eat; he dozed by the fire while she sewed. He lost interest in the theatres and the alehouses. He didn't seem to notice that she was sickly and withered at no more than nineteen years old.

In those early months Gwilym didn't touch her. His reverence had its effect on me too. For some time I contented myself with light embraces or a mild bundling with my new wife. We were haunted by Gwilym's protective presence; if I treated her too roughly, I half expected that he would come thundering into the room and tear me limb from limb. During the day he followed her about like a dog. As I've said, she was no beauty – her shoulders were stooped and narrow; several of her teeth were black; her breath was rancid, and her wheezing shattered into a disgusting cough at the first sign of rain. But Gwilym brightened whenever she entered the room. His health improved. He began to grin in the careless, generous way I remembered from our early days. He even promised to find regular work. When I came home with tales passed on by the merchants and their crews of new lands with limitless gold, Anne teased Gwilym, saying he might earn his passage there if he could pick up an honest penny or two. And he believed her. After ten years of slow ruin with me, he bowed his head and changed his ways for one kind word from this girl.

A wise man would have accepted all this – treasured it. Never mind that I may have been tricked into marrying a beggar. Never mind that she showed me no affection – only deference – while she and Gwilym passed thoughts between them with their eyes. When she greeted him, her dreary cheeks would glow. Never mind. We were a strange family, but a family of sorts. Gwilym was himself again. I should have been happy with that.

iii

I don't know when it started to go wrong. My work was pressing on me – more heavily with every passing week. Supervision was more rigorous. Opportunities for private arrangements were rare. One of my colleagues was caught smuggling and never seen again. There were more goods to check, longer hours to keep, charts to study, standardised measurements to learn. The King's fist closed ever tighter around us all. My wife was obedient but listless in bed. Gwilym was attending church, but still had no steady income.

Sometimes the sight of Anne squinting and humming at her needlework made me all the more ill-humoured. I would snap at her, tell her to stop that tedious noise. And then Gwilym would rise from his chair with a warning in his eyes. He no longer had the full strength of a blacksmith, but he could break my head in a moment.

I saved my frustration for the marriage bed. There, I finally put aside my caution and claimed my rights. I would press my hand over her mouth. I would all but break her in half. Once I made her lip bleed; in the morning it was swollen and blue. That same night Gwilym waylaid me as I returned to the house. Shoved me into a fetid alley. Caught me round the chin and lifted me off my feet. Through gritted teeth, told me to 'Let her be'.

So I lay apart from her again, night after night, and watched the rise and fall of her protruding ribs.

Nights became months became years. Time slips so deviously, if you let it. Gwilym finally found work – making nails in the dockside smithy sheds. I grew more careful and sparing in my deals, and continued my official duties efficiently, invisibly. Mrs Mytton passed away. Her widowed daughter, Mrs Fogge, came to us instead, and had a better time of it, given Gwilym's reformed ways. We could have grown old just by letting the days pass. In the evenings they sat facing each other, Gwilym and Anne, saying nothing, seeing no one else. One hand of Gwilym's would have covered her face completely. I kept to my corner and played dice, squeezing the cubes so hard before each throw that they bit red wheals into the flesh of my hand.

Many nights I lay awake and prayed to regain my gift of prophecy. I screwed up my eyes and cleared my mind and waited for the flight to begin. Waited for it to carry me over the years, far ahead of these dungeon days. What would I see? A quiet, free dotage, eased with contentment and respect? Or a crooked cripple, kept like a dog, begging for scraps from the blacksmith's table? How could I know? My power had gone. I was chained to that bed, to that hour, to that night's jealousy.

Father Sebastian had kept well clear of Gwilym since the marriage, but he was still to be seen flapping back through the lanes at dawn. He had no fear of *me*. Occasionally, if I was alone, he would follow me, jeering at my limp, demanding 'donations for the church', as a price for keeping the secrets of the confessional. I generally shrugged away his insults, his salacious gibes about married life. 'What a holy trinity!' he sang. 'The blacksmith, the slut and their cuckold, Lame John!'

His song reverberated through my head. One night, when the air was heavy and moist, it threatened to stop my ears forever. I was close to madness. I could no longer lie like a corpse in my own marital bed.

God damn you, I muttered. My wife stirred in her sleep. Damn both of you, damn you to hell. Why should Gwilym alone claim her favours? Did he think he could take my wife's affections as freely as he took my food and dwellings? I levered myself on top of her, and she sighed – a thin, hopeless, whistle of a sigh. I knew she would not call out.

iv

There was a child. And yet it was not like a child at all. In such a walking cadaver, we might have expected to see the very first sign of swelling. But there was no curve in Anne's belly until a few weeks before her time. I lurked around my own home, avoiding Gwilym's glowering eye. He held his tongue, though, as well he might – given that it may well have been *his* child growing in her womb. Growing, and sucking away her last remaining energies. It ravaged her. For nine hours she screamed as it was dragged like a demon out of her. It surely *is* mine, then, I reasoned: conceived on a curse. Damned, and its mother with it.

There was death in the silence that followed. Gwilym and I cowered outside the bed-chamber. He seemed about to break into pieces. Then there was a bellow from the midwife, and a crack of noise, which became a long, soulless wail. The door was opened. The midwife wiped her hands. Anne, sickly and glistening, was rumpled among blood-spattered sheets. In her arms lay a limp, fleshless creature with an ancient face. The wail came from Anne's dry mouth.

'May God have . . .'

Before Gwilym could finish, the midwife had given the child's dangling foot a brisk tweak, and one of the ancient eyes opened. The wailing stopped, as Anne slid, senseless, to one side.

'Well,' said the midwife, snatching the child from her arms before it fell. 'You have a baby girl, but for how long . . .' She shrugged.

We stood there, in the half darkness. Presently Gwilym turned, said, 'Do what you must,' and left the room.

I handed the midwife some coins. I was all thumbs; I nearly dropped them.

'Take her away,' I said, 'before the mistress recovers her wits.' It had to be done. The child was barely breathing.

v

Anne was not the same, after the child. She couldn't rise from her bed for several weeks. She would eat only pottage and crumbs, administered by Mrs Fogge. She had no words, no smiles – not even for Gwilym. During her confinement, Gwilym had insisted that I make up my bed in his room. As the weeks passed, he refused to let me return to my own.

'You have crushed her already,' he said. 'Do you want to snuff her out altogether?'

This from the man who – I did not doubt – had helped himself for years.

Eventually Anne found her legs again, and even found a little appetite. She spent her days languishing in her chair at the window. She had neither the strength nor the desire to sew. Gwilym was at her side every possible moment – guarding her openly now against my presence. Any stranger would have taken them for a poor aged mother, protected by her devoted son. Well, he needn't have troubled himself. One look at that broken body was enough to dampen any man's ardour. I may have hankered after the comforts of my own bed, but Anne was not among those comforts. Let Gwilym have her, and God's blessings on them both.

The weeks trickled on. My only conversations of any length were with the merchants and – unless I could avoid it – with Mrs Fogge. Holidays came and went. Gwilym and his charge sat them out by the window. Anne seemed to have resigned herself to her lot; not for the first time in her short life she felt Death's eyes upon her. But I began to detect signs of restlessness in Gwilym. I caught him drumming his fingers, or looking askance at my solitary dice games with something like envy. He even left the house, once or twice – left her there, with only Mrs Fogge and her fiend of a husband! – and 'took the air' for an hour. Aha, I thought. Even an angel's magic can wear off.

Another holiday: Midsummer's Eve. The Vigil of St John. Stray sounds of festivity reached our windows. Anne sat as usual, impassive, surviving from breath to breath. Her chair was pushed back from the sun's heat; Gwilym stood behind it, tapping his fingers idly on the frame.

I wandered out, thinking that I might watch the minstrels' parade, and sauntered among the crowds and the dust and the fumes of scorched meat and ale and stale vomit. I took my time. I wouldn't be missed. I took a look at the mummers and the sweating dancers; stopped to cheer on some wrestlers and cudgel-players; slaked my thirst with a jug of cider. The sun passed its zenith and the sky cooled. The streets grew noisier as people gathered ready for the evening procession. I decided that I would stay out all night among the revellers, rather than return to that tomb. I allowed myself to be jostled by the thickening crowd, and half-heartedly tried to manoeuvre myself into a good place from which to see the triumphal march.

A voice mewed at my shoulder,

'Not brought the fair mistress out to enjoy the fun, then?'

God's teeth! Even in this crowd Father Sebastian had tracked me down. He must have slipped like a snake between legs and under skirts. I looked resolutely ahead and hoped someone would tread on him.

'Poor Mistress Griffith, left all alone, abandoned by her husband *and* her mate!'

Spectators turned in shock or amusement; a woman said, 'For shame.' But the priest had never been cowed by public outrage. He whined on.

'What's up with our old friend Will the Blacksmith, eh, Johnny? Back to his bad old habits, is he? Or does he take communion in the Waterman these days?'

Despite myself, I was curious. The Waterman's Tavern had been a favourite of Gwilym's, in his wayward days. Had he really deserted his post for an evening's relapse? I imagined him fidgeting in my house, alone with Anne's rasping breath, losing sight of the daylight above the rooves, listening to the whoops and screeches and laughter outside, to the lutes and the games and the hurdy-gurdies, and the shouts of sudden anger and rebuke. No great wonder if he'd made his escape again, and hurried off for a taste of wilder times.

With considerable difficulty I elbowed my way back through the crowd, away from Sebastian, stepping on toes, tripping over children and dogs, fending off mouthfuls of abuse, until finally I broke free into a clearing. I took a few minutes to find my bearings, then lumbered into an alleyway, heading for the river.

The Waterman was a foul-aired cellar of a place on the edge

of the mudflats. I knew of it by reputation. Gwilym had spent many a long curfew locked in there. When I arrived, it was already crammed to the rafters, and bursting out on to the bank. I plunged into a storm of belches, filthy songs, passionate arguments, hawks and gobs. Some drunkard was raising toasts:

'Long live the King!'

'A toast to St John!'

'A toast to my dear beloved friends!'

Each one received a hail of cheers and obscenities.

I battled into the middle of the room.

There he was.

Towering over his companions, nursing a tankard, watching two intense players at a game of Primero, with the serious air of a man who might take a wager. It was some time before he noticed me. An ale-wench flung me aside with one broad hip, and my staggering drew his attention. Helpful hands were clutching at my sleeves, preventing my fall. He stared.

'John, man!' He was yelling, unsmiling, over the din. 'Never thought to have seen *you* in a hole like this!'

I felt the press of bodies around me. I took courage from their heat.

'And I didn't know you'd crawled back into it!' I hollered back. 'What about Anne? Have you brought *her*?'

He set his head forward like an angry bull, regarding me from the very tops of his eyes. But he won't kill me here, I told myself. They won't let him. My throat closed. My voice was a squeak,

'Does she know what you are?'

Where you are – I had meant to say *where*.

He slammed his tankard on the card-players' table, to a flurry of protests. I retreated against a wall of drinkers. One or two turned around; there were low words of warning.

Restraining hands on Gwilym's arms.

Suddenly he relaxed. He had lost interest.

'Pah! Go to the devil.'

He was searching for his ale again, laughing to his friends, 'Not worth the trouble. Just a poxy tax-collector.'

This was greeted with groans and insults. He shot me a look of triumph. Go on, it said, tell her. Give me away. Just try it. I'll make you pray for death.

There had been a time, long ago, when this man would have given his life to save mine.

They were still hooting at me, vile names and catcalls. Oh, yes, tax-collectors, straight into hellfire, that's where we'll all go, with our heads up the arses of the priests.

He had turned his fat back to me now, rounding his shoulders into the card-game, as though I had never been there. My lungs filled with rank air. I coughed it out, barking,

'I am not a tax-collector! I am a poet!'

It was a plea: remember, Gwilym.

Around me, laughter and a ragged cheer.

'Ay! a poet!'

Remember.

He stiffened, but did not turn.

'Go on, then, poet' – from behind me – 'give us a verse!'

'A ballad! Sing us a ballad then, rhymer!'

Strong hands were propelling me to a bench, hoisting me on to it, so that I swayed and flailed for support. Still no response from the blacksmith.

'Sing! Sing!' They began a driving chant. I stood, floundering, in a void. Help me, Gwilym. Help me.

'Sing! Sing!'

'He doesn't know how!'

'He needs a purseful of taxes to get him started!'

'*SING!*'

And the lines came in a rush:

 '*Gadael gwlad, gadael glendid – gadael*
 Aelwyd glyd, a golud . . .'

A chorus of squelching imitations.

'He's rhyming in tongues!'

'What's that gibbering, tax man?'

 '*Gwae'r dderwen ddiwreiddyn . . .*'

Higher, louder, I sang; warbling, crooning, diving in melodramatic swoops. The booing grew more impatient.

'A ballad! Give us a jaking ballad!'

'What's he saying? Summoning Old Nick?'

A good-humoured barrowman tried to step on to the bench and guide me down. 'Come on, Taffy, that's right, sit down and have a drink in peace.' But I reared away, almost falling off in the process. I regained my balance. My singing grew more insistent.

 '*Diddosi dyn wna'i dyddyn ef . . .*'

A knot of lads in the corner began to moan and whinny in accompaniment. On an impulse I broke off and turned on them:

'English arseholes! This is poetry! You're too fatheaded to—'
'Run him through!'
'Take the Welsh bastard out and drown him!'
'Villains!' I screamed. 'Cowards! English pricks!'

I toppled forward on to the table. Tankards fell; ale spilled; tempers boiled. And then Gwilym was there. He hauled me over his shoulder and started to wade towards the door. Hostile hands clawing at my doublet and hair; a shower of ale and saliva against my skull and neck. He held me fast with one arm, cleared a path with the other:

'Leave him! I'll deal with him – leave him!'

A couple of my assailants squared up to him as we reached the door, but we passed with no more than a threat and a clout on the ear. Gwilym wrenched us free of the tavern and we were out in the evening air. The sun was low: the mudflats glittered. He set me on my feet and muttered,

'Go on. Scuttle off home. And don't go bothering her – I'll be right on your heels.'

Some boneheads had followed us out to see us off their territory.

'That's right, back to your slum,' called one. They began shuffling back into the inn. We were safe. With Gwilym's help, I had got away with life and limb intact, and that should have been an end to it. I'll be right on your heels, he had said – but in fact he was joining the drift back into the tavern. I could do as he ordered, scuttle away, watch the parade and tend to my wounded pride, and pretend I had never heard Father Sebastian's insidious voice.

Why didn't I go? What did I want? Hadn't I longed to be rid of that savage, who had changed his face so many times along so many years? – my bluff friend, my brave comrade-at-arms, my debauched and parasitic burden, my persecutor, my rival, my enemy. Why not let him slink back into that pit, let him slide back down to damnation? Why should I care? I would have been glad of his ruin. I feared and resented him and often wished him dead. But he had turned to leave me there that evening with such profound contempt. And I could not bear it.

Before they had all passed back indoors, I gave a desperate shout.

'What, are you scared of me?'

They paused; one or two sniggered and cocked an eye at my audacity.

'Scared to show your fists to a Welshman, or what?'

They were slow. Reluctant. The trouble was over now. One stiff-legged runt of a tax man – it was hardly worth the bother. These men had been drinking all day; they dithered between apathy and fire. I bawled,

'Come ON!' – and jutted my two fingers up in deliberate, sober provocation.

That was enough. They were fixed on me again, baring jagged teeth and yellow eyes. Murderous hands groped at the hilts of daggers. I waited.

I saw Gwilym hesitate. I saw him take in the brandished blades, the prowling advance. I saw the appalled realisation. I saw him look at me, and I saw the words he mouthed – 'Run, Ieuan. Run.' – before his face blossomed again into a thousand wounds and melted away to the skull. My gift had returned.

He must have lashed out at them, grabbed at collars, cracked heads together. He must have brought one or two of them down. I heard his roar and their baying as I fled. After fifteen years of limping I was practised and nimble. I hoicked away, collecting speed from the sound of pursuing feet. I veered across waste-ground in the direction of the city. Drumbeats and reflected flames were floating down the river. I locked my mind to them, my whole strength: thudding heart, thudding drums, thudding feet, all overlapped and fastened to each other. For a moment, for a passing moment, I seemed to be running in the air, just above the ground.

The footsteps had gone. They had given me up. I risked catching my breath and peered back across the flat land, to the tavern's battered torchlight.

It was too far away. Maybe my mind played tricks. But I thought I could see him then. Still standing, surrounded, a bull in the ring. I thought I could see the closing circle of killers, the soundless lunge of their arms, and the shadows that leapt in time to their stabbing pulse.

vi

I darted up lanes; I splashed through drains; I careered into holiday-makers, into the blaze of light and the blare of music, and back into rustling darkness. I reached my home, grit-lunged and panting. No sign of Mrs Fogge; she must have seen her chance and sneaked out to enjoy the parade. I climbed the stairs like a spider, on hands and feet, and clutched at the door to the parlour. Anne was struggling to stand; her cheeks and eye-sockets were black in the meagre light.

'What is it?' she said. 'Where's Gwilym?'

I pressed my forehead hard against the edge of the door. My whole frame pounded with terror. I tried to control it, to tell her. As the shaking subsided, I became conscious of something else: a terrible, unthinkable hunger. It wrapped itself around my thoughts and my body. By the time I spoke, I was almost composed.

'He's at the Waterman,' I said. 'Drinking again.'

She leant against her chair. I hobbled towards her. She was as weak as a child.

'Come away,' she said. 'He's not there. I'd know if he was.'

I moved from the window; I couldn't see the road anyway – only myself, in the glass, and the room behind me, picked out by the candlelight in gold and bronze. She was hidden; her voice crackled out from some unlit, cobwebbed corner.

'Come away from the window, and tell me a story.'

Oh, yes – she spoke to me now. Every evening she had something to say – the same request to make. She had taken courage, I think, from my guilt.

It started that same night, that Midsummer's Eve, when I was curled on the bed beside her, wracked with remorse and self-disgust; that same night, she had said my name, for the first time in months.

'Ieuan,' she said. 'Ieuan – tell me a story.'

Her voice was like dead leaves: it had no humanity in it, no hope. I gawked at her bow-back. All I wanted was to beg her forgiveness.

'A story,' she said again. 'While we wait for Gwilym to come home.'

The curtain billowed to a gust of noise from some passers-by. My stomach churned. If Gwilym comes home, I was thinking – if he sees what I've done . . . he'll pull me after him to hell . . .

I tried to collect my wits. 'A story . . .' At least it would occupy my mind.

So the night passed, marked by bells, and by more bells, and by flashes of music, and I told her the tale of the magic cauldron that brought the dead to life, and of the man who cracked its sides with his great bare arms, and cracked his own heart in the process.

Every night since then, she had demanded this penance. Every night she called me away from the window, assuring me that Gwilym wasn't there. Every night I sat by the fire and pieced together another lost legend, while she lolled in her chair and drooled, a ghastly parody of the little girl who had fallen under my spell so long ago.

I tried to explain Gwilym's absence. He'd fallen in with his old cronies, I said. He'd done this before, in his old life – gone off on his adventures, stayed away for weeks on end, then suddenly reappeared. Maybe, I suggested, maybe he'd fallen into the river when he was too drunk to tell earth from water. She agreed. Maybe. She nodded, vaguely. If she fretted after her lover, she gave no sign of it. She only called me to her side and asked for stories.

The fairy of the lake, who could not bear the touch of iron.

The baby who was spirited away, and left by a monster in a stranger's stable.

The secret cave, where a giant blacksmith hammered out mighty shields.

The beautiful woman created from flowers, who betrayed her lord and was turned into an owl.

Night after night I grubbed them all up from the recesses of my mind – the wizards and the kings, and the evil boar, and the lovelorn knights and the warrior giants and the slender-necked, spell-binding maidens. I traced their journeys, their setbacks and victories, with precision, though every creak on the stair, every scribble of mice behind the walls made me jump in my seat like a rabbit. At any moment the door might swing open and Gwilym would be standing there, sliced with wounds, covered in his own blood.

During the day I was slow and clumsy at my work. I expected to be summoned, asked, accused . . . There had to be questions:

from the watchmen, who must have heard of trouble at the tavern that night, and come running . . . from the foreman, who was missing a worker at the smithy . . . A man doesn't simply vanish, like one of my bewitched characters, and leave no questions behind.

But no one came. A month, two months – nobody wondered where he was. He had no real friends, after all – only drifters and alehouse companions, and they had gone their own ways while he sobered up for Anne. The foreman would have found himself another strong pair of hands. And watchmen saw trouble every night. There was only Anne, and she didn't seem to want to know.

I need never have seen the Waterman again; there was good reason not to see it. But in the early evening, after a day's work, I had taken to following the slimy track down to the mudflats. The tavern was always busy – always a band of young dock-workers and boatmen pressing in at the door. I kept my distance, of course, and was careful not to be noticed. I don't know why I went. There was nothing to see.

I had been there again, watching, one evening in early autumn. I was beginning to feel the cold, and I had turned to start back along the bank, covering my nose and mouth against the river stench. A movement ahead made me look up. A featureless, hooded figure stood in my way. I cried out. I almost dropped down dead on the spot.

'Ieuan,' said the parchment voice. 'I came to find you.'

She approached, and I saw the ashen face in the folds of her cape and remembered that first encounter, when I had taken her for a whore. She was even smaller now – an ancient, dwarfish woodland witch.

'How did you . . . Are you here alone? Where was Mrs Fogge—?'

I put out a hand to support her – but hesitated, intimidated by the ghost of Gwilym's disapproval.

'I came to find you,' she said. 'At the quayside. I saw you leave, and I followed.'

'Well, I . . . I'll take you back,' I said. 'You shouldn't . . . I was only . . . I thought I might find Gwilym here.'

We walked, slowly, away from the mudflats. She was ahead of me, picking her way with caution on those feeble legs. The track began to climb to higher, dryer ground, leaving the silt at the water's edge. A little further along a row of small boats, moored to their posts, nudged and rode the swell. Anne stood uncertainly for a moment.

'Where are the boatmen?'

'At the tavern, I shouldn't wonder.'

I stood behind her, while she summoned the will to go on. I said, 'Why did you come to find me?'

She turned, and she took my arm.

'Never mind. I'll tell you another time.'

We continued home, for all the world like a loving man and wife. She asked for no stories that night, but ate quite a healthy supper.

'Well!' said Mrs Fogge as she cleared the dishes. 'Good to see you perking up at long last!'

I stayed away from the Waterman the following evening. I finished my work and went straight home, composing a story in readiness as I went. A tentative future had presented itself. John Griffiths, servant of the Crown, and his devoted wife, Anne, mourning the loss of their friend but finding consolation in each other. Passing the evenings at their fireside, telling tales of miracles and magic. No more bribes. I would give that business up for good. A peaceful, secure, honourable old age.

But she wasn't there. I searched in the parlour, in our bed-chamber, in Gwilym's room (where his hay-and-ale scent still lingered in the air). Mrs Fogge came fussing up the stairs.

'I don't know, sneaking out again in this sharp wind, and never says a word to me – or I'd have put her off going, Mr Griffiths, and her in that state.'

The nights were shorter: the streets were already dim as I limped along, drawing my coat closer about me. God help me – had she gone to look for him? Would she really go to that place, on her own? I kept an eye out for watchmen – they'd be on patrol soon, and wanting to know what brought a gentleman out of doors at this hour.

A low band of light lay over the horizon. I slithered down the bank to the track. Not a soul. From the city, the bells rang the hour. A barge sailed by, and in its wake the moored boats knocked and rattled. I heard a cry, or an indistinct word. I peered at the pale curve of the nearest boat, till the dusk deepened and resolved into a small, seated figure.

As I lugged my bad leg through the mud, she was already inching away from the bank. Somehow she had cut through the mooring rope, and was letting the river do the rest. I fell forward, grabbed the rim of the boat, splashed helplessly after it – up to my thighs, my waist – and finally managed to heave myself on board. The boat pitched and swung to my efforts. For some time, we sat opposite each other, holding its sides, while it settled and turned its nose from the bank and set its own lazy course down the river. When it seemed safe, I groped under the seat to untie the oars.

'I'm sorry – I threw them into the mud,' said Anne.

Another barge washed past and set us rocking. We were invisible to the river traffic. Panic prodded at my bladder. I wailed,

'We'll be drowned!'

No answer.

'If you're looking for Gwilym . . .' I said. I couldn't shake off the suspicion that she knew where to find him.

We drifted on.

Soon there was nothing except the pinprick lights of London, the lapping water and the glimmer of Anne's face. Then, the echo of bells: another hour gone.

'A story,' she said.

'Anne . . . By all that's . . . We must get to the riverbank. Let me call for help.'

'A story. One more.'

'I *can't* . . .'

'The last one. I swear.'

There was a vacancy in her words. An absence. I was afraid of what she might do.

'There . . . Well . . . There was once . . .'

I tightened my grip on the sides of the boat.

'There was once a young bard . . . who strode across field and hill . . . forded rivers . . . braved the forests to sing his song . . . wherever there was anyone to hear . . .'

The night grew colder. The boat followed the water's leisurely rhythm. The blackening sky swallowed the city's last lights, one by one.

The bard proved his love for the girl with the fair, soft limbs; he found his way through the perilous woods, killed the demon prince with his magic sword, set free the fairy princess and took her hand in marriage.

I listened to Anne's gravelly breath.

Presently, she spoke. I had to lean forward to make out the words.

'Ieuan. I am with child.'

A couple of waterside scavengers pulled me ashore, three miles further down the river. I was worth more to them dead than alive, and yet they gouged the filth from my mouth, squeezed the water from my lungs and picked the worst muck and rubbish from my face. They cackled and talked as they brought me back to life. One ale too many, was it? Thought I'd go for a swim, did I, to clear my head?

I spluttered and retched and spat and shuddered, and could not turn my eyes from the river.

'Ay,' said one, 'she's a treacherous bitch. You don't want to sink into *her* arms in a hurry.'

'That's right,' said the other. 'If you don't know her ways, you're better off keeping to dry ground.'

I thanked them and shared their fire, and let them prattle on till daybreak.

But I would have waded out again, if I could have. I would have plunged head-first into the murk with my hands bound behind me, if I could only reclaim that vision. A serene and silvery vision: an angel, hands raised, lips parted, her gown rippling, her hair flowing loose in a fiery cloud.

1

'The market was an exciting place in those days. Not like these supermarkets and shopping malls. It was full of interesting smells and noises. Full of surprises. Like going to the fair.'

Madge Probert's voice rumbles from a speaker in the wall. The volume is high: she seems to have her mouth against the listener's ear. A five-year-old girl stands beneath the speaker, straining her head back, rapt, gazing at a giant sepia picture of Ernest, Florrie and Sid under a huge sign: 'M E Hatchetts, Purveyors of Best Quality Meats.' Cut at an angle into the edge of the picture are smaller images: Madge and Arthur Probert on their wedding day; a startled toddler on a street in Cardiff in 1933; a baby's christening in 1957.

The five-year-old girl's elder brother is rifling through papers and scrapbooks secured with coloured ribbons to a table beneath the display. He closes a notebook marked *'Grateful for your comments'*, having just written 'boring' and 'your ugly' in tiny letters at the bottom of a page. He moves along the table to a fat wedge of paper and begins to read aloud:

'Ex-tr-act of a man-u-script soon to be pub-lished as Madge Probert's first novel, *Tilly Comes to Town*.' He twists himself into an expression of agonised outrage and complains, 'Wot, *this* cra—' before dodging a swipe from his mother.

From within the hall comes the chatter of visitors, the clink of glasses and a confusion of other recorded narratives, criss-crossing, competing, interrupting each other, over and over again.

Elen Rabbaiotti's laugh blankets it all for an instant.

'Bloody 'ell, Harry, it's only one free glass of wine each – innit, Mr G? That's his *third*! – pay up!'

Elsewhere in the hall, Rose Lewis's daughter, Irene, shunts her youngest grandchild higher on to her hip, and tries to direct the child's wandering attention to a photograph of ten-month-old Rose, almost obscured under a vast, nebulous, frilly bonnet.

'Look, Lindy, there's your great-grandma! See the picture? See?'

'Ab-bap!' squeaks Lindy, reaching across Irene's shoulder, apparently trying to throw herself at the passing figure of Gal. Irene, who has brought her own daughter and granddaughter down from Bristol especially for this exhibition, examines the display of pictures, printed to overlap like a deck of cards: Rose as a girl with her parents, outside the grocery emporium; Rose and Freddie and the boys; a badly composed shot of Rose, Len and pudgey Irene on a day trip to the seaside.

'Aah,' Irene sighs, leaning closer to focus on the family group. 'Look – you and me and Dad. He loved a walk on the prom, didn't he, Mum?'

Rose snarls from her chair and tries to remember what Len loved and what he didn't. She has no recollection of that day by the sea; no recollection of the journey there, of the weather, of her daughter's hand in hers. Try as she might to hold her second husband in his proper place, it's the first who slips into step at her side, takes her arm and says:

'When I retire, Rosie, we'll have a garden by the sea, and we'll walk along the seafront just like this, and watch the ships.'

The hall is filling up. Projected across the ceiling are random words and phrases, each in a different typeface and size, many trailing off into enigmatic dots:

'O! Call back yesterday, bid time return . . .'

'Art is long, and Time is fleeting . . .'

'This is truth the poet sings . . .'

'Half to remember days that have gone by . . .'

Hanging across the hall doorway, a painted banner: *Past and Present*.

Three Year-11 girls, still in their uniforms, have surrounded Gal and are firing breathless questions at him. In the far right corner a couple of hesitant women sidle over to the knot of chairs and desks where papers and pens are set out in casual heaps, and cards are sellotaped here and there with exhortations:

'Share your memories!'

'Make your own poem!'

'Did you have a favourite toy?'

'A special pop song?'

Only one person has taken a seat in the Creation Corner so far, and she isn't writing anything.

Gal calls to the volunteers:

'Ladies and Gentlemen, your interviewer has arrived!'

A smattering of applause and a cheer.

Gal strides towards James and Cat, shedding his schoolgirl disciples, and bends to give Cat a kiss.

'Thanks for trogging down all this way again . . .'

'No problem. Don't forget, I was James's beautiful assistant for part of this project. I've got a stake in this event.'

Another circle of fans closes around Gal, and James leads Cat to the drinks.

'Orange juice please,' says Cat, unconsciously patting her stomach.

'Sensible girl.' Elen Rabbaiotti nods chummily. 'Save the booze till after. You'll need it then, with a little 'un driving you up the wall.'

James and Cat wander over to the display on Charles Lightfoot.

'There's old Charles,' says Cat. 'Not a sign of *her*, of course.'

'Who?'

'You know – the Great Love of his Life. Remember?'

James looks blank. Cat rolls her eyes.

'For God's sake, James. You're the one who interviewed him. The woman he had the fling with – Laura, was it?'

The tape crackles and begins its cycle again. Charles's dour voice emerges from the speaker,

'There was five of us in all. Me, Mary Ethel, George, and Emlyn, and Vernon . . .'

Rose has sent her daughter, Irene, to fetch a drink, and has taken up a sentry position, propped against her sticks, near her display. Madge Probert is ushering her own daughter around. 'Ah, Rose, have you met my girl? She's a solicitor in Birmingham. Came down specifically to see *Past and Present*.'

'Nothing much to do in Birmingham, then?' says Rose. Madge pulls her daughter closer to the display screen.

'There's Rose, look – when would that be? During the Great War?'

Rose chews her teeth briefly and addresses the daughter.

'Famous novelist for a mother now, then. Bodice-ripper, an' all. What do you think of that?'

'It's a turn-up, isn't it!' says Madge Probert's daughter. 'A steamy tale of romance and the self-made woman – right, Mum?'

Madge says, 'Oh, look, here's Rose's father, all dressed up in his funny grocer's hat!' And moves away, pressing her daughter's back to prevent her from lingering.

Madge has already noted Rose's little crowd of relatives. All those women – daughter, granddaughter, great-granddaughter – paraded around like achievements. All of them fussing around Rose Lewis, worrying about her comforts, taking an animated interest in the photographs and faces, claiming their forebears with relish. Madge's own daughter is bored. She can't wait to finish her duties and get back to her solicitor's office, a long way away. Madge knows that, and she can't blame her. After all, Madge is the one who protected her from the stories. While her daughter heads off to refill her glass, Madge stands alone, looking at her own display. Ernest. Florrie. Her poor, feeble father, Sid. Arthur Probert. Each ghost marked in its turn, each history locked safely away in Madge Probert's head.

James checks Gal's progress from one group of acolytes to another.

'Going well, then.'

Gal takes a sip of wine, grimaces, and nods.

'It's as I said – immediacy. We're all children at heart. We all like to be told a story.'

'Any new projects in the pipeline?' says James, embarrassed by his own formality.

Gal spots a group of new arrivals over James's head, and gives them a regal wave.

'Possibly . . . I'm thinking of doing something about new patterns of writing. New influences. The Net, new national identities, changes in language . . . You could help me there. Is there such a thing as Techno-Welsh?'

The question is thrown off nervously, without requiring an answer, and James ignores it. Gal is so different, so jumpy, since his accident. Since his overnight stays next door. James longs to ask him about Livvy – but what can he say? He can hardly demand an explanation.

Gal lowers his voice, 'How's Sonia?'

'Oh . . . They offered her the permanent job, in the end. I think she's taking it.'

A ripple of alarm travels across Gal's face. James notes it with satisfaction.

'So – does that mean—'

'That I'm emigrating? Er, no. It probably means *arrivederci* Sonia. At least – she hasn't issued any urgent invitations to catch the next flight over. Put it that way.'

'Sorry about that, honey.' Gal pats James's shoulder. But the comment and the action are forced. Instinctively, they take half a step away from each other. They stand opposite one another, stranded, and scan the crowd. James deliberately avoids looking towards the Creation Corner. He struggles not to think of Gal and

Livvy, in bed. He imagines her nevertheless: pale, cold, slippery as a fish. And he imagines Gal caressing her, tracing serpentine shapes across her torso with his graceful hands. Going through the dance, for courtesy's sake. Degrading, thinks James. But then, that's the trouble with Gal. He doesn't really care, one way or the other. Doesn't love, doesn't hate. All the same to him: all of equal value. With the thought, his eyes involuntarily meet Gal's. Neither of them looks away. Neither of them smiles.

A voice says,

'Gangway. Fat woman approaching.'

Cat is there, between them. Gal turns to her with relief.

'How are you, fat woman? How's it all going?'

'I'm scared witless,' she says. 'It's a very odd experience. There's a stranger in our midst.'

She takes Gal's hand in her right hand, and James's in the left. She lays their hands against her belly.

'Say hello, stranger,' she says.

She keeps them there, linked, until a spectral presence at Gal's elbow makes them drift apart again.

'You're looking well, Cat,' says Livvy. 'Are you going to be down here for a while? Poor old James, he must be so lonely in that house all on his own.' Livvy takes Gal's arm. 'Why don't you come round if you've got the time? We might even have something ready to play you. We've been hard at work, haven't we, Gal? You might be the incentive we need to finally produce the goods.'

Gal drains his glass and becomes business-like. 'Best go and circulate. Say a few words. Enjoy the show, folks.'

'Roll up, roll up!'

'*Shoosh*, Mum,' says Irene. Rose takes no notice.

'Come and have a laugh at Rose Lewis in her baby bloomers!'

'Wouldn't miss it for the world,' says James smoothly, sauntering over with Cat.

Rose raises bald eyebrows at Cat's tummy.

'Didn't know you were starting a brood. Don't get too carried away, now – you'll never be rid of 'em . . .'

'Oh, *Mum* . . .' says Irene. Cat laughs.

James is turning the pages of Rose's poetry scrapbook.

> *The air is a blanket. Try and push it away.*
> *Life is a trap. It crushes your bones.*

Nobody ever breaks free. You have to live
Another day pretending. Even the river
Presses its deadweight over the fish and the stones.

'Aye . . .' says Rose, ducking as Lindy tries to grab a handful of her wispy hair. 'They're either all over you, or they're grown up and gone. You got to love 'em and lose 'em.'

Cat busies herself making 'Oh' and 'Ah' faces at little Lindy. Rose snaps a hand round James's wrist and says in a stage whisper,

'You and that girl – you stick with it now. It'll pep you up no end, having a family.'

James smiles a bright, patronising smile, and thinks, Don't imagine you know anything about me, just because you're old.

Behind him, Madge Probert can be heard blaring an instruction at Gal, 'If you're about to make a speech, Mr Galloway, please don't forget to mention absent friends.'

'That bloody woman,' mutters Rose. 'Thinks 'erself, her. Taking the mickey out of my dad's trade.'

She screws up her eyes to focus on Madge Probert's display, at the other side of the hall.

'And there's that crew of hers at the butcher stall! All lined up like royalty. But they were no better than us. And – mind – they sold poison meat at Hatchetts. It's true. Nearly did for me and my mam.'

2

While Gal is raising a glass to absent friends, Charles Lightfoot is lying in his bed, coaxing his mind into action. Once again, with infinite patience, he paces back with it, hour by hour, fitting together the lucid pieces of his afternoon. He remembers Vernon's arrival. Remembers some to-do about his clothes: hadn't dressed himself well enough, apparently. Buttons all wrong, flies open. Offered inadequate excuses: overslept. Dressed in a rush.

Methodically, he leads his memory on, again, through isolated bursts of recollection. He seems to have spent most of the day – or several years – waking from a doze, at unspecified times, answering a half-registered question as sensibly as he could. Grappling with a sense of dread, scrabbling furiously to gain a foothold in consciousness while Vernon nattered away from the sofa or was suddenly bending over him, repeating his name. Always the undertow of a deeper, lost world, dragging him down.

He rejects memory and resorts to logic. The curtains are open, but it's getting dark. (Or light?) He must have made his way up to the bedroom. He can hear his mother fussing around downstairs. So where are the others?

A curt knock at the door and his father appears with a hot drink on a tray. Smiling. It's Vernon, of course, and time snaps back into order.

'Hot milk and a dash of something else,' says Vernon, easing the tray onto Uncle Eddie's bedside table.

'I'm not ill,' Charles protests, though without vigour.

'Tired, that's all, I 'spect.' Vernon sits on the edge of the bed and Charles, obeying age-old reflexes, recoils against the wall.

'Got someone coming to see you tomorrow,' says Vernon. 'Just to have a word, like. See how you are.'

Again Charles tries to bully his mind into the next step. What happens tomorrow? How does he link all this – room, bed, Vernon – this one-dimensional, disconnected portion of the present, with whatever goes before and after? Vernon's smile is clouded.

Inspiration strikes.

'Have I been talking to myself?' asks Charles. Vernon begins a series of muggings and gestures to imply his toleration and dismissal of Charles's harmless habits. Before he can frame a reply Charles has lost his hold and is scrutinizing the prone body of Peg Farrell, so close and substantial that he *must* be there, standing over her, in the shrubs behind a tacky community dance hall. Her dress has been hitched up around her waist; she's pulling up her underwear, arching her back, so that her head presses into the bushes and disappears. Somebody is there: somebody says something. Charles isn't sure of the words, but finds that he can replay them at will.

'Thanks, darlin'. Give my love to your mother.'

Whose voice? Would Charles Lightfoot really have said that? Even in drink, even in rancour? But then if I'm going doolally, thinks Charles, maybe it didn't really happen at all.

Vernon is still speaking. Charles is sure he hears Mary Ethel on the stairs. He realises that he must sort this out, before his mind caves in on itself. He must ask for the truth.

'Vern,' he says. 'You remember Peg Farrell . . . You know who she was. You remember, someone put her in the club.' He's doing well: Vernon is listening. 'You know that night, at the dance . . . oh, years and years ago . . . Remember? Was I with her? Vern? Was I with Peg?'

He waits, as Vernon considers his answer. Charles has done all he can: he's asked the question, and now he waits. Vernon sniffs, picks up the mug of hot milk, and tests its heat with the flat of his hand. He puts it down again and shakes his head, then smiles at Charles. When Charles recognises the terror in that smile, he understands that his insanity has played one final trick and, instead of spilling words out of his head, has locked them in. All Vernon has heard is gibberish.

Charles surrenders to the tumult of other scenes. He notices someone lounging in his bedroom doorway, army cap askew on his head, fag wiggling in his mouth. This someone is saying something, demanding something from Charles. Charles strains to lift his head from the pillow, trying to understand. He's hardly aware of Vernon taking his hand, grinning desperately, saying,

'All right, Charlie-boy. I'm still here.'

3

He's nearly there. Inch by slow inch, step by drenched step, James is creeping up a high, steep crevice. Water slaps his face and the top of his head, gushes down his neck and back, snakes around his legs and tries to prise them away from the rock. He has to pause, muster his energy, harden his hands against slippery hooks and blades. Soon, soon, he will reach the root of this waterfall, there will be stillness, and he will have the courage to look up. Something solid and deliberate knocks against his ear, his shoulder; after a while, another, and another: a dilatory showering of pebbles. He waits for a gap in this lazy assault and finally, finally, lifts his eyes, which are level with the lip of the ridge. A spirt of laughter propels him back from the rock, tearing his fingers free, launching him out into the abyss. Before falling he sees the single laugh separate into three: three spouts of laughter, shared among the three men who lie side by side, peeking over the edge of the canyon. The crowing of a wiry young soldier; the sardonic snigger of a well-dressed civil servant; the gap-toothed cackle of an evil old man.

By 1507 Ieuan ap Gruffudd was back in Penfynydd, alone and presumably widowed, composing lines that exhumed the themes of an earlier generation. Gone were the drive and aspirations of the government official; gone, too, by all accounts, the material comforts and status of that way of life. The verse that appears from this date, attributed to Ieuan Gloff, hermit of Penfynydd, harks back to the angry nationalism of a previous age, without its optimism.

        Lle bo lladron, bydd llywodraeth –
        Tranc yr heniaith, terfyn gobaith.
        A fynno gyfoeth, ni gâr anrhydedd;
        A droes at Loegr, troes at lygredd.

        Where there are thieves, there is government –
        Death of the language and the end of hope.
        Who seeks wealth loves not honour;
        Who turns to England turns to corruption.

Yet here was a man who, if he had not actively sought wealth, certainly accepted it, and who did indeed 'turn to England' for many years. Why this renewed cynicism? These are, surely, the words of a disappointed disciple. To be fair, Henry VII had not neglected his Welsh supporters: between 1504 and 1508 he issued seven charters of liberty to certain communities in North Wales, formally releasing their inhabitants from the strictures of the penal laws and granting them the rights to buy and to hold land, and to take public office. However, there was more than one catch. The grants were issued at a price; their legal status was dubious; they applied only to a limited number of settlements. Perhaps the former poet, having put his faith in a long-term policy of lifting legal and financial restrictions, had finally tired of waiting. In the years to come, Ieuan would have more cause for bitterness as he witnessed the downfall of those associated with the Bosworth age. In 1521 the Duke of Buckingham, fellow soldier and battle-hero, was accused of plotting against Henry VIII and executed. Ten years later, Rhys ap Griffith, grandson of Ieuan's revered leader, Sir Rhys ap Thomas, also came to grief under a charge of conspiracy. It can only have added to the old soldier's sense of betrayal.

Our last known scrap of evidence is a single line, dated 1535:

Cenfigen, clefyd ein cenedl
– Envy, disease of our nation.

If we have guessed correctly, he would have been 71 when he wrote this and signed it: Ieuan Gloff, Hermit. We do not know whether he survived one more year, long enough to see the implementation of the Act of 1536. At last, the Welsh were granted equal rights, freedoms and privileges. But Ieuan would not have welcomed the so-called Act of Union. This was equality under English laws, English administration, ridding Wales of her own 'sinister usages and customs'. Ieuan had hung on to his fantasy of freedom and independence through 27 years of loyal service to the Crown. For him, this was the last betrayal. Whatever the merits or faults of the Act, whatever its true intentions, to a flag-waving poet of the old order, this must have been the final blow.

'So. Having sifted through the evidence and examined its context – what can we conclude about the progress, or should we say the decline, of our Welsh poet? He's turned his back on a court career. Does he have anywhere to go? Is there still a role, anywhere, for an old-style *prydydd*, towards the end of the Tudor regime? The

Wars of the Roses are over; some may say the medieval nation has given way to the modern state. Can there be any part at all for a romantic, a propagandist, a born-again separatist? Or is he just an anachronism? An embarrassment? Part of a dying world?'

A half-hearted cough; a stifled yawn. It's a hot day; James removes his glasses to wipe away the steam, and blinks at a fuzzy patchwork of ovals, smeared clean of expressions. He knows what the expressions are, anyway: boredom; impatience; hostility. James replaces his specs. He has another ten minutes to fill.

'Any thoughts?'

He lobs his voice across the lecture room; it glimmers over their heads.

'Any ideas from the floor?'

A pattering of papers and muffled titters.

'You could ask Ieuan yourself,' calls a voice. 'He's sitting next to me.'

A sheepish, flame-faced boy, elbowing his companion, explains, 'It's my persona. Ieuan Gloff. On the Middle Ages website.'

James subdues the hilarity with a conductor's gesture.

Cerys Emmanuel, sitting straight-backed in the front row, lifts her hand.

'Why do we have to assume it was a backward step for Ieuan to leave London?'

(A stirring from behind her, a defiant 'Yeah!' and a growl of 'Bollocks'.)

'Maybe he thought it was a *good* move to go back to Wales. Whichever way you look at it, he would have been a bigger fish in a smaller pond, wouldn't he?'

'Fair point, Cerys. But there's nothing to suggest that he took up an official appointment on his return to Wales. And then we must take into account two factors: Tudor policy with regards to Welsh administration – which I'll be covering in Tuesday's lecture – and Ieuan Gloff's description of himself – as a hermit.'

'But—' Cerys again and a groan from the upper tiers of the lecture room. '—he might have reckoned he could have an influence, even as a hermit. Even if he didn't have a position. He might have gone back thinking, I could make things happen here. Make my mark.'

'Nah . . .' Deggy Baker's voice drawls down from two rows behind her. 'He's just dropped out, that's all. Given two fingers to all the money and status crap, and gone back to his roots.'

James glances at the clock on the back wall. 'Well, let's not dwell too long on this one particular case; I'd like us to think about the wider issue of the poet's role in—'

'See, but, I don't reckon you can do that.' Deggy takes his feet down from the shoulder of the seat in front, and leans forward to direct his comments at Cerys, as well as at James. 'You can't make one man into, like, a general rule. You know, it's like opinion polls. They don't *work* – cos – people lie. Or they try and say the right thing. Or they just change their minds. Right, Cezza? You got to allow for it. People change their minds.'

Cerys is keeping her eyes steadfastly ahead. She reaches up to play with a strand of hair. Something going on there, thinks James, and he's shocked by a twinge of envy.

'OK. Let's leave it there, then. Have a good weekend, everybody.'

James files his notes carefully into his briefcase as the students jostle for the door, shoving against each other and calling insults and arrangements. I'll go home, thinks James, pour myself a drink, and put my feet up. Stillness and space. Except, of course, for the next door sounds of repetition and correction, phrases revised and refined, the inflexion of Livvy's voice and, behind it all, the unheard presence of Gal.

For the third or fourth day running, as he switches off the lecture-room lights and closes the door, James is turning sentences around his tongue, preparing them.

Let me talk to you. Let me explain. Let me tell you what I mean.

All this week, he has sampled these sentences, rehearsed them in the car, in the kitchen, as he picks up the receiver – before replacing it and setting them aside.

After the *Past and Present* event, Cat said she would go straight to the railway station. It would be a nightmare of a journey – no good connections – but she insisted she must go, and couldn't stay the night. She was friendly, even kind: she said it was just work, just the way it went, she had to be back in the swing of things, she'd spent too long as it was, beached in James's house.

James saw her off. On the train, she pulled down the window and leaned out. 'It turned out quite well, in the end, didn't it?' she said. 'Gal's project.'

James said, 'Cat, I don't want you to think . . .'

She said, 'Don't worry about me, James. I'll manage. If I need help, I'll ring you. I promise.'

James crosses the campus. It's just beginning to cool off; the students who were draped over the grass in the sun have packed up and are dawdling away between buildings, towards the bar or the city. There are only half-a-dozen cars left in the car park.

Gail Fenwick is unlocking her Citroen. She waves at the weather generally, and calls,

'Let's hope it lasts the weekend, eh! How's the recalcitrant bard-ah? Any more yielding than he was? Come and see me next week, and we'll chat-ah!'

James opens his driver and passenger doors and sits sweltering at the wheel, waiting for Gail Fenwick to drive away, and for the canned air to clear. He reviews his lecture, and the students' comments, and wonders whether Deggy Baker and Cerys Emmanuel really are an item.

People change their minds, Deggy said. You got to allow for it. That's true. He will definitely ring Cat tonight. Just to see how she is. And if she's in the right mood, if the conversation has the right flow, he'll try out one of his sentences. Let me explain myself, he'll say. I'm not being noble. I'm not making an offer. I'm asking you. I'm begging a favour.

James rubs away the sweat that's settled on his nose, where his glasses rest.

She'll tell him where to go, of course. Come to that, he probably won't even ring. But at least, for the moment, he has a plan.

4

This is a strange place. Keep yourself to yourself for a few years and they'll have you marked either as a devil or as a holy man. It's my good fortune that the cattle in these parts are reasonably healthy. Otherwise who knows what they'd have blamed on a ragged old outcast – or what they'd have done about it. As it is, I've lasted longer than I had a right to expect. Long enough to be sought out by the pious and the curious and asked for words of wisdom. I don't turn them away any more. I tell them what they want to hear.

It's not so much that I chose to settle here – more a question of . . . fate, instinct, call it what you will; I wasn't plotting my own course. When I arrived I was dazed and frightened. I hadn't returned to my house, after being dredged from the river. I left Mrs Fogge to draw her own conclusions, and I left the port authorities to theirs: that we were killed by cut-throats. Or that we'd run away to live on my illicit earnings. My one thought was to get out of London.

Throughout my long, befuddled flight across country, I listened for pursuing hooves. No one followed me, though. If they had, it would have been a swift and easy chase. I covered only a few miles a day. My feet had softened, and my flesh had grown dense over the years. I was soon blistered and bent with exhaustion. There was still money in my purse – the river had only hardened the knots that kept it secure. I spent the last of it on lumpy inn food and lumpy inn beds, and after that I took shelter in churches, in barns, in a cell at the monastery in Llandegfa. No more lying at the roadsides under a hedge; in my sorry state, one cold night in the open might have seen me off.

I had made no decisions. I wasn't aware of having picked my destination. But as the country became wilder and higher, and the roads more deserted and rough, my route seemed set. I doubled up to tackle the steep sheep-tracks. I was chilled to the bone, but thankful that the rain held off. The ground chewed at my city shoes. Pain shot through my feet and my weak leg with every step.

When I reached Penfynydd I hardly recognised it. As I climbed the ridge that leads to Bryn Moel, and the ground sloped down and away into the valley, it seemed to me that the place I remembered had disappeared. There had never been more than a scattering of farmhouses and cottages, some nestling on the valley floor, others watching over them from the ring-fort of hills above. Now there was even less to deserve a name. Sheep were grazing around roofless walls. Nettles crept through dead windows. I stood on that high crest, labouring for breath in the evening sun, as the valley filled with shadow. In my youth, at this hour, a map of tiny lights would have fluttered into sight along the fields and up the hillsides. But there were no candles to guide me now.

The nearest church was two miles away, at Nant. I suddenly knew my next task: to seek out Anne's priest. To tell him everything, and seek redemption. I reached the church before sunset. The graveyard bulged with stones, tilting and butting each other from wall to wall. An old woman was crouching over one grave; she eyed my approach and stood up, awkward and astonished. I asked about the priest.

Oh, they hadn't had an *offeiriad* of their own for five years now, not since Father Anian had been taken by the pox. There was only Father Thomas, from Trefair, and he came once in three weeks.

This was a blow. I had intended to confess to that particular priest – the man who had known Anne, seen her grow up, prayed over her family's deathbeds, read her the letter I had sent, with its offer of a future. But it couldn't be helped. Father Thomas would have to do. I would wait for him.

I thanked the old woman and turned back towards Penfynydd. I knew where to go, even without light. I knew the grip of the grass, and the rattle of the scree; I climbed away from the valley and up, up, along the left-hand track, scrabbling over fallen trees, wading through streams and heather, away from the last trails of sunlight.

Partly eaten by the wind and the years, blurred with mildew, the farmhouse rotted patiently in its overgrown yard. The door stood ajar; there was a table inside, covered in chicken shit, and the leavings of a dead fire in the grate – probably set by some other wanderer, or a bored child. Feathery cobwebs hung from the rafters. The settle had gone – dragged away by a neighbour perhaps – and the chair I had taken to tell my stories was broken and upended in a corner. I explored the rest of the house. The bed was in two halves, its ropes frayed and useless. The cribs and the truckle bed had vanished. What little she owned, Anne must have brought with her to London in those saddle-bags, or given away. I squinted up into the chimney, saw no obvious blockage, and set about laying a fresh fire.

I can see now that Gwilym had the right idea. You don't need much, to get by. You don't need to wear yourself out earning your keep. In fact, you don't even need charm or an amiable smile – I could have told him that, and saved him his trouble. People bring me food. When I've been struck with fever, they've brought me blankets and broth, and banked up my fire. Well – they're used to me now. At first, I didn't see a soul. I lost track of time. Even lost the urge to confess. I reasoned with myself: After all, what had I done? What great sin had I committed? As if in answer, came the apparitions. Gwilym's dissolving flesh. Anne's seaweed hair. A tiny package twitching under the midwife's cape.

Some passing shepherd may have heard my screams, as I was flung from another nightmare-vision into the dawn. He may have spread the word that I was possessed by demons. At any rate, months went by and nobody approached the derelict farmhouse where an old tramp ranted and raved. A lost soul. A madman. A seer. With no one else to bear witness, it no longer mattered which I might be. After being free of visions for so long, this torrent was all the harder to bear. But even suffering adopts its own routine. Every morning, I woke. Every day, I survived. Gradually, my physical strength returned. I cleared a square of land and used what was left of the crops. I killed a chicken here and a rabbit there; I did not starve, though in winter I came near it. Before Christmas, Father Thomas took it into his head to visit his whole flock, including the strays. He didn't stay long, and I didn't say much. But the fond old fool must have assured his congregation that I was a harmless enough gathering of skin and bone. Soon I began to find small gifts of bread, cheese and honey at my door. Father Thomas was a good man, God rest his soul.

The youngster was leaning on his stick when I came shuffling out to pee. He was well-built, and had a kind wrinkling about the eyes. Gwilym.

No, no. Gwilym would be as old as I was.

So I ignored him, and went on my way through the morsel of a gate. By this time the locals' doubts had been set aside, and I'd become used to seeing the occasional nosey passer-by. Children liked to throw stones at the door, and run away in raptures of terror when I emerged. As I limped by, this young lad said,

'You're a poet, then.'

I froze. He repeated himself, more loudly.

'Who tells you that?' The question scraped in my throat. I hadn't spoken for some time.

'My father,' said the boy, 'says he remembers you from his childhood. He's got a keen eye for a face, my father.'

Must be keen, I thought, to connect this piteous wreck with the fit, broad-voiced, travelling poet of nigh on thirty years ago. I was suspicious. I scrutinised the lad's face, and said nothing.

'He used to help with the horses at the big house up in Tyddyn-y-Graig,' he said. 'Heard you there one night, that's what he told us: the grooms sneaked him in to listen to you whipping up a storm. Told us about it, many times. Always wishes he could remember the words. He'd like to meet you.'

'I'm no poet,' I said, and let the gate bang behind me.

He was there again, three mornings in a row. His father was unwell, he said. Couldn't I teach him some of the old songs, to take back as a surprise? One day he brought the new priest, who had a quill and paper. They insisted on sitting in my infested den, at the shit-plastered table, and pressed me to recall some of my verses.

'We'd be grateful,' says this pink-cheeked churchman. 'Perhaps you'd like us to bring you some ale?'

Oh, these half-wits made my head throb. I did my best, tempted by the ale and by the prospect of their departure. Words came back to me in shards, broken free of their lines. It was too long ago. The only tale I could remember was the tale that punished me every night, as I squatted by the fire, and stared at the space where the settle had been; and that was a tale I would never tell again.

They brought more paper, these two. My nails were eagle-claws, my hands were twisted by years of cold, but they encouraged me to grapple with the quill and trace a few tentative characters. The boy's interest seemed genuine. Even though his father died seven weeks after our first meeting, he continued to come. Little by little, pieces of verse returned. Hour by hour, I sat in the light of the candles provided by my callers, and scraped the old phrases into place.

'Wonderful,' said the priest.

'Fascinating,' said the boy.

The priest was short-sighted: he held each page half an inch from his nose.

'Ah – "Tudor! Tudor is our King!" – yes, yes, heady days . . .' He actually sniffed back a tear. The boy frowned and said,

'Who was the "mad white boar"?'

I became a sideshow. Among the disintegrating cottages and deserted hills, here was an oddity, an eccentric, a man who shunned society and riches: a wise man. A man of God. Every passing peddlar, pilgrim and outlaw found my door. They asked impossible questions – what is the true path to grace? how can I change my ways? – and accepted any old nonsense for answer. Others came for different reasons: some, like the first lad, wanted to learn of 'the old ways', to hear about the story-telling and the songs and the long march to glory. Between their visits I spent my time patching together as much poetry as I could retrieve, ready to hand to the next ones. In recent years my admirers have even planted me a small garden, sheltered with great blocks of golden stone – brought in a cart all the way from Llandegfa, they tell me. Apparently the monks have fled and the abbey belongs to every grasping hand these days – what's left of it. We have a new pope called King Henry, according to one dimple-chinned young upstart who came hallooing across my gate a week ago. This one was full of himself: spent the last of the daylight eating half my supper and telling me how quaint and out-dated my poems were. All very well for their *time*, he said, but sentimental. Unrealistic. He explained, 'It's all different now. The whole world is opening up to us, if we've only the sense to see it.'

I thought of Gwilym, punching me affably and saying, 'We'll go where the action is, *bachgen*. Food and company. See the world. That'll do for us.'

All such a long time ago. My poetry, my prophecies – all as insubstantial as another man's imaginings. No visions of what is to come, now – only the merciless round of memories, playing and replaying across the years.

For several days I haven't left this sagging bed. I'm vaguely aware of forms, passing through the room, exchanging words, and of the difference between daylight and night. I appreciate your presence. Gentle hands, feeling my brow, trying to give me food. A candle flickers.

I understand what is happening, Father. I sense the departure of ancient guilts and betrayals that were nestling for years in my brain. They lift away like steam. There is more to say, yet – I'm searching, groping for the sense of it, but I know there may not be time. I can't be sure – have I told you the whole tale? Have I traced the right sequence of events? Has any of it been true? I never was much good at confessing – I forget how to distinguish my sins from my stories. But it probably doesn't signify any more.

A feeling of knots untied, the unravelling of words: every word I have ever composed, memorised, manipulated, performed, thought, regretted. All spinning around and away – followed by the songs, heavier, richer and tending to drag. This is more painful. The music sticks to my mind's edges, clinging to remembered landscapes and longings, and has to be wrenched off, note by note.

Now I am empty and clear, and cool as a stone. I've reached the gulf between skin and soul. Light fails around and within me. The last rites rise, and fall, and fade. I'm flying again. Beyond my stories, beyond my prayers, beyond past, and present, and future. Shedding names and occasions for others to gather up. We're all flying. All sloughing off our characters and days: the leather-skinned old woman at her window; the old man in his last convulsions; the brave friend, bleeding and abandoned in the mud. We soar, all of us, without effort, to a pinnacle of indifference. And we're gone.

EPILOGUE

The Story of Alice Day

1

On the third of March, 1898, Alice Day turned down a proposal of marriage.

Her feelings were mixed as she walked across the square, away from her stranded suitor. She had to whap one hand over her hat in the gritty March wind; the other hitched her skirt out of the dirt. Her heart was thundering. She felt sorry for the boy who followed her progress with his tiny pebble-eyes. She felt sorry for his damaged foot and his ravaged skin. She was annoyed and considered the possibility of feeling insulted, because he had asked her with such intensity. But she was grateful to him too, for not teasing her as the other market boys did. She was moved by the gravity of the incident, and by the dignity of her own refusal. She felt very grown-up.

When Alice confided in her sister that night, she managed to wring out a few tears, as seemed fitting for the drama of the occasion. Beatrice played her part, tutting and squeezing Alice's hand under the sheets. When the formalities were over they shook Beatrice's bed with their giggles, and Beatrice whispered,

'Think of being married to Ernest Butterworth! Chopping up pigs by day and snuggling up to a pig by night!'

'Oh, Beatty, don't be mean!'

They stuffed corners of the topsheet into their mouths, in case their father should hear and come upstairs to investigate – and that only increased their paroxysms.

Beatrice was nineteen, sharp-tongued and forthright; Alice was a year younger, and usually smoothed things over. Beatty had always referred to Ernest Butterworth as the Butcher's Beast or Piggy. The girls considered themselves a cut above the market traders. Their father was the stationmaster. The station was small, and he was also the ticket clerk and porter, but he was master none the less. Alice and Beatrice enjoyed turning their noses up at the boys as they strolled arm-in-arm among the stalls, and Beatty was always happy to practise a withering retort.

'Piggy' was a cruel name, being so accurate. Ernest had heavy cheeks; coarse bristles failed to cover the acne-flayed flesh. His little eyes were set wide over a fat nose. As a child he gallumphed along behind his father, letting the ridicule bounce off his stubborn, bowed head. He never lingered around the margins of children's groups; he never hesitated or answered back or complained. I'm different, he seemed to say, and I don't care. Alice noticed him even then, as Mary the Help tugged her briskly by the hand across town. There was a boy who gave his enemies no ground.

She was sixteen when Ernest first addressed her. It was early morning; Alice was accompanying her sister to the florists where Beatrice worked, at the smart end of town. The stall-holders were setting up; Ernest helping his father hoist carcasses from a cart. There was nothing aimless or flirtatious about his opening gambit,

'You should wear a shawl, like the market women,' he said. 'Your ears are red.'

Beatrice was ready, 'And I dare say you'd have her strangling chickens with her bare hands, given half a chance.'

Ernest's reply was gruff and low, meant for only Alice to hear, 'Somebody's got to kill 'em if she wants to eat 'em. There's no shame in it.'

Alice liked his certainty. Despite her airs, she wasn't a squeamish girl: she was impressed by the deft, assured way Ernest and his father went about their work, swiping and skinning and packing.

She had been taken on at the elementary, as a pupil teacher. Her father said it would 'do for now' – until he got her off his hands. Beatrice was being courted by a laconic clerk with a protruding jaw. Alice didn't think much about her future.

She came home one evening to find her father smoking in the stationhouse kitchen, delivering gossip to his wife and Mary the Help. The two women were contemplating the floor, attentive and serious. The smoke from her father's pipe made Alice cough, and she was about to escape into the side-garden when he called her back. Had she heard about Butterworth? Collapsed and died this morning, just like that. She was wan with shock until she realised they meant Butterworth Senior. At seventeen, Ernest was shouldering the business and caring for his mother and two sisters. 'And if I know that lad,' said Alice's mother, 'he'll do it without a whimper. Stoic, he is. Had to be, poor boy.'

Alice repeated the word to herself as she crossed the square on her way to school every morning. Stoic. She would see him, hanging the meat and wiping the stall down, alone; she would call to him – out of charity, she told herself – 'Good morning, Mr Butterworth!' And he would stop whatever he was doing until she had disappeared from view behind the town hall. She knew. She knew he was watching her.

Alice was no great beauty. Her sister, though taller and louder and more buxom, had delicate, fashionable features, and mischievous brown curls. Alice's nose was too long, her lips were too thin; her fair hair refused to curl, and flopped and drooped from under her hat, leaving a trail of hairpins.

Ernest watched her. She kept this as her secret. It triggered something in her: something inexpressible and forbidden. Not lust. Not even attraction. Anticipation. Control. Beatrice would one day take her aside and explain,

'We do have power, Alice. But there's no earthly way of using it.'

That was four years later.

For the present, sixteen-year-old Alice Day made the most of it all: rewarding Ernest with unexpected chats; torturing him with impulsive snubs. Whenever they talked, she was struck again by his solemnity. He was his own man. He knew his trade, and he ran the business well. He would never be a rich man, but neither would he ever be poor, he told her. He would provide for his sisters and his mother as long as necessary. If some swaggering boy flung a comment about his ugliness or his leg, it was Alice who snapped back. Ernest really didn't seem to care about the rest of the world.

So when, two years later, on the third of March 1898, Alice strode shakily away across the market square, pressing against the wind, she was also disappointed. Ernest had set out his case, and clarified his feelings. He had presented them in safe and ritual terms. He had cornered her into a response, and that seemed to be the end of that. Apart from the short-term promise of a rejected and mournful gaze, the game was up.

Alice perched on a stool to wait for Beatrice, drowsing in the ripe scent of early daffodils and hyacinths. Beatty was expecting a proposal soon, herself, and then Alice would be left to romanticise alone. Beatty emerged from a back room, pinning on her hat.

'Come on then, your Ladyship.' She nudged the stool with her foot. 'And to save your feelings, we'll take the long route home, and avoid the square.'

Alice tried to think of a clever response, but Beatty was already sweeping out of the shop. They turned left, towards the church and the round-about route, Alice trotting to keep pace with her sister.

'Well, have you seen Mr Pig-Wig since the Matter was settled?' Beatrice crushed Alice's arm affectionately under her own.

'No, I certainly haven't. Well . . . yes, I have, I have *seen* him, but . . .'

'And did he shed a lovelorn tear? *Do* piggies shed lovelorn tears?' Beatrice began to sing:

'No, 'Arry, don't ask me to marry . . .'

'Oh, stop it, Beatty. As a matter of fact, he was just the same as ever.'

Beatrice made a face, and Alice smiled, but her neck and cheeks flashed crimson. It was true – she had expected him to be mortified, to avoid her eyes when she passed; she had relied on it, and had planned her reaction, polite but aloof. But when she crossed the market square this morning Ernest Butterworth had greeted her and carried on with his work with cool ease. He didn't even stop; he didn't watch her this time. Somehow it made her feel foolish. As if the whole episode had been a joke, at her expense. Alice began to resent Ernest Butterworth.

By June, Beatty and her young man, Robert, had set a date. They took Alice for a picnic by the river. (Someone for Beatty to talk to, Alice suspected.) Beatrice wore a white dress with sleeves that were slightly too large and old-fashioned. It had a tight bodice and sprigs of yellow flowers around the neck and hem. Alice unpacked the food from the hamper while her sister walked along the riverbank, striking poses with the parasol borrowed from her employer's wife. Beatrice, thought Alice, would always be like this: at this instant, she was the real, essential Beatrice. Alice determined to capture that picture of her sister, and store it away.

Later, Beatty sprawled on her side in the sun, overshooting her rug and smudging the yellow flowers with grass stains.

'Isn't it odd,' she said, and then she yawned and stretched like a cat. 'This time next year I shall be giving you tea in my home. *My* home. No trains, no soot, no *pipe* . . .' (This was directed at Robert, who sat apart with his arms around his knees, and ignored her.)

Alice fingered a stray strand of lank hair. Yes, and this time next year, she would be on her own, with no ally to laugh with her as the house quaked in the early hours and soot blotted her window and the adults sat in the kitchen exchanging the same old rumours about the same old neighbours because there was nothing else to say.

Beatrice extended a lazy hand and tweaked Alice's sleeve.

'Who knows – you might have a wedding of your own to plan by then . . .'

But what if she hadn't? What if Piggy was the only person who ever would ask? Alice felt that she was already reaching the end of a pathway: that she would kiss her sister goodbye at the gate and then have no option but to turn back for home. She wasn't particularly clever. She wasn't pretty, or adventurous. She didn't want freedom, exactly – just a space of her own.

Dorian Wilkins was one of the schoolmasters. His hair was completely white, although he was no older than 25. He had flaring nostrils and a neighing laugh that finished every other sentence. The children called him Neddy. His sleeves and trousers were a touch too short, giving the impression that he was taller than he was. He had started to flirt with Alice, in a ponderous way, and before the summer was out he was walking her home after school.

'It's a ten-minute walk. He's never even taken my arm,' she insisted. She was sneaking into Beatty's bed every night now, or Beatty into hers. She wanted to make the most of her sister's warmth and sour, ripe odours while she could.

Beatty said, 'First Mr Piggy, now Neddy. You won't be satisfied until you've turned down the whole farmyard!'

Neddy never walked Alice across the market square. Too noisy, too crowded, and too many torn vegetable leaves and discarded paper wrappings littering the ground. Alice wasn't sure whether to be grateful or not. On the one hand, she quite liked the idea of parading past Butterworth's stall on a schoolmaster's arm. On the other hand . . . well, she wasn't precise about the other hand, but maybe it was best to avoid all contact. She skirted past the square in the mornings too.

And yet Alice dreaded those ten-minute journeys home with Neddy. She dreaded them more with every passing week. She would watch the clock on the classroom wall every afternoon, with welling nausea. From the minute she left the house, she began to fret about it. Her preoccupation began to take form as a distinct plea: Please don't let him ask today. *Don't* let him ask me today . . .

Alice was never convinced that Ernest Butterworth had acted according to a plan. There was no real call to think so, although it would have given the situation more romantic appeal. The Butterworths were not regular churchgoers, but it wasn't unknown for them to attend. When Ernest appeared with his sisters and his mother on a Sunday in September, nobody passed comment. He was probably a reluctant escort. It was Mrs Butterworth who hung back after the service, to tend to her husband's grave. No doubt Ernest would have been off like a shot if he'd had the choice. But he waited for his mother by the churchyard gate, with his thumbs in his waistcoat pockets. He touched his hat to Mr and Mrs Day and the girls, and showed no sign of discomfort, despite the way Beatty nudged Alice. Alice's father wanted to take issue with the minister about some point in his sermon; he led his wife back to the fray, and Beatty took the chance to go swinging her hips up the path towards Robert. It seemed perfectly natural then for Ernest to engage Alice in conversation. He wasn't hasty, or gauche. He didn't try to entice her away for a stroll, or speak with the insinuating, upturned inflexions that Neddy used. He only talked about the sermon and the weather, but he fixed her with his steady focus, and Alice found herself comparing his flat, no-nonsense tone with Dorian Wilkins' insipid whinny.

They all walked away from the church in a loose group: Mr and Mrs Day commiserating with Mrs Butterworth in her bereavement; Beatty showing Robert off and patronising Ernest's sisters. They trailed past the school, past the town hall, past the empty market square and its skeletal stalls. Ernest was rigidly civil and superficial. He asked after Beatrice. He told Alice how well the business was doing. He reported his younger sister's imminent entry into service; he predicted his elder sister's engagement. Without a pause and without warning, he then said,

'Do you remember the farmer's boy, years ago, who disappeared?'

Alice swallowed the wrong way and coughed until her eyes watered. She acknowledged and was thrilled by this unexpected diversion and its promise of artificial danger.

Ernest told her about the flooded quarry, up beyond the woods. He told her about his two friends, Saul the farmer's son, and Alfie the slaughterman's son (who went a bit strange and was sent away). He told her about their day in the sun, ten years back, and how it went horribly wrong. He described the chaos of their plunge into icy water; the splashes and refracted light that multiplied three boys into a mob; the diminution in noise and activity; the puzzled search, growing frantic as he and Alfie realised that Saul had gone. He told it all in his casual, low voice, before they had reached the fork in the road where the two families would part. Only Alice could hear.

'Did they find him?' She reduced her voice too, making this a conspiracy between them.

Ernest put a hand over his eyes, and flicked his shoulders. It was a brief action, quick, uncalculated as a sneeze.

'We never told a soul,' he said. 'We never even said we'd been together. And it's too late now.'

Alice was filled with awe and morbid delight. He had given her a faultless performance. If he had cried, or even betrayed a twitch of remorse; if he had asked her to comfort him, or to keep the secret – it would have fallen short. And that fleeting, ambiguous gesture at the end – suggesting, to Alice, ten years of pent-up grief – that was perfect. Alice was aware of the blood racing through her veins. She knew that this story, and the manner of its telling, would prey on her mind all night. She knew now that Ernest was not like other men. He was a man with secrets.

As the group gathered to itself at the junction and called its goodbyes, Alice let her hand brush like a breath across his.

On the 22nd of September 1898 Ernest Butterworth proposed again, and Alice Day accepted.

2

There was no one reason for the collapse of Alice Butterworth's world. Several times in the middle of the night, or as she was laying the morning fire, or, especially, as she sat through the last leaden months of her confinement – several times Alice ticked off the possibilities in her head, and dismissed them, one by one.

It wasn't Ernest. Alice was romantic, but not to the point of idiocy. She could amuse herself with fantasies. She could embellish married life with rosy ideas and language. But at heart Alice was a realist. Despite everything, she had not married Ernest without weighing up the pros and cons. She knew that she didn't love him in the consuming way of novels, or in the maternal, comfortable way that Beatty loved Robert. But she also knew that they could get along, and – more importantly – that there was a fascination between them. It bordered on passion, but had a stronger element of simple curiosity – which, Alice felt, had a longer-lasting potential. Alice and Ernest Butterworth didn't understand each other, and this, it seemed to Alice, was their strongest bond.

Ernest was courteous and, in his own blunt way, loving towards her. He treated her with respect; if he was sometimes overenthusiastic in his embraces, she wasn't really frightened. When he hugged her desperately and made her cry out, she was touched. She remembered the early days, when he would watch her stalking across the square; she remembered that sense of latent power.

No, Ernest wasn't at fault.

And it wasn't the Butterworths' house, or Ernest's family. One of his sisters had already married and was off their hands before Alice had moved in; the other soon left, to go into service. Within a year, Mrs Butterworth had taken a chill which developed into pneumonia, and died. Alice's parents shook their heads sagely, and said the poor woman had been halfway to the hereafter, anyway, since losing Butterworth Senior.

So Alice had the house to herself, and if it was drab and musty, and had corners that never caught the light or the heat – well, that could be sorted out. Ernest had said as much,

'If there's anything you want changed, say the word. We can afford it. It's *your* home now.'

So what had gone wrong? There was no one reason that Alice

could find and change. She missed Beatty, naturally; but she'd seen her virtually every day before falling pregnant, and even now saw her twice a week. Her mother was with her four or five times a week (which was more than enough) – sitting, knitting, asking Alice if she was tired, or could manage another piece of bread and butter, being a great comfort, with the baby coming.

No – this foreboding had appeared from nowhere. Like a mist. It had soaked up through the floorboards, condensed on the wallpaper and mirror, saturated her skin and seeped into her womb. She couldn't find a single thing wrong with her life: everything was wrong.

Alice was twenty years old. She could see no way of shaking off this depression. She was destined to drag herself through another forty or fifty years, raising children, eating meals, lying beside her husband, and she would never be free of it: this slow, muted terror.

She told no one. She was ashamed, and cross with herself. She hoped that she would pull herself together. She did tell Beatty, once, that she felt as though she'd lost her grip, and had no power over anything any more. But she said it lightly, and rolled her eyes. Beatty sympathised, with the widsom of an old hand at marriage.

'We *do* have power, Alice. But there's no earthly way of using it.'

Alice asked Beatty, on a whim, whether she remembered the farmer's son, Saul Something-or-other, whose family had lived in this area – oh, many years ago – and who had vanished without trace, she believed. Beatty turned her mouth down and considered.

'There *was* some story . . . A family who moved up north . . . there was a scandal of some sort, but I can't remember . . . Didn't they have a boy who went to the bad, and ran away?'

The birth was difficult, but not the worst encountered by the midwife. Alice was dizzy and bemused when they handed her a nine-pound slab of bawling, battling red meat. She took it in her arms and studied it, and felt nothing.

'Ruby red,' she murmured at the swaddled and screeching wound, and then she had to add a comment about the child's pretty lips, for the sake of her mother and the midwife.

Everything was a struggle with Ruby: feeding her, cradling her – it all turned into a fight. Alice decided that the deficiency was not in Ruby. Ruby was only a baby, after all: she couldn't be blamed. And it wasn't in Alice's marriage. It must be Alice herself.

Whatever might be the drawbacks of being a wife and mother, whatever complexities she could attribute to her feelings for Ernest, Alice was certain that she ought to love her own child. After four months she knew that she did not. She was sorry about it. She carried on caring for the child, and showing her every kindness, as she would for anybody's baby. The woman across the street had a new baby too, and came to swap notes: she made saucer-eyes at her own child with an infatuation that Alice couldn't comprehend.

All the same, Alice accepted that life would go on like this, and be feasible. Love was not necessarily required. She went about her chores, she sang to her daughter, she greeted her husband and cooked meat from his stall and moved around her home as if the mist had cleared.

When the time came she had made no plans or preparations. Until an hour before she left, she was Mrs Butterworth, wife of Ernest, mother of Ruby, and she was fully expecting to stay that way. But when the time came there wasn't a doubt or an instant's debate. She had to go. Immediately. Forever. She wanted to see Beatty, but that was not possible: if she saw her sister, she would stay, and if she stayed she would not survive.

She lulled the protesting Ruby to sleep. She tucked her tightly into her cot. She rolled a few necessaries into a bundle. She scribbled a note and took money from the caddy on the mantelpiece. She walked eight miles to the next station down the line, and caught the first train heading south.

3

Spring, 1904. Mrs Alicia Worth, a young widow and schoolteacher, packed her portmanteau, slipped her rent money into an envelope on the sideboard, tidied and swept her room and left.

Mrs Worth's landlady, Mrs Bradley, was hurt and worried by this abrupt departure. Mrs Worth had been a good tenant, always ready with a friendly word, always on time with the rent – ever since she had turned up on the doorstep, shocked and grieving, with only a small bundle for luggage, four years ago. Mrs Bradley had been moved by the girl's helplessness. She had brushed aside Alicia's pathetic apologies for her lack of belongings. Mrs Bradley, a widow herself, had listened on the verge of tears to Alicia's account of the terrible house fire, which had burnt everything she owned to a frazzle, along with her husband. She let her take the room at a cut price – just until the poor lamb could set herself back on her feet. She even helped her find her way around Gloucester, encouraged her in the search for her sole remaining relative (an uncle, who turned out to have absconded from the city years before). Mrs Bradley was proud of Alicia Worth. She took pride in her recovery and growing self-assurance; she took pride in her appointment to the staff of the Intermediate School. They shared a drop of Mrs Bradley's precious port wine to celebrate.

Four years of friendship. Four years of support. And off she hops in the night, without a word. Mrs Bradley was piqued. She swore she would never lend her ear to another sob-story. She counted the money in the envelope, licking her forefinger to gain a purchase on the notes, and was rather crestfallen when it came to exactly the amount she was owed.

In the trap on the way to the station, Alice breathed deeply and knitted her fingers together to stop them trembling. She was being hasty. She was probably mistaken. Why would Beatty's husband be in Gloucester anyway? Even if it *had* been Robert, he hadn't seen her – she was sure of that. And it probably wasn't him. She had caught only a glimpse, as he hurried past in the dusk, with a rolled newspaper under his arm. All the same . . . What if he'd been sent to find her? What if, after four years, they had finally picked up her scent? The trap bucked around a corner, and Alice steadied herself against the side. No – surely, it was just a mistake. Robert wouldn't be here. To soothe her nerves, Alice summoned her mental picture of Beatty in the summer dress with the yellow flowers around the neck and hem. She kept this image as her only souvenir of a past life: a charm, in case of emergencies like this.

It was getting light. Here and there, as the trap jolted through the streets, came the trundle and trudge of early risers going to work. Alice wondered where she would end up next.

Would they really have come looking for her? It hadn't crossed her mind that they would. But they couldn't force her to go back... (Could they?) Alice imagined flinging herself at Beatty's waist, begging her forgiveness. She imagined being clasped to her mother and the two of them weeping on each other's necks. Maybe they wouldn't condemn her too harshly. Alice knew for a fact that her parents had regarded her marriage to Ernest as a backward step. They'd had better options in mind, and would have lobbied hard on Neddy's behalf, if they'd had half an inkling of his interest. Of course they'd forgive her.

Alice thought of Ruby's shallow baby breaths as she tucked her firmly into place, and her hot limbs under the bedding. She thought of those dark mornings, heaving the child – already a solid weight at three months old – to her breast; she and her own mother observing the battle and the suckle; Alice mimicking her mother's pleasure.

As the trap drew up at the station yard, Alice realised with a start that Ruby must be a little girl now – not a baby. Alice had hardly given her daughter a thought in four years. Ruby had just been part of a general discomfort that lay behind Alice's daily routine. Now Alice wondered whether she looked like her father, and thought: I hope she's not mocked.

She handed her portmanteau down and climbed out of the trap. She had decided to go south again. No sense in churning up all the vexations of a life that was over and done with. No sense in seeking anyone's forgiveness: not even her own.

4

She met Daniel Jenkins in a library in 1909. He'd come in to read the paper; Alice was writing herself a reference. She folded the writing-paper quickly, sensing his curiosity from across the table. When she calculated that it was safe, and looked up, he winked. He had wavy dark hair and an inquisitive expression that made her want to look up again. When she left the building, with her unfinished letter in her pocket, he was right behind her. He had a sleepy Valleys accent and when he spoke he seemed amused by some private train of thought.

'Love letter to your sweetheart, is it?'

She didn't answer.

'You've got a neat hand,' he said. 'I envy you that.'

He walked down the street at her side, conducting his one-man conversation. He pointed out his place of work, the funeral parlour – well, he added, that was his place of work *for now*. He told her about a scheme he had cooked up with his brother, Johnny. It was a winner, he assured her. Couldn't fail. They were trying to persuade the funeral director to convert his parlour into a motion picture theatre. What did she think of that? Funerals – fine: regular business, bound to be. But the *pictures* – they were a craze. A boom. You had to grab it while you could. Crest the wave, make your fortune. There were *thousands* of them in America, he insisted, as though he'd been there – *thousands*. 'Nickelodeons'. People can't get enough of 'em. You could always go back to funerals when it was all over – if you really wanted to.

Alice was nonplussed by his zeal. They reached the crossroads, and he extended a hand and said, brazenly,

'I'm very sorry. I'm afraid I don't know your name.'

She could find no polite way to avoid replying. She was Alison Bradley, schoolteacher. Currently living in Newport, but hoping for a better position in Cardiff.

'Oh, you don't want to go *there*,' said Daniel Jenkins. 'All frauds and ruffians down there. *Every* sort coming in, off the ships, out the valleys. No place for a lady like you ... Where you from?'

She looked away, affecting modesty and disapproval, without much success. She said, lamely,

'Nowhere you'd know. The country.'

'There you are, then. Cardiff's no place for a country girl.'

The funeral director had enough of being harangued with Daniel Jenkins' crackpot plans. He sent him off with a flea in his ear.

'Ah, forget him,' said Daniel. 'Stuck in the past, like all the rest of 'em.'

'No-hopers,' grumbled Johnny. 'Don't know what they're missing.'

'Never mind,' said Daniel, slapping his brother on the back. 'We'll move on.'

Moving on didn't worry them: they'd done it before. Pick up a bit of work here and there, sell scrap if needs be, wait for the chance to try out their schemes elsewhere. Daniel was no more daunted by the consistent failure of his plans than he was by Alison Bradley's airs and graces.

And why should he be? reasoned Alison Jenkins, as she packed her bags for another night flit, this time with her new husband and brother-in-law. Maybe Daniel could tell a runaway and a bigamist when he saw one.

5

Daniel was a dreamer. His brother was a gambler. Daniel was good at spotting opportunities: he was right about the motion picture boom, but he didn't know the first thing about the business. He thought eagerness would make up for lack of capital and expertise. Johnny was along for the ride; his heart wasn't in this project, and hadn't been in the others: the boxing hall, the photograph-portrait gallery . . . All Johnny wanted was the cash to see him through another game of cards.

Johnny was smaller than Daniel, hunched and consumptive-looking. Alison hadn't bargained for him as their constant companion, but he was no bother, and he made himself scarce as soon as a day's work was over. Alison liked her new husband: she liked his passing obsessions and his good-humoured acceptance of whatever came along. Above all she liked Daniel's restlessness, his inability to stay put for more than a few months at a time. It made her feel safe.

Trefelin was just another staging post. Somewhere to take stock, make a bit of money here and there – cobbling, selling, a bit of casual labour at the pithead. Then on to the next place. Daniel had a new scheme brewing: a motion-picture-theatre-cum-tea-room. They arrived in July 1910; by September Alison was pregnant.

I can cope, she told herself. As long as we're on the move, chopping and changing, no one will expect me to be sentimental about it. And I can take care of it – I can manage that: I can feed it, clothe it, brush its hair. Nothing more will be required.

Daniel was ecstatic. A baby! A real family! This was the best scheme ever. Overnight, Daniel lost his itch to move on. He charmed his way into a regular job – another funeral parlour. He saw to it that Johnny went to work, on the railway. He found them all a place to live – a narrow, dirty house, shared with the obnoxious Lloyd family. Alison drew the line at Johnny squeezing in with them, so Daniel arranged lodgings for him on the other side of town.

Alison Jenkins, wife and mother-to-be, sitting in a bare room, watching a tide of damp creep up the walls and peel the plaster. Alison Jenkins, thirty years old, waiting for the lid to shut on her life once more.

But everything was different this time. The birth was more painful, but faster: the waves of agony and panic were familiar, and so was the retreat into sick fatigue, the mechanical extending of her arms to take the quacking baby. But this baby was nothing like Ruby. This was a small, diaphanous, nuzzling creature; the cry subsided into an indignant croon. Alison thought the wafer limbs would break but they were astonishingly, impossibly supple. Daniel stroked the down on his daughter's head, and the long, oddly adult fingers. He laughed. Uproariously, irresistibly, until Alison had to join in.

Why this child? Why this one, and not the other?

She didn't know. She wasn't prepared for any of it: the visceral, hardly containable emotion; the avalanche of – what? Excitement? Anguish? She couldn't believe it had a name as sweet and consoling as 'love'.

'She's a little beauty,' said Daniel. 'Pink fingernails. Pink cheeks. She's all pink, like a sugar mouse.'

His daughter was the funniest thing in the world. He wanted to call her Alison, after her mother.

'No,' said Alison, 'we'll call her Rose.'

'Roses are *red*, Ali! This is our *pink* princess!'

'Never mind,' said Alison. 'She's Rose, and that's an end to it.'

Rose was too exquisite for a place like Trefelin. Her mother was ashamed of the squalor and the din and the cockroaches under the range – as if she really did have a princess to entertain. She plotted ways of getting her daughter out of this mess.

When the War came, Daniel volunteered straight away. Alison gawped at him, then began to cry.

'You don't *need* to,' she pleaded. 'You're not a young man. You've got a family. Nobody will judge you.' Daniel was 29; Alison was 34 – five years older than her husband thought she was.

'Better *I* take a bullet than one of those little boys who are falling over themselves to enlist,' said Daniel. She was stunned. It hadn't occurred to her that he might be a *brave* man. She was also furious.

'Courage is all very well – it won't feed a fatherless child!'

She refused to go and see him off. She stood in their gloomy room with Rose on her hip, distracted and tight-lipped, while the girl meddled with her hair.

Within eight months Mrs Lloyd downstairs had lost her son. She cornered Alison in the kitchen and told her they were lies, what they said about a quick war, that it would go on until every last man had been killed, and then what would become of them all? She seemed to find some comfort in this idea, and so did Alison: she rallied, and began to think about teaching again. She would find a way out. She would give Rose a decent home.

As it turned out, Daniel was back home after two years, with a chunk of shrapnel in his thigh. Life threatened to go on indefinitely, as normal.

In 1920 Johnny had a winning streak. He'd had them before: Daniel and Alison would hear of them, after the money had gone.

Johnny had been in an accident on the line. He was too slow, and got his foot caught, and a train ran over it. They thought initially that he'd lose the whole foot, from the ankle down. But Johnny recovered, minus three toes. Since then he had needed a drink to face a day on the rails, and more than a few drinks to face the night's game – although he was always clear-headed when he played his good hands. The winning streaks had become a necessity, rather than a luxury; he needed them to fund his habit, and to put a little by for the next bet.

There was a major gaming session in February 1920. It lasted eight nights, in the back room of the Railwayman pub. The whole town knew about it; reports of the previous night's proceedings spread from door to door as the sun rose, and the players slapped themselves with icy water, and those who had any struggled off to work. Eight nights running, Johnny pocketed other men's savings, wages and promises. People muttered threats. Mrs Lloyd had a bone to pick with Alison.

'There's our miners, taking starvation pay as it is, and your brother-in-law taking even that off 'em.'

It was the first Alison had heard of Johnny's luck.

'Get that money off him.' She held her husband's wrist until it bruised. 'Get it before it goes down his throat like all the rest.'

It was no great fortune – there were no fortunes to be made in that town, at that time. But it would get them started. Trefelin was simmering with bad feeling – towards the coal-owners, towards the government traitors – and Johnny's antics were set to bring it to the boil. One of the other card-players told Daniel he'd heard talk of dirty tricks. Cheating. Fingers were pointed at Johnny Jenkins. Provocative words were exchanged. When Alison tackled Daniel about it, he agreed that it was high time to up sticks.

Rose was eight years old, and now it was Alison who insisted that they settle down. She knew where, too. They would go to Cardiff. Big and busy and elegant – a fitting place for their princess. With the help of Johnny's winnings they scraped together a down-payment on a small, derelict shop not far from the docks.

'It's not perfect, love,' said Daniel, 'but we'll make something of it.'

Alison didn't mind: there were trams and lights and stately, chalk-white civic buildings, and dense, milling crowds. There were possibilities.

6

Mrs Daniel Jenkins of the Jenkins & Jenkins Grocery Emporium was revelling in righteous indignation. Her husband, a wounded war-hero and entrepreneur; her beautiful, fragile daughter; Mrs Daniel Jenkins herself – all struck down, laid low, brought to the very brink of death by a batch of diseased pie-meat for which she had paid good money. As a tradeswoman herself, Mrs Jenkins knew better than most what a responsibility the provisioners' profession had towards their customers. In times such as these, she was all too keenly aware that every penny spent must be on quality and value. She didn't expect to be fobbed off with corrupt produce. She didn't expect to see her family poisoned at her own table. Look at this child – hovering between life and death all night. She'd have them know . . .

Mrs Jenkins put her refund into her purse and snapped it shut with a flourish. She turned on her heel, hitched her coat more comfortably onto her shoulders, gave her daughter's hand an efficient tug and stalked away through the crowd. She was proud. Invincible. She was at the peak of her powers.

Rose related the scene to her father as he swept out the shop that evening,

'You should have seen her, Da. Like *royalty*.'

'A real duchess, your mam,' said her father. 'I always said so.'

Mrs Jenkins' greatest joy was to walk with her daughter through Cardiff's shopping centre. The grumble of carts, the jangling trams, the belch and scrape of the automobiles; the people – flocks of them, all intent on their own business, too many faces to scrutinise or suspect. One day a week, Alison and Rose would leave Daniel and Johnny to the shop and pace out the same long route until their feet throbbed. Past the gloriously pompous castle and its animal wall; all the way to the cool white temples and green spaces of the civic centre, and back to scurry up and down streets, in and out of hushed department stores with Edwardian façades as grand as embassies, through the two-tier arcades and the high-roofed market. Mrs Daniel Jenkins, parading her pink-and-pearl daughter for all the world to admire.

The grocery was doing well. Johnny had smartened up, and

the sheen on his nose had calmed down. In a moment of madness, Alison had her hated, stringy hair cut short. For Christmas Daniel bought her a coat with a high fur collar. She saved up for a cloche hat, and a pair of strapped shoes with Louis heels. Catching sight of herself in the department store windows, Mrs Jenkins decided she was more like a girl of twenty than a wife and mother in her forties.

'You're a regular flapper, you,' said Daniel. He said it admiringly. He had never been a prude. As far as Daniel was concerned, wealth and frivolity were conditions to be attained, not criticised. (He wasn't a political man, either. So when their customers and neighbours began to lose their jobs; when the local kids appeared on the streets with bare feet, wearing underwear made of newspaper; when the grocery takings began their slow but ineluctable slide, Daniel didn't ask why. He clutched at his business and his home like a drowning man, as long as he could. Then he wanted to let it all go and take his chances in the open water. But by that time everything had changed. No more escapes.)

Besides, that was still a world away. For the present, Jenkins & Jenkins continued to flourish, and once a week Mrs Jenkins and Rose went on strutting across the city stage.

Alison never forgot her triumph over Hatchetts. For ten full years she went on basking in its glory, egged on by her husband and brother-in-law.

'Don't give *her* any trouble,' they would say to their regulars, 'She won't stand for any nonsense, this one.'

She liked to pass friendly warnings to new customers about the goods sold at the indoor market.

'You don't know what they'll try and get past you . . .'

She thought of herself as an expert, someone to be consulted about foodstuffs in general. She talked of her family's 'brush with death' and added,

'However tight the money is, quality comes first.'

When she bought her meat at the butchers round the corner, she made a point of examining it scrupulously. The butcher took it in good part, and told the other customers this was 'Mrs Jenkins, the local inspector of vittles.' Alison was becoming a Character.

Rose was a grown woman now, courting Freddie Evans from the baking factory. She still accompanied her mother every so often on the weekly visits to town. Their route was shorter, for the sake of Alison's feet, but it invariably took them into the market and past Hatchetts, at a haughty distance, and Rose's mother invariably said, 'I suppose you were too young, you wouldn't remember the time . . .' and Rose would set her jaw and say, 'Yes, Mam, I *know*.'

When Rose was otherwise occupied, her mother was content to plod round the shops alone. Rose was in love, after all; she had interests of her own – and that was as it should be. Freddie Evans was a bit of wag, had a bit of a tongue in his head, but he reminded Mrs Jenkins of her own husband in his youth. She couldn't help but approve.

One summer week in 1931, Mrs Jenkins wove her lofty way among the market shoppers, pausing at the fishmongers, the bakers, the second-hand book stall. She emerged at a junction – a gap between the stall selling china knick-knacks and the milliners' stall, six feet from M E Hatchetts, Purveyors of Best Quality (huh!) Meats. She relived her moment. She threw out a swift glance of disgust. She turned her head and lifted her chin and looked straight into the piggy eyes of Ernest Butterworth.

The old fear hit her in the midriff like a mallet. Her legs gave way; two or three passers-by caught her by the elbows and manoeuvred her to the milliners' stall, where the stallkeeper let her rest on her stool.

'It's the air,' she gasped, fanning herself with her hand. 'It's so close . . . stifling . . .'

The milliner bent over her, clucking, and the relieved helpers returned to their tasks.

'Oh, I know,' the milliner said. 'If you're not used to it the crush is something awful in here, you'd think there was money to throw away . . .'

Mrs Jenkins recovered a little and asked, conversationally, about the new butcher.

'Oh, I don't know about new,' said the milliner. 'That's Old Hatch, isn't it? Been here since the year dot.'

On the bus going home, Mrs Daniel Jenkins debated the situation with herself. This was nothing to worry about. It wasn't as if it hadn't happened before – these inexplicable 'sightings'. Robert, that time in Gloucester; her father, one Saturday morning in Caerphilly; Dorian Wilkins in a tobacconists in Pontypridd. All mistakes, and well she knew it. Wasn't this just her imagination, bubbling over again?

He had met her eyes. He had seen her. This 'Old Hatch', who'd been selling meat in the indoor market 'since the year dot' – who must have been there, in that case, when she and Ernest Butterworth were swapping their first civilities 80 miles away. For a split second he had looked her full in the face. And yet he registered no hesitancy, no surprise – and there was her proof. She must be mistaken. Ernest would have known her straight away, and shown it. Yes, she was on the stout side now, and her hair was grey, but . . . well, *she* had recognised *him*. And that was the problem. For all her reasonings and rationale, she had *recognised him*. Without a doubt. She had known that florid skin, that broad, short nose, and that fixed, inscrutable stare.

Beatty wavered into sight for the first time in years. Lovely and self-conscious in her white dress with the yellow flowers, sauntering through a lost era. The bus veered round a corner and Alison's stomach lurched.

What if it *was* him? Come back to haunt her, to punish her, and poison her family? Alison had no idea whether Ernest was alive or dead.

Alice Day let herself into her home by the back way, and bolted the door behind her. She drew the curtains, although it would be light for hours. She put more coal on the fire and sat huddled into her old-fashioned coat. Outside, a mist was gathering. She could feel the touch of it in her bones. Soon it would seep under the door and through the cracks in the woodwork. Spread along the tiles and the rugs on the floor. Soak into her shoes and lap around her ankles. There was nothing Alice could do to keep it at bay.

ABOUT HONNO

Honno Welsh Women's Press was set up in 1986 by a group of women who felt strongly that women in Wales needed wider opportunities to see their writing in print and to become involved in the publishing process. Our aim is to publish books by the women of Wales, and our brief encompasses fiction, poetry, children's books, autobiographical writing and reprints of classic titles in English and Welsh.

Honno is registered as a community co-operative and so far we have raised capital by selling shares at £5 a time to over 350 interested women all over the world. Any profit we make goes towards the cost of future publications. We hope that many more women will be able to help us in this way. Shareholders' liability is limited to the amount invested, and each shareholder, regardless of the number of shares held, will have her say in the company and a vote at the AGM. To buy shares or to receive further information about forthcoming publications, please write to:

Honno, 'Ailsa Craig', Heol y Cawl, Dinas Powys,
Bro Morgannwg CF64 4AH.

www.honno.co.uk